PENGUIN BO
The Hypnotist's I

Praise for Liane Moriarty

'The pleasure here is the skill with which Moriarty inhabits her characters as she builds the suspense' *Guardian*

'Will grip you from the first page' *Sunday Express*

'A fantastically nimble writer' *Entertainment Weekly*

'An excellent talent for exposing the dark, seedy side'
Library Journal

'Original, suspenseful, downright brilliant'
Clare Mackintosh

'The twist blew my mind' Marian Keyes

The Hypnotist's Love Story

LIANE MORIARTY

PENGUIN BOOKS

PENGUIN BOOKS

UK | USA | Canada | Ireland | Australia
India | New Zealand | South Africa

Penguin Books is part of the Penguin Random House group of companies
whose addresses can be found at global.penguinrandomhouse.com.

First published 2012
This edition published by Penguin Books 2020
001

Typeset by Palimpsest Book Production Limited, Falkirk, Stirlingshire
Printed and bound in Great Britain by Clays Ltd, Elcograf S.p.A.

A CIP catalogue record for this book is available from the British Library

ISBN: 978-0-241-95506-2

www.greenpenguin.co.uk

MIX
Paper from
responsible sources
FSC® C018179

Penguin Random House is committed to a
sustainable future for our business, our readers
and our planet. This book is made from Forest
Stewardship Council® certified paper.

For George and Anna

'One is very crazy when in love'

Sigmund Freud

I

When people think of hypnosis, they think of swinging pendulums, 'You're getting sleepy' and people clucking like chickens on stage shows. So it's not surprising that many of my clients are quite nervous when they visit me for the first time! In fact, there is nothing unnatural or frightening about hypnosis. Chances are, you've already had the experience of going into a 'trance-like state' in your day-to-day life. Have you ever driven to a familiar destination and found that you have no memory of the drive? Guess what? You were in a trance!

— Leaflet, 'An Introduction to Ellen O'Farrell, Hypnotherapist'

I had never been hypnotized before. I didn't really believe in it, to be honest. My plan was to lie there and pretend it was working, and try not to laugh.

'Most people are surprised by how much they enjoy it,' said the hypnotist. She was all softness and soap; no make-up or jewellery. Her skin had a polished, translucent look, as if she only ever bathed in mountain streams. She smelled like one of those overpriced crafty shops you find in country towns: sandalwood and lavender.

The room we were in was tiny, warm and strange. It was built on the side of the house like an enclosed balcony. The carpet was musty faded pink roses but the windows were modern: floor-to-ceiling panels of glass like those in an atrium. The room was flooded with light. As I walked in, the light seemed to whoosh through my head like a brisk breeze and I could smell old books and the sea.

We stood together, the hypnotist and me, our faces close to the windows. When you stood that close, you couldn't see the sand below, just the sea, a sheet of flattened, shiny tin that stretched out to the pale blue line of the horizon. 'I feel like I'm at the helm of a boat,' I said to the hypnotist, who seemed excessively delighted by this comment and said that was *exactly* how she always felt, her eyes round and shiny like a children's entertainer.

We sat down opposite each other. My chair was a soft, green leather recliner. The hypnotist's chair was a striped red-and-cream winged armchair. There was a low coffee table in between us with a box of tissues – some people must cry; sobbing away about their past lives as starving peasants – a jug of iced water with two perfectly round slices of lemon floating on top, two tall water glasses, a small silver bowl of shiny-wrapped chocolates, and a flat tray filled with tiny coloured glass marbles.

I used to have a big old-fashioned marble that belonged to my father when he was a boy. I'd hold it in the palm of my hand for luck during exams and job interviews. I lost it a few years ago, along with all my luck.

As I looked around me, I saw that the light reflected off the ocean and on to the walls: prisms of dazzling, dancing light. It was a bit hypnotic actually. The hypnotist had her hands folded in her lap, her feet placed squarely on the ground. Flat ballet shoes, black tights, embroidered ethnic-looking skirt and cream wraparound cardigan. Hippie but elegant. New age but classic.

I thought, what a beautiful, calm life you must lead. Sitting in this extraordinary room each day, bathed in dancing light. No emails filling your computer screen. No irate phone calls filling your head. No meetings or spreadsheets.

I could sense her happiness. It radiated off her, sickly, like cheap perfume; not that she would ever wear cheap perfume.

I tasted sour jealousy in my mouth and helped myself to a chocolate to make it go away.

'Oh, good, I'll have one too,' said the hypnotist, unwrapping a chocolate, with warm, girly camaraderie, as if we were old friends. She is that sort of girl. She probably has a whole circle of giggly, supportive, lovely girlfriends, the sort that hug each other hello and have *Sex in the City* DVD nights and long, shrieky telephone conversations about men.

She opened a notepad on her lap and spoke with her mouth adorably full of chocolate. She said, 'Now, before we do anything, I'm going to ask you a few questions. Oh dear, I shouldn't have chosen the caramel. Chewy.'

I hadn't expected so many questions.

For the most part I answered honestly. They were innocuous enough. A bit pathetic even. 'What do you do for a living?' 'What do you do to relax?' 'What's your favourite food?'

Finally, the hypnotist sat back in her armchair, smiled and said, 'And tell me, why are you here today?'

Of course, my answer to that one wasn't one hundred per cent truthful.

He said, 'There's something I need to tell you.'

He had placed his knife and fork on the edges of his plate, and now he was sitting up straight, with his shoulders back, as if he was finally ready to face the music. He seemed fearful and slightly ashamed.

Ellen, who had been smiling, instantly felt a painful cramp knot her stomach. (A part of her mind registered this: the way her body responded first. The mind-body-spirit connection in action. So fascinating.)

Her happy, open smile stayed foolishly frozen on her face.

She was thirty-five years old. She knew what this meant. This nice man, this self-employed suburban surveyor, this single dad who liked camping and cricket and country music, was about to say something that would put her off her barramundi in white wine sauce. He was about to say something that would ruin her day, and it had been such a lovely day, and the barramundi was really very good.

She put down her fork regretfully.

'What's that?' she said, her tone pleasantly quizzical, and every muscle in her body tightened as if she was preparing to be punched. She would cope. It wouldn't be the end of the world. It was only their fourth date. She hadn't invested that much of herself. She barely knew the man. For heaven's sake, he liked country music. That should have been a red flag from the beginning. Yes, she had been indulging in some hopeful daydreams in the bath tonight but that was a common pitfall of dating. She was already moving on, working on her recovery. She would be over it by Wednesday. Thursday at the latest. Thank the Lord she hadn't slept with him.

She couldn't control what was about to happen, only her response to it.

For a moment, she saw her mother, eyes lifted to heaven. *Ellen, tell me, my darling, do you truly believe this facile self-help nonsense you sprout?*

She did, in fact. With all her heart. (Her mother later apologized for her comment. 'That may have been patronizing,' she'd said, and Ellen had pretended to faint in shock.)

'Actually, can you excuse me for a minute?' He stood up and his napkin slid to the floor. He picked it up, his face flushed, and carefully laid it on the table next to his plate.

She looked up at him.

'I'll just –' He gestured at the back of the restaurant.

'All right,' she said soothingly.

'Over there to your left, sir.' A waiter discreetly pointed in the direction of the toilets.

She watched him go.

Patrick Scott.

She didn't really like the name Patrick anyway. It was a namby-pamby sort of a name. You could imagine your hairdresser being called Patrick. Also, his male friends apparently called him 'Scottie', which was . . . well, perfectly acceptable really in that Aussie blokey way.

If he ended it, it would definitely hurt. Just a little sting, but a sharp one. There was nothing extraordinarily wonderful about Patrick Scott. He had an ordinary, pleasant face (long, thin, slightly receding hairline), an ordinary body (average height, quite broad shoulders, but naturally broad, not look-at-me-I-work-out broad), an ordinary job, an ordinary life. It was just extraordinary how comfortable she'd felt with him, almost straight away, within minutes of meeting up with him for the very first time in that embarrassingly empty café. She'd suggested the café and had been horrified to find it virtually deserted, so that their nervous first-date voices seemed too loud, and three bored teenage waitresses stood about the room with nothing better to do but eavesdrop on their stilted conversation. They'd been waiting for their cappuccinos, and he was playing with a packet of sugar, turning it round in circles and tapping it on the table, when their eyes met, and they sort of grinned at each other in mutual recognition of the awfulness of the whole situation, and all of a sudden Ellen felt all the tension in her body drift away, as if she'd been given a powerful painkiller. She felt as if she already knew him, as if she'd known him for years. If she believed in past lives (and she didn't *not* believe in them – in her work she'd seen it all, her mind was wide open to all sorts of bizarre possibilities), then she would have said they must have known each other before.

That sort of instant warmth had happened to her many times before with women; oh, she was the star of female friendship – but never with a man.

So yes, she barely knew this nice surveyor called Patrick Scott, but it would hurt if he broke up with her. Probably more than a little sting.

She thought about the hundreds, maybe thousands of stories of rejection she'd heard from her clients over the years. 'I cooked a three-course dinner party for thirteen of *his* relatives and while I'm doing the washing-up he announces he doesn't love me any more.' 'We had a fantastic holiday in Fiji and on the way home we're drinking champagne and she announces that she's moving out! Champagne – as if it's a celebration!'

Oh, the naked pain that still furrowed their faces, even when they were describing something that happened years ago. Rejection by a lover or even only a potential lover was so tough on the Inner Child. Fears of abandonment, memories of past hurts, feelings of inferiority and self-loathing, all rose to the surface in an unstoppable torrent of emotion.

She was trying to observe her situation objectively, like a client's case history, in the hope that she could stay detached from it. It wasn't working.

Of course, all this panic might be for nothing. Patrick might not be about to dump her at all. There had been no signs, and she was good at reading people. That's what she did for a living, after all. He had said she looked 'gorgeous' when she opened the door for him tonight, with such a pleased expression on his face, as if he'd just been handed a gift, and he wasn't the smooth, charming type who automatically gave the sort of compliments women liked to hear. There had been a lot of eye contact over dinner, some of which could have qualified as 'lingering'. Throughout the meal, she had noted that he was leaning forward towards her (although perhaps he was a bit deaf; it was surprising how many men were just a little deaf – she knew this both from dating and from her work).

She had felt that their body language and breathing rhythms were in synch, and that wasn't because she'd been patterning him, at least not deliberately, the way she would with a client.

There had been no awkward pauses or uncomfortable moments. He had been interested, in a respectful way, about hypnotherapy. He didn't say, 'Show me! Make me cluck like a chicken!' He didn't sneer or, worse, take a gently condescending tone and say he wasn't really into 'alternative medicine'. He didn't say, 'So do you need any *training* for that?' or 'Is there any *money* in that?' He didn't seem afraid. Some men she'd dated seemed genuinely frightened that she might hypnotize them without their knowledge. He just seemed interested.

Also, a few minutes ago, he'd shown her photos of his son! His adorable, blond, skinny little eight-year-old son, on a skateboard, playing the trombone in a school band, fishing with his dad. Surely he wouldn't have shown her those photos if he'd already decided it wasn't going to work?

Unless the decision had just hit him with a flash. Now she thought about it, it had been oddly abrupt, the way he put down his knife and fork to make his announcement, his eyes looking over her shoulder, as if he'd just seen a glimpse of a different future in the distance. She'd been mid-sentence for heaven's sake. (She had been telling him a story about a patient who was obsessed with Jennifer Lopez. It was actually Michael Jackson, but she always changed the details for confidentiality reasons. And the story sounded funnier if it was Jennifer Lopez.)

He'd looked so sad. Even if he wasn't about to dump her, he was definitely about to say something unacceptable or unpleasant.

Perhaps he'd lied about being a widower. He was actually still married and living with his wife, even though they slept in separate rooms.

He wasn't a surveyor at all; he was a mobster. Now the FBI would come after her and insist she wear a wire. Her body would never be found. (She'd watched the entire series of *The Sopranos* on DVD last summer.)

Or perhaps he had a terminal disease. That would be terrible, but at least not personally hurtful.

Whatever it was, she was pretty sure that sunshiny feeling she'd been experiencing all day was about to vanish.

She took a large mouthful of her wine and looked up to see if he was on his way back from the toilets. No. Goodness. He was taking a while. Had he just splashed water on his face and was he now standing at the bathroom mirror staring into his own eyes, his hands gripping the sink, breathing heavily?

He was on the run from the law.

Her own breathing was starting to get a bit ragged.

Too much imagination for her own good. Mrs Pascoe's comment on her Year Seven report card.

She looked around her. The other diners were all involved in their own conversations, cutlery discreetly chinking against plates, the occasional not-too-raucous burst of laughter. Nobody was looking at the woman with the empty chair in front of her.

Was there time? Was it really necessary? Yes.

She sat up straight in her chair and placed her hands palm down on her thighs. She closed her eyes and breathed in through her nostrils, out through her mouth. With each breath she imagined her body being filled with a powerful gold light. The light gave her energy and strength. The light filled her feet, her legs, her stomach, her arms and, finally, *whoosh*, it whirled around her head, so that all she could see was a golden glow, as if she was looking directly into a sunset, and for a moment she felt as if she was floating just a few centimetres above her chair.

I will be fine. Whatever he says will not touch the essence of me. I will cope. On the count of three. One . . . two . . .

She opened her eyes, refreshed and reinvigorated. She looked around. Nobody was staring at her. Of course she knew that she hadn't really levitated above her chair while glowing like a light bulb, but sometimes the feelings were so astoundingly real she couldn't believe they hadn't physically manifested in some way.

Self-hypnosis was such a wonderful tool. She could always tell when a student or client actually got it. They were awestruck by what their minds could achieve. The first time that levitating sensation happened to her it was like she'd discovered she could fly. She could wipe out the drug problem if she could just teach teenagers self-hypnosis.

Patrick still wasn't back. She looked at the meal in front of her. No point letting it go to waste. A waiter gliding by stopped and refilled her wine glass. Good wine, good fish. Pity she didn't have a book.

She thought about her day.

Right up until the moment that Patrick put down his knife and fork, it had been perfect. Exquisite even.

She'd slept deeply and dreamlessly to the rhythm of the rain on the roof and woke late to sunshine on her face. The first thing she saw when she opened her eyes was the branch she'd hung from the ceiling as a reminder of the Buddhist Sutra of Mindfulness. She'd then inhaled and exhaled three gentle breaths while maintaining the 'half-smile'.

(Although she wished she'd never mentioned this practice to her friend Julia, who had asked Ellen to demonstrate her half-smile. When Ellen finally complied, after much cajoling, Julia had rocked with laughter for ten minutes straight.)

When she got out of bed, the windowpanes were icy against her fingertips but the new gas-heating system her grandparents had installed (thanks to Great-aunt Mary's lucky Lotto ticket!) before they'd died had transformed the house into a cosy cocoon. She ate porridge with brown sugar for breakfast while she listened to the ABC news, which was upbeat and wry. The recent flu pandemic was probably not a pandemic after all. (Her mother, who was a GP, had said all along that this would be the case.) A missing toddler had turned up safe and sound. The latest gangland killing was probably just a family feud. The latest political scandal had fizzled. Traffic was moving well. Winds would be south-westerly and light. For once, the world seemed extremely manageable.

After breakfast, she'd rugged up to walk along the beach and come back exhilarated and windblown, licking salt from her lips.

She'd had four appointments that day. She had her last session with a man who had wanted help overcoming his flying phobia so he could take his wife to France for their ruby wedding anniversary. As he left today, he'd shaken her hand vigorously and promised to send Ellen a postcard from Paris. She'd also met two new clients and she always enjoyed meeting new clients. One was a woman who had suffered from some sort of debilitating, unexplained pain in her leg for the last four years, and had been to countless doctors, physiotherapists and chiropractors, who were all baffled. The other was a woman who had promised her fiancé that she would give up smoking by their wedding day. Both sessions had gone well.

Her final appointment was with a client who was probably not going to be one of her success stories. She was having trouble pinning down what Mary-Kate really wanted to achieve from hypnotherapy, but she refused to be referred to anyone else and insisted that she wanted to continue treatment. Ellen had decided not to try anything too complicated today and just gave her a simple relaxation session. She called it a 'soul massage'. Afterwards, Mary-Kate said her soul felt exactly the same, thank you, but that was Mary-Kate.

After Mary-Kate had plodded off, Ellen had cleaned the house, carefully leaving a few things lying about so it didn't look like she'd cleaned up, but that she was naturally this tidy. She had considered taking down some of the Buddhist quotations she had displayed all round her house on pale purple Post-it notes. Her ex-boyfriend Jon used to make such fun of them – standing at her fridge, reading them out in a stupid voice. But hiding her true self wasn't the way to start a potential new relationship, was it?

She also remade the bed with her crispest, nicest sheets. It was probably time to sleep with him. Oh, yes, it was a bit clinical, but that's how it was when you were dating in your thirties. It wasn't hearts and flowers any more. They weren't sixteen. They weren't religious. They had met on the Internet: a dating website. So it was all very clear and upfront. They were both looking for a long-term relationship. They had ticked corresponding boxes to indicate this.

There had been some kissing (quite lovely), and now it was time for sex. She'd been celibate for almost a year, and Ellen liked sex. It surprised some men, who seemed to develop an ethereal, sweetly innocent image of her in the beginning, which she didn't mind; she even played up to it a bit. It just wasn't quite accurate.

(She also liked horror movies and coffee and steak, cooked medium-rare. A lot of people were convinced she was vegetarian, that, in fact, she *should* be a herbal-tea-drinking vegetarian, even going so far as to prepare special meals for her at dinner parties and then insisting that they 'clearly remembered' her saying she didn't eat meat.)

She had taken her time getting ready for tonight: a long, steamy bath with a glass of wine and a Violent Femmes CD. The jarring chords and strident voices were so startlingly different from the chiming, bubbling relaxation tapes she played all day that it was like having a bucket of cold water thrown over her head. The Violent Femmes reminded her of the eighties and being a teenager, and feeling super-charged with hormones and hope. By the time Patrick had knocked on her front door, she was in such a deliriously good mood, the thought had actually flitted across her mind: *You must be heading for a fall.*

She had dismissed that idea. And now . . . *There's something I need to tell you.*

She picked up her fork. Where was that man? She could see one of the waiters giving her a discreet look, obviously trying to work out if he should offer some form of assistance.

She looked at Patrick's half-eaten meal. He'd ordered the pork belly. A poor choice, she'd thought, but she hadn't known him long enough to tease him about it. Pork belly! It sounded disgusting, and now it looked like a big slab of cold, congealing fat.

If he was the sort of man who ordered that sort of artery-clogging meal all the time, perhaps he'd dropped dead of a heart attack in the toilets? Should she send in that concerned-looking waiter to find out? But what if the pork belly had just disagreed with him? He'd be mortified. Well, she'd be mortified in similar circumstances. Maybe a man wouldn't care.

She was really too old for all this dating angst. She should be at home, baking cakes or whatever it was that parents of primary-school-aged children did with their nights.

She looked up again and there he was, walking back towards her. He looked shaken, as if he'd just been in a minor car crash, but he also had a rueful, 'the game is up' expression, as if he'd been caught robbing a bank and was walking out with his hands in the air.

He sat down in front of her and put the napkin back on his lap. He picked up his knife and fork, looked at the pork belly, sighed and placed them down again.

'You probably think I'm some sort of a lunatic,' he said.

'Well, I'm quite curious!' said Ellen in a jolly, middle-aged-lady tone.

'I was hoping not to have to tell you about this until we'd . . . but then I realized that I was going to have to tell you tonight.'

'Just take your time.' Now she was speaking in the calm, slightly sing-song voice she used with clients. 'I'm sure I'll be fine – whatever it is.'

'It's nothing that bad!' said Patrick hastily. 'It's more embarrassing than anything else. It's just that – OK, I'll just come out and say it.'

He paused and grinned foolishly.

'I have a stalker.'

For a moment Ellen couldn't quite understand what he meant. It was as if English had become her second language and she had to translate the words.

I have a stalker.

Finally she said, 'Somebody is stalking you?'

'She's been stalking me for the past three years. My ex-girlfriend. Sometimes she disappears for a while, but then she comes back with a vengeance.'

Glorious relief was washing through Ellen. Now that she wasn't being dumped it was suddenly clear to her how much she actually liked him, how much she was hoping this would work, how she had actually allowed the words 'I could fall in love with him' to cross her mind as she was putting on her mascara. The reason she'd been so deliriously happy today had not been because of the weather or the porridge or the new heating or the news. It was because of him.

A stalking ex-girlfriend was fine!

It was *interesting*.

Then again, stalking . . .

She saw notes written in letters cut out from magazines and newspapers. Messages on walls written in blood. Crazy fans sitting outside celebrities' houses. Violent ex-husbands shooting their wives.

But who stalked a *surveyor*? (Even if he did have an especially lovely jaw line?)

'So when you say "stalking", what does she actually do? Is she violent?'

'No.' Patrick looked as if he were being forced to answer a series of highly personal medical questions. 'Never physically violent. Occasionally she yells. Gets a bit abusive. She makes phone calls in the middle of the night, sends me letters, emails, text messages, but mostly she's just there. Wherever I go, she's there.'

'You mean she follows you?'

'Yes. Everywhere.'

'So, goodness, this must be horrible for you!' There was that middle-aged lady again. 'Have you been to the police?'

He winced, as if at an uncomfortable memory. 'Yes. Once. I spoke to a female police officer. I don't know if she – look, she *said* all the right things, I just felt like an idiot, like a wuss. She suggested I keep a "Stalking Incident Log" recording everything, and I've done that. She said I could take a restraining order out against her, so I was thinking about doing that, but then when I told my ex that I'd been to the police, she said if I took it any further, she would tell them *I'd* been harassing *her*, that I'd hit her – well, you know, I'm the guy, who are they going to believe? Her, of course. So I backed right off. I just keep hoping she'll stop. And the years keep rolling by. I can't believe it's been going on so long.'

'It must be . . .' Ellen was going to say 'frightening' but that might offend his fragile ego; it was her belief that the male ego was as delicate as eggshell. Instead she said, 'stressful'. She couldn't quite keep the undercurrent of joy out of her voice.

'In the beginning I really let it get to me,' he said. 'But now I've sort of accepted it. It's just how my life has worked out, but it's hard on new relationships. Some women get freaked out by the whole thing. Some of them say they're fine with it in the beginning, but then they can't handle it.'

'I can handle it,' said Ellen, quickly, as if she was at a job interview and she was proving she was up to the challenge. Hearing about ex-girlfriends' weaknesses always brought out an embarrassing competitive urge to prove she was better.

Flustered, she took a mouthful of her wine. She'd just put her cards on the table. She had basically just said: I want a relationship with you.

She pretended to be frowning down at her wine glass, as if she was about to make some disparaging comment on the quality of the wine, and when she finally looked up, Patrick was smiling at her. A big crinkle-eyed smile of pure pleasure. He reached out across the table and took her hand in his.

'I hope you can,' he said. 'Because I feel really good about this. I mean, about us. The possibility of us.'

'The possibility of us,' repeated Ellen, savouring the words and the feel of his hand. It was all such rubbish about getting clinical and jaded when you were in your thirties. The feel of his hand was shooting endorphins throughout her bloodstream. She knew all about the science of love, how her brain was currently surging with 'love chemicals' (norepinephrine, serotonin and dopamine), but that didn't mean she wasn't as susceptible as anyone else.

So now all their cards were on the table.

'What made you tell me tonight?' asked Ellen. His thumb was turning circles in her palm. *Round and round the garden, like a teddy bear.* 'About your stalker?'

His thumb stopped.

'I saw her,' he said.

'You saw her!' Ellen's eyes darted about the restaurant. 'You mean, here?'

'She was sitting at a table under the window.' He gestured with his chin over Ellen's shoulder. She went to turn round to look but Patrick said, 'Don't worry. She's gone now.'

'What was she doing? Just . . . watching us?'

Ellen was aware of her heart rate picking up. She wasn't sure how she felt: frightened, possibly a little thrilled.

'She was texting on her mobile,' said Patrick wearily.

'Texting you?'

'Probably. I've got my phone switched off.'

'Do you want to see what she said?' Ellen wanted to see what she said.

'Not particularly,' said Patrick. 'Not at all, actually.'

'When did she leave?' If only Ellen had known earlier, she could have seen her.

'When I stood up to go to the bathroom, she followed me. We had a little chat in the corridor. That's why I took so long. She said she was just leaving, and she did, thank God.'

So she must have walked right past Ellen! Ellen searched her mind for a memory of a woman walking by, but came up blank. It was probably when she was doing her self-hypnosis, dammit.

'What did she say? Wasn't she embarrassed?'

'She always puts on this pathetic act as if we just happened to run into each other. You'd think she'd look like a crazy bag lady with, you know, crazy hair, but she always looks so normal, so together. It makes me doubt myself, as if I'm imagining the whole thing. She's a successful career woman. Well respected. Can you believe it? I always wonder what her colleagues would think if they knew what she did in her spare time. Anyway . . . shall we talk about something more pleasant? How was your fish?'

Are you kidding? There was no other subject Ellen wanted to talk about. She wanted to know every detail. She wanted to understand what was going through this woman's head. She normally understood a woman's perspective in any given situation. She was a girl's girl. She liked women; it was men who often mystified her. But stalking your ex-boyfriend for three years? Was she a psychopath? Had he treated her badly? Was she still in love with him? How did she justify her own behaviour to herself?

'The fish was great,' said Ellen. She tried to suppress her greed for more information. It was a bit unseemly when this was obviously such a distressing part of this man's life. She knew it was one of her flaws: a ravenous curiosity about other people's personal lives.

'Who's looking after your son tonight?' she asked, to help him change the subject.

'My mother,' said Patrick. His face softened. 'Jack adores his grandma.'

Then he blinked, looked at his watch and said, 'Actually, I promised I'd call him to say goodnight. He wasn't feeling that well when I left. Would you mind?' He pulled his mobile phone from his pocket.

'Of course not.'

'I don't normally call him when I'm out,' he said as he turned the phone on. 'I mean, he's a pretty independent kid now. He does his own thing.'

'It's fine.'

'It's just that he's had this really bad cold and then it turned into a chest infection. He's on antibiotics.'

'It's *perfectly* fine.' She wanted to hear him talking to his little boy.

His phone was beeping, over and over.

Patrick grimaced. 'Text messages.'

'From your, ah, your stalker?' Ellen tried not to look too avidly at the beeping phone.

He studied the screen on his phone. 'Yes. Mostly I just delete them without even bothering to read them.'

'Right.' She couldn't help herself. 'Because they're nasty?'

'Sometimes. Mostly they're just pathetic.' She watched his face as he read the messages, pressing buttons with his thumb. He smiled ironically, as if he was engaged in nasty banter with an enemy. He rolled his eyes. He chewed on the edge of his lip.

'Want to read them?' He held out the phone to her.

'Sure,' said Ellen casually. She leaned forward and read as he scrolled through the messages for her.

> Fancy seeing you here! I'm at
> a table under the window.

> You look good in that shirt.

> You ordered the pork belly?
> What were you thinking?

> She's pretty. You two look
> good together.

Ellen recoiled.

'Sorry,' said Patrick. 'I shouldn't have shown you that one. I promise you, you're not in any, you know, danger.'

'No, no, it's fine.' She nodded at the phone. 'Keep going.'

> Nice running into you
> tonight. We should do coffee
> one day soon?

> I love you. I hate you. I love
> you. I hate you. No, I
> definitely hate you.

Ellen sat back.

'What's your professional opinion?' asked Patrick. 'Certifiably crazy, right? Remember, this relationship ended three years ago.'

'How long did you go out together for?'

'Two years. Well, three years. She was my first relationship after my wife died.'

She wanted to ask how it ended, but instead she said, 'Why don't you just change your phone number?'

'I used to change it all the time but it's not worth it. I'm self-employed. I need people to be able to track me down. Hey, I'd better call my son. I'll be quick.'

Ellen watched him as he dialled a number and held the phone to his ear.

'It's me, mate. How are you going?'

'What did I have? Oh, pork belly.'

He glanced down ruefully at his plate. 'Yeah, it wasn't that great.'

'Anyway, how are you feeling? You're OK? You took your antibiotics? What's Grandma doing? Oh, really? That's good. Yeah. OK. Well, maybe if you just tell me quickly.' He stopped talking and listened. His eyes met Ellen's and he winked briefly.

'Is that right? OK, well – right. A volcano? Parachuting? Geez.'

He kept listening, tapping his fingers on the tablecloth.

Ellen watched his hand. It was a lovely hand. Big square-cut fingernails.

'OK, mate. Listen, you might have to tell me the rest tomorrow. I'm being really rude to my . . . friend. OK. See you in the morning. Waffles, of course. Yep, definitely. Night, kid. Love you.'

He hung up the phone, switched it off and put it back in his pocket.

'Sorry,' he said. 'He wanted to tell me every detail of this movie he'd seen. Gets that from me, I'm afraid.'

'Really?' said Ellen.

She was feeling a shot of intense pleasure at the back of her skull. She loved the way he talked to his son, so casual and funny and masculine and loving. She loved the fact that they were going to have waffles tomorrow morning. (She loved waffles!) She loved the way he said 'Love you' so unselfconsciously.

A waiter took away their plates, balancing them on his forearm. 'Was the pork belly all right, sir?'

'It was fine.' Patrick smiled up at him. 'Just wasn't as hungry as I thought.'

'Can I tempt you with the dessert menu? Or coffees?'

Patrick raised his eyebrows at Ellen.

'No, thank you,' she said.

'Just the bill then, thanks, mate,' said Patrick.

Ellen looked at her watch. It was only ten o'clock. 'I've got some nice chocolates at home,' she said. 'If you want to have coffee at my place. If you've got time.'

'I've got time,' said Patrick, and his eyes met hers.

Of course, they never bothered with the coffee and chocolates. As they made love for the first time on the clean sheets, there was a sudden flurry of hard rain on the roof, and Ellen thought briefly of Patrick's stalker, and wondered where she was right now, imagining her standing under a street light in the rain with no umbrella, raindrops sliding heedlessly down her pale, tortured (beautiful?) face, but then all the interesting sensations of a new lover filled every corner of her mind and she forgot all about her.

2

At my age most of my friends are all in long-term relation-
ships, and in my line of work I don't have the opportunity
to meet many new potential partners. I guess this just seemed
like a fun way to make some new friends. I'm a romantic,
but I'm also a realist.

      – From Internet dating site profile of username
Ellen68

Ellen walked barefoot along the beach early the next morning, her trousers rolled up to her knees so she could let the waves break around her ankles, thinking about Patrick (she loved the name Patrick, nothing namby-pamby about it at all!) and everything that had happened the previous night.

His son. (So cute!)

His crazy ex-girlfriend. (Intriguing! Although also possibly somewhat frightening? She wasn't sure.)

His body. *Goodness*, she had thought, as if she was a swooning heroine in a regency romance, when he unbuttoned his unassuming striped business shirt. Just thinking about his chest gave her a shot of pure lust and she pressed two fingers to her tender lips, grazed from all that kissing.

He had left right on midnight. Like Cinderella. He said

that although his mother was staying at his place to look after his son, and would have gone to bed in the spare room, he always felt as if he was somehow taking advantage of her if he stayed out too late.

'I hate doing this. Of course, if we – you know – I'll be able to let her know I'm staying overnight,' he'd said as he buttoned his shirt back up over his caveman chest.

'It's fine,' Ellen had said, her voice thick with sleep. She was happy he was going. She preferred to lie in bed and think about him, rather than have him actually there and worry about what her hair looked like in the morning.

'I'll call you,' he'd said when he kissed her goodbye.

Her phone had beeped with a text message at six a.m.

> When can I see you again,
> please? I think you've got me
> hypnotized!

Which was cheesy. But extremely lovely.

So it looked like it was happening. She was at the beginning of something new. *Here we are again.* She took a deep breath of salty air and felt it catch in her throat. For a moment she felt the weight of all those previous disappointments.

Please let this one work, she thought, pathetically.

And then, with more spirit, *Come on now, I deserve this!*

Ellen had been in three long-term relationships: Andy, Edward and Jon. Sometimes she felt like she was always dragging the memories of these relationships along with her, like three old tin cans on a string.

Andy was a freakishly tall young banker. Their three-year

relationship always seemed vaguely fraudulent to Ellen, as if they were just pretending to be in love but doing a really excellent job of it. When Andy got an overseas posting neither of them even mentioned the possibility of Ellen going with him. The whole affair left her feeling grimy, as if she'd eaten McDonald's.

Edward was a sweet, sensitive high-school teacher. They fell deeply, profoundly in love and became one of those couples with a clear path ahead of them, incorporating children and pets. And then, for complex reasons that were not at all clear to her now, and to everyone's shock, the relationship suddenly imploded. It was quite exquisitely painful.

She met Jon on her thirtieth birthday. So, OK, she thought, *this* is the one. The real grown-up relationship. He was a smart, articulate engineer. She adored him. It wasn't until after he'd pulverized her heart that she finally noticed he'd never actually adored her back.

She'd always thought of these failed relationships as, well, failures. But it occurred to her now that perhaps they were actually essential steps in a pre-destined journey leading to this very moment on this very beach. To a green-eyed surveyor called Patrick Scott.

She thought of Patrick's ex-girlfriend, his stalker. Saskia. An unusual name with its hard spiky little syllables. Ellen rolled the name round in her mouth, like a strange new fruit. Saskia would not appreciate knowing that Ellen's heart was filling with tremulous hope right now.

Ellen kicked out at the water in front of her, sending up a spray of icy droplets. Well, really, what sort of person was this girl? Had she no pride at all? Ellen cringed at the idea of her ex-partners knowing she ever spared them a thought. When, in fact, the three of them were always lolling about in the back of her mind. Every time she got out of the car, she automatically slid the driver's seat back for Andy's long legs; a habit left over from the years they'd shared a car. Every time she cut a tomato she thought of Jon, because he'd once told her cutting crossways made it juicier. Every Boxing Day she remembered it was Edward's birthday.

Of course, it was to be expected that she thought of them. For a while, each had been the person who knew her best, who spoke to her every single day, who knew where she was at any particular time, who would have sat in the front row at her funeral should she have tragically died.

It sometimes seemed so peculiar and wrong to her that you could be that intimate with someone, to go to sleep with them and wake up with them, to do really quite extraordinarily personal things together on a regular basis, and then, suddenly, you don't even know their telephone number, or where they're living or working, or what they did today or last week or last year.

Ellen watched a giant wave on the horizon curl and crash with a distant boom.

That's why break-ups felt like your skin was being torn from your body. It was actually strange that *more* people weren't like Saskia, instead of being so well-behaved and dignified about it.

'Good morning!' An elderly couple walked by from the opposite end of the beach at a brisk pace, elbows pumping. Ellen picked up her own pace so as not to be outdone by octogenarians.

When her grandparents were alive they would walk along this beach every night just before the six o'clock news.

They spent sixty-three years together. Sixty-three years of waking up next to the same person, in the very same bedroom, in fact, where she and Patrick had made love last night. (Which, now she thought about it, was terrible. She liked to think that the spirits of her grandparents still inhabited the house. She hoped her poor grandfather hadn't been trapped in the bedroom, standing behind the curtains, shielding his eyes.)

Ellen had always assumed she would marry young and have a relationship like theirs. She thought she was that sort of person. Traditional. *Nice.* As if nice girls always found nice boys. As if 'niceness' was all that was necessary to maintain a relationship.

In all honesty (and the achievement of genuine self-awareness was her ongoing goal), it wasn't so much her niceness as the fact that she believed herself to be nothing like her own mother: her mother who had brought up Ellen alone, with barely a man in sight.

And yet, here she was, thirty-five and looking for men on the Internet. Each time she clicked on to the website she felt like she was doing something vaguely unseemly.

Unseemly for *her.* That was the crux of it. She didn't think there was anything unseemly about anyone else doing Internet dating. Oh, no, it was fine for the unwashed masses! But Ellen helped people with their personal lives for a *living*.

That was it. She thought she should be the sort of person who was great at relationships and it seemed she actually wasn't. Really, she kept telling herself briskly, why shouldn't she have suffered and had her heart broken like anyone else? Why shouldn't she have found it hard to meet the right man, like so many other women? Why shouldn't she be worried about the ticking of her biological clock, even if it was a cliché? Why shouldn't she be a cliché?

She was ashamed of her shame. As penance she was extremely open about her single status. She told all and sundry that she was Internet dating. She went on each awkward new date with her head held high, her outlook positive and her heart and mind open to all possibilities.

But it was hard work at times.

She reached the rock pool where she always turned back and put her hands on her hips, breathing heavily. She'd been walking faster than she realized.

She looked back along the beach towards her grand-parents' house, now her house, the glass room at the back winking in the morning sun like a diamond stuck haphaz-ardly to its side. 'Fabulous. He's made it even more of an eyesore,' her mother had said when she saw the new room Ellen's grandfather had added on; all thanks to Great-aunt Mary's Lotto win.

Ellen's grandfather's childless, unmarried younger sister, Great-aunt Mary, had won half a million dollars in Lotto and then died just six weeks later, while she was still pon-dering what to do with her windfall. (A new TV, perhaps? One of those 'flat screens'? But really, *Deal or no Deal* would still look exactly the same, wouldn't it? Just bigger.) All her money had gone to Ellen's grandparents, who had used it to put on the extra glass room, install gas heating, and go on a ten-day cruise each year until they died. Great-aunt

Mary's Lotto win had also resulted in their decision to leave their house to Ellen when they died, while her mother and Amnesty International had inherited the capital. This suited everyone because Ellen's mother had no desire to live in her childhood home. 'No amount of money could save it,' she liked to say, with sad authority, as if she'd been asked to give her expert opinion.

It was a strange-looking house, built in the seventies and incorporating all the most fashionable design features that decade had to offer: exposed beams and bricks, a stainless-steel spiral staircase, mirrored arches, lime-green shag carpet and a bright-orange kitchen. But Ellen had always loved it. She thought it had groovy retro charm and she refused to change a thing about it, except for adding an off-street parking spot for her clients. While her career as a hypnotherapist had supported her 'quite remarkably' well (as her mother was always telling people, equally disappointed and proud), she had still been renting an apartment and an office when her grandmother died. Inheriting the house and using her grandmother's sewing room to treat her clients meant that Ellen was now enjoying the most financially secure position of her life.

A white stone on the sand caught her eye and she bent down to pick it up. It had a pleasing shape and feel to it; it might come in useful for one of her clients.

As she straightened back up, she looked out at the ocean and felt a loosening sensation in her chest, as if she'd been released from a corset. You weren't meant to admit, even to yourself, how badly you wanted love. The man was meant to be the icing, not the cake. She was a bit embarrassed by the depth of her happiness. Thank goodness no one could see the champagne corks popping in her head.

When she got home she would answer Patrick's text and suggest they saw a movie that night. Not very original, but still one of the loveliest things to do with a new boyfriend. She would try not to sound excessively eager.

She walked closer to the water and dug her toes deep into the sand. She remembered the feel of Patrick's back beneath her fingers; his collarbone against her lips.

Sorry, Saskia. I think I'm keeping him.

So, he's slept with the hypnotist.

I can tell. I knew as soon as I saw his hand pressed to her lower back as they came out of the movie. It was low, you see, and confident, indicating ownership.

He thinks he's pretty good in bed. It was his wife's fault. She once told him that he was an 'extraordinary lover'. And then she died. So every word she ever said became like the Word of God. The Word of Colleen.

Colleen once told Patrick that the laundry powder should be fully dissolved in the washing machine before you put in the clothes, even though most people just chuck it in on top of the clothes. But Colleen said the clothes wash better if the powder is fully dissolved. And so it was. I still do it, for Christ's sake. Even though it's annoying, because you have to wait until the machine fills up with water and sometimes I walk away and forget about it, and then I suddenly realize I've done half a load without any clothes in the machine.

He was actually pretty good in bed. He probably still is.

Probably still says the same things, makes all the same moves.

I think of him lying in bed with her, breathing in her sandalwood smells, running his hands over her smooth, toxin-free skin.

I would like to see. I would like to be there, sitting at the end of the bed, watching him bend his head towards her nipple. Her breasts are larger than mine. I guess that's nice for him.

I wonder if she hypnotizes him for free.

Her voice sounds like warm honey dripping off a spoon.

They saw that Russell Crowe movie last night. It was pretty good. He should have known what was going to happen because the movie was based on the series we used to watch on a Monday night. I wondered if he remembered and I thought, I bet he doesn't, so I sent him a text reminding him.

Afterwards they went for dinner at that Thai restaurant on the corner where he told me he loved me for the first time.

I wonder if they sat at the same table.

I wonder if he remembered, just for a second. Surely I am worth a fleeting thought?

I couldn't get a table. They must have had a reservation – she must have done it, he would never bother. So I went to a café and I wrote him a letter, just trying to explain, to make him see, and I left it on the windscreen of his car.

I am looking forward to my next appointment with the hypnotist.

3

'We should go,' yawned Ellen.

'We really should,' yawned Patrick.

Neither of them moved.

It was nearly eleven o'clock on a Thursday night and they were lying flat on their backs on a picnic rug on a grassy slope directly under the Harbour Bridge. Earlier, they'd been to the theatre in Kirribilli and seen a silly play. They'd eaten dinner at a tiny, crowded noodle bar, and then they'd walked along the boardwalk by the harbour, watching the traffic zoom over the bridge, while the lit-up ferries slid beneath. They'd agreed tonight would be an early night, and that Patrick wouldn't come back to her place, because a teenage neighbour was looking after Patrick's son – she was a student and had an early lecture the next day, so Patrick didn't want to keep her up too late – but still, neither Ellen nor Patrick wanted the night to end.

They'd been dating now for three weeks, and everything still had that shiny, new-car smell. Even the yawny voices they were using right now still had that self-conscious sheen: *Look, this is how I sound when I'm tired!*

'Have you got a busy day tomorrow?' asked Patrick.

'Just an average day,' said Ellen. 'Five appointments. That's enough for me. I find if I do any more, I get really, well, exhausted.'

She was aware of a feeling of defensiveness left over from her most recent relationship. Jon's contempt for her profession had always been subtle; a faint fragrance she couldn't quite identify, and therefore couldn't ever tackle head-on. He was an even more passionately committed atheist than her mother. (*The God Delusion* was his favourite book.) 'Show me the empirical evidence' was one of his favourite phrases. Whenever Ellen talked about her work, Jon would put his head to one side and give her a patient, avuncular smile, as if she was a charming little girl burbling on about fairy princesses. Then he'd make some humorous, teasing remark that didn't go quite as far as denying the existence of fairy princesses, but was there for the entertainment of any nearby adults. 'Ellen has a Bachelor of Hypnotherapy,' he would tell people, which was his way of pointing out that Ellen didn't have a degree. (She'd enrolled to do psychology and then dropped out halfway through her second semester to study hypnotherapy. Her mother was still in mourning.)

It wasn't until after they'd broken up that Ellen saw how she'd struggled to hold on to herself throughout their time together. It was like every time she spoke, she was simultaneously trying not to take herself too seriously – *hey, I can handle a little gentle ribbing!* – while at the same time justifying her whole existence: *Yes, it is OK to be me. Yes, I do believe in myself and what I'm saying. I am not a frivolous lightweight, except maybe I am.*

'Is it draining because –' Patrick scratched the side of his jaw and frowned up at the stars. 'Ah, why, that is, how exactly is it draining?'

He was respectfully baffled.

'I guess it's because I can't ever just coast,' said Ellen. 'I have to be totally focused on the client. I never use prepared scripts. I tailor every induction –'

'Induction?'

'That's whatever technique I use to induce hypnosis – like, imagining you're walking down a flight of stairs or progressively relaxing your body. I tailor it to the client's interest or background – whether they're more visual or analytical or whatever.'

'Do you have some tricky clients?' Patrick rolled over on his side and rested his head in the palm of his hand. 'Ones who are hard to hypnotize?'

'Nearly everyone can be hypnotized to some degree,' said Ellen. 'But some people have more of a talent for it, I guess, because they're imaginative and they've got the ability to really focus and visualize.'

'Huh,' said Patrick. 'I wonder if I've got the talent for it.'

'I'll give you a suggestibility test,' said Ellen. She got up on her knees, mildly exhilarated; she would never have done anything like that with Jon.

Patrick looked up at her. 'Like a gullibility test?'

'No, no, it's just a little exercise to show the power of your imagination. Relax! It's nothing strange. You've probably done it before at a sales conference or something.'

'OK.' Patrick got up on his knees, facing her, with a brave set to his shoulders. The smell of his aftershave was already familiar to her, but still new enough to arouse. 'Do I close my eyes?'

'No. Just hold your hands like this.'

She interlaced her fingers and straightened out two fingers so they were facing each other. Patrick did the same and looked her straight in the eyes. There was something very sexy about this.

'Now imagine a powerful magnetic force is pulling those two fingertips together. You're fighting it but you can't resist. Watch them. It's getting stronger. Even stronger. It's too strong – *there*.'

Patrick's fingertips closed.

'See! Your subconscious believed the magnets were real.'

Patrick looked at his fingertips still pressed together. 'Well. Yes. I mean, I don't know. I guess it felt real, but that's just because I was going along with what you were saying.'

Ellen smiled. 'Exactly. All hypnosis is self-hypnosis. It's not magic.'

'Do something else.'

'All right. Close your eyes this time and stretch your arms out in front of you.'

He did so, and she paused for a moment, observing the planes and hollows of his face in the moonlight.

'Hello?' he said.

'Sorry. OK. Imagine that I'm tying a huge helium balloon to your right wrist. It's tugging it upwards. Feel it tug. Now in your left hand I'm giving you a bucket. It's very heavy because it's filled with heavy wet sand from the beach.'

Patrick's right arm floated straight up and his left hand dropped down. Either he was doing this to please her or he was, in fact, an excellent subject for hypnosis.

'Open your eyes,' she said.

Patrick opened his eyes and looked at his arms.

'Huh,' he said. He dropped his arms and put them round her waist. He lowered his head as if to kiss her and then he stopped and suddenly spun round to look behind him.

'What is it?' said Ellen, startled.

'I'm sorry,' said Patrick. 'I thought I heard something. I thought it was her.'

There was already no question as to who 'her' was. Ellen looked into the shadowy areas under the bridge for a lurking woman. She noted that she was experiencing a slight buzz: a pleasant burst of adrenaline at the thought of Patrick's stalker secretly observing them.

'You haven't seen her tonight, have you?' asked Ellen. The other night they'd been to the movies and dinner, and Patrick hadn't even mentioned he'd noticed Saskia until they got back to the car and found a letter from her sitting on the windscreen.

Patrick glanced around, his eyes narrowed. Then he sat back down again.

'No, I haven't seen her at all. I think she's giving us the

'night off.' He put his arm round her. 'I'm sorry. It makes me twitchy sometimes.'

'I can imagine,' said Ellen sympathetically. Was there something moving over by that pylon? No. Trick of the light, dammit.

'So your business is all about the power of the mind,' said Patrick.

'That's right,' said Ellen. 'The power of the subconscious mind.'

'I believe in it, don't get me wrong,' began Patrick.

Here we go. Ellen's stomach muscles tightened.

'But there's a limit to it, isn't there?'

'What do you mean?' said Ellen. *He's not Jon*, she told herself. *He's just stating an opinion. Calm down.*

'I just mean, it can't cure everything. When Colleen – that was my wife – when she got sick, people kept telling her to think positively. As if she could just think the cancer away. After she died I saw a woman on TV saying: "I refused to let the cancer beat me. I had two young children, you see. I *had* to live." It infuriated me. As if it was Colleen's fault that she died. As if she should have tried harder.'

Go carefully, thought Ellen. She opened her mouth to speak and then closed it again.

Patrick put his hand on her knee. 'By the way, I don't want you thinking you've got to walk on eggshells whenever anything comes up about my wife. I'm fine about it. I'm not going to go all weird on you, I promise.'

Hmm, thought Ellen. 'My mother is a GP,' she said. 'So –'

So what? So I have some sort of medical credibility because of her? My mother doesn't really believe in what I do either.

'I have looked after clients with terminal illnesses for pain management or stress relief, but I would never, ever promise I could cure them.'

'I didn't mean to imply that,' said Patrick. His hand tightened on her knee.

'I know you didn't.' Ellen put her hand over his, and wondered if he was seeing his wife's face right now.

She didn't tell him that she *did* believe that the mind had miraculous untapped powers.

Show me the empirical evidence, said Jon in her head.

They didn't speak. The sound of a ferry horn floated across to them from the other side of the harbour. There were footsteps from behind them. They both turned to watch a woman wearing a dark business suit and white sneakers walking down the path towards them.

'That's not –' said Ellen.

'No,' said Patrick, his face clearing as the woman was illuminated by a street light.

They were silent. Ellen thought about how she'd closed off such a huge part of her identity during her years with Jon. If this relationship was going to work she needed to throw open those doors! Let in the light! The air! The – *OK, Ellen, enough with the house metaphor.*

'I really love what I do,' she said to Patrick. That defensive tone was still there. She made a conscious effort to let it go, to just *be*. 'I'm quite good at it too.'

Patrick gave her an amused sidelong look. 'Are you the queen of hypnotherapists?'

'I am.'

'What a coincidence. I am the king of surveyors.'

'Really?'

Patrick sighed. 'No, not really. I'm more like the yesterday man of surveyors.'

'Why?'

'I'm not fond of all the new technology. I still prefer to do all my drafting by hand. So that makes me slower. Not as efficient. It's a competitive disadvantage, as my younger brother likes to remind me.'

'Is he a surveyor too?'

'No, he's a graphic designer, but he's very techy. Are you techy?'

'Not really, but I do like to Google. I think I Google every single day. Google is my oracle.'

'What did you Google today?'

Today she'd Googled 'dating a widower: avoiding the pitfalls' and 'stepchildren – disaster?', followed by 'cures for broken capillaries around the nose'.

'Oh, I can't think.' She waved her hand vaguely. 'Something trivial.' She changed the subject back. 'Why did you decide to become a surveyor?'

'Maps,' said Patrick immediately. 'I've always loved the idea of a map, of knowing exactly where I am in relation to everything else. I had an uncle who was a surveyor and when I was a kid he said to me, "Patrick, you've got good where-ability, you'd make a good surveyor." I asked him what a surveyor did and he explained it like this: he said a surveyor determines the location of things on the earth's surface in relation to every other thing above or below that surface. Those were his exact words. It stuck in my head. And for some reason that just clicked with me. I thought, yep, that's what I'll do.'

'I think I must have terrible where-ability,' commented

Ellen. 'I don't have any sense of where I am in relation to anything. Like, right now – I couldn't point in the direction of home.'

Patrick pointed over her shoulder. 'North. That way.'

'If you say so.'

'Have you got any paper?' said Patrick. 'I'll draw you a map.'

Ellen always made a point of having a beautiful hardbound notebook and pen in her bag so she could write down thoughts as they struck her, ideas for her work and so on. She carefully ripped out a page for him. She didn't want him reading any of her random scribbles; most of them were the very essence of uncool.

Patrick pulled a slim gold fountain pen from his pocket. 'My grandfather's Parker pen. I'd run back into a burning house for it.'

He rested the sheet of paper on top of her notebook, leaned it on his knee and drew an old-fashioned compass in the corner. Then he began to quickly sketch the inlets and curves of the harbour. He added a ferry and yachts, the Harbour Bridge and the Opera House. It was like watching an ancient treasure map appear before her eyes.

'Here's where we had dinner.' He drew a little illustration of the restaurant. 'Here's where we saw that ridiculous play. And now we head over to the northern beaches.' He sketched a beach and a two-storey house. 'Here's your house.' He wrote: *Ellen's Hypnotic House*. 'And now we head back over to the leafy North Shore and here's my house.' He wrote: *Patrick and Jack's Messy Men's Hovel*. He had beautiful handwriting; it was like the handwriting of a much older man.

She hadn't been to his place yet. She wondered if it was a hovel.

'And this is where we met for the first time,' he said as he continued drawing. 'And I think that's about everything – oh, except for this.'

He drew a tiny cross next to the harbour and wrote: *WE ARE HERE.*

'That's the most beautiful map I've ever seen,' said Ellen truthfully. She had never had any interest in maps before, and already knew she would keep this forever.

A faint shadow crossed Patrick's face. It came and went so fast she couldn't tell if it was sadness or anger, or maybe embarrassment, or if she'd imagined it.

He smiled at her. 'No charge this time, darlin'.'

Her heart was melting all over the place.

I've got this box.

Sometimes I think if I just threw away the box, I might be able to stop. Once, I got as far as carrying it out to the rubbish bin. I opened the lid of the bin and smelled rotting food and heard the buzz of flies, and I thought, *This isn't rubbish, this was my life.*

I lost them tonight. They were going somewhere near Milsons Point or Kirribilli. I was hungry so I didn't bother driving around looking for his car. I came home and ate sardines on toast while I watched *Cold Case* with the box on the floor next to me.

Every commercial break I dipped my hand into the box and pulled something out at random. Then I would examine it as if it was a clue or a solution, as if I was one of the detectives on *Cold Case* trying to unravel the secrets of the past.

A birthday card, the cardboard still stiff and shiny. Not faded at all. It could have been given to me yesterday:

Dear Saskia,
   Happy Birthday from your boys,
   We love you,
   Patrick and Jack xx

A photo of me and Jack with one of our playdough cities. We spent hours making those cities. I'd spread out cardboard across the dining-room table and we'd put in roads and roundabouts and traffic lights. Shops and houses. We'd spend days working on the one city: Jacksville, Jackland, Jack Town. I loved building those cities as much as he did. It was like being a town planner without the politics or paperwork.

A boarding pass for Queenstown, New Zealand. Patrick and I went snowboarding for a week. His mum looked after Jack. I remember Patrick stopping to kiss me when we walked back inside for a hot chocolate. Warm lips; cold snowflakes falling around us as soft as caresses.

A map that Patrick drew for me when he was giving me directions to a developer's office near the airport.

I remember I said to him, 'That's the most beautiful map I've ever seen.'

4

In this Act, 'stalking' includes the following of a person about or the watching or frequenting of the vicinity of, or an approach to, a person's place of residence, business or work or any place that a person frequents for the purposes of any social or leisure activity.

— Section 8 of the Crimes
(Domestic and Personal Violence) Act

'So she follows you? Everywhere? How is that even possible?'

'Well, not everywhere. The last time, we were at the movies.'

'Maybe she just happened to be there.'

'Maybe, but she tried to get into the same restaurant, and then she left a letter on his car windscreen, which he didn't read. Apparently she waits round the corner from Patrick's house and follows his car. He said if he's going somewhere different, he'll often lose her, but if it's a regular place, like the movies at Cremorne, it's easy for her to work out.'

'Good Lord.'

'I know.'

'This must be awful for you. It's ruining that wonderful time at the start of your relationship. You should be gazing moonily into each other's eyes, not keeping a look-out for his crazy ex.'

'I don't mind. Actually, I find it sort of interesting.'

'You freak.'

Ellen laughed at Julia's decisive tone and stretched luxuriously. It was a Saturday morning and they'd just been swimming at their local pool. Now they were stretched out on white towels in the billowing heat of the sauna. Ellen's legs and shoulders ached from the swim. Julia always made her swim harder and faster than she would if she were on her own. She could feel beads of sweat sliding all over her body: down her back, into her cleavage. She let her hands rest lightly on her thighs, and felt sleek and slippery and sensual. There was no problem practising mindfulness when you were at the start of a relationship. It happened automatically. All that sex. All those chemicals zipping through your body.

And all that *appreciation*. That was what was so wonderful about falling in love. Patrick appeared to highly approve of every new thing he learned about her body, her past, her personality. It made Ellen not just sexier, but funnier, smarter, nicer, kinder, all-round lovelier. She was invincible! Her life seemed to flow and ripple in exquisite harmony, as if she'd achieved enlightenment. Her clients were sweet and grateful, her friends adorable, her mother not at all frustrating. ('So when am I going to meet him?' she said on the phone, her tone warm and pleased, sounding just like a normal mother presumably would.) Whatever grocery items Ellen wanted were always right on the shelf in front of her, traffic lights turned green as she approached, her car keys, sunglasses and purse sat obediently and conveniently on the hall table. Only this morning she'd had just one hour to go to the bank, the motor registry and the dry-cleaner's, and she'd done it with time to spare, and every person she'd dealt with, even at the motor registry, had been charming. She'd had quite an emotional conversation with the bank teller about the weather. (The teller was from the UK and thought that Australian winters were 'divine', and Ellen had felt tearily proud, as if she, in her invincible state, was solely responsible for the Australian climate.)

If only she could bottle this feeling and make it last forever. It couldn't last forever, her rational mind knew that, but her heart, her foolish heart was chirping, 'Oh yes it can! Why not? This is who you are now! This is your life from now on!'

'I would never humiliate myself like that,' said Julia.

What? Oh. The stalking thing.

'Well, I guess she just can't let go,' said Ellen. Right now, she was filled with gentle compassion for all of humanity.

Julia snorted. She was lying on the bench opposite Ellen, a towel wrapped like a turban about her head. She had a long, lean, athletic body and crazy blonde curly hair and she hovered right on the edge of being extremely beautiful. Whenever Ellen walked along a street with her, she saw men's eyes automatically, involuntarily, flicking back to Julia for a second appraising look. Unfortunately, Julia's beauty seemed to attract a certain type of man; the sort who appreciated quality and was prepared to pay extra for it. The problem was these men constantly upgraded their computers, their cars and their women.

That was their nature. They were dedicated consumers, excellent for the economy. After nearly five years of marriage, Julia's husband, William, had decided it was high time he upgraded to the latest brand in a woman: a twenty-three-year-old brunette.

(Ellen always liked to think that the sort of man she herself attracted was automatically superior to those who chose Julia because they didn't let the billboards determine what was beautiful. They weren't superficial; they were *individuals*. Sadly, she couldn't really back this theory up when her relationship history was just as poor as Julia's.)

(Really, when she dug deep, she saw that her whole theory was just her way of making herself feel better because the majority of men didn't feel the need to give her that second flick of the eyes.)

(Although William had been a superficial prat.)

(To be honest, she had been quite fond of him in the beginning.)

'Where's the woman's self-respect?' snapped Julia. 'Just move on, for God's sake. She's making all of us look bad.'

There was a real edge to her voice, as if she was personally offended.

'You mean she's making women look bad?' said Ellen. 'It's normally men who do the stalking. It's good. She's showing women can stalk just as effectively as men.'

Julia made a 'pfff' sound. She sat up, leaned down with one long arm and picked up the ladle lying next to a bucket of water. She threw it on the hot rocks. There was a boiling hiss and the sauna filled with more steam.

'Julia,' gasped Ellen. 'I'm suffocating.'

'Toughen up,' said Julia. She lay back down and asked, 'What's this girl's name?'

'Saskia,' said Ellen, breathing shallow breaths of the hot, heavy air. She felt shy saying it out loud, as if it was a celebrity's name.

'Have you actually seen her yet? Or have you seen photos?'

'No. He never tells me he's seen her until after she's left. I'm desperate to see what she looks like.'

'Maybe she's a figment of his imagination and *he's* the crazy one.'

'I don't think so.'

Patrick wasn't crazy. He was lovely.

'So I assume he ended the relationship.'

'He just said that it ran its course.'

'So he broke her heart,' said Julia sternly.

'Well, I don't —'

'Still, it's no excuse. It happens to all of us. Patrick should take out a restraining order against her. Has he done that?'

Julia believed there were solutions to everything.

'He said he'd been to the police,' began Ellen, but then she stopped and didn't bother to go into further detail. She wasn't entirely convinced that Patrick had told her the whole story about why he hadn't gone ahead with the order.

'Anyway, the silly woman just needs to pull herself together,' said Julia, as if it were up to Ellen to pass on this instruction.

'Yes.'

They lay there in silence for a few moments. Ellen was

planning what she'd cook Patrick for dinner that night. He'd already cooked once for her, on a night when Jack was staying at a friend's place. It had been a very nice, plain roast dinner, nothing too fancy, which was good, because she'd been out with men who fancied themselves as gourmet cooks, and it seemed like such an asset in the beginning but then they were always so vain about it, and hovering round the kitchen criticizing the way you chopped the garlic.

Maybe she should do something with pork, seeing as he'd ordered the pork belly. Some nice tender pork medallions.

'Do you remember Eddie Masters?' said Julia.

'The butcher's apprentice,' said Ellen, remembering a skinny, long-haired boy in a blue-and-white-striped butcher's apron. Julia had gone out with him when they were in their teens. Yes, pork. She would stop by at that expensive butcher in the arcade on the way home from the pool.

'He went out with Cheryl from the chemist after me,' said Julia.

'The scary-looking girl. Actually, I think I just thought she was scary because she had her ears pierced twice.'

'Yes. Well, after Eddie dumped me I used to ring her house all the time. If she answered I'd just sit there, not saying anything, until she hung up. She'd scream all this abuse at me, and I'd just sit there, breathing. Not heavy breathing. Just breathing, so she knew I was there.'

'Julia Margaret Robertson!' Ellen sat up quickly, half pretending and half genuinely shocked. She looked at her friend, who was still lying with her hands clasped on her front. Julia had been school captain of the snooty private girls' school they'd both attended. She'd been slumming it with the butcher.

Julia didn't open her eyes. She smiled devilishly.

'I was thinking about your stalker and I remembered it,' she said. 'I hadn't thought about it for ages.'

'But it's so unlike you!'

'I know, but I was shattered when he dumped me. I couldn't stop thinking about her, about why he chose her over me. I felt as if I didn't exist any more. Ringing her up somehow made me exist. It was like an addiction. I hated myself afterwards, and I'd think "I'm never doing that again", but then next thing I'd find myself dialling her number.'

'How did you stop?'

'I don't know. I guess I just got over him.' Julia paused, then said, 'You know what? Eddie the butcher was a *beautiful* kisser.'

'Didn't he have a goatee?' said Ellen. 'A really wispy one? Like a bit of candyfloss hanging off his chin?'

'Yes, and do you remember how he kept his packet of cigarettes stuffed into the sleeve of his T-shirt?'

'It looked like a growth on his arm.'

'I thought it was unbearably sexy.'

They didn't say anything for a few seconds and then they both dissolved into the sort of helpless, wheezing laughter unique to women who spent their school days together.

'You should look Eddie up on Facebook,' said Ellen, when they'd stopped laughing. 'He probably has his own butcher shop by now.'

'Oh, God, I'm not that desperate,' said Julia. 'Anyway, I am perfectly happy being single.'

You're lying, my dear friend, thought Ellen, covertly observing Julia's body language: clenched hands, compressed lips. It had been two years since Julia's ex-husband had upgraded to the brunette.

Julia lifted her head suddenly. 'You didn't just make up that whole story about the stalker, did you? Is it like a fable you've invented and the subliminal message is that I'm like the crazy stalker and I need to move on and start dating?'

'What are you talking about?' But Ellen knew exactly what she was talking about.

'I remember you told me once about that famous hypnotist, your hero or whatever, the guy who wore the purple cape.'

'Milton Erickson,' sighed Ellen. 'Gosh, you've got a good memory.'

People were always underestimating Julia. It was because she was so beautiful, and also because she had the sense of humour of a fourteen-year-old boy.

'You said he used to treat patients by telling stories,' continued Julia.

'He used therapeutic metaphors,' murmured Ellen.

'Well, I've noticed that ever since William left me you've been casually telling me these little motivational stories about people overcoming obstacles, finding happiness after heartbreak.'

'I have *not*,' said Ellen. She had.

'Mmmmm,' said Julia.

She lifted her chin and smiled at Ellen; Ellen grinned sheepishly back at her.

'So Patrick's stalker isn't a therapeutic metaphor?'

'She is not,' said Ellen.

They lay in silence for a few seconds.

'So this Patrick has a crazy ex-girlfriend and a dead ex-wife,' said Julia. 'Sounds like a real catch. No complications whatsoever.'

'It doesn't feel complicated,' said Ellen.

'Yet,' said Julia.

'Thanks for your enthusiastic support,' said Ellen.

'Just saying.'

Julia sat up and took her towel off her head and dabbed it against her pink, shiny cheeks.

'I bet you love the fact that he's a widower, don't you?' she said. 'It makes him seem like a romantic, tragic figure. It's just like Miles.'

'Miles?'

'Miles. That one-legged boy you fell in love with in high school.'

'*Giles*,' said Ellen. 'And we all fell in love with the one-legged boy. He was gorgeous.'

This was the problem with being friends with someone who knew you when you were a teenager. They never quite take you seriously because they always see you as your stupid teenage self.

It was true that she wasn't unhappy about Patrick being a widower. She quite liked the fact that it made it more complicated. It made her feel like she was part of the rich tapestry of life (and death). Also, it gave her a chance to demonstrate her professional skills. She imagined people saying to her, 'Do you worry about his feelings for his wife?' and she'd say serenely, 'No, actually, I don't.' She would understand completely if he still had feelings for his wife. She would know instinctively when to draw back, when to let him grieve for her.

'*I* never fell in love with the one-legged boy,' said Julia.

'No, you were too busy breathing down the phone line to your ex-boyfriend's new girlfriend.'

'Aha! Touché!' Julia expertly flourished an imaginary sword. She'd been the school's fencing champion. She twisted the towel back round her head and lay down on the bench again.

'Anyway, I've got an excuse for my stalkerish behaviour,' she said. 'I was seventeen. Teenagers don't have properly formed brains. It's a medical fact. How old is your stalker?'

'She's Patrick's stalker, not mine. She's in her early forties, I think.' It was like pulling teeth getting the basic facts out of Patrick about Saskia. Ellen noticed that he always avoided using her name. He called her 'that woman' or 'bunny boiler'.

'There you go. She's a grown-up woman. A middle-aged woman, in fact. No excuse. She's loopy. Loony-bin material.'

Ellen sighed and stretched out her arms and legs as hard as she could, before releasing them and letting her body melt into the bench. 'We're all a little crazy, Julia.'

5

'You will lose weight' / 'You can become just as slim as you choose to be!'

Look at the differences between these suggestions. The first could be described as authoritative, paternal and direct. The second could be described as permissive, indirect and maternal. Milton Erickson believed that the unconscious mind would resist authoritarian suggestions. He was the first to use 'artful vagueness'. Don't you just love that phrase?

> – Excerpt from an advanced hypnotherapy class
> delivered by Ellen O'Farrell. Three students
> nodded, the rest stared at her, artfully vague

The news that she was unexpectedly meeting Patrick's son for the first time that night caused Ellen to feel a completely out-of-proportion sense of panic.

'Sure! Of course, of course!' she said to Patrick, nodding her head like a maniacal puppet when he rang to ask if it was OK to bring Jack along with him to dinner tonight, because the kid from school he'd been planning to visit had come down with some virus.

'He can eat whatever we're eating,' said Patrick. 'Or we'll just order him a pizza or whatever. Don't stress. Oh, and he'll bring along a DVD to watch.'

So, what, should she give the child a sliver off each of their pork medallions? Should she rush out and buy him a lamb chop? But there wasn't time. She was seeing two clients that afternoon and the first one was due in five minutes.

All she had to drink was champagne and wine. She needed Coke or cordial or, at the very least, juice. She had strawberries in liqueur and King Island cream for dessert, entirely inappropriate for a child.

He'd expect ice cream. Cake. Cupcakes? Too childish? She mustn't insult him by treating him like a little kid. Good Lord. She needed hours to prepare for this. She needed to ring her friend Madeline who was the expert on all things children; she needed to text Julia who would tell her she was being an idiot; to email her friend Carmel in New York who would order her a book on Amazon like *The Secret to Positive Step-Mothering*; to Google 'eight-year-old boys and how to talk to them without appearing desperate to be their mother'.

When she and Patrick had talked about her meeting Jack for the first time, they'd agreed that it would be during the *day*, not at night; probably a trip to the aquarium. Some sort of activity to keep the pressure off. She had planned to make funny, interesting, seemingly off-the-cuff (but really carefully scripted) remarks about fish that would appeal to an eight-year-old boy.

She felt a chill as she remembered something else: *her DVD player wasn't working*. The poor motherless child would be bored out of his mind.

Games! They'd have to play games. Did children still play board games? Or should they just sit around and talk? But what about?

For a moment she felt close to tears.

She needed to reframe this problem in a more positive light.

Ellen, he's a kid, not the Queen of England or the President of the United States.

Well, that wasn't at all helpful because, actually, Ellen would be more comfortable meeting the Queen or the President. The Queen reminded her of her grandmother, who she missed every day, and President Obama seemed like a jovial, chatty sort of fellow. Ellen was an only child who had grown up around adults, and her job brought her into contact with new people all the time. She wasn't shy, and although she had a tendency for self-loathing (working on this was an ongoing self-improvement project) she didn't really feel socially inferior to anyone.

Except children. Yes, truthfully, she felt inferior to children.

They were their own species with their own language and culture. They seemed so full of self-confidence these days. When she'd gone to the butcher today after the pool, a little girl who Ellen wouldn't have thought had been more than eight went gliding by chatting away into a pink mobile phone. She was wearing a fur-lined hooded coat, her face was painted like a tiger, and she was gliding because her sneakers appeared to have tiny wheels magically hidden in the soles. Not only that, her shoes had flashing pink lights along the side. Ellen had stared, full of wonder, at this exotic tiger princess on her invisible skates.

A few of her friends had babies, but babies were easy. You could cuddle them and make them laugh just by tickling their palms or blowing raspberries into their soft, sweet necks. Oh, she adored babies, but kids . . .

Actually, in spite of the fact that she was in her mid-thirties, many of her friends of similar age were childless. 'You girls all think you've got forever,' her mother said. 'You do realize that you're born with all the eggs you're going to get? Not that I'm in any rush to be turned into a wrinkly, grey-haired old granny.' A clipped laugh.

OK, so Ellen didn't have much experience dealing with children. But it had to be more than that causing this sense of panic. She peeled back the layers of her consciousness with brutal efficiency to reveal the naked, hairy truth.

She wanted to be this child's stepmother. She wanted him dressed in a cute little suit at her wedding. She wanted him to be a big brother to her own little baby, because she was thirty-five and born with all the eggs she was going to get. She wanted his daddy to be the one because she couldn't stand to look up another profile on that awful Internet dating site and find another middle-aged, bald, chubby man staring smugly at her out of the computer screen, demanding a 'slim lady who takes care of herself, for snuggles and long walks along the beach'. Yes, she wanted this child to love her and approve of her and save her from snuggles with chubby, smug men.

And of *course* that was all too much, and all too soon, and all very embarrassing, and if the kid sensed her crazy desperation (and she suspected that children were like dogs, with an instinct for fear) then he would –

The doorbell rang in an impatient way.

Ellen looked at her watch. It was her two-o'clock client. She ran down the stairs, two at a time, and then stopped at the bottom and recited her standard pre-appointment affirmation: *Breathe in, I am now fully present with this client, breathe out, I will give everything I have to give.*

She opened the door, smiling calmly and professionally. Neurotic Ellen was now safely stashed away in a closed cupboard at the back of her mind.

The client was Rosie: her bride-to-be who had promised her fiancé that she would have given up smoking by her wedding day.

She was a short, curvy woman with big, trusting round eyes and a tiny gap between her two front teeth, giving her an innocent, childlike look. Ellen couldn't actually imagine her smoking. It would be like watching a toddler with a cigarette in her mouth.

At their first session Rosie had mentioned that she was marrying 'Ian Roman' and given Ellen an expectant look.

I'm meant to recognize that name, thought Ellen.

'He's in the media,' said Rosie. 'He's quite, um, prominent.'

And then Ellen thought, *Ian Roman!* It was one of those names that sank into your subconscious via osmosis. He owned newspapers or television stations or something. His name appeared in the financial pages. Not that Ellen made a habit of reading the financial pages.

'So my married name will be Rosie Roman.' Rosie gave an artificial little laugh.

'You don't have to change your name,' pointed out Ellen.

'Oh, no, I'm not a career woman or anything.' Rosie waved her hand dismissively, as if she'd just been offered something far too expensive for her tastes. 'I'm just an ordinary person.'

Rosie seemed in a bad mood today, moving her head from side to side as if her neck was sore, and then pulling hard on the hem of her jumper as if it had shrunk in the wash.

'How are the wedding plans going?' asked Ellen, as she led her up the stairs.

'Don't ask,' said Rosie.

'Oh dear.'

'Stupid time to give up smoking, when I'm stressed out of my mind.'

'Not necessarily. It's often a good time to break a habit when you're out of your day-to-day routine.'

'I guess.' Rosie didn't seem convinced.

Ellen watched Rosie's shoulders relax as they walked into her glass office. The combination of the light and the ocean view was so powerful that sometimes she thought she probably didn't need to do much else for her clients but allow them to sit there.

'So how is it going?' asked Ellen, when they were sitting down.

'I'm still smoking like a chimney,' snapped Rosie.

Before Ellen had a chance to respond, Rosie said, 'I'm sorry. It's not your fault. I know it's my fault. I haven't even been listening to the CD you gave me.'

Ellen had given her one of her CDs with a specially prepared script for breaking the smoking habit. She'd made them years ago, and clients were often effusive about them, although she found it unbearable to listen to her own voice.

'Why haven't you been listening to it?'

Many clients didn't get round to listening to her CDs,

and they always told her this with guilty, defiant looks, as if they were admitting they hadn't done their homework but they knew they couldn't really get into trouble because they were grown-ups and they were *paying* for this.

Rosie shrugged. 'I don't know. I just can't seem to think of anything else besides the wedding. Like, for example, I despise the colour I picked for the bridesmaid dresses. Apricot! It was like I was suffering temporary insanity.'

She lifted a chocolate out of the bowl and then dropped it again.

'My fiancé gave up smoking years ago. He just decided one day when he was driving along the F3. He wound down his window, threw out the half-full packet of cigarettes and never smoked again.'

'Litterbug,' said Ellen.

Rosie looked at her with surprise and giggled. 'Yes.' Then her smile vanished abruptly, as if she'd been caught out.

There was something not quite right here. Ellen had a feeling that Rosie was lying to her about something. People were always lying, of course, whether consciously or not.

'Do you want to give up smoking?' said Ellen.

Rosie widened her eyes. 'Of course!'

'Well, sometimes there are unconscious blocks to letting go of a habit. I'm thinking we might do something a bit different and explore that today.'

'Sure,' sighed Rosie. 'Although I can tell you, there's nothing mysterious about it. I just need more willpower.'

'Well, let's see.' Ellen paused, trying to decide on what

induction to use. Then she knew the perfect metaphor. 'What colour do you wish you'd chosen for your brides-maids?'

'Blue,' said Rosie immediately.

'OK, would you like to choose a spot on the wall to focus on? Anywhere you like.'

Rosie sighed and shrugged and looked around the room. She kept her eyes fixed on the same spot in the far right-hand corner that almost everyone chose and said, 'OK.'

'Soon you will blink.'

Rosie blinked.

'That's right,' said Ellen warmly. 'And sooner or later, your eyes are going to close. It might happen straight away or it might take a little longer.'

Rosie closed her eyes.

Ellen watched Rosie's chest rise and fall and let her own breathing fall into the same rhythm. She spoke rapidly and smoothly, imagining her words pouring into Rosie's mind like liquid from a jar.

'I'm wondering if you can visualize a wall. And I'm sorry to tell you that it's painted apricot. But the good news is you're repainting it an exquisite blue. Your paint-brush is moving up and down in rhythmic strokes. Up . . . and . . . down. Up . . . and . . . down.'

Too complicated? Ellen had found she needed to be care-ful with her metaphors. Men often got too literal. A man might say afterwards, 'You should have had me paint an undercoat first.' Women tended to go off on tangents. One of her earliest clients had said that she loved to sunbathe, so Ellen did what she thought was a pretty safe induction about lying on a tropical beach. Afterwards, the client admitted that she'd spent the whole time trying to choose the best swimsuit.

Ellen watched Rosie's eyes move rapidly behind her eyelids and noted the tension in her body: her shoulders up, her hands gripping the sides of the chair, her fingers pressing hard into the leather. A beam of sunlight caught the diamonds of Rosie's chunky engagement ring.

'Each time you see that paintbrush move, notice your body sink into a deeper feeling of relaxation. You'll probably find your breathing is starting to flow in rhythm with the paintbrush. Up . . . Down . . . In . . . Out. Up . . . and . . . down. In . . . Out.'

She watched Rosie's tiny, pixie-like black boots fall outwards in a v-shape. 'Watch their feet,' Flynn used to tell her. 'That's the giveaway.'

'The wall is nearly finished. By the time it's entirely blue . . . or perhaps a little while later . . . you will be enjoying the most glorious state of relaxation you have ever experienced.'

Rosie's mouth drooped, her face sagged and her head lolled to one side. If some of her clients knew how they looked when they were in a trance they would be horrified. It was something that Ellen had never mentioned to anyone, not even other therapists. It felt like something deeply personal she shared with her clients.

OK, Ellen, just exactly what are you going to do with this blue wall you've got in front of you?

But she knew. Sometimes her work felt clumsy and forced. Other days, like now, it felt natural and fluid. She was in a light trance herself. She was in the 'zone'.

'Rosie, you have the power to turn that wall into a deep rich-blue curtain like you might see on a stage. And behind that curtain somebody important is waiting for you. I don't know who, but it's someone with great wisdom, someone you trust implicitly. You're pulling back the curtain and that person is waiting for you. Maybe they're stepping forward to hug you.'

She waited and watched.

'Are you with that person?'

Rosie lifted her right index finger: the signal they'd agreed upon for 'yes'.

'Now, it's my belief that this person has something to share with you. They might be able to tell you why you're finding it hard to give up smoking, or give you the resources or strength you need to break this habit. I'm going to be quiet now while you listen to what they have to say.'

Ellen could feel her own chest rising and falling in perfect rhythm with Rosie. Rosie's face remained impassive, but she was chewing at her lip.

After a few moments, Ellen spoke again.

'Rosie,' she said. 'I'm wondering if you would like to share with me what you've learned. It's entirely up to you.'

For a moment Rosie said nothing and then she spoke. Her voice was a husky, slow monotone.

'I don't want to marry him,' she said. 'That's why I don't want to give up smoking, because I don't want to be married.'

Ellen's eyebrows shot up and her eyes went to the cluster of shimmering diamonds on Rosie's finger.

'I don't really like him all that much,' said Rosie.

*

'So, *this* is my son, Jack!'

Patrick stood in Ellen's hallway with his hands resting on his son's skinny shoulders.

'Well, *hi*, Jack! How are you?' Ellen sounded exactly as she'd been afraid she would: like a librarian at story hour.

'Good, thanks.' The boy glanced briefly up at Ellen and then looked away again. He had his father's slightly almond-shaped, pale-green eyes. His thick blond hair was long and messy, cut over his ears, like a 1960s rock star.

'Good! Well, so . . . great! So I'm hoping you like sausage sandwiches.' To her joyous relief, Ellen had discovered some sausages in the freezer before they'd arrived.

Jack didn't appear to have heard her. He had his chin down and was tugging at the front of his T-shirt as if he was checking the fabric for strength.

Patrick cleared his throat. 'Ellen asked you a question, mate.'

'No, she didn't.'

'Yes, she did. She asked if you liked sausages. You *love* sausages, don't you!'

Jack shrugged his shoulders away from his father's hands. 'I don't *love* sausages, actually, Dad. Also, she didn't ask if I liked sausages. She said, "I'm hoping you like sausage sandwiches." That's not a question. It's, like, a sentence. See. She said, *I'm hoping you like sausage.*'

'OK, well –' began Ellen.

'I love pizza. You said I could order a pizza tonight.'

'I said *maybe* we'd order a pizza tonight, but if Ellen has made sausage sandwiches for you, then that's what you're having.' Patrick gave Jack a stern, paternal and somewhat panicky look.

'I haven't actually made them yet,' interrupted Ellen. 'You can have pizza, Jack, if that's what you prefer, of course you can.'

'Yeah. Thanks, that's what I'd prefer.' Jack sighed gustily, as if someone was finally talking sense. 'So, can I watch my DVD now?'

'Jack. Please. You don't need to watch your DVD straight away. That's not good manners.'

Ellen saw that Patrick's cheeks were sucked in as if he was clenching his jaw. He was desperate for Jack to make a good impression on her. Her own nerves vanished.

'It's all right,' she said to Jack. 'My DVD player isn't working, but you can watch it on my laptop if that's OK.'

'Yeah, that's OK,' said Jack kindly. 'I can work your laptop.' For the first time he tilted his head up to look at her properly.

'You must be disappointed about your friend being sick,' she said to him.

'Yeah,' he said impatiently. 'Hey, will you please hypnotize me? Also, could you teach me how to hypnotize my friends? Like, so they do whatever I command? That would be so cool! They could be my slaves.'

'That's sort of unethical,' said Ellen.

'What?'

'OK, let's get that DVD on.' Patrick clapped his hands together.

'You're acting really weird, Dad.' Jack frowned.

Patrick gave Ellen a self-conscious grin. 'Weirder than usual, hey, Jack?'

Jack shook his head gravely. 'Seriously, Dad.'

They headed down the hallway and Jack stopped to

touch a fingertip to the metallic silver polka-dots on the orange wallpaper.

He looked back up at Ellen. 'This is a cool house.'

'Thank you.' She was so smitten she only just managed to stop herself from calling him 'darling'.

Twenty minutes later, Jack was sitting in Ellen's living room with the laptop on his knees, headphones over his ears, his eyes fixed on the flickering images on the screen and his big, chunky sneakers up on Ellen's beautifully restored retro coffee table.

Patrick didn't tell him to take his feet off the table, and Ellen didn't know how to ask him to take his feet down without sounding like an evil stepmother. What did a few scuff marks matter?

'Well, he's gorgeous,' she told Patrick, when they were sitting at the dining-room table. She had laid out a platter of sourdough bread and dips and big green olives. They could see the top of Jack's head where he sat watching his DVD through the dining-room door. She lowered her voice slightly even though he obviously couldn't hear them.

'He has his moments,' said Patrick. He cleared his throat and smiled at her. 'You're the first woman I've introduced him to since his mother died.'

'Well, that's an honour. But wait, didn't you introduce him to Saskia? I mean, you said you lived together for a couple of years? So she must have lived with Jack too.'

She hadn't thought about that before. Saskia had known Patrick's little boy as well.

Patrick's nostrils twitched as if he'd just smelled something unpleasant. He spat an olive seed out into the palm of his hand. 'I don't count her.'

Ellen was unsettled. He couldn't just pretend Saskia had never existed. He must have loved her once, in the beginning. And Ellen was not the first woman he'd introduced to his son. That was factually incorrect. She didn't like that.

'How old was Jack when Saskia lived with you?'

'He was a toddler, I guess.'

'And did they . . . get on? Was he upset when she left?'

'He doesn't even remember her,' said Patrick dismissively, which didn't answer her question at all. His eyes lost their focus on her and he suddenly called out, 'Jack! Get your feet off the table!'

How could he see that Jack had his feet on the table from here? Or had he noticed before and not bothered to say anything?

'Excuse me.' Patrick stood up and went into the other room.

When he came back he was all set for a new subject. 'So, how was your day today? You had a couple of clients, you said, were they good – ah – sessions?'

If she knew him better she would have said, *I haven't finished talking about Saskia and Jack*, but she was always struggling to contain her possibly voyeuristic interest in his ex-girlfriend. After all, he didn't seem to want to know anything about her ex-partners.

So she told him about her session with Rosie and how she'd discovered that the reason she didn't want to give up smoking was because she didn't really want to get married. Of course, she carefully didn't reveal any names, or the fact that the cancellation of the wedding would probably make the social pages of the Sydney papers. She thought it was an interesting topic of conversation that showed her in a good light.

Patrick listened intently, and then he squinted at her, as if he was trying to see through the sun. It made him look older. He had deep lines on either side of his eyes, she guessed from all that outdoors work as a surveyor.

He said, 'So she's calling off the wedding? Because of you?'

'Well, I don't know exactly what she's going to do next. That's up to her. I guess I just helped her see how she really felt.'

'But imagine how that poor bloke is going to feel. Are you sure it's not just a case of cold feet? Or maybe she's just looking for an excuse for why she can't give up smoking?'

Ellen felt irritated. She had been expecting fascination and even awe over what hypnotherapy could achieve. She scratched at a spot on her wrist. (Irritability always manifested itself as an itchy feeling on her right wrist, in the exact spot where she had suffered dermatitis as a child.)

'I don't make my clients *do* anything,' she said. 'I *help* them to bypass the critical factor and directly access their unconscious minds. My client had what's called a mini *satori*. It's the Zen word for enlightenment.'

Ellen thought back to the end of her appointment with Rosie. After she had come out with the revelation about her marriage, Ellen had given her a post-hypnotic suggestion: 'When you come out of this trance you will feel calm and in control as you make your decisions about what you want to do next.'

When Rosie had emerged from her trance, she had

blinked and immediately held up her hand to look at her engagement ring. She'd slid the ring from her finger and held it up to the light with her fingertips, looking at it curiously like it was a strange and unpleasant scientific specimen. Then she smiled at Ellen and said, 'You know what? I don't even like the *ring*.'

'I'm sorry. I didn't mean to imply any criticism,' said Patrick. 'I guess I just identified too much with the man.'

'It's OK,' said Ellen. This was the first time there had been the slightest hint of tetchiness between them. It had to happen, she told herself. There was no need for alarm.

'I saw one of those stage shows once,' he said. 'You know, where they call people out of the audience to hypnotize them. I have to admit, and I hope this doesn't offend you, but I'm assuming stage hypnotists are very different from, you know, *proper* hypnotherapists like you, but the thing is, I sort of hated it.'

Ellen smiled at his guilty expression.

'That's fine,' she said. 'It's completely different from what I do.'

'I hated the stupid looks on their faces.' He demonstrated by slumping back in his chair and letting his chin drop to his chest. He straightened back up and took a sip of his wine. 'They looked so pathetic. It was like he'd drugged them and he could make them do whatever he wanted.'

'He couldn't really. They were still in control. He just helped them lose their inhibitions,' said Ellen.

'I like to be in control,' said Patrick. 'That's why I've never been a big drinker, and I've never taken drugs. I want to be in the driver's seat all the time, so to speak.'

He paused, took another olive with his fingertips and then delicately placed it back down on the plate in front of him. He kept his eyes fixed on the olive. 'That's what I hate most about this thing with Saskia. She's in control. She affects my life and I don't get any say in it and there's not a thing I can do about it. So I'm sorry if I sometimes seem a bit weird about her. It's just that when we're talking about her, it's like she's in the room with us.'

He was looking at her with the same pleading, desperate expression as the many clients who came to her looking for a solution they didn't really believe she was capable of providing, and Ellen experienced a sudden tiny shock of sympathy. It had been all false bravado on that first night when he'd told her about his stalker. Of *course* he was damaged by it: he was a stalking victim! It had been incredibly insensitive of her not to even think about this before. She had been so interested in Saskia and trying to understand her motivations, she hadn't even really considered the potential impact on Patrick. She was behaving as if only women felt real emotions, as if men were somehow a less complex life form.

'I'm sorry,' she said. 'When I was asking all those questions about Saskia I hadn't really thought about how she's the last person you want to talk about. I mean, the way this must affect you – it must be – well, obviously, I've got no idea what it must be like.'

Patrick was looking at her, straight in the eyes. There was some complex feeling he was trying to convey to her. Perhaps he was having his own mini *satori*.

He leaned forward. She leaned forward too. Good. He

was going to share. This was going to take their relationship to a new, deeper, more spiritual, more profound level.

'Do you want to go upstairs for a few minutes?' he said.

'And I think he's going to tell me something profound and meaningful, and it turns out he just wants a quickie! With his son, right *there*. Sex was the furthest thing from my mind!'

'It's always the closest thing on their mind,' said Ellen's friend Madeline.

They were talking on the phone. Ellen was filing paperwork in her office and she could tell by the hissing and clattering that Madeline was cooking, probably something elegant and organic, and probably with a floral apron tied round her pregnant waist. Madeline was glowingly pregnant with her second child. She and Ellen had shared a flat when they were in their twenties, back when Madeline would have fallen about laughing at the thought of ever wearing a floral apron.

Ellen would have called Julia but she'd found that Julia's interest in hearing about Patrick had ever so slightly cooled as the relationship progressed. Even before Julia's divorce, she had always been the sort of friend you called when things were going badly, rather than when they were going well. Now that Patrick was officially Ellen's 'boyfriend' there was just the tiniest hint of contempt in Julia's voice when Ellen mentioned anything about him; unless it involved his crazy ex-girlfriend – she *loved* hearing about Saskia. It wasn't that she didn't want Ellen to be happy; it was just that she didn't think there was much to say about happiness.

Madeline, on the other hand, was the sort of friend who cared deeply but was hopelessly inept when things were going badly, who panicked and changed the subject fast if someone's voice so much as trembled with emotion.

'That's not true. That's a cliché,' Ellen said to Madeline. 'I've been out with men who never think about sex. Anyway, I'd just that moment had this revelation that I needed to stop thinking of him as a man, and think of him as an individual, as just another human being.'

'Just because he felt like sex doesn't mean he's not human.'

Madeline seemed to be missing the point.

'Yes, but with his son in the house?'

'Well, if you're going to live with him then you might have to get over that.'

'Don't parents wait until their children are asleep?'

'Wasn't the whole point of this story something to do with the expression on his face?'

'Yes, that's right. So when I declined his charming offer, he got this *look* on his face, and I *think* it might have been a sulky look.'

'What do you mean, "you think"?'

'Well, the expression was only there for a flash. I think those people who specialize in detecting lies call it a "micro-expression". After that, he was fine. We had a lovely dinner, and afterwards we played Monopoly with his little boy and that was fun. But I kept thinking about that face he pulled, that micro-expression, and I thought: Is this a sign? Am I going to look back one day and say that was the moment I should have got out? Because that's what micro-expressions do! They reveal your true self!'

'Ellen, this is the most ridiculous thing I've ever heard. The poor man is so enamoured with you he wants sex every second of the day, and then when you turn him down, he shows the briefest look of disappointment –'

'I know, I know, I'm awful. Over-analytical. Hysterical. It's just that I want this one to work, Madeline, I really want this one to work.'

'Well, of course you do,' said Madeline crisply.

So it's serious. The hypnotist has met Jack. As far as I know that's the first woman he's introduced Jack to since me.

I wonder what he thought of her.

She doesn't really seem like a kid person. Too spiritual and floaty. Children like earthy, real people who get down on the floor and play with them. I can't imagine someone who talks about 'light filling your body' sitting in a sandbox.

I guess Jack is too big for sandboxes now, although it's still there in their backyard. Sometimes, when Patrick is at work and Jack is at school, I go to the house and eat my lunch in the backyard. I sit there on the garden seat we bought on eBay, where I used to have my morning cup of tea, and I remember when this was my home and this was my backyard and this was my life.

I always told him we needed a padlock for that back gate.

I used to sit in that sandbox with Jack and we'd play with his Matchbox cars for hours. His dad did better sound effects than me but I was more patient. Patrick was too much like a kid himself. He'd build this amazing racetrack through the sand, with tunnels, bridges and lakes, and then he'd get all frustrated when Jack suddenly decided to stand up and stomp it all to the ground. I'd say, 'Patrick, he's two years old.'

Jack looked so tall and lanky when he got out of the car at the hypnotist's place. I was parked across the street. I'd just stayed there after my appointment with her. I'd had a feeling that Patrick was coming over for dinner. When she'd taken me upstairs, I'd smelled a garlic and wine sort of smell, like something marinating. I didn't expect to see Jack come too. It gave me a shock. A sudden shock of indescribable pain, like when you're a kid, and you're hit on the nose with a basketball on a cold morning, and you *CANNOT BELIEVE* how much it hurts, and your friends all laugh and you want your mother so bad.

I don't think Jack was especially excited about meeting the hypnotist. He didn't look too happy. His shoulders were all slumped. I thought I saw him blowing his nose. I hope he doesn't have the flu. It's bad for people with underlying conditions like asthma.

Once, when he'd just turned three and Patrick was away for work, Jack had an asthma attack in the middle of the night and I had to take him to Emergency. I can still remember the terror I felt seeing his little ribcage caving in as he tried to suck in enough air, and the way his beautiful green eyes fixed on mine, begging me to help him, and then sitting there with him on my lap, trying to stop him from pulling off that stupid little plastic mask while they gave him Ventolin. The doctors and nurses all assumed I was his mother. 'How is Mum coping?' 'Does Mum need a cup of tea?'

It would have been stupid to have corrected them and say I was just his stepmother. 'Does Stepmum need a cup of tea?'

Jack called me Sas, because that's what Patrick called me. Each night when I went in to say goodnight, he'd take his dummy out of his mouth (we didn't wean him off his dummy until he was nearly four; which was very bad, we were soft with him) and say 'I lub you, Sas', and quickly pop his dummy back in, and every time I felt like my heart just about exploded out of my chest.

Jack was more than I'd ever hoped for, more than I'd ever dreamed.

The night he had the asthma attack, they finally let us go home when the sun was coming up. I didn't want to put him in his cot, so I took him into our bed and we both fell asleep. When I woke up, Patrick had got home from his trip, and he was just standing there watching us, with this look on his face, this look of tenderness and love and pride, and he said, 'Hello, family.' I'll never forget that look.

Two years later, three weeks after Jack started school, Patrick said, 'I think it's over.'

'You think what's over?' I said cheerfully. That's how unexpected it was. I didn't have any idea what he was talking about. A TV series? The summer?

He meant us. We were over.

6

'The rejected stalker is often a former intimate partner, with a complex, volatile mix of desire for reconciliation and revenge.' ?!! (Revenge for what? What did he do to her?)
 – Scribbled note by Ellen O'Farrell while Googling
'motivations for stalking'

There were no more 'micro-expressions', or if there were, she didn't catch them. Her doubts drifted away like candle smoke.

The first two weeks of July were glorious that year: shiny, blue-skied winter days as crisp and crunchy as apples. It was the perfect weather for a new relationship, for holding hands on public transport, for the sort of behaviour that makes the recently broken-hearted want to weep and everyone else roll their eyes.

Ellen collected memories: a remarkably lustful kiss pressed up against a brick wall like teenagers outside the Museum of Contemporary Art; a Sunday-morning breakfast where she made him laugh so hard other people in the café turned to look; a mildly drunken game of gin rummy that ended in bed; coming home from yoga to find an enormous bunch of flowers lying on her doorstep with a note that said, 'For my girl'.

They stopped being quite so careful with each other.

'Jesus,' said Patrick, the first time he saw Ellen polish off a giant steak.

'Aren't you meant to be a good Catholic boy?' said Ellen.

'I wasn't using the Lord's name in vain. I was saying, Jesus, did you see what that woman just ate? I thought I was dating a hippie, dippy vegan chick, not a bloodthirsty carnivore.'

'Hurry up or I'll eat yours.'

There was no sign of Saskia for a while.

'Maybe I've scared her off,' said Ellen, who was still idly researching the psychology of stalking whenever she had a spare moment.

'Maybe!' Patrick patted her arm in a kindly, worried fashion, like a doctor responding to a terminal patient who says, 'Maybe I'll be the exception to the rule.'

The words 'I love you' began to hover in Ellen's thoughts, like a song lyric she couldn't get out of her head. She remembered reading somewhere, probably in a stupid magazine article, that it was fatal for the woman to say 'I love you' first. Which was the most ridiculous, sexist, superstitious thing she'd ever heard . . . but still, there was no rush. They'd only been dating for six weeks. The right moment would present itself.

She thought back over her previous 'I love you' history.

She'd been the first to say 'I love you' to Andy. He'd looked momentarily terrified, before he quickly, dutifully, said that he loved her too.

She said it first to Edward too, after drinking a particularly delicious strawberry daiquiri. She hadn't really meant it at the time, to be honest. She meant that she loved strawberry daiquiris.

Actually, now she thought about it, she always took the lead! She'd written 'I love you' on Jon's thirty-eighth birthday card and he'd taken forty-two humiliating days to say it back.

It might be safer all round if Patrick said it first.

And then he did.

He stayed at her place one week night, and in the morning he was running late for an early appointment. He leaned over the bed, kissed her cheek and said, 'OK, gotta go, love you,' before rushing off.

He'd said it in the exact same casual voice that he used to tell Jack that he loved him on the phone. It was clearly a slip of the tongue.

She was pondering this, half amused, when she heard the sound of his footsteps pounding up the spiral staircase. She sat up in bed as he reappeared at her doorway.

'Sorry,' he said breathlessly, his hands gripping the door jamb. 'That was a mistake. Well, no, not a mistake! I was waiting for the perfect moment with moonlight and rainbows or whatever, and now I've blown it. Fool.' He slapped his forehead.

He came and sat down on the bed next to her, and looked at her in a way that she didn't think she'd ever been looked at before, by anyone, lover or friend, as if nobody else had ever concentrated that hard.

He said, 'I would like to make something very clear.'

'All right.' Ellen made her face serious.

'I am making this comment on the record. I am, of course, prepared to put it in writing if necessary.'

'Right.'

He cleared his throat. 'Ellen. I love you. I officially love you.'

'I love you too,' said Ellen. 'Officially, that is.'

'Right. Good. Well, this has all worked out extremely well then.'

He held out his hand and they shook hands formally, as if at the conclusion of a satisfactory business deal, except that before she could let go, he pulled her to him, rolled her on to her back and kissed her as they laughed.

They sat back up, grinned idiotically at each other, and then Patrick looked at his watch. 'OK, so this sounds bad but –'

'Go.'

He kissed her again and then left. She lay down again and felt drenched with happiness. *This* was how love was meant to feel: simple and peaceful and funny. Obvious. There was nothing to analyse. It seemed to her that she had never loved or been loved like this before. All those other times had been a wishy-washy imitation of the real thing.

Just imagine if she'd gone her whole life without knowing that!

(Also, not that it mattered, it was just something interesting to note for future reference: *he* said it first.)

I had to cancel my appointment with the hypnotist because I had to go away to Melbourne for work.

I tried to get out of it, but Trish supposedly came down with some terrible virus, and I was the only one available at short notice. Single, childless woman. What else have you got to do? That's right. Nothing.

Patrick and I never went to Melbourne together, so there were no memories lurking on street corners. At first it seemed like the trip was a good idea. The brooding skies and cruel breezes were a relief after Sydney's relentlessly cheery weather. Work kept me busy and distracted. I was tired at night and fell asleep straight away.

But the longer I was away from Sydney, the more my desire grew to see Patrick and Ellen again. On Thursday morning I woke up early, ravenous for information. *What were they doing right that moment?* Had he stayed at her place? Had she stayed at his? My need to know felt physical, like a nutritional deficiency.

I flew back to Sydney on the first flight out on Friday morning, my hands clenched round the armrests, leaning forward as if I could will the plane to go faster. I was a vampire and I needed blood.

It was Friday afternoon and Ellen was taking a moment in between appointments for some deep breathing and positive affirmations.

She had a somewhat stressful weekend ahead of her.

That night, Patrick was meeting Ellen's mother and godmothers for dinner, and the following evening Ellen was being introduced to Patrick's family. On Sunday, Patrick was meeting Julia for the first time. They were having fish and chips at Watsons Bay, and Patrick's friend 'Stinky' was coming along too, to meet Ellen, and also as a possible match for Julia, although his name obviously didn't bode well. ('Oh, he doesn't actually *stink*,' Patrick had said, all chuckles at the thought of Stinky actually stinking. 'That's just what we call him.' 'So why do you call him that?' Ellen had asked, but Patrick just laughed. Men were so strange sometimes.)

They hadn't meant for all these introductions to happen on consecutive days. It had just turned out that way because of various reasons such as Ellen's mother suddenly rescheduling their dinner, and Stinky unexpectedly being in Sydney for the weekend.

The weekend loomed in front of Ellen like a week of exams and dental appointments. She'd woken up that morning with a vague sense of dread, manifesting itself in an unpleasant feeling of nausea. It felt like a crowd of people were about to come stomping through the middle of their delicate new relationship, throwing about their opinions, asking questions, digging up flaws. Patrick and Ellen would see each other through the eyes of other people; people who mattered. Their perspectives would be like harsh, unflattering spotlights illuminating shadowy corners.

Breathe in.

She didn't give a fig what other people thought!

Breathe out.

Rubbish. She gave a whole fig tree. She wanted everyone she loved to love Patrick and everyone he loved to love her.

Breathe in. Breathe out. Breathe –

'Forget it,' she said out loud.

She gave up trying to access her higher self and instead took a chocolate from her silver bowl, letting it dissolve slowly in her mouth. The chocolate was there for therapeutic purposes. It released neurotransmitters like endorphins and serotonin, leading to a sense of well-being, and even euphoria. Which, as Julia said, was all just a complicated way of saying it tasted good.

Ellen closed her eyes for a moment and felt the warmth of the sun on her face. She was sitting in the recliner chair that her clients used. She often sat here and tried to imagine what it must be like for them, seeing her sit opposite them. Did they ever catch a glimpse of her doubts, or worse, her vanities? Did she look silly sitting there, with her legs so professionally, elegantly crossed? Did the sun shining through the windows show up the little hairs and lines around her lips?

She would bet that when Patrick was out on a job, leaning over to peer into his 'theodolite', lifting one arm high, he never felt a moment of self-consciousness. But it was different in a 'soft' profession like hers, where there were still some people who thought she was akin to a magician or a faith healer or a fraud. She remembered meeting an old friend who said, with genuine surprise, 'You're not *still* doing that hypnosis stuff, are you?' as if it had just been a funny little phase. 'It's my career,' Ellen had told her, but the friend, a corporate lawyer, thought she was joking, and laughed politely.

In fact, it was more than a career. It was her passion, her calling, her *vocation*.

The recliner was still warm from the last client who had sat there: Deborah Vandenberg, the woman who suffered from unexplained, debilitating pain in her right leg if she walked for more than ten minutes. Before coming to Ellen, she'd tried physiotherapists and chiropractors and sports doctors; she'd had X-rays and MRIs and exploratory surgery. There appeared to be no physical reason for the pain. The medical profession had basically shrugged their shoulders and said, *Sorry, we don't know.*

'I was very active,' she'd told Ellen. 'I loved bushwalking. Now, some days, when it's very bad, I find it hard to *shop*. This pain has changed almost everything about my life.'

'Chronic pain does that,' said Ellen.

She'd never experienced it herself, but over the years so many clients had brought her stories of how pain was a corrosive substance that cruelly ate away all of the simple pleasures of a life.

'But I may be able to help,' she'd said.

'Everyone thinks they can help.' Deborah gave her a politely cynical smile. 'Until they give up on me.'

She reminded Ellen a little of Julia. She was tall and confident, with short dark hair and a tomboyish grace as she sat back in her chair, one long black-jeaned leg entwined about the other.

She had mentioned that she enjoyed cooking, so at their previous session Ellen had got her to imagine a stove dial she could use to turn her pain down. Today, as soon as they sat down, Deborah told Ellen that it was 'possible' she'd turned her pain down one notch while walking through a car park that morning.

'But I probably imagined it,' she said, as if suddenly doubting herself. She had made it clear from the beginning that she was a sceptic. At the end of her last session, she'd said, with some pride, 'You didn't put me under, I was fully conscious the whole way through.' 'That's fine,' Ellen had told her. (She got that a lot, and often from clients who had just moments ago been drooling and slack-jawed, quite clearly in deep trances.)

'We're going to work on another dial today,' Ellen told her. 'I think we'll call it your "Good Energy Dial".'

Deborah's lips pulled back in a slight sneer. 'That sounds very . . . cute.'

'I think you're going to like it,' said Ellen firmly, ignoring the sneer. Negativity hid fear.

She'd used a quick, simple induction that involved feeling a deeper sense of relaxation with each step taken down a flight of stairs and watched as Deborah's sharp features relaxed. She looked much younger when she was in a trance (because in spite of her scepticism, Deborah most certainly did go into a trance). The lines on her face smoothed out, and there was a vulnerable, naked look about her, in contrast to her conscious edgy confidence. It made Ellen feel motherly towards her.

'I want you to think of a time when you felt filled with confidence or joy,' she said. 'Sift through your memories until you find that one perfect moment. Nod when you're there.'

She waited and watched and, as she did, she travelled back through time herself to her own perfect moment, where she had first practised hypnosis. She was eleven, sitting in this very room, with her grandmother, her mother's mother, who believed that everything Ellen did was spectacular. Ellen had just finished reading a book she'd found at the library, *How to Hypnotize Anybody*, and her grandmother had agreed to be her first patient. She'd used a necklace as a pendulum, and watched her grandmother's wrinkled brown eyes follow it, back and forth, back and forth.

'You're very good at that,' her grandmother said afterwards, blinking with what Ellen could tell was genuine surprise: it was quite different from her generous clapping after Ellen played her the recorder. 'I think you might have a gift.'

I think you might have a gift . . .

The sweetest, most surprising words imaginable. It was like that moment in the movies when superheros discover their powers, or perhaps it was how nuns felt when they first heard the spooky, charismatic voice of God whispering in their virginal ears.

Deborah, her eyes still shut, her cheeks slightly flushed, nodded to signal she had her moment. Ellen wondered, briefly, what Deborah was remembering.

'That feeling you're remembering right now, that's the feeling that I want you to be able to call upon, whenever you need it. Whenever you press your thumb into your right hand you can generate that feeling. The harder you press, the more you can increase the feeling, until it's flowing like electricity through your body.'

Ellen let her voice rise with the vigour and power she wanted Deborah to feel.

'So next time you feel pain, this is what you can do. First you can use the pain dial to reduce your level of pain, and then you can use your energy dial to recreate that feeling of power.'

She saw a flicker of hesitancy on Deborah's face and immediately switched to a more authoritative, paternal tone. 'You have the ability to do this, Deborah. It's all there, inside you. You are going to excel at these techniques. You can be pain-free. *You can be pain-free.*'

A few minutes later, she brought Deborah out of her trance. She blinked in a disorientated, bleary-eyed way, like a passenger waking up on a plane, before quickly checking her watch. Then she ran both her hands through her hair, and said, 'I didn't go under again,' and briskly pulled out her wallet from her handbag.

Ellen just nodded and offered her the bowl of chocolates, but later, as they were standing at the front door and Deborah was putting on her coat, she said slowly, without looking at Ellen, concentrating on doing up her buttons, 'You know, you might actually cure me.'

'I'm not curing you,' Ellen reminded her. 'The physical cause could still very well be there, whatever it is. I'm just helping you find a way to manage the pain.'

'Yes, but it might actually *work*,' said Deborah, and the surprise and respect in her eyes was just like the look on Ellen's grandmother's face all those years ago.

Ellen smiled now, remembering that moment. That was job satisfaction.

She opened her diary and her smile faded when she saw her last appointment for the day: Mary-Kate McMasters. Oh, well. No more surprised, respectful looks today.

She glanced at her watch. There was still time for Mary-Kate to cancel. On three previous occasions she had called at the last minute to say that she couldn't get away from work. She was a legal secretary and always sounded full of breathless self-importance when she called to cancel, as if the law firm she worked for couldn't operate without her.

Ellen chided herself for that uncharitable thought. Maybe Mary-Kate was indispensable. And she always insisted on paying the fifty per cent cancellation fee that Ellen specified on her price list (for cancellations with less than twenty-four hours' notice), even though Ellen never tried to enforce her own policy. She hated accepting the money for doing nothing.

The doorbell rang and Ellen swore, as if she'd stubbed her toe.

So she was annoyed when Mary-Kate cancelled and she was annoyed when she turned up. For some reason she was feeling a strong antipathy towards this poor, sad woman. What was that about? She'd had annoying clients before, and clients she liked more than others, but she'd never experienced such a visceral feeling of displeasure when a client turned up for an appointment.

If she wasn't careful her dislike would seep its way into Mary-Kate's therapy and that would be unconscionable.

She reminded herself of the Buddhist doctrine: *We are all one.* She was Mary-Kate and Mary-Kate was her.

Mmmm.

She opened the door with a warm, welcoming smile. 'Mary-Kate! Wonderful to see you!'

'I'm sure it's just glorious to see me,' said Mary-Kate with a bright, sarcastic smile.

She couldn't have heard Ellen swear, could she?

As usual, Mary-Kate was dressed entirely in black. She was a dumpy, lumpy woman with long, lank hair parted in the middle like a seventies flowerchild, except that she didn't have the fresh baby face to carry it off. Her face had a resentful, hangdog look.

Oh, you're a depressing sight, thought Ellen. She longed to give her a make-over, to cut her hair off, give it some volume and colour, to dress her in something other than black. Her face was quite pretty really. Even a touch of lipstick would brighten her up!

Good Lord, she was turning into someone's awful mother.

'Would you like to use the bathroom?' she asked Mary-Kate.

She always asked clients if they wanted to use the toilet first; a full bladder was the worst thing for a good hypnosis session.

'No, thank you,' said Mary-Kate. 'Let's just get on with it.'

When Mary-Kate was sitting in the green recliner, somehow managing to make it look like the most uncomfortable chair ever, Ellen opened Mary-Kate's file on her lap.

'How have you been since we last met?' she asked.

'Same as ever. Fat as a whale. How have *you* been?'

Ellen glanced up at her. 'You're worried about your weight?'

'No, well, yes, of course, *obviously*, but whatever.' Mary-Kate sighed and yawned. 'So, Friday today. Got anything interesting planned for the weekend, Ellen? Seeing friends? Family?'

'No particular plans,' said Ellen. 'So, tell me, is weight loss something you'd like us to work on?'

At Mary-Kate's first appointment she'd said she wanted hypnosis because she'd started to become panicky whenever she drove through the Sydney Harbour Tunnel and she wanted to put a stop to it before she became one of those 'nutty, fragile' types. She hadn't mentioned anything about her weight, but that was often the case with clients.

The real reason they were there didn't emerge until after a few visits.

'Perhaps I went through the potato famine in a past life,' said Mary-Kate. 'And now I'm trying to make up for it. That's why I crave potatoes.'

'Well, hypnotherapy can be very useful –'

'I don't believe in past lives,' said Mary-Kate truculently. 'That's such *crap*.'

'I think we talked about this at our last session,' said Ellen mildly. She was not fond of the word 'crap'. Also, they had talked at some length about Mary-Kate's lack of belief in past lives.

'So you don't take people back to their past lives?'

'I don't specifically offer past-life regression,' began Ellen. 'But I certainly have had clients who believe they have re-experienced past lives under hypnosis. I have an open mind about it.'

Mary-Kate snorted and gave a little sneer.

'Have you had to drive through the tunnel since I saw you last?' said Ellen.

Mary-Kate shrugged. 'Yeah, I did. I was fine, actually. I must have got over it.'

Ellen studied her. 'So, then, what are you hoping to gain from today's session, Mary-Kate?'

Mary-Kate sighed again. She looked disdainfully around the room, as if it was a cheap hotel room, leaned over, took a chocolate, then changed her mind and dropped it back in the bowl again.

Finally she spoke. 'Actually, I think I do need to use your bathroom.'

*

It felt like relief to see her again.

I don't know how she feels about me, but I sort of like her. I mean, I'm sickened by her existence obviously, but I find her strangely compelling.

It's sort of a perverse crush. Like when you meet a man and you find them repulsive but you still want to go to bed with them, and when you do, it's great, but afterwards you feel ill with regret. Like that ape-like guy I met at one of the client Christmas parties last year. He wore too much aftershave and more jewellery than me. The sex was fine, but afterwards I was like a rape victim scrubbing myself in the shower and sobbing for Patrick. I guess it's like that self-loathing you feel after eating bad, greasy junk food.

Ellen wouldn't eat junk food. Tofu and lentils, I imagine. I wonder if she is lovingly appalled by Patrick's pizza habit yet.

It's not like I want to go to bed with her. I just want to know everything about her. I want to watch her, in every imaginable situation. I want to get inside her head and inside her body. I want to be her, just for a day.

I haven't felt like this about any of the other girls Patrick has dated.

The thing about Ellen –

It makes me feel good that I can use her name.

I used her name a lot at our last session. 'Thanks, Ellen.' 'See you next week, Ellen.' Each time I use her name it's like I'm slapping Patrick across his self-satisfied face.

Don't think you've moved on, boy. Making a new life that has nothing to do with me. I'm still here. I'm tossing her name about. I've been in her house. I've used her bathroom. I know what brand deodorant and tampons she uses. She's nothing special.

Except maybe she is. She might even be too good for you, buddy. She might be out of your league. Out of our league.

The thing about Ellen is that it seems like she is exactly the same person on the outside as she is on the inside. That's the impression she gives anyway, as if she is without artifice or affectation, as if she doesn't have to filter every word that comes out of her head to make sure it gives the impression she wants to give.

Of course, she must have some sort of filter. Everyone has a filter. It's just that her filter is something quick and simple which carefully discards anything that might accidentally offend anyone. Whereas my filter is a labyrinth of pipes and funnels and sieves that converts everything I think into something acceptable to say, depending on the situation and the person and what I'm trying to prove at that particular moment.

She has nothing to prove. She really believes all that 'power of the mind' crap. She's passionate about it. It's like her religion.

She comes across as a bit sanctimonious at first but I think she is actually a genuinely good person – in the old-fashioned sense of the word. She wishes only good for the world. Whereas you and I, we're sort of flawed. We don't wish everyone well, do we?

I feel like such a fake when I'm with her, not just for the obvious reasons. If I met her as my true self I would still be aware of that difference between us.

I can understand why you think you might love

her, Patrick. I do understand. I love her a little bit too.

It's just that on our first Christmas Eve together you and I fell asleep flat on our backs, like sunbathers; we were holding hands, with the taste of raspberries in our mouth from that wonderful liqueur Stinky gave us, and the ceiling fan whirled above us, and the room seemed to rock, just gently, and I remember thinking it was like we were two children on a raft, floating down a magical river.

That night happened. I don't care how sweet or pure-hearted Ellen is, that night happened. To us.

When she didn't even exist.

Remember how we both had a crush on Cameron Diaz?

Well, that's how it should be with Ellen. We should have met her at a dinner party, and on the way home we could have talked about how lovely she was, and how interesting and weird all that hypnosis stuff was, and by the time we got home we should have forgotten all about her.

She's extremely nice, but she's like Cameron Diaz, Patrick. She's not meant to be a real person in our lives. She's nothing to do with us.

Ellen and Patrick were driving to her mother's place. Patrick was behind the wheel. He was the sort of man who automatically assumed it was his job to drive, which was fine with Ellen, who was a nervy driver. (She remembered how Jon always carefully, correctly, shared the driving. 'Your turn,' he'd say, tossing her the keys, and then he'd sigh and snort and criticize her driving the whole way.)

'So your mother never met anyone else after your dad,' said Patrick. 'Jesus. This traffic is out of control.' He banged his foot on the brake and the car jerked. 'Sorry.'

He was clearly nervous.

It was such a pity that Ellen couldn't reassure him by saying something like, 'Oh, my mother is going to adore you!'

Her mother probably wouldn't adore him. Out of all of Ellen's past relationships, she'd liked Jon the best, with his witty, caustic remarks. Of course she had. Jon was the one who had done the most damage to Ellen's self-esteem, the one she'd loved, who hadn't really loved her back.

If only she had one of those sweet, slightly plump, chatty mothers, who was sort of vague about politics and business and anything outside the domestic realm. If only she had a grey-haired, bespectacled father who would warmly shake Patrick's hand and ask him man-to-man questions about surveying, while the sweet mother fussed about, trying to get the 'fellows' to take a second piece of cheesecake.

It wasn't going to be like that at all.

'Mum has had a few long-term relationships over the years,' she told Patrick. 'But not for a while now.'

'And your dad is just . . . not in the picture?'

'Never anywhere near the picture,' said Ellen. She paused, aware of a slight flash of irritation. 'Like I said.'

She had told him her family history a few weeks after they started dating. She had perfected the telling of the story over the years, so that it was the ideal party piece or dinner-party anecdote, unusual and interesting and intimate, just the right length, with no embarrassing emotion likely to cause guests to shift uneasily in their seats.

She always started the same way. 'My mother was a woman ahead of her time.' Then she would explain that early on the morning of the first of January 1971 the intensely pragmatic Doctor Anne O'Farrell made a new year's resolution to become a single mother. She was a successful, independent woman in her thirties and she didn't especially want to be married, but she did (oddly) want a baby. With the help of her two closest female friends, she made a list of potential candidates to father her child, along with their positive and negative attributes: their education levels, their medical histories and personality traits.

Anne had kept these lists and given them to Ellen when she was a teenager. Her 'father' was a list of bullet points in her mother's scrawly handwriting with the figure 'eighty-five per cent' circled next to it. The highest score by ten per cent.

Her father's positive attributes included 'post-graduate education level' (he was a surgeon; Anne had met him at university), 'good teeth', 'small ears' (her mother abhorred large, flappy ears), 'excellent skin', 'no family history of heart disease, diabetes or respiratory problems' and 'good social skills'.

His negative attributes were 'eyesight (glasses)', 'spiritual tendencies', 'mother who reads tarot cards', 'somewhat strange sense of humour' and 'engaged to be married'.

Over recent years, Ellen had started leaving off the 'engaged to be married' part. She didn't know if it was the whole world that was becoming more moral – a sort of increasing level of global prudishness – or if it was just her own social circle that appeared to be becoming more conservative.

Apparently her father's engagement hadn't been an obstacle. It had been as easy as pie to seduce him, not just once, but the optimum number of times, and on the appropriate days before and after ovulation.

'It was the seventies after all,' said her mother.

And that was that. A job well done. Her 'father' got married a few months later and went off to live in the UK, and never knew of Ellen's existence.

'What if I wanted to go and find my dad?' she'd said to her mother when she was going through her extremely tame, short-lived rebellious teenager stage, and she quivered a little at the unfamiliar, almost sexual word in her mouth, 'Dad'.

'I'm not stopping you.' Anne didn't even look up from the newspaper she was reading. 'It would be a very cruel, hurtful thing to do to his wife.'

And, of course, Ellen would never knowingly do anything cruel or hurtful, and besides, the thought of actually meeting this middle-aged man filled her with shyness. Her friends' fathers were big and hairy and deep-voiced, sometimes funny, but mostly boring, and somehow essentially irrelevant to real life.

Her mother's friends, Melanie and Phillipa, had never had children of their own. They had been Ellen's godmothers, and for much of Ellen's childhood had shared a house with her mother. There had been various boyfriends who arrived to take them out on dates, who sometimes turned up at breakfast time (unshaven and croaky-voiced at the kitchen table), but mostly they were just an amusing sideshow in Ellen's life; their mannerisms and appearances were dissected with much hilarity before they vanished. (Although Mel had finally got married in her fifties to a shy, inscrutable man, who seemed to make her very happy, and didn't overly impact on her social life.)

'It was like having three mothers,' Ellen would tell people, which was true. Three successful, opinionated single women had all had an equal say in her upbringing.

'It was like growing up in a lesbian commune,' she'd continue, but she'd stopped saying that as she got older, because she'd just been trying to sound sophisticated and edgy, and maybe it was a bit disrespectful to lesbians and she actually had no idea what it would be like to live in a lesbian commune or even if they existed.

'So my father was basically a sperm donor – he just didn't know it.' That's how she always finished the story, and it normally generated lots of stimulating discussion, and people would say things like, 'Aha! That's where you get your hypnotism thing from – your spiritual dad and your tarot-card-reading grandma!' (as if they were the first people in the world to have thought of that), and some would applaud her mother's actions, and others would politely, or not so politely, express their disapproval.

She didn't mind when people disapproved. She wasn't sure if she approved herself, but she knew her mother didn't care less what anyone else thought, and Ellen had told the story of her conception so many times now, she felt quite detached from it. It was like Julia's story of how her father kidnapped her and her brother during a bitter custody dispute between her parents, and he'd dyed their hair brown, and there had even been a thrilling police chase. Ellen knew that Julia must have once felt some sort of emotion about this memory, and probably at some subconscious level she still did, but now it was just an excellent story. A party piece.

Patrick had listened to her story carefully, and at the end he'd said, 'Good for your mum, but I'm sorry you missed out on having a father.'

'You don't miss what you don't have,' said Ellen, which wasn't something she really believed at all, but she certainly hadn't spent her childhood sobbing into her pillow for 'Daddy'. 'Maybe it would have been different if I'd been a boy.'

'I think daughters still need their dads,' said Patrick gravely, and his seriousness had made her fall a little bit further in love with him, and imagine him tenderly holding a baby girl (yes, all right, her own baby girl), like a man in a baby-powder commercial.

And now he was saying, 'And your dad is just not in the picture?', as if he hadn't really concentrated on the story properly, as if he'd heard her story at a dinner party many years ago and couldn't quite remember the details. It was so disappointing. Ellen felt that nauseous, anxious feeling again. What if she just *wanted* to be madly in love with this man? What if it was all a gigantic self-delusion? What if he was actually a superficial, selfish prat?

Would she have been better equipped to pick out the good men if she'd grown up with a father? Probably. In fact, almost definitely. After her mother had called her bluff about contacting her father, she'd researched the psychology of fatherless daughters and left photocopies with the relevant sections marked in yellow highlighter. 'What exactly do you want me to do about this?' her mother had said. 'Go back in time and never conceive you?' 'Feel guilty,' Ellen had answered.

Anne had laughed. Guilt wasn't in her emotional lexicon.

'I'm sorry,' said Patrick, as the light changed green and the car inched further forward. 'I know your dad wasn't in the picture. I'm just nervous. I've got that job-interview feeling. I'm not great at job interviews, especially when I badly want the job.'

She glanced over at him and caught an expression of almost terrified vulnerability flash across his face. For an instant he looked exactly like his son.

'When I'm nervous I just start coming out with all this crap that doesn't even make sense.' He frowned as he looked in the rear-vision mirror. 'Also, I'm sort of distracted because our friend is back.'

'Friend?' said Ellen.

'Our bunny-boiler friend. Behind us.'

'Saskia is following us again?' Ellen swung round in her seat and scanned the cars behind them. 'Which one is she?'

'Yeah, that's great. That's fantastic. That's one thing you really need, your ex following you to meet your girlfriend's family for the first time,' muttered Patrick.

'Yes, but *where is she*?' The seatbelt pulled hard across Ellen's neck. Directly behind them was a man in a truck, his eyes closed, thumping his hands against the big steering wheel, his mouth moving as he sang along to an unheard song.

'She's in the lane next to us, a couple of cars back,' said Patrick. 'Don't worry. I'm going to lose her.'

He slammed his foot on the accelerator and the car shot forward. Ellen turned round in time to see the lights change from orange to red. When she turned back they were crossing the intersection, leaving a bank of stationary cars at the lights.

'What *colour*?' she said desperately. 'What colour car?'

'Lost her,' said Patrick happily. 'Look. We're moving again.'

'Great,' said Ellen, and rubbed at her sore neck.

I lost them at the lights and I couldn't guess which way they were going.

Maybe they were meeting up with friends of hers. Patrick doesn't know anyone down that way.

I saw her turning round in her seat. I wonder if she was trying to see me. Patrick probably knew I was behind. I know when he knows I'm behind him. He drives faster than usual, erratically. Sometimes he sticks his fingers up at me. Once I saw him getting a ticket for doing an illegal right-hand turn trying to get away from me. I felt bad about that because he'd always been proud of the fact that he'd never got a ticket in over twenty years of driving. I sent him a bottle of wine to his work to apologize. I picked it out especially. A Pepper Tree white. We'd discovered that wine on a trip to the Hunter Valley during our last summer together. We bought a whole case and we got addicted to it. I don't see how he could drink that wine without thinking of me. But I waited outside his office that night and I saw one of the girls he works with walking to her car carrying my bottle of wine. I recognized it, because I'd wrapped it up nicely in blue tissue paper. He didn't even bother to open it. He just handed it to that girl.

I try to imagine how he describes me to the hypnotist. To *Ellen*. I guess he tells her I'm 'psychotic'. He yelled that at me once. I was walking behind him at his local shops, when he suddenly swung round and walked straight back towards me. I stopped and waited for him, smiling. He was smiling too. I thought we were finally going to have a proper conversation. But then, when he got closer, I saw it was a sarcastic, angry smile. He stuck his finger in front of my face, and yelled, 'You're a psychotic lunatic!'

Which . . . you know, might have been funny in other circumstances, except that I was worried he was going to hit me.

He was so angry he was shaking.

Actually, I sort of longed for him to hit me. I needed him to hit me. If he wasn't ever going to hold me in his arms again, at least he could hit me. There would be a connection again. Flesh against flesh.

But he didn't. He locked his hands behind his neck and rocked his head like an autistic child. I just wanted to comfort him. He didn't need to get so worked up. It was only me. I'm still only me. That's what he can't seem to get. I said, 'Darling.'

He dropped his hands and I saw that his eyes were red and watery. He said, 'Don't call me that,' and he walked away, and I stayed where I was, looking at the specials pinned up on the window of the shop where we always got fish and chips on a Sunday night.

That's the thing. I'm permanently stuck in this crazy-person role now. He will always think of me as a crazy person. He used to think I was a 'funny bugger' and I had 'beautiful eyes' and that I was 'one of the most generous people he'd ever met'. Those were all things he said to me, things he meant at the time.

But now I'm just crazy.

The only way for me to not be crazy would be to disappear from his life. Like a proper ex-girlfriend is expected to do. To discreetly vanish into the past.

And that's what drives me . . . crazy.

Ellen could see Patrick's 'fight or flight' response kick in as soon as they walked across the doorway of her mother's home.

Oh, my poor darling, she thought. She remembered the first time she'd taken Jon to meet her mother; the way he'd looked about with those lazy, hooded eyes, so certain of his own superiority. Patrick's clear green eyes were darting about as if looking for possible escape routes, and he was clearing his throat over and over.

It mattered to him what Ellen's mother thought. It mattered, and that meant Ellen mattered.

Poor man. It was understandable that he was nervous. Jon was an exception; most men would find this intimidating.

Three immensely elegant, immensely confident women in their sixties, all holding the delicate stems of their glasses of wine with their fingertips, all bizarrely dressed almost entirely in white, to complement her mother's all-white theme – white couches, white walls, white accessories – all swooping down from the high stools on which they'd been perched to kiss Patrick on both cheeks, who only expected to be kissed on one cheek and kept offering the wrong one, and having to bend awkwardly at the knees so they could reach him.

'Why are you all dressed in white?' asked Ellen. 'You're blending into the furniture.'

There were peals of laughter.

'We couldn't believe it when we saw each other!' gurgled Pip.

'We look like that Bette Midler movie. *First Wives Club*. Not that we've ever been wives.' Ellen watched her mother's eyes rest on Patrick's tradesman-out-on-the-town outfit of blue jeans and long-sleeved checked shirt rolled to the elbows. Jon wore Armani and Versace and some other Italian men's designer label that was so very special Ellen had never heard of it.

'Ah, Anne, Mel is a wife,' pointed out Pip.

'Of course she is. I just never think of her as one. Which is a compliment, Mel.'

'I'm so flattered, Anne.'

'Who else was in that movie?' mused Pip. 'Bette Midler, Goldie Hawn and somebody else. Someone I like. Do you know, Patrick?'

Patrick looked startled. 'Ah, I'm not –'

'We finally worked out it was because we'd all read the same article in *Vogue*,' said Mel. 'About flattering colours for women in their fifties. Not that we're *technically* in our fifties.'

'Speak for yourself,' said Anne. Ellen's mother found it genuinely insulting to be reminded of her actual age.

'You're thirty-four days older than me, Anne O'Farrell.'

'*Diane Keaton!*' cried Pip. 'That was the third wife. Thank goodness I got it. That was going to drive me crazy for the whole night.'

'Patrick, what can we get you? Beer, wine, champagne, spirits? You sound very dry.' Ellen's mother fixed her violet eyes upon Patrick, like a bird on its prey.

(Anne's eyes were her most striking feature. Her friends had wanted her to enter an Elizabeth Taylor lookalike competition when she was young, and she probably would have won if she hadn't thought such competitions beneath her. Unfortunately she hadn't seen fit to pass on her beautiful eyes to Ellen. Obviously this wasn't really her decision, except that Ellen had always suspected that if her mother *did* have the choice, she might have decided to keep all the glory for herself. She was very vain about her eyes.)

Patrick cleared his throat again. 'A beer would be great, thanks, ah . . .'

'You haven't actually introduced us properly yet, Ellen. The poor man probably thinks he's stumbled into some sort of elderly harem.'

'You haven't stopped talking,' said Ellen. She put her hand on Patrick's arm. 'Patrick, this is my mother, Anne.'

'Can you see the resemblance?' Anne fluttered her eyelashes up at him as she handed Patrick a glass of beer.

'I'm not . . . I'm not sure.' Patrick clutched his hand round his beer.

'And my godmothers, Mel and Pip,' continued Ellen, ignoring her mother. 'Or are you Phillipa tonight? She switches back and forth.'

'Depending on whether I'm skinny or fat,' said Phillipa. She beamed at Patrick and waved a hand up and down her plump body. 'So it's perfectly obvious who I am right now, hey?'

An expression of pure panic flew across Patrick's face.

'Phillipa,' remonstrated Ellen.

'Aha! So not thin enough for Pip! I have to come back to you for some more hypnotherapy sessions, Ellen.' Phillipa turned to Patrick with a deadly serious expression on her face. 'I suffer the most debilitating addiction to carbohydrates.'

'That's . . .' began Patrick. He obviously had no idea how to finish the sentence, and drank his beer as if his life depended on it.

'I have tried to get Ellen to hypnotize my addiction away.'

'She giggles the whole way through,' sighed Ellen, as her mother passed her a glass of white wine without asking what she wanted; she would have preferred a juice.

'Come and have a sensible conversation with me, Patrick,' said Melanie. She patted the stool next to her. 'Ellen said you were a surveyor, right? My grandfather had a wonderful collection of old maps he left to me. I think the oldest dates back to about 1820.'

Patrick took his beer glass away from his lips and spoke in his normal voice. 'Is that right?'

Mel got Patrick settled next to her, and pushed a plate of bread and salmon dip towards him. Ellen watched Patrick's shoulders relax as Mel chatted calmly to him, steering him on to stable, factual, masculine conversational ground where he could be sure of his footing. She always thought that Mel should have been a diplomat's wife because of her ability to talk graciously and knowledgeably on any subject.

(Although Mel herself would have found that a very sexist remark. 'I'd be the diplomat, thanks very much,' she would have said.)

'Let's go help your mother.' Phillipa grabbed Ellen by the arm.

'Why, how kind of you, Pip,' said Anne, her violet eyes still on Patrick.

'Oh, darling, he's just adorable!' said Phillipa as soon as they were in Anne's pristine kitchen. 'I bet he's one of those strong, silent types, isn't he? I can just see him on a mountaintop with his surveying equipment, squinting into the sun.'

'No,' said Ellen (although that was exactly the way she liked to imagine him). 'He's not like that at all. He's very chatty when he gets a chance to be. And he mostly does surveys on houses.'

'Oh, to be young and in love,' said Phillipa nostalgically. 'I loved being in love. I always lost so much weight.'

'I remember you sitting in this kitchen and saying "Oh, to be young and in love" to Julia and me when we were seventeen,' said Ellen. She paused. 'And that means you weren't that much older than me now!'

'Speaking of Julia,' said her mother, who never required anyone's help and was now giving the last-minute touches to delicately constructed meals on giant square white plates that would be divinely flavoured but would no doubt leave Patrick suggesting pizza on the way home, and Phillipa reaching for the bread basket, 'I saw Julia's mother at yoga on Saturday. She said your new boyfriend has a stalker.'

'The grapevine is so efficient,' said Ellen. It sometimes felt like she'd never left that closed little private-school world of her school days where all her friends' mothers were on the same committees.

'A stalker!' Phillipa's eyes popped. 'How exciting!'

'Oh, yes, it will be all very exciting, Pip, when my daughter is found dead in a ditch.' Anne spoke from inside her walk-in pantry.

'Is it an ex-lover?' continued Phillipa, ignoring Anne. 'A woman he *spurned*? Or just a random homicidal maniac who has taken an interest in him?'

Anne came out of the pantry and put a bottle of vinaigrette down on the worktop with unnecessary force. 'Has this person shown any violent tendencies?' she asked. 'Has Patrick reported her to the police?'

'It's just an ex-girlfriend who hasn't quite moved on,' said Ellen. 'There's really nothing to worry about.'

She wondered how her mother would react if she knew Saskia had been following them tonight, or if she knew that Ellen had felt a discernible sense of disappointment when they lost her at the lights.

Anne said, 'Just promise me you'll be careful. You always see the *good* in people, Ellen, which is all very adorable but also naive.'

Ellen smiled at her. 'I must get that adorable tendency from my father.'

Anne didn't smile back. 'You certainly didn't get it from me.'

'Too right,' said Phillipa and giggled so hard she snorted.

I couldn't decide where to wait for them.

Patrick's place or hers. I knew it would depend on what they were doing with Jack for the night. Mostly Patrick's mum seems to go over to Jack's place and mind him, but sometimes Jack goes to her place, and I guess he stays in the room out the back. It's not very fair to Maureen. I remember she used to get exhausted when we left him with her when he was a toddler. He had her wrapped round his little finger. Although of course it would be different now he's eight. I guess he probably just does his own thing – watches TV or whatever. I hope Patrick doesn't let him watch too much TV. I hope he reads. He used to love his books. I remember once I decided to see how many times I could read him *The Very Hungry Caterpillar* before he got sick of it. I had to give up after I'd read it to him fifteen times. Every time I finished he'd say 'Again?' with the same enthusiasm. I can still see his little fat, flushed cheeks as he sat there on my lap in his red Thomas the Tank pyjamas, his lips pursed in concentration as he poked his fingers through the holes that the caterpillar had bitten through the apples.

I could have babysat Jack tonight, while Patrick and Ellen went wherever they went. That would have been fine. 'Bye!' I could have said cheerily, like a teenage babysitter, sitting on the couch, snuggled up with Jack under a duvet with a bag of crisps.

Maybe I should text Patrick and offer. Ha ha.

I could have been babysitting for years. I sometimes think that could have made all the difference – if Patrick hadn't decided to rip Jack out of my life, my little boy, my darling little boy.

I remember one of the mothers I knew from Jack's preschool ringing me up when she heard and saying, 'He can't do this to you, Saskia. It's got to be illegal. You must have rights. You're Jack's mother.'

Except I wasn't his real mother. Just his dad's girlfriend.

What court would care about that? A relationship that lasted three years. I didn't even officially live with them for the first year. Not all that long.

Long enough to see him get out of nappies, learn to swim and tell knock-knock jokes and use a knife and fork. Long enough for his hair to go from curly to straight. Long enough for him to call for me whenever he had a bad dream. Me. Not Daddy. He always called for me.

A sudden shriek slicing through my sleep and I'd be halfway down the hallway before I even woke up properly. I remember once I went to him and he was sitting up in bed rubbing his eyes and sobbing his heart out. 'I just wanted to blow out the candles!' he said to me. And I said, 'It's OK, you can blow them out,' and held out an imaginary cake. He puffed out his cheeks and blew, and that was it, problem solved: he smiled at me with his eyes still full of tears and then put his head back on the pillow and fell straight back asleep. Patrick didn't know anything about it until the next day.

I guess Jack's nightmares aren't so sweet and simple these days.

This is the thing. When do you cross the line from babysitter to mother? If you look after a child for a night, you obviously don't suddenly become his mother just because you bathed him and fed him for a few hours. The same goes for a week. Or a month. But what about after a year? Two years? Three years? Is there some point where you cross an invisible line? Or is there no line except the legal one, the one you sign on the adoption papers? Foster children can be claimed back by their real parents at any time, even after years.

I should have adopted Jack. That was my mistake.

But it never even occurred to me.

I saw looking after Jack as a privilege, a gift. It was just another wonderful part of being in a relationship with Patrick.

So when he broke up with me, I knew that I'd have to lose Jack like I'd have to lose everything else that I loved about Patrick, like the veiny tops of his hands – I loved his hands; and his handwriting, he had such beautiful handwriting for a man; and the particular way he smiled at me after sex; and his singing, he sang country music songs quietly to himself when he did stuff around the house. I hate country music but I loved hearing that quiet singing. It was the soundtrack to my life.

I never found out if I did have rights to Jack. Maybe I did.

But I went into shock when Patrick said he didn't love me any more.

I couldn't get out of bed. I couldn't talk. Couldn't eat. It was like I'd been hit with a terrible illness. It was like a bomb had exploded through my life, shattering everything I thought I knew.

If Patrick had just let me see Jack on weekends. Like a divorced dad. That might have been enough.

Maybe then I wouldn't be doing this thing, this whatever it is, that I cannot seem to stop doing no matter how hard I try. And I have tried. I have. I never understood alcoholics or gambling addicts before. Just stop it, I always thought, when I heard about somebody wrecking their life because of a stupid addiction. But now I get it. It's like telling someone to stop breathing. *Just stop breathing and you'll get your life back on track.* So you hold your breath for as long as you can but it doesn't take long before you're gasping for air. I know it's humiliating. I know I'm pathetic. I don't care. It's just not physically possible to stop.

And so I sat there in my car outside Ellen's house. She told me her grandmother left it to her when she died, which sort of sums up the differences between us. My grandmother left me a fruit bowl. I had the window down and I could hear the sounds of the waves breaking on the beach. That's what Ellen must hear when she goes to sleep. That's what Patrick must hear when he stays over.

I fell asleep, eventually, and when I woke up my back had seized up and the sun was rising and I couldn't see Patrick's car. So that meant they'd stayed at his place.

I thought of them asleep in the bed that was once mine, probably lying on sheets that I'd chosen, and I wondered if he was reaching out for her now in the dawn light, running a fingertip so delicately down her arm she wasn't sure if she was dreaming it. Dreamy, half-asleep lovemaking at dawn was his thing.

I opened the car door and got out all hunched over, like an old lady. The kookaburras laughed like crazy.

7

Remember...
1. All hypnosis is self-hypnosis.
2. You can't get stuck in hypnosis.
3. You are always in control. You can stop
at any time.
4. Hypnosis is a natural state of mind.
5. Help yourself to the chocolates!
— Laminated card stuck to Ellen O'Farrell's
office wall

Ellen woke to the feel of Patrick's fingertip running slowly, delicately up the length of her arm.

The fingertip on the arm was always his opening move.

Jon used to kiss the back of her neck. Tiny butterfly kisses.

Edward would lick her earlobe, enthusiastically and wetly, which tickled unbearably. He mistook her shrieks and convulsions for crazy sexual excitement and she never got round to clearing up the misunderstanding.

Andy would whisper in her ear, his breath hot and irritating, 'You feel like . . .?' ('What?' she always wanted to say. 'Do I feel like *what*? Finish the sentence!')

She wondered if Jon was kissing the back of someone's

neck right now, and Edward was licking an earlobe and Andy was whispering his unfinished question.

Why are you thinking about ex-lovers?

With her eyes still closed, she rolled towards Patrick to give him easier access to her arm. She liked the fingertip thing. She loved the fingertip thing.

She'd loved Jon's butterfly kisses too.

So what? Concentrate on the fingertip.

Presumably, Patrick had used the same techniques on Saskia, in this very same bed, possibly on these very same sheets.

Which was interesting, but not at all relevant.

Once you'd perfected your sexual moves you didn't tend to change them. She herself still kissed exactly the same way that boy in the caravan park had taught her to kiss when she was fifteen. He tasted of beer. Disgusting and delicious. What was that boy's name? Chris? Craig? Something like that.

Patrick tugged at her nightie. 'Let's get this off.'

She wanted to be in bed with Patrick right now; there was nowhere else she wanted to be. On the other hand, it didn't especially please her, the idea of Jon kissing someone else's neck.

She helped Patrick pull the nightie off over her head.

She wondered what Saskia was doing right now. Where did she go last night, after she lost them at the lights? Did she go home and look at old photos of herself and Patrick? Did she cry?

Was Ellen responsible for another woman's pain? Should she give him back? Of course, she had no intention of giving him back. He didn't want Saskia. He wanted Ellen.

This was the way the world worked. Relationships ended. If they didn't, she'd still be with the beery-breathed boy in the caravan park.

Julia was right. Saskia needed to be a grown-up and move on.

But, on the other hand, wasn't there something noble about Saskia's refusal to let go? She was crazy with passion. Ellen had never let passion make her do anything crazy.

'What are you thinking about?'

Patrick was up on his elbow, looking down at her, smiling. He brushed back her hair from her forehead.

'Saskia,' she answered honestly, without thinking.

Patrick retracted his hand. 'I cannot get away from that woman, can I?'

'I'm sorry,' said Ellen. She went to pull him back towards her, but his lips had compressed into a thin line and he looked like a grumpy schoolteacher who has just about had it up to *here* with you lot.

He said, 'Now the bitch is in bed with us.'

He got out of bed and walked into the en suite bathroom, closing the door behind him unnecessarily hard.

Ellen settled herself back on her pillow and gazed up at the slowly whirling ceiling fan. (Round and round and round. She saved it up as a good image for an induction. 'Imagine you're watching a ceiling fan.')

Look, Saskia. You stopped us from having sex. He's angry with me because of you.

Every time she was with Patrick, part of her was imagining how Saskia would react if she was there, watching. It was as if she were performing in her own reality TV show with an audience of just one. If Patrick knew how much time she was devoting to thinking about Saskia, he'd be furious.

Outside the window, the kookaburras burbled with laughter.

If you stare at someone for long enough from behind, they will sense your gaze and turn round. They don't actually see you, but they feel something different in the atmosphere.

That's why I've always believed that if I thought about Patrick for long enough and hard enough, he would sense it. If someone can feel a gaze across a room, then shouldn't they be able to sense a torrent of true emotion, a *tsunami* of feeling, from across a handful of suburbs?

I imagine my feelings like a dense cloud, floating above the streets of Sydney, and one day Patrick is standing in the shower (he likes his showers long and red-hot; steam billowing) with the window open and all of a sudden he senses it – my love – he's breathing in the cloud of my feelings, and he turns off the taps and thinks, 'Saskia.'

And while he's drying himself he thinks, 'I made a mistake.'

And then, before he even gets dressed, he calls me. And everything is right again.

People get back together. It happens all the time. Why shouldn't it happen to us?

Ellen could hear the sound of Patrick's shower running.

She must have upset him; he'd been looking forward to this morning. Jack had stayed with his grandparents and Patrick wasn't picking him up until they went there tonight for dinner. He'd talked about how they would sleep in till late this morning, and eat breakfast and read the papers in bed. He'd bought croissants especially. Now she'd ruined his morning.

Was it any wonder that the poor man didn't want to hear his stalker's name mentioned when he was trying to make love to Ellen?

Overcome with remorse, she threw back the covers.

Without putting her nightie back on, she got out of bed and tried the bathroom door. It wasn't locked. The shower was pounding. There was so much steam she could hardly see.

'Are you going to join me?' said Patrick from the shower. He didn't sound like an angry schoolteacher any more.

She pulled back the screen.

A few minutes later her legs were locked round Patrick's waist and she wasn't thinking about Saskia at all.

I wandered around for a while in the hypnotist's front garden.

I picked a daisy and stuck it behind my ear; as if I was that sort of girl, the sort who knows she will look whimsical and pretty with a flower stuck behind her ear. It was like I thought the daisy could transform the whole situation, make me cute and endearing, as if this was a funny little love triangle, as if Ellen and I were two girls at a party trying to get the attention of the same boy. Then I walked on to Ellen's front porch and caught sight of my own reflection in the glass panel next to her front door. I looked middle-aged and seedy. I took the flower out and crushed it in the palm of my hand, and then I knocked, quite loudly, on the front door, even though I knew she wasn't home. I knocked again, angrily. I seemed to be making some sort of a point. *I'm here!*

Then I shrugged, as if we'd had an appointment and she'd let me down. I stepped off the porch and noticed a path running straight down the side of the house and on to the beach.

I went down it and took my shoes off and walked barefoot on the cold sand.

Imagine that. Walk out your back door and you're on the beach.

I wonder if she appreciates it. She doesn't seem like an especially sporty type. I can't imagine her sweating or puffing. I guess she sits cross-legged and meditates and chants. Or she does yoga. Salutes the sun and all that crap.

The beach was deserted and silent, except for the lap of the waves and the occasional squawk of a seagull; still too early for the joggers and power walkers and dog walkers. It was high tide and the pearly sky seemed to hang very low.

Without stopping to think about it, I took off all my clothes and ran out into the ocean and dived straight under a wave.

The water was so shockingly cold it made all the air rush out of my lungs. When I came back up, I screamed out loud, and dived under again and again. I opened my eyes each time I went under and saw swirling eddies of sand and shafts of filmy light.

Forget him.
Let him go.
Be free of him.

The words came into my head, crystal clear, each time I went under, as if mermaids were whispering messages in my ear.

Afterwards, as I walked naked along the beach towards my clothes with the early-morning sun gently caressing my shoulders, I decided to have coffee and read the paper at one of the cafés and I suddenly felt a strange feeling that I hadn't felt in a long time and it took me a few minutes to work out that it was happiness. Plain, simple happiness. I'd forgotten how much I liked swimming in the sea. It's been ages. I don't know why. The weather had to be scorching and the water had to be practically tepid for Patrick to swim. 'You wuss!' I used to yell at him from the water, and he'd lift a hand in ironic acknowledgement without even looking up from the paper.

His mother told me once that he'd always been funny about water temperature. She had to write him notes to get him out of school swimming events. When he was in the shower his brother used to throw cups of cold water over him and he'd scream like a girl. 'Big girl's blouse,' his dad would say.

I wondered if the hypnotist had met his parents yet. His mum was fond of me. One Christmas, after she'd drunk too much punch, she told me that I was like a daughter to her.

I might listen to the mermaids and have a night off from Patrick and the hypnotist. I might go to that work party tonight after all. I might wear the red dress I keep putting off wearing.

And on the way there, I might drop by on Patrick's mum. Just to say hi. I could show her that I've moved on.

'So you're a hypnotist, Ellen,' said Patrick's mother. 'I must admit I've never met a hypnotist before.'

'She's a hypnotherapist, Mum,' Patrick corrected her.

'Oh, I'm sorry!' His mother looked stricken.

'It's all right!' Both Patrick and Ellen rushed to reassure her.

Maureen Scott was an off-the-shelf mum and grandma. She had the nondescript, colourless hairstyle, the softly sagging face, the formless figure, the pastel-coloured, elastic-waisted clothes.

'My mum is a lot older than yours,' Patrick had said when they were driving over. 'She's a different generation.'

'How old is she?' Ellen had asked.

'She's turning seventy this year.'

Ellen's mother was sixty-six, only four years younger, but Ellen hadn't pointed it out and now she was glad; Maureen did seem as if she was at least twenty years older than Anne. Whereas Ellen's mother was all sharp lines and angles, Maureen seemed without definition. She could imagine Maureen as one of Anne's patients. Anne would be brisk and condescending, and tell her to take calcium to avoid osteoporosis and have regular mammograms, as if these old-lady problems were a long way in front of her.

'So, a hyp-no-therapist,' repeated Maureen carefully. 'Now I'm just so interested to hear more about this, Ellen.' She passed Ellen a tray with a picture of the Sydney Harbour Bridge containing a dish of French onion dip and rows of crackers.

'We'll have to watch ourselves,' said Patrick's dad. 'She might hypnotize us over dinner.' He clapped his hands and chuckled.

George looked disconcertingly, comically, similar to Patrick. Ellen had to stop herself from staring. She didn't think she'd ever seen a parent and child who looked so alike. If Patrick wasn't in the same room, she might have suspected Patrick was playing a joke on her and pretending to be an old man with a not especially convincing disguise. George's hair was white instead of brown, but seemed to be cut in an identical style, and Patrick's eyes looked out at her from a more wrinkled face. Everything was the same: the shape of his nose, the jaw line, the set of the shoulders, even the way they sat in their chairs, their legs stuck out straight in front of them, cradling cans of beer in big hands.

'They're actually clones,' said Patrick's brother in her ear, as he reached down beside her to place a coaster in front of her. The coaster had a picture of Ayers Rock on it.

Patrick's younger brother, Simon, was small and dark with a neatly trimmed goatee like a fashion designer. He was only twenty-four, and looked to Ellen like he should have been taking drugs in a nightclub, instead of passing round drinks in this redbrick bungalow with the crucifix hanging above the television silently playing a game show, and the china cabinets stuffed with knick-knacks and collector plates.

'Ellen is going to teach me how to hypnotize my friends,' said Jack without looking up from his spot in front of the television, where he was lying on his stomach playing with a small computer game.

'I can teach you, mate,' said George. He picked up a

teaspoon and let it swing back and forth between his fingertips. 'You're ... getting ... sleepier.'

He slapped his knee. He was one of those self-applauders.

'Yeah right, Grandpa,' said Jack.

'I bet Ellen's never heard that joke before,' said Simon.

'George!' said Maureen. 'I'm sure there's more to hypnotizing people than that!' She looked anxiously at Ellen. 'That is – is there?'

'A little bit,' smiled Ellen. The French onion dip was made from sour cream mixed together with a packet of dried French onion soup. It took her right back to her schooldays.

'Sometimes I feel like I've been hypnotized after I've been watching too much television,' said Maureen. 'I feel like I'm coming out of a daze.'

'Well, that actually is a form of hypnosis,' said Ellen.

'Is it really?' said Maureen, looking gratified.

'Ellen helps people give up smoking, or lose weight,' announced Patrick. 'Things like that. She helps high-powered business executives overcome their fear of public speaking.'

He was quoting verbatim from one of Ellen's brochures. She hadn't even known he'd read it.

She felt like their relationship had reached a new level today: a deeper, more complex, more profound level. Their love-making in the shower this morning had been so extraordinary, she kept wanting to tell people about it. The man at the fruit and veg shop had said chattily, 'What have you been up to today?' and she'd wanted to say, 'Well, actually, I had a *particularly* enjoyable sexual experience in the shower this morning! Thanks for asking!' Afterwards, they got back into bed and talked, and Patrick had apologized for snapping at her and said that Saskia made him feel so crazy at times that he'd *even* thought about counselling.

'So, you help people with public speaking. I have to do talks in front of clients for work,' said Simon, who was a website designer. 'I always think I'm not nervous at all, but then this weird thing happens.'

He stood up to demonstrate. 'It's like an involuntary spasm in my left leg.'

He made one knee knock against the other one.

'Huh!' said Patrick. 'The same thing happens to me. Except for me, it's more like this.' He stood up and made his leg twitch.

'You boys look like Elvis impersonators,' chortled Maureen.

Jack had rolled over on to his back to watch. 'I'm great at doing speeches,' he said. 'That doesn't happen to me. Does it happen to you, Grandpa?'

George shook his head. 'Nope. You must get your nerves of steel from me.'

'Nerves of steel,' murmured Jack to himself. 'I have nerves of *steel*.'

'What about you, Maureen?' said Ellen.

'Actually, I'm rather good at speeches,' said Maureen unexpectedly. 'I've been doing the speech at our tennis club Christmas party for over forty years. It normally goes down quite well.'

'Mum tells a good joke,' said Patrick.

'Most mothers are hopeless at telling jokes,' said Simon. 'Not ours.'

Both men looked proudly at their mother. Maureen beamed.

'Sometimes they're pretty dirty,' said George. 'My wife tells a good dirty joke.'

'Oh, I do *not*,' gurgled Maureen.

'I've got a joke! Knock knock!' cried Jack.

There was a knock on the door. Everyone laughed.

'I haven't said the punchline yet,' said Jack, offended.

'Someone knocked when you said "knock knock",' explained Maureen. 'We were laughing at the coincidence. I wonder who that could be. I'm not expecting anyone. Are you boys expecting someone?'

'Probably some door-to-door salesman,' said Patrick. 'Bet they'll try to get you to change phone companies.'

'Well, I just don't know,' said Maureen without moving, as if they really needed to work this puzzle out first.

'Might be one of those Jehovah fellows.' George didn't move either.

The person knocked again.

'I just can't think of anyone who would visit at this time,' mused Maureen. 'It's such a funny time. Just before dinner.'

'Man! This is the craziest thing that has ever happened to us!' said Simon with such authentic astonishment that Ellen thought at first he was serious. 'This is life on the edge! This is –'

'I'm going to answer the door.' Patrick put his hands on his knees.

'*I'll* get it.' Jack leaped to his feet and ran out of the room.

There was the sound of the door opening and then the unintelligible sound of a woman's voice.

'Probably some beautiful woman desperately trying to track me down,' said Simon behind his hand to Ellen. 'Happens a lot.'

'Happens a lot in his dreams,' said Patrick.

They could hear Jack talking at length.

'I think he's telling the mystery visitor the knock-knock joke,' grinned Simon.

'Well, I suppose I really should – but I just can't think who it would be!' Maureen left the room, patting down her hair.

They heard the sound of a woman laughing and suddenly Patrick banged his drink down so hard on the coffee table that beer sloshed over the sides. 'You're kidding me.'

'Kidding you about what?' said his father.

Patrick stood up and pulled back the curtain of the window that looked out on the street. He shook his head with a nasty, bitter smile, dropped the curtain and went striding from the room without looking at Ellen.

Ellen felt her heartbeat pick up. Patrick had spent the drive over with one eye in the rear-vision mirror. 'No sign of bunny boiler,' he'd said happily as they pulled up in front of his parents' house.

'What's going on?' said Patrick's father.

'I think you-know-who has stopped by,' said Simon. He gave Ellen a rueful, curious look.

'Bloody hell,' said George. 'I'd better go see if they need my help refereeing.'

'I guess you know about her,' said Simon carefully, when they were alone in the room. 'About his ex-girlfriend.'

'Yes,' said Ellen. She was pressing her hands to her

stomach to stop herself from leaping out of her chair to run to the door. *I just want to see what she looks like!*

She strained to hear what was going on.

Simon shook his head. 'Must be a bit weird – upsetting for you?'

'Oh, not really,' said Ellen. 'I've never even seen her.' She tried not to make it sound like a complaint.

Patrick's voice carried loud and clear into the room. Ellen had never heard him speak like that, his voice so rough-edged and unpleasant. He sounded like a big, beefy, red-faced man holding his palm up to the camera on one of those early-evening current affairs shows. 'Saskia. If you don't leave now, I am calling the police. You've crossed the line. This is unacceptable.'

And then Jack's voice, high with fear or excitement: 'Daddy? Why are you calling the police?'

Simon winced. 'I might just try and extricate Jack.'

He left the room. Ellen stayed pinned to her seat. There was no valid excuse for her to get involved.

She wondered if she should be frightened for their safety, if Saskia was about to pull out a gun or a big shiny kitchen knife. The book she was reading said that the vast majority of stalking victims weren't even physically assaulted (just mentally terrorized) but it was filled with horrific real-life case studies where the poor victims did end up dead.

Or perhaps her mother was right and she should be frightened for her *own* safety: maybe she was Saskia's target. Ellen's mother would be so cross if Ellen ended up dead.

'OK, let's everyone just calm down.' It was Patrick's dad. Ellen still hadn't actually heard Saskia's voice.

She put her drink down on the Ayers Rock coaster on top of a crocheted doily and wandered restlessly about the room. There was a bookshelf crammed with framed photos.

She recognized one of Patrick with another woman and picked it up greedily. Could this be Saskia?

Then she saw that the photo was taken in a hospital and that the young, blonde-haired woman sitting up in bed holding a baby in a blue bunny shawl must be Colleen. Patrick's wife. His dead wife. Ellen wondered if the cancer cells that would take her life just a year later were already there in her body, gathering forces for their malignant attack.

Patrick must have climbed up on the bed next to his wife. They were squashed close together, with their backs propped against the bars of the hospital bed. Colleen had one arm round the baby and the other hand lay on Patrick's lap. You could tell he was holding it tightly.

Colleen was smiling at the baby; Patrick was smiling at the person taking the photo. It was only eight years ago, but Patrick looked so much younger and different: his eyes seemed rounder, his cheeks chubbier, his hair thicker and longer, his T-shirt a younger person's T-shirt. Colleen's hair was messy and Patrick was unshaven. It must have been taken only hours after Jack was born. They had that amazed look about them that Ellen had seen in other people's first baby shots. *Look what we did!* The birth of a first baby. One of those everyday events that only seems incredible to the people involved.

Ellen felt vaguely embarrassed. She'd spent the day thinking about *sex in the shower* with that young woman's husband. How tacky. He'd had a *real* relationship with Colleen. He'd married her, had a child with her. It had been a grown-up relationship. You could tell how much Patrick had loved Colleen by the way his body was curved round hers.

Ellen felt a sense of kinship with poor, silly, crazy Saskia standing at the front door, still holding on, making a fool of herself. If the lovely Colleen (you could tell she was lovely, just from the photo) hadn't died, Patrick would never have spared a glance for Saskia or Ellen.

Dying was such an elegant way to leave a relationship. No infidelity, no boredom, no long, complicated conversations late into the night. No 'she's still single, I hear'. No running into each other at parties and weddings. No 'she's stacked on the weight' or 'she's showing her age'. Dying was final and mysterious and gave you the last word forever.

'That's my mum.'

Ellen started. Jack was standing next to her, looking at the photo in her hand. 'That's the day I was born. My mum is dead.'

'Yes.' Ellen carefully put the photo back in its place. She wondered if Jack felt the same way about his dead mother as she did about her non-existent father: a sort of emotion without emotion. 'I know.'

'My dad's ex-girlfriend is at the front door,' said Jack. 'Saskia. She lived with us for a while.'

'Do you remember her?' asked Ellen curiously.

Jack looked shifty. 'Sort of. Like, I remember her picking me up from school, and she used to say, "Welcome back, Jack!" She always had this little plate ready with biscuits and fruit and stuff.' He gave her a quick, warning glance. 'Dad doesn't like to talk about her.'

'I know,' said Ellen. *Why was Saskia picking him up from school? Didn't she have to work? Why wasn't Patrick picking him up after school?*

Outside the front of the house, there was the sound of a woman's raised voice, and then a car door slammed and tyres squealed.

He said he would call the police if I didn't leave.

I hadn't even known he was going to be there. I was so pleased with how good I looked in my red dress and I still felt so cleansed from that naked swim at the beach, and I had this idea that going to visit Patrick's mum and dad was just a normal, social, everyday thing to do. I was half thinking that maybe it was time to start looking up some old friends, and they seemed like a good place to start.

I didn't think of it as part of my 'habit'. My dirty, nasty little habit.

The proof is that I didn't even notice that Patrick's car was parked out the front! And I'm fixated on that car. I've got so used to following it, my vision telescopes in on it, even when I'm stuck in traffic miles behind.

All I was thinking about as I walked up the front path was about the first time Patrick brought me here to meet the family, Jack running up the path ahead of us. I was nervous because it had been less than a year since Colleen died and I thought they might think I was too quick to snap up the grieving widower.

I remember Simon was in his last year of school. He was still wearing his school uniform and for some reason he'd got hold of some elastic bands and done his hair in a whole lot of tiny little pigtails sticking up all over his head, like a hedgehog's quills. Maureen kept apologizing for him.

That's what I was thinking about as I walked up the driveway: how nice they'd all been to me. The front door looked exactly the same.

Stupid. For an intelligent woman, sometimes I'm so, so stupid. Did I really think that just because their *front door* looked the same that the last few years had never happened, that I was just a regular old friend dropping by? My capacity for self-delusion is enormous.

Then I knocked on the door and I heard a burst of laughter, as if they were all laughing at me. It made me snap back to reality and that's when I turned my head and I saw Patrick's car, and I couldn't believe I'd missed it, and I thought, 'He's brought Ellen over. He's introducing them to Ellen.'

I thought about running away, except that they would have seen me, and anyway, part of me wanted to march into that house, to say, 'How can you meet this new woman as if I never existed? How can you do it all, the interested questions, the careful pouring of not very good wine, the special Harbour Bridge tray, I bet, with the crackers, all exactly the same, except with a different woman? Doesn't that seem bizarre? Wrong?'

And then Jack opened the door. Of course I've seen him, more often than Patrick knows, but I haven't got this close to him since the day I left. I could have approached him many times, but I never wanted to confuse him or upset him.

He smiled at me. The loveliest open smile. His beautiful

eyes are still exactly the same. And then he started chatting to me, perfectly naturally, telling me about how I'd knocked at the same time as he'd said 'knock knock' to tell a knock-knock joke, and what were the chances of that happening, like one chance in a thousand, in a million? And I was laughing when Maureen appeared and she had a polite, perplexed expression on her face, and it vanished as soon as she saw me. She looked horrified, as if I was a home invader.

And then Patrick appeared, his face so ugly with anger, and then his dad, all serious and frowning, as if there had been a car accident, and Simon, all grown up, no pigtails, not even looking at me, just grabbing for Jack's hand, as if he needed to rescue him from me.

Nothing I said could make any difference. They just wanted me to go.

I wanted to scream: But I loved you all. You were my *family*.

'We loved her,' said Maureen to Ellen. 'We really did.'

'Can we please change the subject to something more interesting?' said Patrick, but everyone ignored him.

They had finished dinner and Jack had fallen asleep on the couch in the living room, and Ellen thought that everyone had maybe drunk a little more than they normally would have, following the stress of the Saskia incident, and their tongues were loosening up nicely.

'Of course we were upset when Patrick broke up with her. I felt absolutely terrible for her,' continued Maureen. 'She didn't have any family here, you see, she grew up in Tasmania, so we were like her family.'

'I'm sure Ellen doesn't want to hear all this,' said Patrick.

'I don't mind,' said Ellen, which was the understatement of the century.

'People fall out of love,' said George. 'You can't blame him for how he felt.'

'I *know* that, George,' said Maureen irritably. 'It doesn't stop me from feeling for the poor girl.'

'She needs to let Patrick be now,' said George. 'This has gone on long enough.'

'She was like a mother to Jack.' Maureen ignored her husband and talked directly to Ellen.

'You should have let her keep seeing Jack,' said Simon to Patrick.

'How many times have I had to say this? She never *asked* to see him,' said Patrick. 'As soon as I said I wanted to end it, she just went crazy, completely, certifiably crazy.'

'Her heart was broken,' said Maureen.

'Whatever, I didn't think she was safe around Jack.'

'Also, her mother had just died,' said Maureen.

'Yeah, your timing sort of sucked,' said Simon.

'She was very close to her mother,' said Maureen to Ellen. 'They spoke on the telephone every single day. My boys would go crazy if I tried to speak to them every day! Although, of course, I'm sure it's different with daughters.' She looked wistful for a moment. 'Do you speak to your mother every day, Ellen?'

'No,' smiled Ellen, although, actually, they did email or text or have some form of communication nearly every day.

'Saskia's father died when she was very young, you see, and she had no sisters or brothers, so her mother was all the family she had,' said Maureen. 'She took her mother's death very hard.'

'It was a month after her mother had died,' said Patrick. 'Her mother had been sick for a whole year. How much longer was I meant to wait? I didn't think it was fair to her to keep pretending.'

'A month is nothing,' said Simon.

Ellen privately agreed.

'Listen to Mr Sensitive here. You broke up with your last girlfriend by *text message*!' said Patrick.

'It was a very caring text message. Anyway, I wasn't living with her.'

'When Patrick first went into business for himself he was very busy, obviously, and Saskia started working part-time so she could look after Jack.' Maureen was directing all of her conversation at Ellen. 'She really was a wonderful mother to him.'

'*Colleen* was his mother,' said Patrick.

'Well, of course she was, darling, but Colleen wasn't there.'

'Which wasn't her fault.'

'Of course it wasn't, I'm just trying to be fair to Saskia, and to say that she did a wonderful job.'

'Colleen would have done it better. And Colleen wasn't crazy.'

'You never dumped Colleen,' said Simon. 'So you don't know.'

'I do know,' said Patrick. 'I *do* know. And, anyway, I would never have dumped Colleen.' There was a perceptible tremor of emotion in his voice that caused a hush round the table. Ellen saw that everyone was trying not to look at her. She felt Maureen's excellent roast lamb and baked potatoes sitting lumpily in her stomach. *Well, of course he's still in love with his dead wife. The damned girl had to go and die before she had time to get boring or annoying.*

Patrick's father took a deep breath and smiled at Ellen without quite meeting her eyes. 'Well, I want to hear more about the hypnotism business.'

Ellen smiled weakly. They had already talked at length about the 'hypnotism business' over dinner.

'I read somewhere that Hitler used hypnosis,' said Simon.

'Most politicians are experts at conversational hypnosis patterns,' began Ellen, automatically. She was asked this question all the time when she did speaking engagements. 'Simple things, like repetition –'

'There's an ad on TV at the moment,' said Patrick, looking down at the table. 'I don't know what it's for, but it's got a man in a swimming pool and someone's old bloody Bandaid is floating in the water and it gets stuck to his mouth, and he pulls it off and throws it away, with this sort of all-over shudder, like, get it off, *get it off*.'

'I know the one. It's for a car,' said Simon.

'What's an old Band-Aid got to do with cars?' frowned Maureen.

'The point is that every time I see Saskia's car in the rear-vision mirror, or I get another one of her letters ranting and raving about God knows what, or an email, or a text, or I have to listen to her voice on my answering machine, or she delivers a *bunch of fucking flowers*, I'm sorry for swearing, Mum, but *roses*, to my work, I feel like that guy in the ad, I just want to get it off, *get it off*.'

'She sent you roses?' said Maureen. 'She sent flowers to a man?'

'So that's why I don't want to hear that Saskia was a great mother, or that my timing sucked when I broke up with her,' said Patrick. 'If I did wrong by her, I have paid the price. I have paid and paid and *paid*.'

With that, he stood up from the table and left the room.

'Oh, dearie me,' sighed Maureen.

'Welcome to our family, Ellen!' said Simon brightly.

'He started up with Saskia too soon after he lost Colleen,' said Maureen. 'That was the problem. Much too soon. He never grieved. Men are terrible grievers. Whenever they feel anything bad they just try and stomp it down.'

'Whereas women talk and talk everything to death,' said George.

'Talking helps!' said Maureen. She turned her attention back to Ellen. 'After we lost Colleen, Patrick got this thing in his head that he had to be a good provider for Jack. He was obsessed with it. He threw himself into work. That's why Saskia ended up doing so much for Jack. Patrick was working all the time.'

'Mum, I think we've probably shared enough with Ellen for one night,' said Simon.

'Maybe you're right,' said Maureen. She stood up and began to stack plates, and without looking at Ellen she said quickly, 'Tell me, Ellen, are you a Catholic by any chance?'

Simon snorted.

'I'm not actually,' said Ellen apologetically.

'Oh! Well, that's – and do you mind me asking what religion are you?' Maureen took her husband's plate. 'Not that it matters, of course, I was just curious.'

'Well, I'm not really anything,' said Ellen. 'I wasn't brought up in any particular religion. My mother is a staunch atheist.'

Maureen looked startled. 'A staunch –? You mean, she doesn't believe in God? Not at all? But you do, of course?'

'Isn't there some rule about not discussing religion or politics at the dinner table?' said Simon.

'I guess I'm more of a spiritual person than my mother,' said Ellen. 'I'm very interested in Buddhism for example. I like its philosophies – practising mindfulness, that sort of thing.'

'Oh, yes, I've heard that's all very "in" at the moment,' said Maureen. Ellen could sense that she was losing points.

'Ommmmm,' chanted George. He placed his palms together under his chin and bowed his head. 'That's what you Buddhists do, isn't it. Ommmm. Ommmmm.'

'George! She's not an *actual* Buddhist,' said Maureen. She gave Ellen a frantic look. 'That is, are you, darling?'

Simon rocked with laughter.

'I just find it interesting,' said Ellen meekly.

'Well!' Maureen squared her shoulders, as if to say that life must go on whatever it throws at you. She tapped a finger to her mouth. 'Do you like babies, Ellen?'

'Mum!' Simon slapped a hand to his head.

Ellen caught the roguish glint in Maureen's eyes. She knew exactly what she was doing.

'I adore babies,' she said firmly.

'Lovely,' said Maureen. 'Me too.' They understood each other perfectly.

'Having one for dessert, are we?' said George.

Maureen rolled her eyes. 'We're having apple crumble with cream and ice cream.'

'Maybe just a very small portion for me,' said Ellen.

'Oh, you're as thin as a rake,' scolded Maureen. 'I'll get you a nice big plate.'

Later that night, she and Patrick lay in Ellen's bed, flat on their backs, both of them sucking on antacid tablets. At Maureen's insistence, Jack had stayed with her for another night. Patrick had carried him from the couch into her spare bedroom, and he hadn't woken at all. Then Patrick and Ellen had caught a taxi back to her place, because they'd both had too much to drink.

'I'm sorry about tonight,' said Patrick.

'It was fine,' said Ellen. 'I think your family are lovely.'

It was true. There was something about the Scott family that had made her feel surprisingly comfortable, as if she'd sat at the dining-room table and passed round the baked potatoes many times before.

'I shouldn't have let that conversation about Saskia go on like it did,' said Patrick. 'I just get resentful when they seem to be on her side.'

'I know,' said Ellen. She touched his shoulder. It felt rock-hard, as if all his muscles were contracted. She kneaded his flesh with her fingers, trying to ease his tension. 'I understand.'

'And I should never have yelled at Saskia in front of Jack,' said Patrick. 'I just felt this sort of crazy fury when I heard her voice. I thought for a while there that I could just accept her in my life, like a disability. But now, I seem to be going in the opposite direction. It's like I'm reaching the end of my tether. Sometimes I think I could kill her. I understand now, how people get to that point. The point of murder. I could kill her.'

'Please don't,' said Ellen. She stopped massaging him. It didn't seem to be helping. 'I don't want to visit you in jail for conjugal visits.'

'I'd make sure I didn't get caught,' said Patrick. He removed another tablet from the roll he was holding on his chest and chewed on it grimly.

Ellen rolled her head to glance with concern at his face. He saw her looking and smiled.

'It's all right,' he said. 'I'm just joking. Anyway, I would get caught. I'm the sort of person who never gets away with anything. I do an illegal right-hand turn and the cops are waiting round the corner.'

'Speaking of the police –'

'Yes, I know.' Patrick's jaw shifted convulsively. 'I just – I don't know. I'm just not sure if that's the way to go.'

He obviously didn't want to go back to the police again, but she couldn't quite pinpoint his reasons. Was it just his fear that Saskia would do what she'd threatened and make accusations against him? Or something more than that?

'Think about it,' she said.

'I will.' But she could tell that he wouldn't.

She yawned, suddenly and hugely. 'I can't believe how tired I feel.'

'I'm going to be awake for hours,' said Patrick. 'With my thoughts going round and round like a merry-go-round. Could you just hypnotize me to sleep?'

'Ha,' said Ellen.

'Seriously. Can you do that?'

'Hypnotizing your partners isn't considered such a good

idea, you know, ethically,' she said, feeling prudish. It had come up before, in previous relationships, but mostly the requests had been flippant and she'd been able to brush them off.

'I won't report you,' said Patrick. 'I just want to switch all these thoughts off in my head.'

Her heart went out to him. She wavered. 'I thought you didn't really like the idea of hypnotism. You said you hated the idea of losing control.'

'That was before I met you. I understand more about it now. And I trust you.'

Ellen thought of her mentor, Flynn, an old-school hypnotherapist in his sixties, who hated stage hypnotists with a passion, and believed that the only way to protect their professional integrity was to never, ever practise their craft outside the therapist's office. She thought of the cool young guy she was mentoring, Danny, who proudly told Ellen that he used the hypnotic handshake to help pick up women in bars (with huge success apparently, so Ellen knew that it didn't matter how strenuously she disapproved). If she ever told Flynn about what she let Danny get away with, he'd be horrified, like a grandparent who thought she was spoiling her child. She guessed that on a scale of ethics she was somewhere in the middle of Flynn and Danny.

'I suppose there wouldn't be any harm in just doing a relaxation exercise,' she said.

8

By the way, I'm not 'stalking' you. Please stop using that word, you know it's ridiculous. I just want to TALK to you, that's all.

> – From an unopened email to Patrick Scott

'So this guy in the US goes to court because he is being stalked by his ex-girlfriend,' said Patrick. 'And the judge says, "You should be flattered by the attention," and a few days later he ends up dead. His stalker shot him, or stabbed him or something. True story.'

It was Sunday afternoon and Ellen, Patrick, Julia and Patrick's friend 'Stinky' (his real name still hadn't been confirmed, and both Ellen and Julia were too much their North Shore mothers' daughters to bring themselves to call him 'Stinky') were eating fish and chips on a picnic rug at Watsons Bay.

It was Julia who had brought up the stalking issue: 'So I hear you have a stalker, Patrick,' she'd said, within minutes of them all sitting down, in the same sociable tone as if she was saying, 'So I hear you're a surveyor, Patrick.' Ellen had been surprised that Patrick hadn't tried to change the subject, especially after the previous night with his family. In fact, he responded almost enthusiastically. It was interesting seeing the slight variations in his personality when he was around different people. With his family he was chattier, softer, boyish. With Stinky and Julia he was a laid-back, nothing-worries-me Aussie bloke.

'But you're not in fear of your life are you, Scottie?' asked Stinky.

Stinky was chunky and balding, with two dimples creasing his cheeks, so he looked like a giant baby with grey stubble and a deep voice. He was also quite short for a man, something Patrick had neglected to mention, and Ellen had neglected to mention that Julia was quite tall for a woman. When Julia, who was looking especially cosmopolitan with a fitted jacket and scarf and spike-heeled leather boots that made her look super-model tall, had shaken hands with Stinky, who was wearing a rumpled country shirt and faded jeans with scuffed workman's boots, she had raised one eyebrow across the top of his head at Ellen, who had shrugged back. This would become a story Julia would exaggerate for years to come: *The time you tried to set me up with a bald midget called 'Stinky'*.

But, in a way, it was better that Julia had obviously written off Stinky because she was completely relaxed, eating the hot chips like a machine and even flirting a bit with Stinky. If she'd actually seen him as a prospect she would have been avoiding eye contact, acting aggressively non-interested, and she would have lost her appetite completely.

'I'm not in fear of my life,' said Patrick. 'Just my sanity at times. My point was that people don't take male stalking victims seriously.'

'Did you ever meet this girl, ah, you over there?' said Julia to Stinky. 'Look, I just can't call you "Stinky", and you seem to smell perfectly acceptable.'

'It's Bruce.'

'It's not.'

'What's wrong with Bruce? I'm offended.'

'OK, Bruce, did you ever meet her?' said Julia. 'Patrick's stalker?'

'I knew her well,' said Stinky. 'I liked her. I liked her a lot actually.'

He glanced at Patrick, who shrugged and said, 'You want her phone number? You're welcome to her, mate.'

'So you wouldn't have thought she was capable of this . . . crazy stuff?' said Julia.

'Oh, I don't know.' Stinky's dimple deepened. 'Aren't we all capable of it? I always think love is a kind of madness.'

'Love is a kind of madness,' repeated Julia. 'That's a very, mmm, poetic thing for a man called Bruce to say.'

'He's trying to impress the *laadies*,' said Patrick.

'The point is,' said Julia, 'we've all been hurt by someone, but we just have to get on with it, don't we? That's life.'

'You've never Googled an ex? When my last girlfriend broke up with me, I spent hours cyber-stalking her,' said Stinky. 'Even if I didn't physically stalk her, I stalked her in my mind.'

'So what? I might have raised my voice at my ex-husband, but that doesn't mean I'm in the same category as someone who murders their ex.'

'But doesn't it give you an understanding of how it could happen?'

'Nope,' said Julia.

'Oh, you're a hard woman.'

'You sure are.' Ellen gave Julia a pointed look.

'OK, fine,' said Julia. 'I once made anonymous phone calls to an ex-boyfriend's new girlfriend. Just for a few weeks and I was *seventeen*!'

'Aha!' Stinky pointed his chip at her triumphantly. 'You've got a history as a stalker yourself!'

'I was not a stalker, I was just a silly teenager.'

'You're not in the same league as my bunny boiler,' said Patrick. He paused. 'Sometimes I think she comes into my house when I'm not home.'

'You never told me that!' Ellen turned to look at him.

'Report her to the police, for God's sake!' said Julia. 'And change the locks!'

'What makes you think she's been there?' asked Stinky.

'I've changed the locks more than once,' said Patrick. 'And I don't know what makes me think it. Just a feeling when I get home. Nothing is moved or anything. I just sense she's been there. Something in the atmosphere. Maybe I smell a trace of her perfume.'

Ellen noticed that Patrick had avoided responding to Julia's comment about the police.

Julia shuddered theatrically. 'Oh God, that's like something out of a horror movie.' She pointed her chin in Ellen's direction. 'Lucky your new girlfriend likes horror movies.'

'Do you?' Patrick put his hand on Ellen's knee. 'I didn't know that. I'm a wimp. They scare me to death.'

'I like my horror with popcorn and a choc-top,' said Ellen. 'I don't like the idea of Saskia going through your house! I don't like that at all.' She shuddered, although part of her knew she was shuddering because it seemed like the acceptable response. She felt deeply sympathetic towards Patrick and understood his fear and anxiety, but for some reason she genuinely didn't feel any fear for herself. Perhaps it was because she hadn't met Saskia and she still didn't feel quite real to her. Or perhaps it was just that Saskia was a woman, and she didn't really believe that women were capable of violence, even though she knew, of course, that they were. Whatever the reason, she still found everything about Saskia more interesting than frightening.

'Sorry,' said Patrick. 'I never actually meant to tell you that. Anyway, I'm probably imagining it.'

'She'd never hurt anyone,' said Stinky to Ellen. 'If that's any comfort to you. She was a pacifist. She marched against the war in Iraq.'

'That was political,' said Patrick. 'This is personal.'

'Didn't she work for an animal shelter for a while?'

'An animal shelter,' snorted Julia.

'What's funny about working for an animal shelter?' said Ellen.

'I don't know,' said Julia. 'It's such a cliché.'

'Not for the poor little kitties and puppies.' Stinky looked mournful.

'What is this?' Patrick reached out and punched Stinky on the arm. 'I'm surrounded by people who want to defend my stalker.'

'Sorry, Scottie.' Stinky held up both palms. 'I was trying to make Ellen feel better, let her know she's not in danger.'

'Well, "*Scottie*", unlike "*Stinky*" here, I'm not going to defend your stalker,' said Julia to Patrick. 'I think she's an absolute nutcase and you and Ellen should both be scared out of your minds.'

'Thank you,' said Patrick.

I went to the beach again today and fell asleep on the sand in my red dress.

Not the beach where the hypnotist lives, or any of the beaches I'd been to with Patrick. I went to Avalon. I'd actually never even set foot on that beach before, so no memories.

I made myself ill on memories last night. I overdosed on them.

After I left Patrick's family's house, I didn't go to the party. Maybe I knew all along I wasn't going to the party. I don't do parties. I drove for six hours without a break, except once, when I stopped for petrol and a bottle of water.

I drove to every place in Sydney I'd ever been to with Patrick.

I drove back and forth across the Harbour Bridge at least thirty times.

I was so in love with this city when I first came here. Sydney. Even just the name sounded exciting to me, like 'New York' probably sounds to more sophisticated people, who didn't grow up in a tiny grey smidge of a country town right in the middle of Tasmania.

'You're from Tasmania?' Sydneysiders used to say, with a lifted eyebrow and a half-smile, like they wanted to say, 'Really? That dear little place?' And I would duck my head humbly, as if I was apologizing, as if I was saying, 'Don't hold it against me.' That doesn't happen any more. Now people murmur, 'Oh, beautiful countryside in Tasmania.' I don't know if it's me who has changed, or Tasmania.

Sydney is my big, brash, jewellery-wearing, credit-card-flashing ex-lover. Sydney dazzled me with beaches and bars and sunshine, with restaurants and cafés and music, and that big, hard, glittery sapphire of a harbour.

Like a silly, besotted girlfriend I threw myself into finding out everything there was to know about this place. I know my way round Sydney better than any Sydneysider or taxi driver. I can tell you where to go for the best yum cha and sushi and tapas. I know the theatres and the museums and the cool pubs. I know where to scuba dive, where to bushwalk, where to park. I'd only been living in Sydney for six months when I met Patrick, who has never lived anywhere else, and he didn't even know half the places I took him to existed.

Patrick and Sydney gave me the best, the most blissful time of my life. We kissed on ferries and drank champagne by the harbour. We saw plays and movies and bands. We took Jack, grinning down at me from Patrick's backpack, on long walks through the green dappled light of the national parks. We held his hands on the beach and said 'One, two, *three*!' and scooped him up high over waves that frothed round our ankles.

I was so in love with both of them. I remember saying to my mother, 'I didn't know it could be so easy to be this happy.'

And she'd say, 'Hearing you say that just makes my day.' I could imagine how she'd be smiling as she scrubbed energetically away at her kitchen with a dishcloth and a bottle of Spray'n'Wipe.

Because all Mum ever wanted was for me to be happy.

I always thought she was just weirdly selfless, until I started taking care of Jack, and that's when I began to get an inkling of how your child's moods dictate yours and how maybe that becomes a habit.

I do remember that once she said, 'Do you think Patrick is as happy as you?' and I said that of course he was just as happy as me.

There was a pause and then she said, very carefully, tentatively, 'It's been less than a year since he lost his wife. He must still be grieving, Saskia, it takes such a long time, just maybe . . . keep that in mind.'

She was qualified to talk on the subject because my dad died when I was a toddler. I don't remember a thing about him. I certainly do not have any repressed feelings of abandonment by my daddy.

I know my father was the love of my mother's life, according to her, and I know she said she missed him every day of her life but that doesn't mean Patrick was the same. For one thing, Mum didn't meet anyone else who could have made her happy. Patrick met me. I made him happy. I know I made him happy. I'm not stupid. I didn't imagine it.

Of course I knew part of him was still grieving for Colleen. I was deeply respectful of Colleen's wishes about Jack's upbringing. She had written down a list of things for Jack. Her writing was shaky because she must have been quite ill by then. Her spelling wasn't the best. It was uncharitable of me to notice that, I know, but there you have it, I have never held myself out to be a particularly nice person. Colleen believed in vitamins, so I gave Jack his vitamin tablets every day. Colleen believed that vests somehow protected children from all evil, so I put vests on him even when I knew he was probably going to be too hot. I'm sure Colleen didn't mean the poor child had to wear a vest on warm days, but Patrick took everything on that list literally.

But Patrick was happy with me. He said he was happy. He said, 'You saved my life.' He said, 'I'm keeping you forever.' He said, 'I would have been lost without you.'

Today, I lay on the beach and I dreamed of Colleen. In my dream I was screaming at her, 'There is no need for an apostrophe in the word "vitamins"!' So that's a pretty embarrassing nerdy dream: screaming at a dead person about their grammar.

Somebody said, 'Big night?'

And I opened my eyes and there was a man standing on the sand next to me staring down at me. I was looking straight into the sun so I couldn't see much of him except that he was wearing a knee-length wetsuit and carrying a boogie board under one arm and he had woolly hair that seemed too young for him.

I sat up, and looked down at my red dress. I guess I did look like someone who has passed out after a big party, except I'm too old for that sort of behaviour. I said, 'Sort of.'

And then he didn't seem to know what else to say. He smiled and put his fingers to his forehead in a sort of salute and kept walking down to the water. I sat on the beach and watched him on his boogie board. He wasn't very good at it. He kept trying to paddle for waves and then missing them but each time he finally managed to catch one, he got such a funny excited look on his face, his woolly hair lying flat against his head sticking out of the wave.

This afternoon I went into one of those surf shops and I don't know what came over me but I somehow walked out carrying a wetsuit and a boogie board.

I guess I'm going to have to learn how to ride it now. Or surf it. Or whatever the right terminology is. I'm quite chuffed about it.

Ellen woke up on Monday feeling drained and wrung-out and was horrified when she opened her appointment book to find her day was filled with back-to-back appointments and she hadn't even allowed herself a lunchbreak.

She could vaguely remember thinking blithely to herself, 'Oh, I'll manage!' when she'd scheduled so many appointments. Now she thought longingly of her bed and how truly, amazingly glorious it would be to slide back under the blankets and sleep the day away. If only she felt properly, contagiously ill, with proper symptoms, then she could get on the phone and cancel all her appointments. But she knew she was just worn out. There had been too much eating and drinking and nervous socializing on the weekend. Too much heightened emotion. Too little sleep and too much sex. She suspected she was coming down with a bad case of cystitis.

She was also out of milk, which, for a few moments, as she stood at the open fridge, seemed like the end of the world. She actually stamped her foot. She *needed* the crunch of cereal contrasting with the coolness of milk.

She put stale bread in the toaster with fast, sulky

movements, as if the person responsible for the lack of milk was watching and feeling guilty. She went and picked up the newspaper from the front yard, where the delivery person had considerately thrown it straight in the middle of her front hedge, so she had to rustle through unpleasantly damp, dewy leaves to retrieve it.

And then, to top it all off, as she was eating her toast (which tasted weirdly acidic) and reading the paper (which was full of bad news: murders, fatalities, wars and suicide bombs – the world was adrift on a sea of tears) she came upon an article under the heading 'A-List Turns Out for Society Wedding'.

And there was a picture of her client Rosie. It had been about two months since Ellen had last seen her and during that time she'd lost a lot of weight. All her curves were gone. Her shoulders were bony and hunched, in a strapless wedding dress, surrounded by four tall, skinny bridesmaids in floor-length gowns. So she'd gone ahead with the wedding. Her revelation under Ellen's supposedly skilful hypnosis that the reason she wasn't having any luck giving up smoking was because she didn't really like her fiancé had meant nothing at all. Either she'd decided that she didn't really feel that way, or she was marrying him anyway, maybe for the money or the prestige or because she didn't have the courage to cancel the wedding after all the invitations had gone out to the 'A-list'.

Either way, it left Ellen feeling even more depressed. It made her feel pointless and incompetent.

The phone rang and Ellen quickly answered it, hoping for a cancellation; ideally of the morning's first appointment, so she could go back to bed.

'Good morning,' she said briskly. 'This is Ellen.'

'It doesn't sound like you're having a very good morning at all!'

It was Harriet; her ex-boyfriend's younger sister. They had stayed friends after Ellen and Jon broke up.

Harriet was a tiny, brittle, bossy woman, and very occasionally her somewhat malicious conversation was exactly what Ellen felt like, in the same way that she sometimes found herself oddly craving the sharp, sour taste of liquorice.

But right now, the sound of Harriet's slightly nasal voice shredded Ellen's nerves like a cheese grater.

She took a deep bracing breath as if she was about to run up a steep hill and said, 'How are you, Harriet?'

'Fine, fine, just thought I'd call for a chat. It's been months.'

Only Harriet would think that 7.30 on a Monday morning was an appropriate time for a chat.

'Yes, yes, too long,' said Ellen and let her eyes briefly close. She felt an absurd desire to scream.

Whenever she spoke to Harriet, Jon suddenly jumped to the front of her consciousness. She could hear his voice in the similar speech patterns of Harriet's voice. She could see his heavy-lidded half-smile, half-sneer. Harriet reminded her that Jon still existed.

She preferred to be bright and bubbly and moving-full-steam-ahead-with-her-life when she talked to Harriet, so that the appropriate messages would get back to Jon. (She knew that Harriet would make sure she mentioned every conversation to Jon. That's what she did: collected information and then shared it round, little pellets of power.)

Ideally, Ellen should mention Patrick right now (*Have you heard? Ellen has a new boyfriend*), but she didn't have the energy to give him the enthusiasm he deserved.

'How's Jon?' she said instead. Let's bring him out on centre stage, instead of letting him lurk about in the corners of this conversation.

'Funny you should mention him. You're not going to believe this, but my eternal bachelor of a brother is getting married. We're all in a state of shock. Can you believe it?'

'No,' said Ellen. She cleared her throat. 'Goodness.'

She had lived with Jon for four years and the word 'marriage' had never been mentioned. It had been her understanding that he didn't believe in the institution and it never seemed to occur to him to ask how Ellen felt about it. In fact, he just didn't believe in marriage to *her*.

Her feelings were quite badly hurt. She actually felt them break, like a row of delicate, fragile porcelain cups that had exploded all at once. There were shards of pain flooding her body; tiny ones prickling her sinuses, a huge sharp one lodged in her chest. *Oh, for heaven's sakes, you don't care! You're in love with another man! You're properly in love for the first time! You don't care, you don't care, you don't care.* Except she did.

'He's only known this girl for a few months,' continued Harriet. 'She's a dental hygienist.'

A few months. After just a few months. Maybe Jon was properly in love for the first time. And it was fine that Ellen had never properly loved Jon, but it was not fine that Jon had never properly loved her. Why? Because she was the *nice one*!

'Anyway, we're sure it won't last,' said Harriet. Her voice faltered a little as if she was pulling back now that the damage was done.

Had she deliberately called first thing on a Monday, when any normal person's defences are down, to pass on this information just to hurt her? She must have known it wasn't going to be welcome news, and yet Ellen knew that Harriet was genuinely fond of her.

'Oh, well, I hope for their sake that it does.' Ellen was impressed with the cool, detached tone of her voice. 'Listen, Harriet, can I call you back another time? I'm having one of those mornings. I'm out of milk, and I woke up in such a bad mood.'

'Touch of PMT?' said Harriet. She'd always been one of those women far too happy to talk about her menstrual cycle.

'Just got out of the wrong side of the bed,' said Ellen.

She put down the phone and cried. Harsh, jagged, angry sobs. It was ridiculous. It was way out of proportion.

'This is your ego,' she said. Her voice sounded loud, childish and broken, in the kitchen. 'This is nothing but your ego.'

She could think of nothing worse than to be married to Jon. She did not miss him. It had taken a long time for her to reinstall her personality after he'd systematically taken it apart, making her doubt her every thought.

He was a selfish, pompous, egocentric, nasty man and yet she had loved him desperately. She did not want to be married to him, and yet she did not want him to marry someone else. She did not want him, but she wanted him to want her.

It was stupid and immature and yet there it was, she couldn't seem to wrestle control of her feelings. She cried and cried. It was an orgy of inappropriate sobbing and wailing. She wanted to pick up the phone and call him. She wanted to scream, 'What was wrong with me?' She wanted to see this girl. She wanted to watch them together. She wanted to listen in on their conversations.

Oh, Saskia. I understand. I know. I get it.

Finally, after much heaving of the shoulders, loud snotty sniffs and sudden fresh flurries of tears, it was over, and she felt remarkably cleansed; exhausted, shaky and pale, but fine, as if she'd just vomited up the last of a rancid meal.

Good Lord. How ridiculous. How peculiar. Maybe Harriet was right and she really did have PMT, although her hormones were normally well behaved and didn't cause such dramatic waves of feeling.

She picked up her diary to check when her period was due.

She flicked back and forth through the pages: slowly at first and then faster and faster. It wasn't possible, was it?

Finally she put the diary back down and stared out the window of the kitchen at the sea.

I'm going to stop. I'm over it. I'm done.

Ironically, those were the actual thoughts going through my head when I went for my appointment at the hypnotist's today.

She didn't look that great when she opened the door to me. Her skin looked blotchy, and her hair seemed sort of lank, and there was a greasy food mark on her top. I felt quite cheered by the sight of her.

And then, before we had our session, when she asked if I needed to use her bathroom, as she always did, I said yes, because I actually really did.

Out of habit, I automatically opened the mirrored cabinet above her sink. I wasn't really that interested. I knew exactly what I'd see: the supermarket brand moisturizer, the contact lens solution, the deodorant and razors, the handful of lipsticks and the little bottles of essential oils.

I nearly missed it. I was about to close the cupboard door when something different caught my eye: a long, flat, rectangular box.

I picked it up, without much interest, and then I felt something snag in my chest, like a sharp hook dragging and tearing at my heart.

It was a pregnancy test. I recognized it immediately because I've used this same brand myself. Many times.

The box was open.

I opened it and pulled out two long white plastic sticks. She'd already done both tests, wanting to double-check the result.

The little window on both tests showed the same symbol. The symbol I had longed for but never ever seen.

The hypnotist is pregnant.

9

You shall see nothing, hear nothing, think of nothing but Svengali, Svengali, Svengali!
   – Svengali's instruction to Trilby O'Ferrall in the
classic novel *Trilby* by George du Maurier

She kept forgetting for minutes at a time and then remembering.

It was only seven hours since she'd done the test. After putting down her diary and staring out the window for at least ten minutes, she had suddenly gone into a frenzy, as if someone else had taken over her body. She'd thrown on dirty clothes, driven into the village and double-parked in front of the local chemist, which was only just opening. The chatty grey-haired lady who normally sold Ellen hay-fever medication had kept her face politely uninterested when Ellen asked her for a pregnancy test and double-sealed the top of the white paper bag while talking about the funny weather for this time of year.

Her first appointment of the day had been knocking on the door while Ellen was still sitting on the edge of her grandmother's bathtub, holding both undeniably positive pregnancy tests in her limp hand.

The morning had passed in a blur. She had no idea whether her work had been abysmal or brilliant. She had chatted and listened and induced trances and written out receipts while an amazed voice in the back of her head chanted over and over: *I'm pregnant, I'm pregnant, I'm actually pregnant.*

It was much too soon. Only three months! Their relationship was far too new for the words, 'I'm pregnant.' It felt tasteless and tacky. Like something that happened to a teenage couple on a soapie.

Also, it was too medical. *My period is late as a result of your sperm accidentally colliding with my egg, through something faulty or slippery or otherwise relating to our condom usage, and I did a test that confirmed the level of pregnancy hormones in my urine and there you have it.*

Putting that aside, did Patrick even *want* another child? At all? Ever? She thought he did, but now she considered it, she saw that her beliefs were based on ridiculous, flimsy evidence, such as the fact that he adored his son, and she'd once seen him smile tenderly at a stranger's baby, and his *mother* wanted him to have more children, and he seemed very fond of his mother. Also he was a lovely man, and lovely men should automatically want more babies because it was a biological imperative that they pass on the loveliness gene.

In fact, it was quite possible he'd smiled at that stranger's baby because he was thinking, *Thank God that's all behind me.*

She felt a cold chill at the thought. It was ridiculous. She knew so much about him – he was frightened of spiders, he couldn't see the point of cucumber, he'd once punched a boy called Bruno – but she didn't know this one essential point.

And let's assume he did want another child, what would they actually, literally *do*?

Would they move in together? Into her house or his? Get married? She didn't want to live in his house. The bath was too shallow and the kitchen too small and the colour of the living-room carpet was bad for her soul. She loved her grandmother's house and working in this room and falling asleep to the sound of the sea. But maybe it would be disruptive to Jack to move him out of his home? And what about Jack? Was he ready to have a little brother or sister?

A little brother or sister. That gave her another fresh start. The baby was either a boy or a girl. That was already decided. Oh my goodness, she was having a *baby*. She suddenly felt weak with a strange feeling that she thought might be equal parts hysterical terror and blinding joy. A baby.

'Ellen? Could we get started?'

It was her two o'clock. Luisa. She had just returned from using Ellen's bathroom and was looking at her with a faintly angry expression on her attractive, sculpted face. Ellen had always sensed an undercurrent of barely controlled fury in Luisa. She was a relatively new patient, a daughter of a friend of Julia's mother. She was seeing Ellen for 'unexplained infertility' and she had made it quite clear that although she didn't actually believe in 'this dippy-hippie stuff' she had got to a point where she was willing to try anything. She said she was also seeing an acupuncturist, a herbalist and a dietician. Imagine if Luisa knew that Ellen had *accidentally*, clumsily, foolishly, inconveniently become pregnant. The world was an extremely unfair place.

*

I was in my late thirties when I met Patrick so I knew if I was ever going to have a baby he was my only chance. It wasn't like I had to beg him or anything. He said yes straight away. He even seemed excited by the idea – he kept talking about how he didn't want Jack to be an only child – but then, as the months went by without anything happening, he seemed to lose interest.

He didn't want to talk about it and he refused to see any doctors. He didn't even want to try on the right days. He said, 'I don't want to hear that you're *ovulating*.' As if ovulating was something disgusting.

In all honesty, he was a bit of a bastard about it.

I forgave him. I understood that it was different for men. They don't have the biological drive.

He said, 'Saskia, my love, if it's not meant to be, it's not meant to be.'

Which was true. We had Jack.

Except that it wasn't true. He had Jack. I didn't have Jack at all. And I wasn't his love.

Turned out that it was meant to be. He was meant to have another baby, just not with me.

'Sorry? What did you say? You're inviting me to a Tupperware party?' Ellen was on the phone to Danny, the young hypnotherapist she'd been mentoring over the past year.

'Ha! Yeah right!' shouted Danny. He appeared to be calling from a nightclub. He reminded Ellen of Patrick's younger brother, Simon. That generation seemed to have a different dialect or accent or something. They all sounded ever so slightly American, and there was an amused casualness about the way they saw the world, as if nothing was beyond them. Maybe it was technology. It put power in their fingertips.

Or was that the way Ellen had sounded when she was twenty-four too? No. She'd never been casual about anything.

'Let me just go outside for a moment,' said Danny.

I'm pregnant, Danny. Pregnant. That means I'm having a baby. And I've only been dating the guy for three months. What would you do if your girlfriend told you she was pregnant after only three months?

'OK, is that better?' The background noise vanished. 'No, what I'm saying is, you know how you've got Tupperware parties, right? So I was just standing at the bar and listening to these two women, middle-aged, like, mothers I guess, and they were talking about how much weight they needed to lose, and their personal trainers, and how long you need to run on the treadmill to work off a roast potato, and you could tell they were, like, *passionate* about this shit.'

'I'm having trouble following,' said Ellen.

'Hypno-parties! I'm going to run weight-loss hypno-parties! So all these women get together and I give them a group hypnosis session for weight loss. I'd use Flynn's rapid induction techniques you were telling me about, he wouldn't mind, would he? These chicks would be in the perfect receptive state anyway. Then a standard script with a few positive affirmations – maybe an aversion suggestion for every time they look at a roast potato or open the fridge? But they've got to cook dinner for their kids, I guess. Anyway, I can work out all the details. What do you think?'

'I'm not exactly –' began Ellen.

'It's perfect! How much do you think I could get away with charging?'

'Well, I don't know,' said Ellen. 'I always prefer to individually tailor treatment to –'

'The money they spend on these personal trainers. I could get them better results.'

'Maybe you could.'

All the women would fall in love with him. He'd been the only male in the Introduction to Hypnotherapy course Ellen had taught, and he was attractive and charismatic, but in an understated way that made you think you were the only one to have noticed. When he was doing Ellen's course, he always took a seat at the far right of the room, and Ellen had noticed the way all the other students unconsciously leaned towards him, like flowers bent by a breeze.

She could hear a girl's voice in the background now calling out, 'Danny! I've been looking everywhere for you!'

I bet you have, thought Ellen. When Danny looked at you, he held eye contact. It was a gift. Not many men could do that without appearing psychotic.

'So, anyway, I've got to go, the idea just hit me and I wanted to see what you thought! I'll call you, OK? How are you, anyway, Ellen? Sorry. I never even asked.'

He didn't sound perfunctory. He sounded as if he genuinely cared. Maybe he did. Or maybe he was the ultimate salesman.

'I'm fine, Danny. You go.'

*

It was later that night and Ellen was slouched on the couch watching *Beauty and the Geek* and eating with her fingers from a plate containing nothing but roast potatoes, which was all she felt like for dinner.

It wasn't like it was the first time in her life she'd ever felt a strong desire for a particular type of food but now she was pregnant she felt entitled to label it as a 'craving'. Perhaps the baby needed potato.

Or perhaps it was just that Danny had mentioned roast potatoes and her subconscious had obediently responded to the suggestion.

She allowed these thoughts and words to cross her mind – *Now that I'm pregnant . . . the baby . . . craving* – and felt as though she were doing something slightly illegal. She couldn't just waltz into that whole complicated world of motherhood without some sort of official entry pass, could she? What was the entry pass? A marriage licence? It seemed crazy that as of yesterday the thought of having children was still something far in her future, and then today, after one trip to the chemist, she was craving roast potatoes and thinking about 'the baby'. Next she'd be having pickles and ice cream for dessert.

The carbohydrates and the bad television were putting her into a sort of half-comatose state. Her head felt as if it was stuffed full of cotton wool.

Baby brain.

Enough, Ellen!

The phone rang and she put her plate to the side and heaved herself off the couch with a grunt. Now she was walking like a pregnant woman, with one hand supporting the small of her back. She made herself stand upright.

She really was the most suggestible person in the world.

It was her godmother, Melanie. That was good. Mel didn't really like talking on the phone and was always in a hurry to finish up the conversation. She would be quick, and Ellen could get back to the enjoyably stupid beauties and endearingly geeky geeks.

'I just wanted you to know how much I liked Patrick,' said Mel. 'I really, really liked him. And such an improvement on that Jon. Such a self-satisfied prick. I hope you don't mind me saying that.'

'The self-satisfied prick has just asked someone to marry him,' said Ellen.

'Oh, that poor girl,' said Mel with genuine feeling. 'What a lucky escape for you.'

And just like that Jon was safely locked away in the filing cabinet at the back of her memory where he belonged. Ellen felt a surge of gratitude and affection for both of her godmothers. Pip had also called earlier today and left a long, rambling, giggling message on Ellen's voicemail all about soulmates and wedding bells and was she too old to be a bridesmaid? Of course, Ellen's own mother hadn't called yet.

'Your mother liked him too,' said Mel.

'Did she say that?' said Ellen.

'Well, no,' admitted Mel. 'But I could tell. Speaking of your mother, did she seem herself to you on Friday night?'

'I think so.' Ellen dragged her mind with difficulty to her mother's behaviour on Friday night. Hadn't Anne been her normal self? Ellen had been so focused on Patrick and herself, she hadn't really spent much time observing her.

'Why?'

'Oh, nothing, really. She's just been a bit, hmmm, secretive lately, as if there's something she's not telling us.'

Look, I am currently dealing with a very big secret myself. I don't have time for my mother to have secrets too. I am meant to be the young, interesting one. Why couldn't her mother be dull and safe, with the major upheavals of her life firmly behind her, like Patrick's mother?

These were the childish thoughts that crossed Ellen's mind as she looked longingly at her roast potatoes and the flickering television set.

'You don't think she's sick or something?' she said in a sudden panic, as if she was about to be punished for her selfishness.

'No, no,' said Mel. 'How stupid of me to worry you. She's in perfect health. She flogged me at tennis just the other week. I'm probably imagining the whole thing, or I'm just desperate for gossip. Ignore me. The whole point of this phone call was to tell you that I really liked Patrick. Now I must let you go. Talk to you soon!'

She was gone. Nobody ever finished phone calls more abruptly than Melanie, unlike Phillipa, who spent at least twenty minutes wrapping up each conversation. If it had been Pip saying she'd noticed something strange about her mother, Ellen would have put it straight out of her mind, but Mel wasn't the type to imagine things. Her mother must be hiding something. Of course, that wasn't necessarily a bad thing. People were allowed to have secrets.

'I myself have a secret,' said Ellen out loud. It was an unusual feeling. She couldn't remember the last time she'd had a secret of this magnitude, if ever; one that would give people a little shock.

Just you and me, kid. We're the only ones who know about this.

She would keep it that way for a while longer.

She was halfway through another roast potato when the phone rang again. This time it was Julia.

'I can't believe you set me up with a guy who comes up to my armpits!' she shrieked.

'Sorry,' said Ellen with her mouth full. 'I didn't know.'

It was so tempting to make Julia shriek even louder with the two little words: I'm pregnant.

'And he looked like he stepped straight off the set of *The Farmer Wants a Wife*!'

'I thought he was sort of sexy, actually,' said Ellen. Of course she must resist. Patrick had to be told first.

'I didn't say he wasn't sexy,' said Julia.

Ellen's eyebrows popped. 'I *see*.'

'After you and Patrick left he walked me to the car and asked me out for a drink.'

'What did you say?'

'I said yes. Just as friends, obviously.'

'Obviously.' It warmed her heart to hear the change in Julia's voice. The brittleness was gone. She hadn't sounded like this in years.

'And I found out his real name. It's Sam. I knew it wasn't Bruce. Oh, hey, I forgot to say that I loved Patrick! He's gorgeous. A real man sort of man. Don't mess this one up.'

'Thanks for the vote of confidence.'

'I'm serious, Ellen. He's a keeper.'

'OK.' *Well, that's handy, seeing as I'm having his baby.*

'I mean, Jon was so pleased with himself,' mused Julia.

'Why does the truth always come out later? Everyone behaved as if they adored Jon when I was with him,' said Ellen. 'You all used to fall about laughing at his jokes.'

'Yeah, he was sort of witty,' said Julia distractedly. 'Are you watching *Beauty and the Geek?* See the blonde girl with the bulgy eyes? Don't you think she looks sort of homicidal? Speaking of homicidal, you didn't tell me that Patrick's stalker breaks into his house!'

'I didn't know.' Ellen watched the bulgy-eyed girl on the television screen. She'd quite forgotten about that new revelation regarding Saskia. What would she think if she knew Ellen was pregnant? Would that be enough to cure her? Or would it tip her over the edge into insanity? Had *she* ever wanted to have a baby with Patrick?

'Anyway, I've got to go. My mobile is ringing. Might be Sam! I'll talk to you later!'

She hung up. As soon as Ellen sat down on the couch with her roast potatoes the phone rang again.

'Hello, darlin'.' It was Patrick. For some reason, it had become one of their rituals that he always put on a deep American cowboy voice whenever he said hello. 'What are you doing?'

'Watching television and . . . eating potatoes.' Ellen felt guilty, as if every second she didn't tell him about the pregnancy was a betrayal. But it would be wrong to tell him over the phone, wouldn't it? And, frankly, she didn't want to hear what Patrick thought about it just yet. It was already confusing enough working out how she felt about it. *His* feelings would add a whole new layer of complexity to the situation. If he was thrilled by the news she would back off: it was too soon, it was all wrong, the sensible thing would be not to let this pregnancy continue. If he was horrified, if *he* suggested a termination, she would be devastated. She wanted this baby! If he said, 'I'll stand by you whatever you decide,' she would be annoyed. It was *their* problem, not just hers. Basically, she couldn't think of any way the poor man could react that would please her.

'How was your day?' she said, trying to keep her voice natural.

'It was fine, until you-know-who showed up at the office.'

'You-know-who?' said Ellen. 'Oh, of course. I do know who.' Poor Saskia. He always refused to use her name.

'She was even crazier than usual. Crying. Talking about babies.'

'Babies,' said Ellen. Her blood ran cold. Did Patrick already *know*? Was this some creepy way of him letting her know that he knew?

'What did she say about babies?' she asked. She laced her fingers through the curly cord of her grandmother's phone. (The phone was green, over thirty years old, with the old round dial that you slowly dialled with one fingertip.)

'Oh, I don't know. Seriously, I don't listen. I told her she needed psychiatric help. She handed me yet another letter and begged me to read it.'

'Did you?'

'Of course not. I stopped reading them years ago. It's always the same old crap. Anyway, look, do you want to get out of Sydney for a long weekend? I just had this sudden desire to get on a plane and escape this cold weather and then I got an email about cheap flights to Noosa. It felt like a sign that we should have a romantic long weekend. After the weekend we just had I'd like you to myself for a couple of days.'

Ellen didn't say anything for a moment. She felt an overwhelming wave of tiredness at the thought. She would have to pack a bag. One of those big broad-brimmed hats that girls wore on romantic long weekends. She didn't know where her sunglasses were. They had been missing for days. The lost sunglasses seemed like an insurmountable problem.

'You know, cocktails by the pool, sleeping in, lying on the beach,' Patrick continued. He hesitated and sounded unsure of himself. 'Or, I guess, when you live by the beach, maybe going somewhere like Noosa doesn't sound so exciting?'

Ellen roused herself. Her lovely new boyfriend was suggesting a weekend away. She should be thrilled.

'No, no, it sounds perfect. Just what we both need.'

Relief smoothed out Patrick's voice. 'I already asked Mum if she could take Jack for the weekend and she's fine with it. Oh, my whole family loves you, by the way. My brother said you were hot. I said hands off, kid.'

'Did he?' Ellen was flattered. Simon was so young! *Take that, Jon.*

What would Patrick's family think if they knew she was pregnant? She remembered the crucifix hanging over the television. They were old-fashioned Catholics, Patrick had said. Presumably in this day and age they would assume she and Patrick were sleeping together but they probably didn't want to have it shoved in their faces quite so soon. Would his mother suddenly call her a wanton hussy?

'Can you take next Monday off?'

'I've got a few appointments but I should be able to move them.'

'Good. I'm really looking forward to it. I love you.'

'I love you too.'

When she hung up, she went straight to the plate of roast potatoes to throw them away.

She would tell him at the weekend. It made sense. A neutral location; not his place or hers. They would be lying on a king-sized bed, tangled in crisp white hotel sheets, without any of the clutter of their day-to-day lives, and as a result they would come up with a correspondingly clean, elegant solution.

'Patrick, my love,' she would say, with the white sheet pulled up over her breasts and tucked under her arms like they did in the movies, her hair sexily tousled. 'There's something I have to tell you.'

As she straightened up from scraping the potatoes into the bin she caught sight of her missing sunglasses sitting on top of the fridge.

Yes, everything was going to be just fine.

I drove straight to work after my appointment with the hypnotist. When I walked into the office I moved carefully and slowly, because I was in a million pieces and any tiny movement might have made me disintegrate like a special effect in a movie.

'You look like you're in pain,' said my boss. He thinks I'm seeing a physio for a bad back. I chose this deliberately because he had problems with his back all through last year, and now he finds anything to do with bad backs a fascinating topic of discussion.

I said I *was* in pain, and then we talked about slipped discs and stretching and anti-inflammatory tablets before he remembered he was late for a meeting.

Then I worked.

I answered emails, returned phone calls, cleared my in-tray and wrote the first five pages of a report.

I worked well. I was crisp and efficient and diligent. I am highly respected in my professional world. I wonder what my colleagues would think if they knew I spent my lunchbreak crying in my ex-boyfriend's office. I wonder what they would think if they knew that underneath that veneer I am broken.

I gave him a letter I had written sitting outside the hypnotist's office. It was full of rage and probably didn't make much sense.

It was pointless because I have a feeling he doesn't read my letters any more.

And that's the problem with this rage. There's nowhere for it to go, because he no longer sees me. It's like I am smashing my head against an enormous, impassive, silent cliff face, over and over, until I'm dripping with blood. Nothing I do will change his opinion of me. Nothing I do will make him see me again.

And I can't seem to accept that.

If he were dead, like my mother, then I would understand. He would be gone. But he's not gone. He's still there. He's living his life as if *I* had died, like his wife. As if he is perfectly entitled to move me, to replace me, to make another woman pregnant.

If somebody would just tell me what to do to make the pain and the rage stop, I would do it.

It's strange. Sometimes when I'm sitting in the hypnotist's office with all that light bouncing round the walls, I want to ask her. 'Ellen,' I want to say, 'please help me.'

She would, I think.

10

Want to lose weight? Tried everything? Now you and your friends can THINK YOURSELF SLIM in the comfort of your own home with the help of a fully qualified, experienced Clinical Hypnotherapist! Host a HYPNO-PARTY! (Special Gift for the hostess!)
– Full-colour leaflet (print run: 10,000) produced by
Danny Hogan

On Thursday night, while Ellen was trying to pack for her weekend away, there was a knock at the door.

'What happened?' said Ellen when she opened the door and saw her mother holding a bottle of wine and smiling socially as if she was arriving for a dinner party.

'I'm "dropping by",' said Anne. 'Stop looking so panicked. I had dinner in the area and I made an impromptu decision to stop and see my daughter. For heaven's sake, you've gone completely white. It's not that unprecedented, is it?'

'Yes it is,' said Ellen, standing back so she could come in. 'You don't drop by.'

'I can't believe you still haven't got rid of this wallpaper,' said Anne, running her fingertips disdainfully down the wall in the hallway. 'I'd be ripping it off –'

'And painting it a nice neutral colour,' finished Ellen. 'I know. You've told me, and I've told you, I like it. It reminds me of Grandma.'

'Exactly,' murmured Anne. She walked into the kitchen and winced as she always did at the orange worktops as if she'd never seen them before. It was all some sort of performance to prove how she'd moved on. Her mother had enjoyed a perfectly idyllic childhood in this perfectly lovely, spacious house, on the *beach* mind you, but for some reason she liked to behave as if she'd spent her childhood in a white trash ghetto and she now lived in Paris.

'Glass of wine?' said Anne.

'No, I won't actually,' said Ellen. 'I overindulged last weekend, and I'm trying to be alcohol-free this week.'

And I'm pregnant, Mum.

The thought crossed her mind but felt strangely meaningless. Although nothing had changed since she'd done the test on Monday, now the initial shock had worn off, it had begun to seem less and less likely that she really was pregnant. For one thing, apart from that night when she'd had the roast potato 'cravings', she hadn't experienced any symptoms; she felt completely normal. It had also crossed her mind that she would probably miscarry. She was in her thirties after all, and you were meant to take vitamin supplements when you were planning to get pregnant and make an appointment with the doctor and have blood tests. As soon as this had occurred to her, she had become positive that it would happen. If she didn't make too much of a fuss about it, or overthink it, this pregnancy would probably just slip quietly away, until her body was ready for a properly organized pregnancy.

'Oh, well, I won't either then,' said her mother. She put the bottle of wine down and rapped her knuckles gently on the table. It seemed an uncharacteristically pointless gesture and Ellen remembered Melanie's call earlier in the week about her mother seeming 'secretive'.

'How are you?' she said.

'Me? I'm well. Very well.' Her mother stopped rapping and shook her head slightly. 'Shall we have a cup of tea then? What were you doing when I interrupted you so shockingly?'

'Packing,' said Ellen, as she put the kettle on to boil and carefully selected two of her grandmother's most flowery, old-ladyish china cups and saucers. 'I'm going away with Patrick for the weekend. To Noosa.'

'Ah, Patrick,' said Anne. She settled herself down at the table. 'I really don't need the whole teacup and saucer palaver. I'm not eighty.'

Ellen ignored her and took out the teapot.

'A tea bag will do! Are *you* eighty?'

'So, what did you think of Patrick anyway?' said Ellen, warming the pot just to annoy her mother. 'Both Mel and Pip called to say how much they liked him.'

'Did they?' said Anne. She raised her voice over the bubbling of the electric kettle. 'Well, I certainly didn't dislike him. You really should replace that kettle.'

Ellen put down the teapot. 'What's that supposed to mean?'

'I mean it's so loud. It's like a plane taking off.'

'No, what do you mean, you didn't dislike Patrick?'

'He's perfectly innocuous,' said Anne.

'That is so insulting!' Ellen was half laughing in disbelief.

'If you want to know the truth, I just felt that there was something not quite right about him. A sort of coldness.'

Coldness! This, from her warm, cuddly, motherly mother.

'Oh, and you're such a discerning judge of character.' Ellen sat down at the table and watched her hand shake slightly as she poured the tea. It was rage. She was filled with rage on Patrick's behalf.

'Well, you asked me,' said Anne. 'I'm not saying I'm right. I'm just telling you how I felt.'

'You thought Jon was wonderful.'

'Jon was good company.' Anne smiled fondly, as if Jon was a dear old friend.

'Mel said the other night that he was a self-satisfied prick. He was brutally sarcastic. He treated me like I was an idiot. He was bordering on verbally abusive.'

'Oh, Ellen, he *wasn't*. Don't try to rewrite history. Especially don't rewrite it to make yourself the victim. I hate that victim mentality women have these days. It was just a relationship that didn't work out. He wasn't an evil monster.'

'Jon made me very unhappy,' said Ellen. *He was SO an evil monster!* Her voice trembled. She was reminded of the year she turned fifteen when her hormones went crazy and it seemed like every conversation she had with her mother ended up with Ellen crying. 'And Patrick makes me very happy.'

'Well, then, that's all that matters,' said Anne in the

same brisk, sensible, placatory tone that used to drive Ellen to distraction when she was fifteen. 'You don't need to listen to me. Look at my history. What do I know about men?'

'Nothing,' said Ellen. 'You know nothing.'

Her mother raised her eyebrows and lifted her teacup. 'I didn't mean to upset you.'

'Well, you *did*,' said Ellen sullenly. She really was behaving like a teenager. Where was all her advanced emotional intelligence today?

'I am sorry. I'm truly sorry.' Anne clumsily patted Ellen's shoulder. 'You still look very pale.'

'Probably because I'm *pregnant*,' said Ellen and dissolved into a luxurious flood of salty tears.

I called in sick on Tuesday and went to Avalon Beach again with my new boogie board.

I have never done such a thing before. It's not how I was brought up. My mother would be bewildered. She thought a regular pay packet was a wonderful thing; something a woman especially should never take for granted. I can still hear the reverence in her voice when she told people about my very first position out of uni. 'Saskia has got herself a *job*.'

I remember how baffled she was when I once said something about 'job satisfaction'. 'But, darling, they pay you!' She was worried I would be rude to the boss. She would have thought taking a sickie was crazy, risky and very bad-mannered.

Sorry, Mum. I needed a 'mental health' day.

'Mental health,' she would have snorted.

She didn't believe in modern maladies like depression or anorexia. A friend's son was diagnosed with clinical depression and Mum was disgusted. 'What's the silly man got to be sad about? He's got a good *job*! A wife! A baby!'

She believed in grief over death and joy over birth and love and marriage and plain wholesome food and a spick-and-span house. Anything else was just 'being silly'.

I wonder if she would have said I was being silly when I fell apart after Patrick broke up with me. She adored him, and Jack too, of course. She thought of Patrick as her son-in-law and Jack as her grandson.

I assume that Patrick would have met the hypnotist's parents by now. The thought of him chatting to the hypnotist's mother, being polite and trying to impress her, as if my sweet mother never existed, as if my mother was just practice for the real mother-in-law – well, that just fills me with an almighty torrent of rage.

I've stopped picking up the phone to call my mother. I did it for months after she died. I even dialled the number a few times before I remembered and quickly slammed down the phone before some stranger answered. I don't hear the phone any more and think, 'That will be Mum.' But I still miss her. Every day.

I understand, intellectually, that the death of a parent is a natural, acceptable part of life. Nobody would call the death of a very sick eighty-year-old woman a tragedy. There was soft weeping at her funeral and red watery eyes. No wrenching sobs. Now I think that I should have let myself sob. I should have wailed and beaten my chest and thrown myself over her coffin.

I read a poem. A pretty, touching poem I thought she

would have liked. I should have used my own words. I should have said: *No one will ever love me as fiercely as my mother did.* I should have said: *You all think you're at the funeral of a sweet little old lady, but you're at the funeral of a girl called Clara, who had long blonde hair in a heavy thick plait down to her waist, who fell in love with a shy man who worked on the railways, and they spent years and years trying to have a baby, and when Clara finally got pregnant, they danced round the living room, but very slowly, so as not to hurt the baby, and the first two years of her little girl's life were the happiest of Clara's life, except then her husband died, and she had to bring up the little girl on her own, before there was a single mother's pension, before the words 'single mother' even existed.*

I should have told them about how when I was at school, if the day became unexpectedly cold, Mum would turn up in the school yard with a jacket for me. I should have told them that she hated broccoli with such a passion she couldn't even look at it, and that she was in love with the main character on the English television series *Judge John Deed.* I should have told them that she loved to read, and she was a terrible cook, because she tried to cook and read her latest library book at the same time, and the dinner always got burned and the library book always got food spatters on it, and then she'd spend ages trying to dab them away with the wet corner of a tea towel. I should have told them that my mum thought of Jack as her own grandchild, and how she made him a special racing-car quilt he adored. I should have talked and talked and grabbed both sides of the lectern and said: *She was not just a little old lady. She was Clara. She was my mother. She was wonderful.*

Instead I said my brief acceptable little poem and then

I sat back down and held Patrick's hand, and afterwards he helped me bring cups of tea to my mum's friends, and chatted so charmingly to the old ladies, and I never thought *I no longer have a family* because Patrick kept holding my hand, and Jack was going to be running into our arms at Sydney airport, and I knew that Patrick's mum was planning on leaving a big bowl of her beef stroganoff in the fridge because she knew it was my favourite.

Four weeks later he said, 'I think it's over.'

My mind kept going round in endless circles. If I ring up Mum to tell her about Patrick I'll feel better, but Mum is dead. If I tell Patrick that I can't believe my mum is gone, I'll feel better, but Patrick doesn't want me any more. If I take Jack to the park or a movie, then I'll feel better, but I'm not his mother any more. If I go and see Maureen then I'll feel better, except she's not part of my life any more.

I didn't have enough people in my life to cover the loss of this many people at once. I didn't have any spare aunties or cousins or grandparents. I didn't have back-up. I didn't have insurance cover for a loss like this.

The pain felt so physical: as if huge patches of my skin were ripped off and have never healed.

And now the hypnotist is having a baby.

So, Mum, I know, it's a good job and they *pay* me, but ever since I saw the hypnotist's pregnancy tests, I've had these strange images running through my head at work. Sometimes I imagine throwing a hot cup of coffee straight at a colleague's face, or tearing off all my clothes and running naked into the boardroom shouting obscenities, or picking up a pair of scissors and driving the sharp edge over and over into my thigh. You would not understand that. Crazy thoughts didn't run through your head.

So I called in sick and went to the beach to learn how to boogie board.

It was harder than I expected. The board was slippery. Why was it so slippery? I couldn't seem to keep it in position under my stomach. I kept sliding off. That had never looked like a problem when I saw other people doing it. I got mad and swore. I thought, even the boogie board doesn't want me.

And then when I did manage to hold the board still, I couldn't see to get my timing right to actually catch a wave.

I thought, six-year-old boys can do this, what's wrong with me?

I thought, other people find love and have babies and make families, what's wrong with me?

I thought, other people don't obsess over their ex-boyfriends, what's wrong with me?

I considered letting the board float away to sea in a fit of petulance, but it seemed too wasteful, and I was already ashamed enough about my day off.

When I was walking up to the car, sniffing and cold and cranky because I couldn't even seem to fit the stupid board comfortably under my arm, I saw that woolly-haired man who had seen me the day I fell asleep in my red dress. He was walking down to the beach with his boogie board stuck comfortably under one arm.

'How's the surf?' he said.

'Stupid,' I said, and kept walking.

When I got to my car, my mobile phone was ringing.

It was the hypnotist.

*

The experience of flying together for the first time made Ellen and Patrick chatty and overexcited. They both got the giggles as a flight attendant did an especially grim-faced safety demonstration, although nobody else seemed amused by her. They had bought novels to read on the plane but they both kept putting them down on their laps to talk.

Patrick seemed especially high-spirited.

'I didn't even ask if you've been to Noosa before,' he said, as the plane took off.

'I haven't,' said Ellen. 'What about you?'

'Just once,' said Patrick. 'Actually, it's where I met Saskia.'

Ellen noted that it was one of the rare times that he actually spoke about her as if she were just a normal girl.

'How did you meet?' she asked, trying to keep her voice light and not overly interested.

'We were both up here for a conference,' said Patrick. 'She's a town planner, have I mentioned that? Anyway, I sat next to her at one of the sessions. It's strange, because I felt like I was a bit insane then, I think I was still in shock over Colleen's death, and Saskia seemed so *sane*. She was into bushwalking and she took me on these great long hikes through the national park. I hadn't been doing any exercise and all of sudden my heart was pumping and I was getting air into my lungs, and looking at these stunning views made me feel like it was possible to be happy again.'

'Endorphins,' said Ellen. 'We'll have to do some walks this weekend.'

And when you're pumped full of happy endorphins, I'll tell you about the baby.

'Yeah, I'd like that. For a while there, Saskia and I were bushwalking every weekend, but then she got this problem with her leg. She couldn't walk for hardly any distance without getting pain. It really affected her.'

'What was wrong with it?' said Ellen. There was something strangely familiar about this story. Had Patrick already told her about Saskia's leg? She was sure she would have remembered. She'd carefully hoarded all the information he'd handed over about Saskia.

'Nobody could tell her. She went to doctor after doctor, physiotherapists, nobody could tell her. One specialist suggested it was all in her mind and Saskia was so angry she walked straight out.'

Ellen was aware of a strange slippery feeling of panic, as if she'd just remembered she'd forgotten to turn off the stove.

'Sometimes she had to bring a chair into the kitchen so she could sit down to cook dinner,' mused Patrick. 'It changed her personality. She used to be so sporty. I tried to be sympathetic but then I got so frustrated, because there was nothing I could do about it. She thought I was losing patience with her, but I wasn't. I felt for her, I did. It just frustrated the hell out of me because I couldn't fix it. It reminded me of when Colleen was sick. That useless feeling. Like you're losing a fight and you can't even take a swing.'

Patrick was distracted by the approach of the flight attendant. He twisted his head to look. 'Should we have a drink? Except we'll have to pay for it, so it doesn't seem as decadent. That's the problem with these cheap flights.'

It couldn't just be a coincidence, could it?

She nearly said it out loud, to test the possibility: 'Huh! That's funny, I have a client who has exactly the same problem.' Except she knew it wasn't a coincidence, and she knew he would know it wasn't.

Deborah.

What was her last name?

Deborah Vandenberg.

She could see Deborah Vandenberg's face so clearly. She ran late for her very first appointment. She had seemed a little odd, a little shifty-looking, but then, many of her clients seemed odd and shifty at their first appointments. It was because they had never seen a hypnotherapist before and didn't know what to expect. They kept looking about warily, as if they suspected someone was about to play a practical joke on them.

'I've had this pain in my leg,' she'd told Ellen, and ran her palm down the length of a long, slender, blue-jeaned thigh.

She told Ellen that sometimes she had to sit down to cook dinner. She told her about a 'smarmy doctor' who asked if she'd been experiencing any 'stress' lately, and she'd been so furious at the implication that she could be imagining the pain that she'd walked out without saying another word.

Deborah was Saskia.

Saskia was Deborah.

All this time obsessing over Saskia and she'd already met her, she'd talked to her, *she'd been in her house*. She was tall and striking. Interesting-coloured eyes. Hazel. Almost gold. Like a tiger's eyes. (Ellen noticed eyes. It was because she'd been brought up in the shadow of her mother's violet eyes.) Well-dressed. Articulate. She would never ever have picked her as a stalker. She had not had a definite picture in her head of Saskia, but she'd been imagining her as small, with squinty eyes, a scurrying, insane little mouse of a person. (Why did she think tall people couldn't be crazy? Because they looked like they ruled the world? Because she admired them and coveted their legs?)

She felt Patrick's hand on her arm. 'Ellen? Did you want a drink?'

The interesting thing was that she quite liked her. Deborah – Saskia. She'd enjoyed their sessions. Their chats. She'd admired her boots once, and Deborah – Saskia – had told her about how they were actually comfortable, as well as beautiful, and Ellen had gone out and bought exactly the same pair, spending more money than she'd ever spent on shoes.

She was wearing those boots right now.

'No, I'm fine,' she said to Patrick, tucking her boots under her seat.

So did Saskia really need help with her leg? Or was that just an excuse? And what exactly was her objective? Did she just want to observe Ellen? (In the same way that Ellen would have quite liked to have secretly observed Jon's new wife-to-be, the dental hygienist, except that she would never actually make an appointment, because she wasn't *that* interested and, more to the point, how embarrassing if someone found out.)

Patrick sighed and stretched out his legs.

'The best part of leaving Sydney is knowing that I don't need to worry about Saskia suddenly turning up anywhere. I didn't even bring my mobile phone. I gave Mum and Jack the number at the hotel and your mobile number. I hope that's OK, I meant to ask you.'

'Of course it's OK.' *Oh no, no, no.*

'So that's the last thing I'm going to say about that woman for the rest of the weekend. I'm not going to talk about her; I'm not going to think about her; I'm not going to see her. We are now entering a Saskia-free zone.'

Oh God. Ellen tapped two fingers rhythmically against her forehead. If it wasn't so awful it could nearly be funny. Or at least slightly amusing.

'What's the matter?'

'I just remembered something. Something I meant to do before I left.'

She had told Deborah, or Saskia, exactly where they were going this weekend. She had even told her where they were *staying*.

She'd called her the other day on her mobile phone to ask if they could reschedule their Monday appointment. 'I'm unexpectedly going away,' she'd told her. 'For a long weekend to Noosa.'

'I'm envious,' Saskia had said, in her cool Deborah voice. 'I love Noosa. Where are you staying?'

'I think my partner has got us booked in at the Sheraton,' Ellen had answered. Partner! She'd called Patrick her partner! Why had she done that? She didn't even like the word. It was because Deborah seemed like the sort of woman who would find 'boyfriend' too juvenile a term. But why had she even needed to mention Patrick at all? For some reason she had wanted Deborah to know that she was in a relationship. Because Deborah had seemed liked an attractive, professional, fortyish woman who would be in one of those elegant relationships involving vineyards and boating and really high-quality sex, with no accidental pregnancies, obviously. She had wanted Deborah to think that she was in one of those relationships too.

So because of her foolish, unprofessional desire to impress a *client* (who she should not have wanted to impress in the first place) she had helpfully let Saskia know that they were going away for a romantic, impromptu weekend to the same place where she and Patrick had *met*.

She glanced at Patrick. He had leaned his head back against the seat and let his face relax.

'I don't even realize how tense she makes me until I get away,' he said without opening his eyes.

Ellen dropped her head and hit the heel of her hand against her forehead in silent anguish. Instead of making life easier for Patrick, she'd actually aided and abetted his stalker. Her mouth went dry and she lifted her chin. Saskia wouldn't *follow them all the way to Noosa*, would she? She couldn't, for example, have booked tickets on *this very flight*?

Ellen unbuckled her belt and lifted herself slightly up in her seat to glance over the top of her seat at the faces of passengers sitting around them. People avoided her eyes, or had their heads bent reading or talking. Only one little girl, sitting on her mother's lap and sucking crazily on a dummy, stared back curiously. Ellen plonked herself back down, repressing a hysterical desire to giggle or cry.

Now she was going to spend this weekend lugging around not one, but two major secrets. At any moment she could open her mouth and instantly wipe that relaxed expression off the poor man's face.

He opened his eyes, and the sunlight pouring in from the window made them look very green. 'You OK?'

'I'm great.' She patted his knee and turned to look out of the window at the wing of the plane. 'I'm just great.'

So I managed to get myself on the same flight as them.

They walked straight past me. Patrick was in front, frowning at the seat numbers on his boarding pass. Ellen was walking behind, looking dreamily about. *I don't need to frown at my boarding pass because my 'partner' will find our seats. I'm so new age and happy and pregnant.*

She's going away with her 'partner'. I hate that word. It's so Sydney. What's wrong with 'boyfriend'? When he was with me he was my boyfriend. I was his girlfriend.

And we're all off to Noosa for the weekend. A jolly threesome.

I dropped the boogie board when she said 'Noosa'. Just when I think there are no new ways for him to hurt me. Why Noosa? They've got a whole country full of places for a romantic weekend away and he chooses Noosa.

I thought my memories of that week were safe. I thought nothing could touch that time. I feel like I can remember every minute. Every taste, every sound, every smell.

I can still feel the exact shape of my room key in the palm of my hand and taste the exact combination of salt and ice and alcohol in my mouth from the margaritas we'd drunk, as we stood together in the hotel lift looking up at the flashing floor numbers, both of us knowing that we were going to my room to make love for the first time. I can still see the sunburnt face of the young boy who wheeled in the clunky trolley with breakfast the next morning: the smell of fresh coffee and bacon. I can still see the croissant flakes scattering the front of the newspaper we read in bed.

He's even staying at the Sheraton. Why would he book there? I can't help but wonder if it's because his memories of that week are just as special, and he thinks – he could be so *stupid* sometimes – that he can get back that happiness with someone else.

He can't. He can't just delete me from all his memories and replace me with another woman.

That's why as soon as I got the call from the hypnotist I knew I had to go. I had to be there. I have to let him know that I'm there too. I'll always still be there.

I'll choose the perfect moment to let them know that I've come along too. He'll be angry but that's OK. I'd rather his fury than his indifference. I'd rather he was yelling at me than not to exist at all.

Patrick was in the bathroom cleaning his teeth and Ellen was already in bed watching a movie they'd paid for and eating chocolate from the mini-bar.

The room was perfectly lovely. King-sized bed with crisp white sheets, big fluffy towels, soft shadowy lighting and neutral colours.

Exactly like other hotels where she'd stayed with other men.

'Where did you stay when you were here last?' Ellen had asked as they were going up in the lift.

'Here,' Patrick had answered, his eyes on the numbers of the floors flashing above them.

'So this was the hotel where you met Saskia?'

'Well, I knew it was good,' said Patrick, and then he laid a finger across her lips. 'We're not mentioning her name this weekend, remember?'

So poor Saskia had to hear that Ellen and Patrick were going to stay in the same hotel where she'd first met him. For heaven's sake, it was no doubt the same hotel where they'd made love for the first time. What would hearing that have done to her twisted mind?

Ellen looked at the door and thought of horror movies. They would order room service and Saskia would dress up as a staff member and wheel the trolley in with her head lowered and the music would be letting the audience know that something really terrible was about to happen, and then, just as the music reached its terrifying crescendo, she'd suddenly *leap* at them with a carving knife held aloft and –

'Did you remember toothpaste?' Patrick put his head round the door.

'Yep. There's some in my make-up bag.'

He was still too polite to go through her stuff without permission.

And she was having his baby.

Too soon. Too soon.

'Well, of course you'll have the baby,' Anne had said.

'Not necessarily,' Ellen had said, surprised by her mother's definite tone. She had assumed she would say something along the lines of: *I'll support you whatever you decide and what form of contraception were you using anyway?*

'It depends on what Patrick says. And, you know, I'm . . . pro-choice.' It was an American phrase. For a second, she wasn't even sure she'd picked the right team. What was the other side called? Pro-life. Well, she was all for *life*.

Anne snorted. 'You're thirty-five, not sixteen. You're desperate to have a baby –'

'What? Where did that come from? I am not desperate to have a baby.'

'I saw the expression on your face at Madeline's baby shower, when you were holding what's-her-name's baby – and I have to say that was a particularly ugly baby.'

'Mum.'

'He looked like a little toad. Anyway, my point is that you do want to have children and you're financially secure and you like the father, you might even love the father. If you had an abortion and then you found you couldn't get pregnant, you would never forgive yourself. Of course you're having the baby. You just tell him, you're having a child, neither of you meant it to happen, but it has, and it's not nineteen fifty so he doesn't have to marry you, and he can be involved as little or as much as he likes. It's all very simple. He will have legal obligations in regard to child support but, if I were you, I wouldn't worry too much about that. You've got your grandmother's house. You've got me and your godmothers. You don't need his money.'

'I suppose not,' said Ellen. Patrick's money had been the last thing on her mind.

'It's all very simple,' said Anne again, while her fingertips did a joyful little tap-dance on the table top, and Ellen saw that she was actually pleased about the baby. She might even be thrilled.

There was a pause.

The soft expression vanished from her mother's face. 'Of course, it's early days,' she said briskly. 'At your age, the chances of a first-trimester miscarriage are relatively high.'

'Thank you, Mother.'

'Well, you're the one talking about terminating the pregnancy, you can hardly get all sensitive about the possibility of a miscarriage.'

'I didn't say . . . well, yes, OK.'

Her mother was right. There had never been any doubt. She was going to have the baby. The complicated part wasn't whether she wanted a child. The complicated part was how it would affect her relationship with Patrick.

Because Ellen didn't just want a baby. She wanted the whole kit and caboodle. The husband. The daddy. The man holding her hand in the delivery room.

That's what she couldn't say to her mother: *I don't want to do it your way. I never wanted to do it your way. I don't want to raise a child alone. I don't want to be different. I just want to be the same as everyone else.*

Patrick came out of the bathroom and hopped into bed with her. He took a piece of chocolate from the bar she was eating.

'You just cleaned your teeth,' said Ellen.

'I know. Don't tell Jack. Bad Dad.'

Speaking of which, how do you feel about another child? She was so close to just saying it, except that she really didn't have the energy to talk about it. Tomorrow. They would talk about it tomorrow. It was lucky he wasn't a big drinker. When she'd said she didn't feel like wine with dinner, he'd said, 'Oh, that's fine. I won't have any either.' Sharing a bottle of good wine had been such an integral part of her relationship with Jon, he would have noticed immediately if she wasn't drinking.

They watched the movie together. The plot was too complicated. They couldn't get the characters straight. They both kept saying, 'What? Who's he?' Finally they switched it off, agreeing they were either too tired or too old, and turned to each other.

Their lovemaking was sleepy and tender, as if they were an old married couple. Ellen felt teary. Everything was going to be perfect.

'Will you hypnotize me to sleep?' said Patrick, as they switched off the lights.

'I'm pretty tired,' yawned Ellen.

It had so quickly become a habit. She would give him a five-minute relaxation exercise before he went to sleep. He seemed genuinely amazed by it. He said he loved it, it was like magic, and that listening to her voice was his favourite part of the day and he hadn't slept that well since he was a teenager and that she was helping him deal with the stress of 'that woman', his work, everything. She'd never been with anyone who was so impressed by her skills before.

'That's all right,' said Patrick. 'I've been exploiting you, haven't I? I wouldn't be up for doing a survey right now.'

Oh, he was nice, and she did want him in a relaxed frame of mind tomorrow.

She sat up and laid a hand on his forehead. Sometimes

this felt more intimate than sex. She so rarely used touch on her clients, although she knew other therapists who did. Lying in bed in the private inky blackness, knowing that her words had the power to place images in his head, to slow his heartbeat, to lower his blood pressure, she felt powerful, nurturing, mystical. A good witch, a sorceress. Not a hypnotherapist, a hypnotist.

'I'm going to count to ten. By the count of three or four, you may feel your breathing slow and your eyelids become heavy. By five or six you will probably be struggling to keep them open. By seven or eight or even nine, it will most likely be irresistible, and you'll let your eyelids close. By ten, your eyes may be shut, your breathing deep and regular.'

She saw the shine of his eyes in the darkness. Already she could sense his breathing slow. She used a different induction technique each time, whatever came to mind. She was freer, looser and more creative than she was with her paying clients.

She began to count, increasing the pressure of her hand on his forehead as she did, and making her voice softer, slower and yet more insistent.

His eyes were shut by the count of seven.

'And now, I want you to imagine this: warm honey drizzling off the edge of a spoon.'

He loved honey. He put huge glops of it on his breakfast cereal, and she'd taken note of the way he would stand there in the kitchen, seemingly mesmerized as he watched the honey slowly drip from the spoon he held up high.

'This honey isn't just ordinary honey. This honey is the

colour of morning light. This honey is warmth and sweetness and security. This honey is every happy moment in your life. Every beautiful memory. Every second where you felt truly alive.'

She knew he could see the honey. She could see it too. She was in a light trance herself. When the work was going well, it happened, and it was always a pleasure when it did.

'Keep watching the honey. Keep watching until there is nothing else in your mind.'

She paused and felt the curve of his skull beneath her hand and the warmth of his body against hers, and thought, *He's the father of my child. He'll be the Daddy and I'll be the Mummy.*

It was possible she was overly romantic when it came to the whole concept of fatherhood.

'And now I want you to take your attention to your feet. Imagine that your feet are dissolving into the bed like warm honey. They're dissolving . . . liquefying.'

She continued with the honey metaphor as she slowly worked her way up his body, encouraging him to sink deeper and deeper into his trance. This was the deepest she'd ever taken him.

She pinched his arm and he didn't flinch. Spontaneous anaesthesia.

If he was a regular client, now was the point where she would plant a post-hypnotic suggestion. If she was treating a smoker she might say, 'Every time you go to open your packet of cigarettes, you will feel an overwhelming sense of revulsion and disgust.' If she was treating an overeater, she might say, 'You will eat slowly and mindfully and only what your body needs.'

But Patrick hadn't asked for help with any particular problem. He just wanted stress relief. He just wanted a good night's sleep.

As a therapist, she would only know what he told her.

As his girlfriend she happened to know that this weekend had the potential to be extremely stressful.

She said, 'Throughout this weekend, you are going to maintain a wonderful sense of relaxation and well-being.'

Nothing wrong with that. He was already in that frame of mind anyway.

She said, 'If anything goes wrong, if you hear or see anything that upsets you or worries you, the touch of my hand on your right shoulder – like this – will immediately bring about a sense of deep relaxation.'

She laid her hand on his shoulder.

'Whatever life throws at you, you'll be able to handle it. If something unexpected happens, you will have the resources to do what you know, in your heart, is right for you. You will not remember these suggestions. And now, on the count of three, you will come out of your trance, and you will immediately fall asleep, and you will sleep throughout the night without dreaming or waking, and in the morning you will feel refreshed and reinvigorated. One. Two. Three.'

His breathing changed, became shallower, and he made a comical sound that was halfway between a snort and a snore.

'Thank you,' he mumbled, as he turned over on one side and pulled one of the pillows into a vertical position and shoved it under his head. 'G'night, darling.'

And then he was asleep.

Ellen turned on her side so that her back was pressed against his.

Had she just crossed the line, ethically speaking?

Flynn would say that she'd crossed it the first time she agreed to perform any form of hypnosis on Patrick.

Danny would laugh and say he didn't believe there were any lines to cross. That was what being in a relationship was all about: trying to manipulate the other person to do what you wanted. 'Everyone tries to hypnotize their partners,' he'd said to her once. 'We're just better at it than the average person.'

What did she think herself? Well. She didn't believe she'd crossed the line, exactly, but perhaps she'd edged her toe over it.

The tip of her toe. She thought of Saskia. Now she could put a face to her. An intelligent, attractive face. Saskia wasn't afraid to cross any line to try to get Patrick back.

Lines were there to be crossed.

So maybe Ellen was just doing what she needed to do for her *unborn child*. She was a lioness protecting her cub; a mother rushing into a burning building to save her child. Or maybe that was rubbish and she was trying to rationalize doing something that she knew was wrong.

Well. Look. She just wouldn't do it again. She'd teach him to do his own self-hypnosis. That was the solution. There was something ever so slightly . . . unsavoury about this habit of theirs. She enjoyed it too much. That was the last time.

She felt like an altar boy promising not to masturbate any more.

She fell asleep, and dreamed of Deborah-who-was-now-Saskia. She was sitting cross-legged in Ellen's recliner chair for clients, dipping a spoon into a huge jar of honey. She took a spoonful of the honey and held it far above her head, and let a long thin line of it drizzle into her open mouth.

Then she closed her mouth and looked at Ellen, and slowly, sensuously slid her tongue over her sticky lips.

'You crossed the line,' she said. 'You know you did.'

'Don't get honey on my chair,' said Ellen, briskly, to cover her shame.

After we got off the plane, I stood in a far corner of the terminal next to a big pillar where I could see them waiting at the baggage carousel but they couldn't see me.

Ellen kept looking about her, as if she was expecting to see someone she knew. Patrick was completely focused on the carousel, eyes narrowed, his whole body poised, ready to leap. He was always like that when we travelled. He seemed to think collecting luggage was some sort of test of strength and agility, as if he had to crash-tackle his bag the moment it appeared and wrestle it to the ground. It always made me laugh.

It made Ellen laugh too. I saw her smiling when he suddenly shot forward and pounced on both their bags at once, re-emerging triumphant with his prey.

I gave him that bag as a birthday present the last year we were together.

Ellen is one of those people who ties a ribbon round the handle of her bag so it's easy to spot. Her ribbon was a big floaty shiny-blue bow, feminine and whimsical and yet so sensible. That ribbon sums up everything I love and hate about her.

I watched them walk off to the car-rental counter. He was carrying both of their bags. I guess he's being especially caring and chivalrous now that she's pregnant.

I thought it was my birthright as a woman to have that time, at least once, where a man treats you like a princess, rubbing your feet at night, pressing his hand to your stomach, masterfully ordering you not to pick up anything too heavy.

But apparently not.

It probably would have driven me crazy anyway. I just like the idea of it. I'm too tall to be treated like a princess.

When they stopped at the counter, I saw him kneading the back of her neck as they talked to the car-hire woman. At one point all three of them laughed heartily over something. After they left the terminal I went to the carousel to pick up my bag. It was the only one left. Slowly revolving round, alone and ignored and invisible. No pretty ribbon. Old and tired and sagging in the middle. Now I wonder who that could remind me of?

'Don't look so sorry for yourself,' I snapped at it, and a man walking by quickly looked away.

I went to the same car-hire place. No hearty laughs from the woman for me. Just grim slapping down of paperwork and dire warnings about the excess on the insurance and how it was my responsibility to look carefully for any damage on the car before I took it.

'Actually, I think it should be your responsibility,' I said.

The woman stared, and I said, 'Oh, forget it.'

I drove to the Sheraton and steeled myself for the

memories as soon as I walked into the lobby, but they'd renovated. The place looked completely different. It was like they'd done it on purpose. *You don't exist any more, Saskia. We've brought in interior designers to wipe away all trace of you.*

There was no sign of Ellen and Patrick.

I went for a walk on the beach and tried to use Ellen's dial technique for my leg pain. Maybe it works. I'm not sure if I'm imagining it. She would say that's exactly the point: to *use* my imagination so that I don't actually experience the pain.

I guess she will have the chance to use her techniques for a pain-free childbirth. She said that women have been known to have caesareans without painkillers, 'using their body's own natural anaesthesia'. Sure. Someone cuts open your stomach with a knife and you don't feel a thing. All you need to do is *believe*. Sounds like something from a Christmas movie.

It never really occurred to me that she might actually help me with my leg pain. It was just the first thing that came into my head when she said, 'Why are you here today?' Instead of answering, 'I'm here because you've been on a few dates now with Patrick and I've seen the way he looks at you and I'm thinking you could be the first serious contender, so I followed you home, and there was your cute little "Ellen O'Farrell Hypnotherapy" sign sitting on the front lawn outside your house, with your phone number conveniently listed, so I rang up and made an appointment. How do you do?'

After each of our sessions I told her that I didn't think I'd been hypnotized, but she just smiled her smug Mona Lisa smile, as if she knew better.

To be honest, I wasn't really sure *what* happened in that sunny glass room. Each time I sit in that green chair I start out thinking that I don't really need to listen to her instructions, I should just think of something else, it's not like I'm really there to be hypnotized. I'm there for the before-and-after chat, where we've discussed everything from hay fever to the difficulty of finding comfortable shoes. But then her words always seem to trickle into my head, and I start to listen, and I think, 'Oh, well, it won't hurt to let my eyelids feel heavy,' and next thing, my whole body is sinking into the chair and she's telling me to try and open my eyelids and I can't. Well, presumably I *could* if I really wanted to.

Once she starts talking, I don't think about Patrick at all.

Last time she asked me to remember a 'fleeting perfect moment' when I felt filled with confidence or joy or peace or power, and so I remembered Sunday-morning break-fasts in the summer with my mum when I was a child. I'd make a whole stack of pancakes and Mum would always act so impressed and then we'd sit on a picnic rug in the backyard and read our books and eat the pancakes with lemon and sugar, and sometimes we'd stay there until lunchtime.

I'm meant to be using the 'power of that memory' to help with my leg pain.

It's a load of crap, of course.

I think.

I can remember the first time I experienced the pain in my leg. It was just after Mum told me her diagnosis. I was buying groceries with Jack, and it was taking ages because he kept seeing things he wanted, which we had to argue over, and we were having a dinner party with one of Patrick's clients and I was trying to impress, so I was looking for obscure ingredients. 'Just do something simple,' Patrick always said, but I said that people feel special when you go to some trouble, when you have the table set with a good linen tablecloth, with fresh flowers and cloth napkins and gleaming glasses. I loved a beautifully set table. Now I eat sitting on the couch, with the plate on my lap, or standing at the kitchen counter, or in bed.

I noticed this ache creeping up the side of my leg. It wasn't excruciating, just annoying, as if I'd pulled a muscle, and eventually I had to sit on the edge of the frozen foods' cabinet and rest it, and Jack said, 'What are you *doing*, Sas?'

Then it happened again the next day. I still didn't give it much thought. It certainly never crossed my mind that five years later I would still be dealing with it.

I was so confident when I went to see that first physiotherapist that she would be able to fix it. I thought it was something that needed to be crossed off my 'to do' list, like getting my car serviced or my legs waxed. Quick, fix this pain please, it's annoying me.

Patrick was sympathetic at first, but then he seemed to lose patience and interest. We couldn't do our bushwalks any more. We couldn't walk through the city to a restaurant for more than two blocks without me having to find a bus stop to sit down. We couldn't stand in a group at a party without me saying I needed a chair. I caught a flicker of impatience cross his face once when he came home and found me sitting on the kitchen floor with the chopping board on my lap, slicing up carrots. I guess it was just so boring for him to have a girlfriend who behaved like an elderly person.

Then Mum died, and then he 'ended the relationship'. Perhaps he'd been getting bored and my leg was the final straw.

The pain in my leg isn't as bad as it was, but it got to a certain point and then it never got any better. It's like a permanent physical reminder of that time in my life, when everything changed forever. It's the marker between the person I am now – strange, obsessive, flabby and unfit – and the person I was before – normal, happy, very fit, could go for years without seeing a doctor. As soon as I start to feel that creeping ache, I feel a corresponding creeping sense of hopelessness and pointlessness and nothingness.

And of all the people I've been to see about this pain, Ellen is the first person who seemed even remotely interested in how much it's affected me.

'It must be incredibly frustrating,' she said, and she seemed so sympathetic, for a horrifying moment I thought I might cry.

Yes, Ellen, it is incredibly frustrating, especially when one of my hobbies is following my ex-boyfriend, who, by the way, happens to be your current boyfriend, often on foot, and it makes it very difficult, although I'm proud to say that I've never given up, I just keep going, no matter how bad the pain is, and people stare, because I guess I'm grimacing. There she goes, a twisted old witch, hobbling after her old pain-free life with outstretched clawed hands, trying to snatch it back.

I I

From the moment we're born everyone is hypnotizing us. We are all, to some degree, in a trance. Our clients think we're 'putting them to sleep', but our ultimate goal is the opposite. We're trying to wake them up.
– Excerpt from an article written by Ellen O'Farrell
for the journal *Hypnotherapy Today*

The Saturday was wonderful. They slept late. Breakfast and the papers in bed. A long walk on the beach and a quick swim. (Very quick; Patrick started shivering after only a few minutes.) Coffee and cake by the river. Lunch by the pool. An afternoon nap.

Ellen's senses seemed sharper. The sun and the sea breeze caressed her skin. As they walked down Hastings Street, she could smell everything: coffee, the ocean, the perfume and aftershave and sunscreen of passers-by. She heard every fragment of conversation, every burst of laughter.

There appeared to be some sort of baby boom happening in Noosa. The place was crowded with babies and toddlers and roundly pregnant women. Every baby was gorgeous: their big melting eyes seemed to fix on Ellen as if they knew her secret. The pregnant women seemed to know too. They gave her gentle, mysterious smiles from behind their sunglasses.

She'd felt so excluded from this club of mothers and children. She kept catching herself thinking: Would it be allowed? For *me* to push a big complicated-looking stroller like that? For *me* to pick up a baby without first asking someone else's permission? For *me* to grab hold of a toddler's hand while crossing the street?

Why not you? she asked herself. *Why not?*

But still she didn't tell him.

Moment after moment slipped by where she could have told him. They had all the time in the world. She'd never seen him so relaxed. His forehead seemed smoother. He touched her constantly.

There was no sign of Saskia. Ellen's stomach slowly unclenched and she stopped scanning the crowds. She was so relieved for Patrick. The poor man deserved a weekend without having to constantly look over his shoulder.

And how did *she* feel about the fact that Saskia had been in her home? Did she feel frightened, furious, violated?

She pondered this when she woke up first from their afternoon nap, Patrick's body still curved round hers, their fingers still interlaced from when they'd fallen asleep together.

All of those feelings felt like possibilities. Yes, when she thought about Saskia sitting in her glass office, deceiving her, secretly observing her, there was most certainly a tremble of genuine fear and a flare of rage. What did she want from her? What was she planning? And how dare she? The *audacity*.

But she was still intrigued. Even more so than before. Fascinated. Beneath the fear, she still felt . . . no, surely not. But, yes, as inappropriate as it was, that's what she felt: a mild sense of pleasure. She liked the fact that someone was that interested in her. It gave everything a definite edge. A spark. Maybe it was a tiny seductive taste of life as a celebrity: the feeling that everything you did was important and worth noting. Or maybe Ellen had some sort of personality flaw that perfectly complemented Saskia's. She was the yin and Saskia was the yang, and together they formed a psychopathic whole.

(Or was she just trying to make herself seem as interestingly peculiar as Saskia?)

At any rate, Patrick would have to be told about Saskia's subterfuge at some point. But she wouldn't ruin this little interlude from real life. She would wait until they were back in Sydney. Also, there was still the pregnancy. *The baby.*

She felt Patrick's hand tighten round hers as he stirred and woke up.

'Hello, you,' he yawned, running his other hand over her shoulder, down her waist and letting it rest on her hip. 'Sleep well?'

'Like a baby,' she said, without even a tremor in her voice.

'Mmm. Me too.'

After they got up, Patrick suggested a walk. He pulled her to the window. 'See the headland? There's a spot just by the entrance to the national park where I thought we could watch the sun go down. How does that sound?'

'Perfect,' said Ellen.

And it was.

There was a table and chairs right on the headland. The lush green of the national park contrasted with the deep blue of the ocean. The sky was all soft pastels: pink and blue and orange.

Patrick had bought an expensive bottle of champagne and cheese and biscuits and strawberries. He'd carefully wrapped two champagne glasses from the hotel mini-bar in his beach towel.

'Very impressive,' said Ellen.

'I know!' said Patrick proudly.

Ellen decided she'd have one glass of champagne. Her mother had told her that the 'occasional glass of wine is hardly going to cause foetal alcohol syndrome'.

'To us.' Patrick clinked his glass against hers. 'May we have many more weekends exactly like this.'

'May we drink many more glasses of champagne exactly like this,' said Ellen. The champagne was excellent; dry and creamy.

'May we – oops, just let me get that.'

'What did you drop?' asked Ellen, confused, as Patrick scrabbled about at her feet.

He didn't answer. He seemed to be getting back up in an extremely awkward, slow manner, like an old, arthritic man.

'Have you hurt yourself?' Ellen stood up and went to help him.

'Sit down, woman! I haven't hurt myself.' Patrick seemed to be trying not to laugh.

'What are you *doing* then?'

'Ellen,' said Patrick, and his voice changed, become deep and ponderous. His face had a silly, self-conscious look about it, as if he was playing a game of charades.

He had one knee on the ground and the other propped out in front of him. He held up a little black velvet case in the palm of his hand.

Oh my Lord in heaven, he was *proposing*. He was doing

one of those proper, bended-knee, ring-already-purchased proposals. How wonderful.

And yet how strangely excruciating.

Her eye was caught by something behind him. A slight movement. There was somebody standing at the lookout, taking photos of the sunset.

'Ellen,' said Patrick again. He cleared his throat. 'OK, I feel sort of stupid. And there's something digging into my knee. It looks so much easier in the movies.'

Ellen laughed and put down her champagne glass with slightly trembling fingers. She blinked back tears, overcome with flattered self-consciousness. *A man is proposing to me at sunset.*

She saw the woman with the camera turn round and face them. She was smiling.

'Ellen, will you – I mean, could you – I would be honoured . . . would you, that is, marry me?'

'There are two things I need to tell you first,' said Ellen. She was surprised at the clarity of her voice.

'OK.' Patrick immediately dropped his hand holding the black velvet case and then almost lost his balance. He gripped on to the side of the picnic table for support. 'Umm. Should I get back up?'

'I'm pregnant,' said Ellen. She paused. 'Also, I'm pretty sure that woman over there is Saskia, and she's coming this way.'

Then she laid one hand firmly on his right shoulder and hoped for the best.

I 2

One of the effects of increasing urbanization is the increasing isolation and loneliness of the individual. It has therefore been suggested that psychiatrists and psychologists be invited to join town-planning committees to contribute their thoughts on this complex issue.

– Excerpt from a paper delivered by Saskia Brown
at *Urban Development for 2004 and Beyond* conference,
Noosa, 2004

'Hi, Patrick. Hi, Ellen! I thought I recognized you!'

Saskia came striding towards them and stopped at the picnic table, removed her sunglasses and smiled brightly down at them. She was wearing shorts (Ellen noted beautiful, long, smooth legs) and a T-shirt and a baseball cap, and her whole demeanour seemed perfectly sane and ordinary. She looked sporty and attractive. No one watching would ever guess that she was anything other than a woman out for a walk who had happened to run into some friends. If anything, they would think that Ellen and Patrick were the ones behaving strangely. Neither of them spoke; they stared dully up at Saskia.

'It's such a beautiful evening.' Saskia polished the lenses of her sunglasses with the edge of her T-shirt and put them back on, gesturing out at the sky. 'It's one of those sunsets that should be on a postcard.'

'Saskia,' said Patrick hoarsely. He went to stand up, his back hunched, like an old man.

'Oh, no, Patrick, please don't let me interrupt!' Saskia made friendly, flapping gestures with her hands, indicating that he should kneel back down. 'You get right back to proposing. Lovely to see you both!'

She went striding off.

Patrick sat down heavily on the bench opposite Ellen, picked up the champagne glass and drained it.

Saskia stopped and called back. 'I'll see you on Friday for our appointment, Ellen!' She slapped her thigh. 'The leg is doing pretty well!' She waved.

Ellen's hand automatically went up and she waved back.

'You *know* her?' said Patrick. A panicky expression flew across his face. 'Have you always known her? Is this like some sort of weird set-up between the two of you?'

'No, no, no!' Ellen rushed to explain. 'I knew her as Deborah. That's what she called herself. Deborah Vandenberg. She's been coming to see me about her leg pain.'

'Deborah,' repeated Patrick and his eyes brightened with suspicion. 'But you knew it was Saskia. Just then! You knew it was her.'

'I worked it out on the plane,' said Ellen. 'When you told me about her bad leg. But I didn't want to upset you by mentioning it. It's my fault she's here. I told her we were coming to Noosa . . . when I thought she was Deborah. I'm sorry. I'm really sorry.'

She felt as if she had actually been part of a wicked conspiracy with Saskia.

Patrick lifted the lid of the jewellery box and snapped it shut again. He laughed disbelievingly, as if to himself. 'I was sure I was safe. I thought I'd be able to propose without her watching, but I couldn't even do that.'

'May I see the ring?' asked Ellen.

'It's an antique,' said Patrick. 'I thought you'd like that. It's got a history. Someone else's history, I mean. It's not like it's from my own family, but I thought you'd like that.' He opened the box again and flipped it shut without looking at it. 'I thought you weren't the type for one of those standard, shiny diamond rings. Jack helped me choose it.'

He was talking sadly and nostalgically, as if about something that had happened a long time in the past.

'It sounds perfect,' said Ellen. 'So, could I –?'

He pushed the ring across the table to her and she opened the box.

'Oh, Patrick.' The ring was white gold with a small oval aquamarine stone the colour of the ocean. 'It's beautiful. It's exactly what I would have chosen for myself.'

Ellen had never been especially interested in jewellery. She was not one of those women who could speak authoritatively about carats or cuts. 'Ooh, sparkly!' she would say when newly engaged friends drooped their left hands at her. To her, their rings all looked identical.

But the absolute rightness of Patrick's choice made her want to cry. It was like tangible evidence that he really saw her. It was a ring she could never have envisaged, or described, but one that said, 'Didn't you know? *This* is who you are.'

Ellen regretfully closed the lid, unsure what to do next; she hadn't actually said yes to his proposal yet. For the first time since she'd heard about Saskia's existence, she felt a satisfying, righteous flash of rage. That moment had been *hers*. Right now she was meant to be doing that half-sobbing, half-laughing thing that women did, burying her head in Patrick's chest, stopping every now and then to hold up her hand and examine her ring. It was meant to be a memory to cherish, and now it was gone forever.

'It was probably too soon to ask you,' said Patrick. 'But it just felt so right and I thought, to hell with it, I know she's the one, so I –'

He stopped and blinked slowly, like one of her clients coming out of a trance.

'Did you say you were pregnant?'

So he's going to be the hypnotist's husband.

He was doing the whole movie-scene deal. The pink-sky sunset. The champagne. The bended knee.

I thought: they're actually going to live that life. See, it really does happen to some people. They're going to have a beautiful, elegant wedding, probably on the beach, and it won't rain, but if it does it will be funny, the men will hold up big umbrellas and the women will giggle and run in their high heels. She'll only have one glass of champagne because she's pregnant. And then the baby will be born, and everyone will gather in the hospital room, with flowers and jokes and cameras. Then they'll have another baby, of the opposite sex to the first one. They'll have dinner parties with friends and such *busy* weekends, and they'll brush away sentimental tears at their children's concerts, and when the kids are older they'll travel and take up hobbies, and eventually they'll move into a friendly retirement village, and when they die their children and grandchildren will gather round and mourn them.

Who would mourn me, if I died today? My colleagues? I think they'd get over it pretty fast and then they'd be fighting for my office. Friends? In the space of a few years I've got myself crossed off everyone's Christmas-card list. It was my fault. I couldn't be bothered. I never returned their calls or answered their emails. I was too busy following Patrick. It's quite a time-consuming hobby. My hairdresser seems fond of me, but who would tell her that I'd died? She'd just think I'd left her for another hairdresser. Which I would never do. Maybe I should leave a note: *In the event of my death, please let my hairdresser know.*

There will be no grief or pain for the hypnotist and her husband, and if there is, it will always pass. They'll support each other until they're over it. The doctor will give them prescriptions to fix the pain.

It's strange, but now this has happened I find I can no longer imagine getting back together with Patrick. Something has changed. He never proposed to me. We never even talked about it. He'd already had the big white wedding with Colleen. I spent ages looking through their huge leather-bound rectangle of a photo album, staring at Colleen and her big white boofy-sleeved dress, wondering what she would have thought of me.

One morning when we were lying in bed, Patrick said, out of the blue, 'I'm keeping you forever.'

And that was all I needed. That was my romantic proposal and engagement ring and wedding ceremony and honeymoon all in one. As far as I was concerned, we were married from that moment.

But obviously not as far as Patrick was concerned.

Ellen is the sort of woman who makes a man feel the urge to go down on one knee and propose, whereas I am not.

When I walked over to them at that picnic table I felt like some sort of hideous half-human creature. I could smell my own ugliness.

I accept it. It's fine. They will be forever on the inside, and I will forever be on the outside.

But I'll make sure they always know I'm still there, looking in, peering through the glass, tapping on the window. I will never go away.

'She'll never go away,' said Patrick. 'If you marry me, you'll have to accept that she's part of the package. My son. My mum. My dad. My brother. My stalker.'

'Yes,' said Ellen. 'I understand.'

'I hope it's a girl,' said Patrick. 'The baby. I hope it's a little girl. I'd love a beautiful little girl. Would you like a little baby girl?'

'Sure,' said Ellen.

Patrick wasn't drunk, but his words were softening round the edges. They were sitting on the balcony of their hotel room and he was drinking the rest of the champagne bottle.

It appeared they were engaged. Ellen was wearing the ring on her left hand. It kept catching her eye. She had said 'yes'.

Patrick was thrilled about the baby. Ecstatic, even. When the news of her pregnancy had finally sunk in, he'd pulled her into his arms and held her as if she was something precious. 'A baby,' he murmured. 'Bloody hell. Who cares about anything else? We're having a *baby*.'

Everything was perfect, except that Saskia's face seemed to be permanently floating on the periphery of Ellen's vision, like the shocking memory of a bad car accident: the crunch of metal, the flinging back of the head. She kept replaying that moment when Saskia walked towards them: the wide, friendly smile, the eyes made blank by her dark sunglasses.

Ellen's righteous fury had abated, and now she felt strangely spent, empty of feeling, as if she really had been in some sort of traumatic accident.

'It's strange, but I didn't feel as angry as I usually do when Saskia turned up today,' said Patrick. 'I just felt this calmness. A sort of acceptance.'

So her post-hypnotic suggestion had worked a treat. Ellen felt both professional pride and professional guilt. She said nothing. Her back ached. She wriggled around in her chair, trying to get comfortable, and fiddled with the ring.

'Is it too tight?' asked Patrick, watching her. 'We can change the size.'

'It's perfect,' said Ellen. 'I'm just not used to wearing rings.'

Patrick emptied the last of the champagne into his glass and settled back into his chair, stretching his legs out and entwining his toes round the bars of the balcony fence.

'Yes. A beautiful blonde-haired little girl who looks just like you,' he said happily, looking out at the moonlit night.

'Except I don't have blonde hair,' laughed Ellen.

'Of course you don't.' Patrick rolled his eyes at his own stupidity and reached out to lightly touch his hand against Ellen's hair. 'I think I was imagining her looking like Jack.'

Ellen thought of the photo she'd seen at his parents' place of Colleen sitting on the hospital bed holding Jack. Her hair, she remembered, was long, wavy and very blonde.

When they got back to Sydney they told all and sundry about the engagement, and just their closest friends and family about the – shhhh – pregnancy.

People seemed surprisingly happy for them. They got tears in their eyes. They sent flowers and cards. They turned up with bottles of champagne and flamboyant hugs.

'Why do you find it surprising?' asked Patrick.

'I don't know,' said Ellen. 'I guess I didn't think anyone would care that much, at our age.'

'They're just happy to hear some good news for a change,' said Patrick. 'People love happy endings.'

For some reason Ellen didn't really like all the fuss and good cheer. She preferred to be the observer than the focus of everyone's attention. All the questions – 'When are you due?' 'When will the wedding be?' 'Where will you live?' – made her jittery, because they hadn't worked out the answers yet. Also, it worried her that she would some-how let people down now.

There hadn't been any tears in her mother's violet eyes when she'd heard about the engagement, just a lift of her eyebrows, before she quickly swept on her most gracious persona – the one where she appeared to channel the Queen – and completely seduced Patrick with her well-mannered charm, 'I really couldn't be more thrilled', and a cheque for five thousand dollars.

Privately she said to Ellen, 'He doesn't need to marry you just because you're pregnant! You've only known the man for all of five minutes!'

'He asked me before he knew I was pregnant,' said Ellen. 'And I know everything I need to know about him.'

'So you think,' said Anne under her breath, and Ellen pretended not to hear. She took a deep breath and rose above it.

It was hard to tell exactly what Julia thought about the news. She screamed and hugged Ellen when she heard about the engagement, and said all the right gushy, girly things about the ring, but a fleeting shadow crossed her lovely face when she heard about the pregnancy.

'What do you mean it was an *accident*?' she said. 'Teen-agers get accidentally pregnant! Were you using mind power as contraception?'

Ellen didn't tell her that after her first appointment with the very nice obstetrician that her friend Madeline had recommended, she'd worked out that she probably got pregnant after that drunken game of gin rummy, when they'd sort of 'forgotten' about contraception. It did make them sound like teenagers.

'Have you been out for that drink yet with Stinky – I mean Sam?' asked Ellen, changing the subject.

'He cancelled at the last minute,' said Julia shortly. 'He said he had the flu. Couldn't get out of bed.'

'So he postponed?'

'Whatever,' said Julia. 'Don't put on your soft, soothing voice, it drives me nuts. If he's not interested, he's not interested.'

'Julia, he probably really did have the flu.'

'Stop it! You've got that condescending, *tranquil* look on your face.'

Ellen gave up and told her instead about Saskia's appearance at Noosa, and how it was all Ellen's fault, which cheered Julia up considerably.

Patrick's family were lovely. His mother admitted that she'd been praying for an engagement from the very first night she'd met Ellen.

'And did you pray for a new baby too?' asked Patrick innocently.

'Of course,' said Maureen. 'Admittedly I didn't think it would happen quite so soon but if you're thinking I disapprove, Patrick, I'm sorry to disappoint you. I'm not that old-fashioned!' She beamed at Ellen. 'Of course, you will get married *before* the baby is born, won't you?'

Patrick's dad gave her a big fatherly hug, enveloping her in the fragrance of some aftershave that reminded her so strongly of her grandfather she'd had to stop herself from clinging on to his shirtfront. Patrick's brother, Simon, gave Ellen flowers and cooked them an excellent celebratory dinner (he was a much better cook than Patrick) at his flat. He teased Ellen in a brotherly way she'd never been teased before. She loved it.

Ellen had been worried about how Jack would react to the news that she was going to be his stepmother, especially when he heard about the pregnancy, but he seemed perfectly nonchalant about it all. 'I hope that the baby is a boy,' he said. 'I'll teach him stuff. Like how to drive a car. Fly a plane.' He paused and gave Ellen a sidelong look. 'Shoot a gun.'

'Shoot a gun!' Ellen put on her most horrified face.

'Just messing with your head,' said Jack, delighted. It was his new favourite phrase.

And it seemed that all the logistics were going to work out just fine.

Both Patrick and Jack said they were happy to move into Ellen's house. 'If you're happy to have us,' said Patrick. 'We'll keep our house as an investment and rent it out. We'll be property tycoons!'

'I'll go to the beach every single day of my whole life!' said Jack. 'Even when it's raining. Even when there is hail! Nah, not really. Just messing with your head.'

Jack would still go to the same primary school. The twenty-minute drive was of no consequence because Patrick's office was in the same direction.

So that was that.

Ellen was part of a new family and her whole life was about to be transformed. She kept wandering through the house, twisting her new engagement ring round and round on her finger, and imagining it filled with new people and new stuff. A room for Jack. A room for the new baby. She would be a mother of two. There would be newsletters from Jack's school on her fridge. Patrick's collection of prints of old surveying equipment would have to go on the walls somewhere. There would be a cot, a changing table, a baby's bath. Jack's bike would lie on its side in the front yard. There would be a baby seat in the car, a stroller and a school bag in the hallway.

talking about this, but for some reason Ellen still hadn't managed to identify, he never actually got round to doing it. She was sure it wasn't just about his pride, there was something else behind his procrastination, but she didn't push the issue. From what she'd read, restraining orders didn't offer much protection against truly committed stalkers anyway.

In the end, Patrick decided to go to work, because it turned out that Ellen wasn't going to be alone in the house anyway. A large plumber would be there replacing the hot-water system, which had unexpectedly died the day after they returned from Noosa.

The large plumber was a friend of Patrick's and he promised to stay within hearing distance the whole time, should Saskia turn up. (Although what if Saskia swiftly removed a gun with a silencer out of her handbag and shot her, or plunged a syringe into her arm that caused total body paralysis, including her vocal chords? Ellen had seen too many horror movies to believe that even the largest plumber could offer any protection from a real psychopath.)

As the time drew nearer for Saskia's appointment, Ellen sat at her desk and pretended not to care either way. She tried to do some paperwork, but her heart was hammering too hard to concentrate.

She won't come, she thought.

But, actually, she didn't really believe that. At their last session, Ellen had lent Saskia one of her books about hypnosis for pain management. They'd talked about how they both resented people who didn't bother to return books. 'Don't worry,' Saskia had said. 'You'll get it back.'

The minutes ticked by and the doorbell stayed silent. Was she disappointed or relieved? She felt she could convince herself that either emotion was authentic.

At twenty past eleven, the phone rang and Ellen snatched up the receiver.

'Ellen O'Farrell Hypnotherapy, how can I help you?' There was only the tiniest tremor in her voice.

Silence. Ellen thought she could hear the muffled sound of traffic on a busy road.

'Hello?' she said.

Nothing. She pressed the phone hard against her ear. She could definitely hear traffic. A horn tooting.

She said quietly, 'Saskia?'

The line went dead.

My car broke down on the way to my appointment with Ellen. In the middle lane of the highway. Everyone angrily tooted their horns at me, over and over, as if their tooting would finally convince me to make my car work again.

I got out of the car and screamed at the tooters: 'JUST WHAT DO YOU EXPECT ME TO DO? DO YOU THINK I'M DOING THIS ON PURPOSE?'

They wouldn't have been able to hear me over the sounds of the traffic. They would have just seen my mouth moving silently and furiously, my arms waving about. 'Crazy,' the tooting motorists probably muttered to themselves.

Yes indeed.

While I waited for the breakdown truck to come, I decided to call Ellen to let her know that I wasn't going to make it. It felt like the polite, normal thing to do. That's what I would have done for any other appointment. After all, that's what I would have done if I were still Deborah.

I had been looking forward to surprising her by turning up as normal for the appointment. I was interested to see how she would handle it. I was wondering if she would even let me in the house. Would she slam the door in my face? I didn't think so; I don't think door slamming is in her sweet, spiritual nature. I suspected that Patrick might be there with her, waiting for me, ready to call the police, ready to finally take out that restraining order he's threatened so often, ready to be protective of his precious, pretty, pregnant *fiancé*.

But if Patrick wasn't there, and she did let me in, I was going to admire the ring and ask her when the baby was due and if she was planning a big wedding. I was going to ask did she mind if I wore white too or would that be offensive, or was I not on the guest list? Ha ha ha. I was going to ask her if Patrick still liked sex in the shower and Sunday morning blowjobs. I was going to watch that serene expression of hers shatter like broken glass.

Or else I wasn't even going to mention Patrick. I was going to continue in my Deborah role and hand back the book she'd lent me and enjoy watching her pretending not to be 'totally freaking out'. I have been watching a lot of television this week. Television featuring young American girls. Their language is catching.

I was playing it by ear. I could have handled anything, done anything, said anything. That's what I thought anyway, but as soon as I heard her voice on the phone, my own vanished.

My vocal chords were paralysed. It was literally physically

impossible for me to say, 'Oh, hi, Ellen, it's me, Saskia. I'm not going to make my appointment this morning because my car has broken down.'

I couldn't act like a normal person again when she now knows me as a crazy person because that would imply I have a choice. That I can choose to be crazy or normal. And if I have a choice then that would imply that I'm not really crazy at all, and I should just stop it and get on with my life.

But what life? Patrick and Ellen *are* my life. Without them, there's just a job and a flat and a car that needs a new automatic transmission, and that's about it.

The doorbell rang that afternoon, after the plumber had left, when Ellen was studying the fancy control panel for the new hot-water system.

Patrick had chosen a system where you could pre-set the water temperature that came out of the tap. He said it would be perfect for bath time with the new baby. Ellen hadn't even known such systems existed. (Also, *bath time*! She marvelled at his casual reference to something so ordinary and yet extraordinary.) He'd put together a long list of things that needed doing around the house to prepare for the baby: the sockets had to be child-proofed, the spiral staircase was a 'death trap for toddlers' and so on and so forth. 'So, I guess we'll have to get quotes.' Ellen's stress levels had risen as she looked at the list.

'I'll take care of all that,' said Patrick. He puffed his chest out and jutted his jaw like a superhero. 'Don't you worry your pretty little head about it.' She put a hand to her forehead and pretended to swoon in his arms. (Actually, it was almost a genuine swoon.)

Ellen looked at the time. She wasn't expecting any clients. *Saskia*, she thought, as she walked down the stairs. *And now there is no large plumber to protect me.* Just in case, she picked up one of her grandmother's heavy glass candlestick-holders from the hall table, laughing at her serious reflection in the hallway mirror. Ridiculous. But, still, she didn't put it down.

She opened the door.

It wasn't Saskia. It was a thin, short, nervous-looking girl smoking a cigarette and smiling up at her apologetically.

Ellen knew her face perfectly well, but for a moment she couldn't place her; she'd been so sure it was Saskia, she couldn't get the name 'Saskia' out of her head.

The girl dropped the cigarette and crushed it beneath her foot. Then she picked up the butt and held it in her cupped hand.

'I can't believe I lit this up while I was waiting for you,' she said. 'I'm an idiot. Anyway, as you can see, I'm still at it.'

Ellen stared at the crushed cigarette and said, 'Rosie.'

'Yes,' said Rosie. 'I'm sorry. I know I don't have an appointment. I just got back from my honeymoon this morning, and I came by on the off chance you had some free time . . .'

'I saw your wedding photos in the paper last week,' said Ellen, trying not to sound resentful. *You still married him after our breakthrough! Why did you marry him if you knew you didn't even like him?*

'Those photos were awful,' said Rosie. 'I looked so ugly, and you saw the colour of the bridesmaid dresses?'

'The pictures were black and white.'

'Oh, right, yes, of course. Well, they were awful. Anyway, do you . . . could you fit me in?'

'Of course I could,' said Ellen warmly, guilty about her resentment. She stood back and ushered her in, discreetly replacing the candlestick-holder on the table.

'You're probably wondering why I still married him,' said Rosie, when she was settled in the green recliner.

'Here,' said Ellen, offering a tissue in the flat of her hand, so that Rosie could finally dispose of the cigarette butt she was still holding.

'It was the most stupid of all reasons,' said Rosie. 'You'll be horrified.'

'I'm sure I won't be.' Although she might very well be.

'When I left here after our last session, I was so ready to call off the wedding. I knew it would be a huge deal. The invitations had gone out. You know, the *Prime Minister* was on the guest list. He had to be in Japan or something, but you know . . . And my mum had lost twenty kilos and bought the most expensive dress she'd ever owned, and my dad had spent days working on this terrible speech, and my friends were all so jealous, which isn't the reason to marry somebody, but, you know, everyone was acting as if I was marrying out of my league, which I was, which I *did*, but anyway, that's not why I did it – it was something that happened after I left here.'

'What happened?' asked Ellen.

'I thought I'd go for a walk on the beach,' said Rosie. She was tapping at her lips with two fingertips in a v-shape:

the way of a smoker longing for a cigarette. 'I wanted to clear my head, to think about how I could possibly explain it to Ian, and I saw this couple sitting on the beach, and they were kissing, really kissing, you know the way people kiss when they're at the beginning of a relationship?'

'I know,' said Ellen. She remembered that kiss outside the museum.

'And I thought, oh, that's sweet, but then as I got closer, I thought, that's Joe! My ex-boyfriend. We broke up a year ago. I thought I was over him. I thought I didn't care less, but the *way* he was kissing this girl, as if he'd never experienced such bliss, it just killed me.'

'Ah,' said Ellen.

'And just like that, I thought, I can't do it, I can't call off the wedding,' said Rosie. 'We were going on our honeymoon to this expensive resort in Malaysia, where my ex-boyfriend and I had always wanted to go, but we couldn't ever afford it, and I wanted him to hear about it. I wanted him to imagine me there with another man. I wanted to wipe that blissful expression off his face. He'd always had a thing about money and wealthy people being somehow better than him, and I knew that we had mutual friends who would tell him all about the wedding – and, I don't know, it was like I lost my mind. And I just went ahead with the wedding, and decided that I did love Ian, of course I did, how could I not? I convinced myself that I'd just got confused in my session. I sort of blamed you, to be honest. So I got married, and that was all fine, but you know what?'

'What?' said Ellen.

'Two things. The resort in Malaysia wasn't that great, it

was actually pretty awful, and we had to cut the honeymoon short because of some merger or coup or something or other. And then, do you know what I heard this morning? My ex only went out with that girl for a few weeks. He's single again now. But I really couldn't care less, either way! I never actually wanted to get back together with him, I just couldn't bear to think of him being so happy with someone else and then hearing that I was single again. Isn't that the most pathetic thing you ever heard in your life?'

'Of course not,' said Ellen. 'We all have the most peculiar motivations for what we do.'

There was a pause. Rosie fidgeted and then said suddenly, 'You're engaged!' She pointed at Ellen's ring and Ellen realized she'd been drawing attention to it by twisting it round her finger. It had very quickly become a habit.

'Congratulations! I bet you love him. I bet you love him properly.'

'Well.' Ellen smiled foolishly. She didn't want to sound smug.

'Anyway,' said Rosie. 'Ian wants to try for a baby straight away.'

'So you're ready to give up smoking once and for all,' guessed Ellen.

'No,' said Rosie. 'I want you to hypnotize me into falling in love with him. I mean, love is just a state of mind, right? I don't want to have a baby with someone I don't love. You can do that, right? Make me believe that I love him? So I haven't made the worst mistake of my life?'

13

A woman's relationship with her father will have a profound impact on all her future relationships with men. The fatherless daughter lacks a template. Fatherless daughters are more likely to be promiscuous – so GREAT, thanks, Mum, I'm going to be a slut!!!!!!!!!!
　　– Entry in Ellen O'Farrell's diary, written a week before her fifteenth birthday

Ellen's mother was nervous.

It was suddenly perfectly clear. Ever since they had got to the restaurant for lunch, Ellen had been observing Anne, trying to work out what was different about her. Anyone else would have said that Anne was perfectly calm and at ease as she chatted with Ellen about the pregnancy, argued amiably with Ellen's godmothers about the choice of wine and asked the waiter probing questions about the specials. Yet, there was something odd about the way she was sitting: her back was unnaturally straight, even for someone who was a passionate advocate of good posture, her chin too high, her shoulders too braced. Her beautiful violet eyes kept sweeping over Ellen. Normally Ellen was aware of her mother's eyes discreetly giving her a rigorous health-check: monitoring her skin tone, her weight, the whites of her eyes. She had always thought that Anne would have preferred to strap a blood-pressure monitor round her arm and shove a thermometer in her mouth each time they met, rather than hugging her.

She turned her attention to her godmothers. Phillipa had an air of suppressed excitement, as if she was about to see a slightly risqué show. At first, she couldn't see anything out of the ordinary about Melanie, but then she saw the way her eyes kept returning to Anne, as if waiting for something. Ellen remembered Mel's phone call, only two weeks ago now, when she'd said that 'Anne was behaving oddly'. With the pregnancy and the engagement she'd forgotten all about it.

As soon as the waiter left after taking their orders, Ellen spoke up. 'OK, what's going on?'

Anne's hand went straight to her neck, and Ellen saw that she was wearing a lovely, expensive-looking necklace that Ellen had never seen before, and also that the skin of her neck seemed older and more vulnerable than the rest of her, like a crumpled piece of silk; Ellen wanted to reach out and smooth it.

'Where did you get that necklace?' asked Ellen.

'You really can't put anything past this one,' said Phillipa proudly. 'She's always been like that. Remember that time we tried to convince her that –'

'Pip,' said Melanie. 'This is between Anne and Ellen.'

'Exactly! I agree! I don't even know why we're here! Would you like us to go off somewhere and give you two some privacy?'

Anne sighed. 'The three of us brought up Ellen

together. That's why I wanted you two here as well. You've both been like mothers to Ellen. The four of us are a family. We're a family and this is . . . a family matter.'

Ellen was horrified. Her mother did not talk like this.

'It's cancer, isn't it?' she said.

'It's good news.' Anne smiled. Suddenly she looked radiant. 'I came round to tell you the other night actually but then we got distracted, didn't we?'

'OK,' said Ellen.

'Well, it's just that I've met up with your father, that's all.'

'Well, not quite all,' said Phillipa.

'I'm sort of . . . in a relationship with him,' said Anne.

'It's *so* romantic,' said Phillipa.

'I don't understand,' said Ellen. 'I thought he was married and living in the UK.'

'Divorced,' said Anne blissfully, as if divorce was one of life's sweetest pleasures.

'And he's moved back to Sydney,' added Melanie. 'Your mother has been seeing him for weeks. She never told us. I *knew* something was going on.'

'It's all due to me,' said Phillipa. 'He found me on Facebook! He asked if I'd kept in touch with Anne O'Farrell, and when I told your mother I could tell by the expression on her face that she still had a thing for him, even after all these years!'

'A *thing* for him?' said Ellen. She could feel the most profound sense of irritation rising in her chest. The three of them were acting like teenagers. 'But you picked him from a list!'

'Yes, yes, all that happened,' said Anne. 'Don't worry.

It was amazing.

It was absolutely terrifying.

'Deborah Vandenberg' was scheduled for an appointment at 11 a.m. Friday morning.

'I assume she won't come,' said Ellen. 'Now that she knows that I know she's Saskia.' (Although she had said, '*See you Friday.*')

'I'll have to take the day off work,' said Patrick. 'I don't want you alone with her.'

'She won't come,' said Ellen. 'But if she does, I'll be fine. She's never been violent.'

She didn't want Patrick there. If Saskia did turn up, she wanted to talk to her. She longed to have a proper woman-to-woman chat with her. 'Why do you do this?' she would say. 'Help me understand.'

Obviously Ellen could no longer see her on a professional basis, but she could refer her to someone else, who could help her both with her leg pain and her inability to let go of Patrick. She would be kind and firm and put an end to all this nonsense.

(Part of her recognized the folly of her own thinking: if only Saskia saw how very *nice* and understanding Ellen was, she would graciously step aside.)

'This is my problem, not yours,' fretted Patrick. 'You're pregnant, remember, you should be avoiding stress.'

'She won't come,' insisted Ellen. 'I'm sure she won't come.'

'I've got to do something about that restraining order,' he said.

Ever since they'd returned from Noosa, he'd been

Your life isn't based on a lie. The part I didn't ever tell you was that I did actually have a little crush on him.'

'More than a little,' said Melanie. 'Pip and I saw right through her, of course.'

Now all three of them were chewing at their expensively lipsticked mouths, as if they were trying not to giggle in class. Anne refilled their wine glasses and Ellen, who was drinking mineral water, felt like their middle-aged mother. They were all being so *silly*.

'And it turns out that he's always had a thing for me too,' said Anne with pride. 'He thought about me throughout his marriage. I was always popping up in his dreams apparently.'

'That poor woman,' said Ellen.

'What poor woman?' Her mother frowned.

'His wife! The one he was engaged to when you slept with him to conceive me!'

'Oh, don't be so . . .' Anne stopped and flicked her hand as if to wave away a harmless insect. Ellen suspected she'd been about to say 'boring'.

Mel spoke up. 'Ellen, your mother had nothing to do with their marriage breakdown. There is nothing untoward going on here.'

Ellen thought about some poor woman in London, sleeping next to her husband each night, while he dreamed of a violet-eyed girl back in sunny Sydney. Nothing untoward indeed.

'So.' Ellen tried not to sound snappish. 'You've told him about me?'

Anne's moony expression vanished and she looked nervous again.

'He was very shocked of course, and so cross with me for not telling him. He said he would have called off the wedding if he'd known and married me. Imagine! I could have been quite the little housewife.'

'Oh, Mum,' said Ellen.

There was something cosy and self-satisfied about her mother's tone. It made Ellen's whole existence seem tacky and trite, instead of bohemian and brave.

'You'll meet him of course, won't you, Ellen?' said Phillipa. 'It will be just like that television show where they reunite lost families. I'm crying already, just thinking about it.'

'I will meet him, of course I'll meet him, but there's nothing romantic or heart-wrenching about this,' said Ellen. 'We just share the same DNA.'

'But now you know your parents were in love!'

'We thought you'd be thrilled.' Mel gave Ellen a curious, analytical frown, as if she was an accounting discrepancy she needed to solve. 'You were always so desperate to meet your father. You were obsessed with him for a while.'

'When I was fourteen,' said Ellen. Now it just seemed like an awkward sort of social obligation.

'Don't you want to see what he's like?' asked Phillipa.

'I'm curious, of course,' continued Ellen, except she wasn't particularly. She was too focused on her own life at the moment: her baby, her soon-to-be 'stepson' and 'husband'. Her husband-to-be's ex-girlfriend. She didn't have time to devote to building a new relationship.

'Well, there's no rush,' said Anne. 'Whenever you're ready.' Her hand kept returning to her neck, to caress the stone of her new necklace.

'So the necklace is a gift from him?' asked Ellen. 'From, ah . . . David?' Surely she wasn't meant to call him Dad?

Anne removed her hand. 'Yes. It's for our one-month anniversary.' She flushed. 'I know we're too old for that sort of thing.'

'Awwww,' said Phillipa.

Ellen's mother was clearly in love, and she was in love with Ellen's father, which in most cases was considered appropriate and convenient, and the way the world was meant to work. Ellen couldn't understand why she felt so unhappy about it. Was it just resistance to change? Did she not want her mother to love anyone else except her? She would have to think about this when she got home.

'I'm happy for you, Mum.' She did her utmost to sound sincere.

'I'm not counting my chickens, it's early days of course,' said Anne briskly, but then she smiled her bizarre new smile and reached out to touch Ellen's hand. 'Your dad is the loveliest man I've ever known.'

I live in a three-bedroom duplex.

I've never been fond of duplexes, and yet, here I am.

When Patrick and I broke up I needed somewhere new to live fast, and I asked a real estate agent I knew to find me the first available rental property in my price range. So he found me this bland, sterile little place, in a street crammed with identical duplexes and three twenty-storey apartment blocks. The people who live here are hard-working mid-level professionals. They are the worker bees of society, on their way to something better. This is an area where 'convenience' is what counts. The railway station is an easy walk and it's only a ten-minute trip into the city. There are dozens of perfectly adequate but not that great restaurants and 24-hour dry-cleaner's and ATMS and cab ranks. People stride along checking their Black-Berrys and gulping down takeaway coffees. It's not a place for lovers. There are no buskers or bookshops or galleries or cinemas. It's good. It's like an extension of the office.

For the last three years a man called Jeff has lived in the other half of my duplex. He is short, bald, with a neat ginger-coloured beard, and the most personal fact I know about him is that he doesn't feel the cold. He wears short-sleeved shirts all year round. When he is inside I rarely hear a sound from him through our shared walls: no music, no television. Once I did hear him crying out, as if in anguish, 'But that's *not* the way you do it!' Do what? But I was only mildly intrigued. I didn't care enough to actually have a proper conversation or make eye contact with him.

If we see each other at the letterbox or walking in and out of our front doors we both immediately speed up and walk away fast as if we have suddenly remembered we are running very late, or we develop an intense inter-est in one of the letters we have just received, tearing it open as if it's of the utmost importance. We call out things in a distracted, busy tone like, 'Hot, isn't it?' and 'Cold, isn't it?' or if the weather is difficult to label, 'How are you?' and we never wait for the other person to answer because we don't care about the answer. Some-times in my head I answer: *Still obsessively stalking my ex-boyfriend, grieving for my dead mother and suffering unexplained leg pain, thanks, how about you?*

So, yes, Jeff is the perfect neighbour for a duplex. We have managed to live next door all these years, and collect each other's mail when we're away, and negotiate shared issues about garbage collection and lawn mowing, while maintaining the most delightfully superficial of relationships.

And then today, when I'd just got home from collecting the car from the mechanic, Jeff suddenly marched up to me and stood far too close. I tried to take a discreet step backwards. 'Hi, Saskia,' he said. I think this was the first time he'd ever used my name.

'Hi, Jeff,' I said. Likewise.

'I wanted to let you know that I'm moving,' he said. 'I'm having a sea change.'

'Sea change,' I repeated.

'Yes, I'm moving to a little town down the south coast. I'm going to run a café. I'm calling it Jeff's Jetty Café.'

I was stunned. I'm not sure why. I think I just never expected him to be important enough to make any significant changes in his life, but of course he doesn't know that he's only a minor character in my life. He's the star of his own life and I'm the minor character. And fair enough too.

'It's not on a jetty, but I'm going to give it a jetty sort of look. Ropes and anchors and ... buckets, that sort of stuff.' A flash of uncertainty crossed his face. He has no idea what he's doing.

'Sounds wonderful,' I said. It will be a spectacular failure.

'Yeah, decided it was time to get out of the police force,' he said.

'You're a *policeman*?' I couldn't believe it. I'd never seen him in uniform. I thought he was an auditor or an IT consultant or even a librarian. Shouldn't policemen be forced to disclose their careers to their neighbours? What if I'd casually revealed a crime to him at the letterbox? Offered him an illegal substance?

And there is the matter of Patrick. He's always threatening to call the police. Ridiculous. Why would the police be interested in what is essentially a private matter between two adults? But still. Technically, I do enter his house without his permission.

'I had no idea you were a policeman,' I said. I couldn't keep the resentment out of my voice.

'Undercover,' said Jeff. 'Pretty stressful. Messes with your head. Impossible to form a relationship with anyone. I'm not getting any younger. I'm desperate to meet that "special lady". Want to be a dad one day!'

I did not want to hear that Jeff was desperate to meet that special lady. It was like he'd shared an intimate, slightly revolting sexual secret.

'A nice young family is moving into my place,' he continued. 'Two little kids. Boy and girl. You'll find them a bit livelier than me.'

And that suddenly seemed to remind him of the sort of neighbours we'd been, and he took an abrupt step backwards.

'So,' he said. 'I've kept you long enough. Just thought I should let you know, so you didn't get a surprise when the removal van arrives tomorrow. The young family will be moving in the day after.'

'Best of luck with everything,' I said.

'Thanks,' he said, and smiled, and he had an unexpectedly nice, shy smile, and I was filled with a strange, sad regret. I could have been his friend. I could have invited him over for a drink or a coffee. Maybe then he wouldn't have needed his silly sea change.

Before Patrick, I would have been the sort of person who would have done that. This is all Patrick's fault.

And now there will be a 'nice young family' living next door. My bland little duplex will no longer be my safe haven from other people's happiness. The thought of having to hear and see this smug family loving each other every day of my life is unbearable and unacceptable. I hate families with one boy and one girl, like a family in a car commercial. It's so *tidy*. They're always so pleased with themselves.

I can feel this explosive pressure building in my head. Something has to happen. I have to make something happen. Soon. I'm just not sure what.

When Ellen got home from lunch with her mother and godmothers she sat on the front step with her bag on her lap. She didn't want to take the keys out of her bag and open the door to an empty house. She wanted to ring the bell, and wait for the sound of the slow, shuffling footsteps. Her grandfather always opened the door with a wary, almost belligerent expression on his face that would vanish when he saw it was her. 'She's here!' he'd call out jubilantly to her grandmother, and he'd open the door wide and Ellen would smell baking.

They'd been dead for over a year but today for some reason it didn't seem possible that they weren't inside.

They must have opened that door to her hundreds of times. It didn't feel like she was just recalling memories. It seemed perfectly reasonable that they were still there, somewhere, on some other plane of existence, and if she just sat here quietly for long enough and really concentrated, she could slip through time or matter or something and rest her head on her grandfather's shoulder just one more time and see him redden slightly the way he always did whenever she hugged him.

'What's on your mind, Ellie?' Her grandmother was the only one who had ever called her Ellie. ('I did not, and never would have, named my child "Ellie",' Anne would shudder.)

She longed to tell her grandparents about this new development in her life, that David Greenfield, that strange, enticing name on her birth certificate, was no longer the carefully selected sperm donor of her youth, but the 'loveliest man her mother had ever known'. It was like hearing that Santa Claus really did exist after all, when you no longer cared or believed in the possibility of magic, when it was just plain confusing.

'That mother of yours,' her grandmother would say with a shake of her head, and put the kettle on again. Ellen sighed and smiled. Yes, that's what this was really all about. She wanted her mother reprimanded for creating this upheaval in her life. Her grandparents were always on her side.

And the reason she wanted her mother reprimanded was just fear. Fear of change. Fear of the unknown. The same fear that caused her grandfather to look wary when he opened the door. *Is that change knocking on my door?*

She sighed, took her keys out of her bag and stood up. Her eye was caught by something on the wrought-iron mosaic table near the front door. Her grandmother had made that table after she'd done a mosaics course. (It wasn't actually very good. The green and orange rectangles were all out of alignment. The teacher had to keep scolding her grandmother for talking too much during class.)

A book had been placed upright in the centre of the table, carefully displayed as if it was for sale in a bookshop. There was a pink camellia flower lying diagonally next to it.

An icy thumb caressed Ellen's spine. It was the book she'd lent Saskia. She'd returned it, as promised. Ellen picked up the book and flicked through the pages. No note. Just the creepy, careful way it was displayed. And the flower. What did the flower mean?

'Is this the hypnotherapy place?' A voice interrupted her thoughts.

Ellen jumped and gave a startled, girly shriek.

'Oh! I'm *so* sorry to frighten you like that!' A man in his late forties or early fifties with a humble, apologetic look on his face stood at the bottom of the porch stairs looking up at her. He was carrying a notebook with a pen carefully clipped to the side, and wearing a business shirt that appeared two sizes too big for him, without a tie. He looked like a man running late for his new bible study group.

Ellen pressed her hand to her chest to calm her thumping heart.

'I'm sorry,' she said. 'I was just very deep in thought.'

She smiled and held out her hand as she walked down the steps to meet him. 'This is definitely the right place. You're Alfred, right? Alfred Boyle. I'm Ellen.'

Alfred was a new client who had found her on the Internet and emailed a few weeks back to ask for written confirmation of her pricing. He'd said in his email that he was a partner in an accounting firm and that he 'required help improving his public-speaking skills in a professional setting'.

As Ellen opened the front door for him, and led him up the stairs, she glanced round hoping for a fleeting glimpse of her grandparents (what would they have to say about Saskia?) but the house was empty, and no matter how hard she sniffed, hoping for the scents of her grandmother's baking, all she could smell was the Thai chicken curry she'd made the night before.

She left the book and the camellia flower on the hall table, to think about later.

14

Freud always said that the reason he stopped using hypnosis was that a patient jumped up and kissed him. Apparently the real reason was that his false teeth no longer fitted properly after his gums had been ruined by his cocaine use and he couldn't speak well enough to easily induce trances. The lesson for us? Floss!

– Excerpt from a speech delivered by Flynn Halliday to the Northern Beaches Hypnotherapists Meeting, August, 2010

'Ellen, my dear. You are looking well.'

'Thank you, Flynn.'

Flynn Halliday bent to brush his cheek against hers.

It was a month since Ellen had returned from Noosa and she was attending the regular local chapter meeting of the Australian Association of Hypnotherapists. Flynn was president and Ellen was treasurer. They ran the meetings at a small room in a local community centre, and Flynn and Ellen had arrived half an hour early to set up the room. 'How have you been?' asked Flynn, as they dragged tables and chairs into a horseshoe shape. 'Any news?'

Ellen hesitated. She was feeling guilty. She always felt guilty around Flynn, because she felt like she'd let him down in many ways.

She'd known him since she was in her early twenties. He'd employed her for many years in his hypnotherapy business as an assistant, a trainee therapist and finally as a hypnotherapist. He'd wanted her to go into partnership with him, and she knew he'd been very hurt when she'd decided to go out on her own.

There was also that *thing* she'd never ever spoken out loud, or even properly admitted to herself; the thing about the way Flynn sometimes looked at her. Sometimes she thought she was imagining it, and she was behaving like a typical fatherless daughter by misinterpreting the perfectly acceptable fondness of an older man for a younger colleague. Other times she was quite sure that if she'd ever given Flynn the slightest encouragement he most certainly would have courted her: with poetry, probably, elaborate compliments and thoughtful gifts.

Flynn, who had never married, or even been in a relationship as far as Ellen knew, was in his late fifties, with fine, thin, fair hair and a rosy, cherubic face. He looked like an elderly choirboy. The idea of sex with Flynn seemed illegal.

There was no need to mention the pregnancy yet. Although over the last few weeks she had begun to feel profoundly different (strange little poking sensations in her belly, tender breasts, mild nausea that lasted all day long and a permanent sense of quivering on the verge of tears), she looked exactly the same, and anyway, she thought that Flynn would prefer to think of her as a virgin.

But it would be strange not to mention the engagement.

'I do have some news, actually,' she said, pressing her thumb to her ring. 'I'm engaged.'

Flynn had been facing away from her. He waited just a beat too long to turn round.

Ellen's eyes filled. *Oh, Flynn, you silly man.* If only it was possible to live a parallel life, a spare one, where she could have let Flynn court her and marry her, and she could have made him happy. Except without the sex.

'Congratulations!' Flynn came across the room and gave her another clumsy, vaguely peppermint-scented kiss.

He stood back and clasped his hands together like a country vicar. 'Wonderful.'

As Flynn groped about for something else to say, Ellen thought about Saskia. If only her relationship with Flynn wasn't so complicated she would have asked his advice. She had a lot of respect for his opinions when it came to the human psyche.

Ellen wished she'd never told Patrick about Saskia returning the book. He'd been battling insomnia ever since, pacing the house, frustrated with his own powerlessness.

'I hate that you have to deal with this,' he'd said, his face looking older, weighed down with stress. 'I'm meant to make your life better. Not more complicated.'

'She just returned a book,' said Ellen. 'I'm not frightened.' She wasn't. Not really. Just a mild, fluttery sense of unease, that could have been nothing more than a natural reaction to all the changes going on in her life, nothing to do with Saskia at all.

'So, that's just wonderful news,' said Flynn again. Then

an expression of panic flew across his face. 'It's not that Danny fellow, is it?' he said.

'No. I'm marrying a surveyor actually,' said Ellen. 'I shall be a surveyor's wife.' *What?* The oddest things came out of her mouth when she was feeling awkward.

'Surveyor! Man of the land, right, wonderful.' Flynn kept his hands clasped and shook them as if he was giving himself a warm handshake. 'Yes, yes, because that Danny. Have you heard what he's doing?' Danny and Flynn had been introduced only once by Ellen at an industry function, and there had been instant mutual dislike.

'I haven't talked to him for a while.'

'He's treating hypnotherapy like *Tupperware*. He's running these parties and he's calling them –'

'*Hypno-parties!*' Marlene Adams sailed into the room. She was another hypnotherapist of a similar generation and mind-set to Flynn. (Why hadn't he fallen for her?) 'Isn't it *dreadful*! I heard him talking on the radio just yesterday, and I thought to myself, *What? I beg your pardon? HYPNO-PARTIES?* Well, that's just going to do wonders for our professional credibility, isn't it!'

'So, next Sunday is the last Sunday of the month,' said Patrick, later that afternoon.

'Old jeans,' said Ellen. 'This box says "old jeans".'

She had stopped in the hallway to look at the neatly written notation in black marker on a large dusty cardboard box. Patrick and Jack had been officially living at her place for just on a week now. However, the process of moving in their possessions was proving to be complicated.

Apparently Patrick didn't believe in removal men. They were 'overpaid thugs'. Instead, every couple of days, whenever he got a chance, he picked up a few boxes in the back of his company van.

Ellen would have preferred him to have taken a few days off work and hired some overpaid thugs and done the job properly. Instead, her hallway was rapidly filling with giant cardboard boxes, which Patrick didn't have time to move, and which were too heavy for Ellen to lift. Her clients had to shuffle sideways every time they walked down her hallway.

'Does that mean this cardboard box is filled with old jeans?'

'Is that a trick question?' asked Patrick.

'Why do you keep old jeans?'

'For doing stuff around the house, working in the garden, that sort of thing,' said Patrick, in a patient, manly tone.

'OK, but a whole box of them?' Ellen ran a fingertip over the layer of dust on the box. She had a feeling this box had been sitting in Patrick's garage for years. These jeans would never be used, and he would never throw them out. Her nose tickled and she sneezed.

'Bless you,' said Patrick. 'So as I was saying . . . it's the last Sunday of the month.'

She looked at the next box. It said 'old shirts'. She could smell a damp, mouldy smell. Actually, she could see a patch of furry, green mould growing on the side of the box.

He was a hoarder. She hadn't known this about him. His house had looked perfectly acceptable when she visited. Very tidy and organized, in fact. All these boxes must have been crammed behind cupboard doors and stacked up to the ceiling in his garage.

Her throat tickled and she sneezed again.

'How many more boxes do you think you'll be bringing over?' she asked, trying to make it sound like she was just casually interested.

'I've barely scratched the surface,' said Patrick cheerfully. 'I've been in that house for over twenty years. Collected a lot of stuff.'

Ellen felt a rising sense of hysteria.

'Why? Is it bugging you? Obviously this is only temporary. I'm not planning on using your hallway as a permanent storage area if that's what you're thinking.'

He put his hand on her waist.

'You should have driven a lot of this, this . . . *stuff* straight to the tip from your place.' Ellen moved slightly so that his hand fell away. 'You would never have missed it.'

She recognized that cool, precise voice. It was her mother's voice. Just recently Julia had said that she had found herself speaking more and more like her own mother and Ellen had said, 'There's no danger of that happening to me.'

Anne had a violent dislike of 'stuff'. (She always spat out the word 'stuff' as if was a profanity.) Ellen's possessions were always disappearing when she was a child. 'You hadn't touched that *stuff* in weeks,' her mother would say, when Ellen discovered some toy or piece of clothing had been donated to the 'poor people'. Ellen had always felt envious when she visited friends and saw their kitchen worktops laden with the detritus of their chaotic family lives, the framed photos on bookshelves overflowing with books, the strawberry-shaped magnets holding up school merit awards and colourful drawings on the refrigerator. Her home, and therefore her life, seemed so sterile in comparison. She equated messiness with love and warmth and those sweet, vague, plump mothers who distractedly offered her peanut-butter sandwiches before hurrying back to the stove or the laundry.

On the rare occasions when Anne wasn't at work and Ellen's friends visited, her mother would take far too much notice of them, skewering them with her violet eyes, offering lime juice (what kid drinks *lime juice?*), asking them their opinions on current affairs (they didn't have any opinions of course, except for Julia, who thought Ellen's mother was fabulous) and then making sarcastic little jokes they didn't understand.

Ellen couldn't believe that she'd just used the word 'stuff' in the same context as her mother; it just went to show how your childhood experiences were imprinted on your subconscious. When she found the time, she would need to do some serious work on this, and delve into her true feelings on the matter, or otherwise she'd find herself offering lime juice to her child's friends one day.

'It *is* bugging you,' said Patrick. 'Look, I promise it will all be gone by the weekend.'

He looked so sweet and apologetic that Ellen felt a rush of love for him and her eyes filled with guilty tears. (Pregnancy hormones! It was quite fascinating observing their impact on her emotions.)

'That's fine, there's no rush, I'm just being silly.' She

blinked rapidly, and continued down the hallway without looking at the boxes. 'What were you saying about Sunday?'

They went into the kitchen, and Patrick put the kettle on. He always put the kettle on the moment they walked into the kitchen, taking it for granted that they would be having a cup of tea. There was something old-fashioned and ceremonial about it, and it reminded her of someone. Who? Of course, it was her grandfather. Her lovely grandfather making tea for her grandmother.

Yes, she did adore Patrick. Thank God. She knew it was ridiculous and unrealistic but she felt panicky whenever she experienced even a moment's irritation with him. They were having a baby together. She had to remain vigilant; any cracks in their relationship had to be patched up immediately. It was absolutely vital. This child, her child, was going to grow up with a mother *and* a father.

'So what were you saying about this Sunday?' she said, as Patrick placed the cup of tea in front of her.

This Sunday she was meeting her father for the first time. Her stomach clenched on cue as the thought crossed her mind. It was impossible to pretend that she didn't care, or that she wasn't nervous. Her body gave it away every time she thought about it.

'It's the last Sunday of the month,' said Patrick. He turned away to the refrigerator. 'Have we got any crumpets?' He spoke with his back to her, as he burrowed through her refrigerator shelves. 'Oh, good, here they are. So, I wondered if you'd like to come along with us. Wholemeal? Why ruin a good crumpet by making it wholemeal?'

'What are you talking about?' said Ellen. He was going

to eat all the crumpets now and she wouldn't have any for her morning tea tomorrow. Also, he wasn't making any sense. 'Why do you keep saying "the last Sunday of the month" as if it means something to me?'

Patrick looked up with surprise as he put the last two crumpets into her toaster. 'You know – on the last Sunday of the month, Jack and I always visit Colleen's parents for lunch. In the mountains.'

'You still visit Colleen's parents?' said Ellen confusedly. 'Every month?'

'They're Jack's grandparents,' said Patrick. 'We always stop at Colleen's grave along the way.'

'You have never told me that before,' said Ellen. She was aware that her heart rate was up. Just slightly. 'Never.'

'I'm sorry, I thought I had,' said Patrick. 'Anyway, doesn't matter –'

'You've never mentioned it,' said Ellen. There was no way in the world that she would forget something like that. She was a woman. She was Ellen. She might have forgotten what model car he drove, or what football team he followed, but she would not have forgotten that he visited his dead wife's grave and family every month.

'It doesn't matter,' began Patrick again.

'It does matter,' said Ellen. 'You've never mentioned this before. I know. I would have remembered.'

'I didn't say I had mentioned it. I *thought* I had mentioned it,' said Patrick. 'Obviously I didn't. But it really –'

'When?' said Ellen. 'When did you think you had mentioned it?'

The crumpets popped up. Patrick went to lift them from the toaster and burned the tips of his fingers.

'Ow. Look, I don't know. I genuinely thought I had!'

'You didn't.' Ellen knew she was being horrible.

'Fine! I forgot to mention it. I'm sorry. Can we let it go now?'

'I can't *stand* it when you say that!' said Ellen, and it immediately struck her that he'd never said it before. It was *Edward* who used to say that. 'Can we just let it go?' he'd say, in that exact same exhausted tone. It was amazing that long-lost memory had somehow floated to the surface of her consciousness after all this time.

'You can't stand it when I say what?' Patrick looked taken aback.

'Nothing,' said Ellen. 'Sorry.'

She wondered if he'd deliberately or subconsciously avoided mentioning Colleen too much before they were engaged. She'd noticed that ever since she'd accepted his proposal, her name had been cropping up more often. Just the other day, he'd walked by the laundry when she was putting in the laundry powder and he'd said that Colleen had always said that it was a good idea to put the laundry powder into the machine before the clothes, so that it was fully dissolved or something. She'd felt a tremor of irritation. It seemed that Colleen had been something of a domestic goddess. She also sewed. One of the boxes in the hallway said 'sewing machine'. 'Colleen made her own wedding dress on that machine,' Patrick had said when Ellen asked him about it. 'Well, I won't be making my own dress,' Ellen had said lightly, 'I can't even thread a needle', and Patrick had said, 'Oh, no, I wouldn't expect you to.' Which had somehow made Ellen feel as if he was saying, 'Of course I wouldn't expect you to ever be as extraordinary as Colleen.'

Bloody beautiful blonde-haired laundry-powder-dissolving Colleen.

'So, anyway, I thought, now that we're engaged, and with the baby and everything –' Patrick cleared his throat and didn't quite look at her – 'I thought maybe you could come along and meet them this Sunday?'

Ellen took a deep, soothing breath. This was important to him. He was nervous about asking her.

'Well, that would be nice, but I can't this Sunday,' she said. 'I'm having lunch with Mum and with – my father. I'm meeting him for the first time, remember?'

Patrick had been excited about the sudden appearance in Ellen's life of a father. They'd talked about it at length, wondering together what he would be like (would there be a resemblance to Ellen?), wondering how he must be feeling, the strangeness of it, the awkwardness of it, the weirdness of Anne's behaviour.

'Oh, of course,' said Patrick now, frowning as he buttered the crumpets with far too much butter. 'I'd forgotten. Could you change that, do you think? Meet him for dinner instead?'

She didn't want to change it to dinner. Dinner was more intimate, more formal, more momentous. Lunch was just right. Light and breezy. 'Hi, Dad, nice to meet you!' And she didn't want to go through all the bother of changing it anyway. Her mother would have a fit. Ellen had never seen her so tightly wound up about anything (and that was saying something, because her mother's natural state was uptight), as if everything depended on this one event going right. There had been a lot of uncharacteristic dithering about the choice of venue. A restaurant had been booked and then cancelled. Another restaurant had been chosen and then discarded because she couldn't get a table with a view. When she'd finally settled on a Malaysian restaurant, she'd confirmed and reconfirmed the time and place with Ellen. Pip and Mel were on tenterhooks. Ellen's friends were demanding immediate updates as soon as she got home. She couldn't just casually *change* it.

'This lunch is a really big deal for me,' said Ellen.

'I know it is,' said Patrick. He came and sat down next to her, placing the plate of crumpets on the table. He gave her a pleading look. 'But your dad wouldn't mind if you changed the time, would he? What about the Saturday instead?'

'Your dad.' His very choice of words showed that he didn't understand the enormity of this meeting. She wasn't just having lunch with 'her dad' in the same casual way that he would have lunch at the local shopping centre with his own sweet father.

'Well, why can't you change your lunch with Colleen's family?' Ellen kept her voice neutral and pleasant. This should be easy. This was just negotiating timing. This was the sort of thing that might lead to conflict with other couples but not with someone as emotionally evolved as her.

Patrick winced and scratched the side of his jaw. 'It's just that this is when we always meet. The last Sunday of the month. Even when Colleen was alive. It's a tradition. It's never changed. Her parents are quite old and conservative – they like things done a certain way. Also, I sort of –'

He looked shame-faced, and put down his crumpet.

'I sort of told them you were coming. This is huge for them. It's huge for me. I've never introduced another woman to them. It will be hard for them – they'll feel like you're replacing Colleen. They're still grieving, of course. You never get over the loss of a child. But they're really keen to meet you! Millie said, "Ellen is going to be a part of Jack's life, so we want her to be a part of our life too."'

Patrick shook his head in an amazed sort of way, and gave Ellen a sad, sentimental smile, as if she would be equally amazed by Millie's bravery.

Ellen felt a surge of resentment against everyone. She didn't particularly want to meet the strange man who was her father this weekend. She didn't particularly want to meet Patrick's dead wife's family. (How could she not feel guilty for being alive when their only beloved child was dead?)

She was pregnant. She had never felt so tired in her life. Her hallway was crammed with *stuff*. She just wanted to be left alone to sleep and sleep and sleep, and while she slept she would like Patrick to get rid of those boxes.

That's what she wanted to do on Sunday.

Patrick licked honey from his fingers. 'Jack is excited about you meeting Millie and Frank. He told them you'd hypnotize them.'

'You told Jack I was coming before you even invited me?' said Ellen.

'I know. I'm really sorry. I'm an idiot. I just had in my head that you were coming.'

'But I can't come!' said Ellen.

'But if you ask your dad –'

'He's not my *dad*,' said Ellen. She noticed her teeth were

clenched together and made a conscious effort to relax her jaw. 'I've never met the man. Please don't call him my dad.'

'Fine, I know that meeting your father is important to you. Obviously! It's huge. But I'm positive that he wouldn't mind if –'

'I'm not changing it,' said Ellen. 'Just explain to Millie and Frank that I can't make it this time. I'll come next month.'

'Is it that you feel awkward about meeting them? Because they won't make you feel awkward. God, they were even nice to you-know-who – and that was only a short time after Colleen had died.'

'You-know-who? You mean *Saskia*? You just said two seconds ago that you'd never introduced another woman to Colleen's parents!'

Patrick's voice rose. 'Another *sane* woman. She doesn't count.'

Ellen's voice rose to meet his. 'She counted then!'

Patrick's face took on that particular look of controlled fury he got whenever Saskia's name came up. 'Why are you taking her side?'

'I'm just saying –' began Ellen.

'Forget it. Forget about Sunday. Forget I ever mentioned it. You're right. We'll do it another time.' He stood up. 'I'm going to get some more stuff from the house.'

He slammed out of the kitchen without looking at her.

'Thanks for eating all my crumpets!' Ellen yelled after him.

Then to her complete astonishment she picked up the plate and threw it against a wall.

*

Everyone is moving.

Jeff from next door is moving down the coast. The lively new family will soon be moving in next door.

Patrick and Jack are moving in with Ellen.

I'm the only one standing still.

Tonight after work I sat in my car outside Patrick's place while he loaded boxes into the back of his van. He obviously still doesn't believe in removal companies. I remembered the day that I moved into his house. He insisted on moving all my stuff. He got Stinky to help him, while I looked after Jack. We went to the park down the road. There was another little toddler there about the same age as Jack, so we had to practise sharing. Jack thought the park belonged to him. The little girl was exactly the same. They both kept saying, 'Mine! Mine!' while the other mother and I chanted those inane things parents say, 'Share!' 'Play nicely!' 'Take turns!'

The other mother sighed, 'This stage is just so exhausting, isn't it?' and I agreed, except of course I didn't think it was exhausting, because I was giddy with happiness. I was in love with Patrick, and I was in love with Jack, and the three of us were starting our new life together.

That night we had pizza and beer and we let Jack have a piece of pizza. His first ever. Patrick took photos. He said it was a historic moment. Jack had the funniest, wide-eyed, blissful expression – as if he couldn't believe that he'd lived on this earth for three whole years without knowing about the existence of this extraordinary thing called pizza. He chomped his way through it like a machine. 'I know, mate, I'm with you,' said Patrick. 'Just wait till you have it with a nice cold beer.'

I was there when your son ate pizza for the first time, Patrick. I helped teach him how to share. I cannot be deleted. I was there, and I'm still here.

He didn't look too happy tonight as he dumped his boxes in the back of his van. He didn't look like a man who was getting married and having a baby. He looked sort of grumpy and middle-aged, to be honest.

I guess it could have been the fact that he knew I was there watching him. I know my presence infuriates him, but I don't know, I sensed there was something else. I know him better than anyone.

When he put the last box in the van he came over to my car. I wound down my window and he bent down and leaned in and said, 'Hi, Saskia.'

I was taken aback. He hasn't said my name in such a long time. Or if he had said it, he'd yelled it, as if even the very word 'Saskia' was something evil and disgusting.

This time he said it in such a normal way, as if I was an old friend.

And for a second I was filled with jubilant, insane hope. He's leaving her, I thought. He's back. It's him again. It's all over. All I had to do was wait it out.

But then he spoke, and I saw that he was actually angrier than I'd ever seen him before. It was like he was carrying a bomb and he had to walk and talk very quietly and carefully, so it wouldn't detonate. He said, 'I don't want you going anywhere near Ellen again. Do you understand me? Follow me, if you must, but *leave her alone*. She's done nothing to deserve this.'

He was going all knight-in-shining-armour, protecting his fair maiden from the dragon. Me. I was the dragon.

'I haven't –'

'The book.'

'I was returning it!'

'The *flower*.' He spat out the word 'flower' as if I'd left her a dead animal.

'Patrick, I like Ellen,' I said. I wanted to reassure him that I wasn't any danger to her. The flower was meant to be a sort of friendly, even apologetic gesture. I wanted her gone, somewhere far away, yes, but I didn't want to hurt her.

'Don't,' he said sharply. 'Don't even talk about her. Don't – Jesus.'

He took a deep breath and puffed out his cheeks to blow out. I remembered how we used to say to Jack, 'Deep breath, deep breath,' when he was having a tantrum, and trying to learn how to control his anger.

'Do you remember –' I started to say.

'When is this ever going to end?' Now he was using this fake, flat, reasonable voice.

I said, 'I won't ever stop loving you, if that's what you mean.'

He said, 'You don't love me. You don't even know me any more. You love my memory, that's all.'

I said, 'You're wrong.'

He sighed and said, 'Fine, you love me, but what's the point? I'm marrying Ellen.'

I said, 'I know. Congratulations on the baby too.'

His face changed again, and he said, 'How do you know about the baby?' And then he said, 'Don't tell me. I don't want to know.' He pushed himself away from the car and walked off.

I called after him, 'Do you remember when Jack ate pizza for the first time?'

And then suddenly he stopped and went still, and he turned round and yelled, 'Yes, I remember! We had some happy times! So what? So *what*?'

He lifted his palms in the air, with his fingers splayed, and I saw his hands were trembling.

'This can't go on,' he said, and he really sounded quite strange. 'This has to stop.'

'I know,' I said, and I sounded and felt perfectly calm. 'You have to come back to me.'

The plate Ellen had thrown against the wall was one of her grandmother's. It was part of a set that her grandmother had received as a wedding present from her own parents. Ellen loved that dinner set. If there were a fire, she'd run back to save it. She couldn't believe that she'd thrown one of those precious, irreplaceable plates against the wall. And over such a silly, trivial thing. It wasn't like Patrick had just announced he was having an affair. They'd just had a disagreement over conflicting social engagements!

She did not behave like that. Imagine if her clients could see her!

She knelt down on the floor and regretfully picked up the broken pieces.

'I'm sorry, Grandma,' she said out loud. 'That was really embarrassing.'

She saw an image of her grandmother in the spirit world (she would be busy helping out on some spirit-world committee; she had always been a very civic sort of person), looking up from her paperwork to observe Ellen over the rims of her glasses. 'That's not like you, darling.'

'I know,' said Ellen. 'It's so strange!'

The phone rang. It was her mother.

'I just broke one of Grandma's plates,' Ellen told her. 'The wedding present set.'

'Those plates always gave me such a musty, fusty feeling,' said Anne. 'I'd keep them handy for throwing against the wall whenever you have an argument with Patrick. Not that you'd ever do anything like that, would you? I guess if you two have an argument you just meditate together or chant or align your auras or something.'

'I did throw it against the wall,' said Ellen.

'You did?' Her mother sounded impressed.

'Yes,' said Ellen. She was suddenly furious with her mother. 'And Patrick and I do not chant or meditate together and I do not believe in auras, well, not as an actual physical manifestation, and anyway, you don't align your auras, you align your chakras. If you're going to be cutting, at least get your terminology right.'

There was a pause.

'I didn't mean to be cutting,' said Anne in a softer, placatory voice. 'I'm sorry. I thought I was being witty. Actually, your father, ah, David, made a comment last night. He said I could be a bit "sharp" at times. Perhaps he has a point.'

For some reason her mother's apology made Ellen feel even angrier. 'Well, I assume you're not going to change your personality to suit a man!' she snapped. 'You drummed that into me from when I was eight years old! When Patrick Hood wanted to sit next to me at lunchtime

I told him that he couldn't because he might repress my personality. He said he wouldn't press anything and then he blushed and cried and ran away.'

Anne giggled. 'Actually, I never said anything of the sort. You would have got that whole repression lecture from Melanie. I never believed any man was capable of repressing my personality, thank you very much.'

'You might be right,' sighed Ellen, although she was sure it had been her mother. That was the problem with having three mothers; they all got mixed up in her memory. She pressed a fingertip to her forehead. 'I think I have a headache. What were you calling about?'

'Well, I just wondered if we could change this weekend's lunch. David and I have been invited to go up to the Whitsundays for a long weekend on a yacht, a sixty-foot yacht, if you can believe it! Some friends of his from the UK are in Australia at the moment. Bankers, apparently. Very wealthy. By the sound of it they're weathering the financial crisis rather well.'

There was an undercurrent of pure pleasure running beneath her mother's normal clipped, cool tone. It occurred to Ellen that this was the sort of life Anne had always been meant to lead. Drinking champagne on a yacht, chatting with bankers. Next it would be shopping in Paris.

'David didn't want to put off our lunch but I said you wouldn't mind. Of course, I didn't tell him that you were totally blasé about the whole event.'

'It's fine,' said Ellen, but she was hurt. Her father had got a better offer. After all, he could meet the daughter he'd never met any old time. And now she would have no excuse not to go up to the mountains on Sunday and meet Colleen's parents. Wonderful.

'Are you sure?' said her mother. 'You sound upset. You're not upset, are you? Because it was me who said we should accept the invitation. I know it's horribly superficial of me, but I have to admit it just sounded so wonderfully . . . decadent, I guess is the word.'

Her mother's honesty and slight embarrassment made her sound vulnerable. She was never embarrassed. Ellen's heart softened. She took a deep breath. For heaven's sake. Her emotions were skidding about all over the place.

'It's perfectly fine. It's good, in fact. Patrick had something he wanted me to do.'

'Excellent!' said her mother. 'Oh, by the way, I thought you'd be interested to hear that I've had not one but three patients tell me they've lost weight through hypnosis over the last week.'

'Is that right?' said Ellen, not especially interested.

'Yes, apparently they've been going to these "hypno-parties". They're all the rage in Sydney at the moment. They're like Tupperware parties but instead of handing round plastic containers they all get hypnotized. Then they drink champagne and eat carrot sticks I guess. Ladies of a certain age and income bracket are going crazy for them.'

'Fancy that,' said Ellen. Well, good for Danny.

Although it gave her an obscurely depressed feeling. What was the point of stock-standard hypnotherapists like her, when there were dynamic young guys like Danny shaking up the industry?

'Well, I have to run,' said her mother. 'We're off to the theatre.'

'OK. Say hi to Pip and Mel.'

'I'm going with David actually.'

'Oh,' said Ellen. 'What are Pip and Mel doing?'

'I don't know, but David and I are seeing the new David Williamson play. It's opening night. We've got front-row tickets.'

'Of course you have,' said Ellen.

'I beg your pardon?'

'Nothing. Say hi to Dad!'

'Ellen?'

'Sorry. I'm in an extremely peculiar mood. I'm fine. Have fun.'

She hung up the phone and looked at the tiny pieces of broken plate glinting on the floor.

Everything she had ever believed would make her happy was happening. She had a father and a mother going to the theatre together tonight. She had a fiancé and a stepson and a baby on the way. Why wasn't she in seventh heaven? Why was she feeling so skittish and irritable? It couldn't just be pregnancy hormones combined with a simple fear of change, could it?

She couldn't be so ordinary, could she?

Aha! So you think you're extraordinary then, do you, Ellen?

There was an enormous crash in the hallway and Ellen jumped. She ran out of the kitchen and saw that two of Patrick's boxes that had been piled on top of each other had toppled over and split open, spilling their contents in a great jumbled mess across the hallway floor.

She could see an old dirty sneaker, CDs that had fallen out of their cases, tangled extension cords, a travel hair-dryer, Christmas decorations, a frying pan, a Matchbox car, a bulging photo album that had fallen face down, an old dustpan, coins, receipts . . . stuff.

As she went to pick up one of the fallen boxes she saw that Patrick had carefully written 'miscellaneous' on the side. She laughed. It was meant to be a gentle, loving laugh at her imperfect but adorable husband-to-be, but it came out an unpleasant, bitter-sounding bark, as if she'd been unhappily married to him for years and this was the last straw.

Then she said, 'Oh, please *don't*,' as the bottom of the box broke and another flood of 'miscellaneous' items crashed to the floor.

She dropped the soft dusty sheets of cardboard and stamped her foot. Her home would never be hers again. It was going to disappear under a mountain of rubbish. She scratched viciously at her wrist as an itchy feeling of rage enveloped her, as if tiny bugs were crawling all over her body.

This is an inappropriate reaction. You need to breathe. In and out. Imagine a white light is filling . . .

'Shut up! Shut up! Shut up!' she screamed in the empty hallway.

She looked about for something, anything, to distract her.

She bent down and picked up the photo album.

The first photo she saw was of an impossibly young-looking Patrick wearing a puffy-sleeved white shirt with a blonde girl sitting on his lap. She had white jeans tucked into her boots, padded shoulders, earrings with dangling orange feathers. Patrick and Colleen. Young love in the late eighties.

She flipped the pages.

Photo after photo of Colleen posing for the camera, presumably held by Patrick. Hands on her hips, pouting her lips, opening her eyes wide, giggling uncontrollably.

Ellen's seventeen-year-old self, the one who had worn a very similar pair of earrings when she was a schoolgirl, but would never have had the confidence to model like that for a boyfriend, responded bitchily. 'Yes, you're pretty hot stuff.'

Her better self spoke up: *Ellen! What's wrong with you? She's a little girl! Seventeen and she's going to die young. Give the poor girl a break.*

She turned the page.

'Oh, lordie me,' she said, this time in her grandmother's voice.

She was looking at naked photos of Colleen. Her blonde hair slick against her head as if she'd just stepped out of the shower. Without the dated clothes and hairstyle, she'd lost that faintly silly look that people have in old photos. Now she wasn't just a pretty eighties girl, she was a classic beauty, with high cheekbones and big eyes. Ellen studied each photo, feeling both weirdly excited and slightly sick. Colleen had a perfectly proportioned body, slim and curved in all the right places. She could have been a model.

There wasn't anything pornographic about the photos. They were innocently sensual; Ellen could feel the raw intensity of first love.

There was one beautiful photo of her lying completely naked on a single bed with her eyes closed, sunlight across her face. Ellen imagined how Patrick must have felt, as a horny teenage boy, looking at this gorgeous girl. Ellen had been perfectly attractive as a teenager, a 'pretty' girl – but she'd never had a body like this, and now her skin was aging and her body was thickening with pregnancy and she was filled with a feeling of pure envy. She wanted to be that young girl, lying naked on a bed with the sunlight on her face, and the truth was she never had been and she never would be.

Stop looking, she told herself. *This is highly personal, private stuff! You have no right! It's disrespectful. Your reaction is emotionally immature. Everyone has photos of their high-school sweethearts tucked away in old boxes, it's no big deal! Shut the photo album, put it somewhere safe where Jack can't find inappropriate photos of his dead mother, and go and research prams for the baby on the Internet, or do your taxes or something.*

She sat down cross-legged on the floor amongst all the miscellaneous junk and kept looking, and as she did, she felt a strange longing to have a girl-to-girl talk with Saskia.

'Do you think he's still in love with his wife?' she could ask her. 'Do you think he ever really got over her? Do you think neither of us really ever had a chance with him?'

She felt like Saskia would be the only person who would truly understand why she couldn't stop looking at these photos.

15

You'll never forget your first age regression!

— Flynn Halliday

'Describe what's going through your mind,' said Ellen.

Alfred Boyle, the humble accountant who wanted help with public speaking, was sitting in the green recliner displaying all the signs of an ideal hypnotic state: his cheeks were flushed, his eyes moved restlessly behind his eyelids, his well-polished, black business shoes splayed outwards.

It was Ellen's second session with him and she was doing an age regression.

After their first appointment it had become obvious to Ellen that Alfred's fear of public speaking was a full-blown phobia. He trembled and stammered just talking about it. It was having a serious impact on his life. He regularly called in sick on days he was due to give a presentation.

Alfred had already regressed to his first job as a trainee accountant, when he'd made such a hash of a short presentation that his boss had eventually interrupted, 'Don't worry about it, mate.'

Now Alfred was describing an incident in high school where he'd had to give an impromptu speech on the topic of 'music'.

'I feel sick,' said Alfred. His voice sounded younger. Not as deep. Even the awkward way his jaw moved reminded Ellen of a teenage boy. 'I've got nothing to say about music. Music. What is music even? Like, sounds and shit? I cannot think of a single word to say about music. They're all staring at me. They think I'm an idiot. I *am* an idiot.'

'Where do you feel the fear?'

'Here.' Alfred pressed his hand to his stomach. 'I'm going to vomit. Seriously. I'm going to vomit all over the classroom floor.'

Ellen looked at him uneasily, and felt her own nausea rise.

'We're going to use that feeling like a bridge,' she said firmly. 'And we're going to follow that bridge to the *very first time* you felt that way.'

She was on the hunt for what was called the 'Initial Sensitizing Event'.

'As I count backwards from five to one, you will travel back in time. Five, you're becoming younger, smaller, four, you're following the feeling, three, you're nearly there, two, one.'

Ellen leaned forward and tapped Alfred lightly on the forehead with her fingernail. 'Be there.'

She waited a beat.

'Where are you?' she said.

'Pre-school,' said Alfred.

At the sound of his voice Ellen felt a cold shiver. It never ceased to amaze her when this happened. There was a fifty-two-year-old man sitting in front of her but she was talking to a small child.

'How old are you?'

Alfred held up his palm and tucked back his thumb.

'Four?' said Ellen.

Alfred nodded shyly.

'And what's happening, Alfred?'

'It's quiet time, but Pam is crying in the reading corner. She's really sad. I think I should cheer her up.'

'How?'

'I'm giving her a present.'

'Ah, that's a good idea. What is it?'

'My snail.'

Oh dear. This was clearly not going to work out well.

'Your snail?'

'Yeah, I found it on the footpath this morning and I put it in my pocket. It's *huge*! And guess what?' Alfred's face filled with boyish enthusiasm. 'His shell is *hairy*! I've never seen a hairy-shelled snail before.'

'What are you doing now?'

'I'm saying, "Look, Pam, this is for you."'

'What's Pam doing?'

By the expression of shocked horror on Alfred's face, it didn't look like the snail had been a hit. 'She's screaming and pushing me away!'

Oh, Pam, thought Ellen.

'I'm falling back against the bookshelf and it's crashed to the floor with everyone's Easter Eggs we painted this morning! And Miss Bourke is yelling like she's on fire, and I can't find my snail and *everyone is looking at me*.'

Alfred's shoes drummed against the floor. 'Miss Bourke is hitting my legs!'

Bitch, thought Ellen.

Four-year-old tears were running down Alfred's fifty-two-year-old face. 'Now I have to stand up in front of everyone and say sorry to Pam and sorry to the whole class for breaking their Easter Eggs and everyone is looking at me, like I'm . . . like I'm a bank robber.'

Ellen wanted to march straight back through time and remove Alfred from the pre-school and take him out for an ice cream.

But there was only person who could do that.

She raised her voice. 'I want to talk to grown-up Alfred now. Are you there?'

Alfred straightened up. He cleared his throat and lifted his chin. His voice deepened again. 'Yes.'

'All right, Alfred, I want you to go back to that pre-school now and see your four-year-old self with your grown-up eyes. I'm going to count backwards from five. Five, four, three, two, one . . . be there.'

Alfred stretched his neck.

'Are you there?'

'Yes.'

'Can you see four-year-old Alfred?'

'Yes.'

'What would you like to say to him?'

'It's all right, mate. Girls don't like snails. They're strange like that. You were just trying to help. None of it was your fault.'

Ellen checked her watch. The session was running over time and she had Mary-Kate McMasters booked for the next one, assuming of course that she turned up. Time to wrap up with a few positive suggestions.

An image of Mary-Kate's sad, dumpy face appeared in Ellen's mind.

She looked thoughtfully at Alfred Boyle.

Mary-Kate and Alfred were both single.

'Single,' they'd both said immediately, with exactly the same resigned, well-what-would-you-expect intonation in their voices when she'd asked about their relationship status on their intake paperwork.

They were of similar ages. She couldn't think of anything else they had in common, but still, who could ever really predict the magical combination of personality attributes and backgrounds and chemistry that caused two people to fall in love?

So why not give them just the tiniest nudge? The barest flick of her fingernail could roll them together like two marbles. What would be the harm? Before she could change her mind she started talking.

'You've been carrying around the feelings from that day in pre-school for a long time now. It's time to start rewriting history. The next time you run into a sad-looking woman you might feel a strong desire to pay her a compliment –'

Ellen paused. Assuming Mary-Kate was the next sad-looking woman he saw, how would she respond? Presumably not like four-year-old Pam, but still, this was Mary-Kate. Ellen actually had no idea how she'd react. Was this a crazy idea?

'– and *no matter how she reacts*, you'll feel good about yourself. In fact, you'll feel great.'

Ellen hesitated. How far should she push this?

Oh, to hell with it.

'You may even find yourself asking her out. You'll speak clearly and confidently and you'll look her straight in the eye, and if four-year-old Alfred starts to get in the way, grown-up Alfred will take charge. You'll ask her out for a drink. Tonight, if she's free. To the Manly Wharf Hotel perhaps. You could sit at one of those seats right out –'

OK, now she was getting carried away. She hurriedly finished off.

'And even if this woman says no, you'll be filled with optimism and confidence and positivity, because all that matters is you took that leap. Nod to show me you understand.'

Alfred nodded once. His head had dropped forward towards his chest. He looked like a drunk who was agreeing that someone should call him a taxi.

Well, thought Ellen. *What would be, would be.*

She brought him out of his trance.

'How do you feel?' She poured him a glass of water. Alfred took the water from her outstretched hand, tipped his head back and drank deeply. Then he put the empty glass back down on the table and grinned at her. He actually had quite a nice smile.

'Good, I think,' he said. He shook his head and chuckled. 'Yep, I've always been such a hit with the ladies. Just what every girl wants. A hairy-shelled snail. I hadn't thought about that in years.'

'A tomboyish girl might have appreciated the snail,' said Ellen.

'But you're not saying *that* was the cause of my problem with public speaking, are you?' said Alfred.

'I'm not saying anything at all.' Ellen folded her hands on her lap and smiled at him.

'It's just –'

'What?'

'Well, it's so trivial. It's embarrassing. It's not like we discovered I had a past life where I was, I don't know, stoned to death by Egyptian monks because I gave a boring speech.'

'*Egyptian* monks?'

'I don't know, I'm an accountant, not a historian! Anyway, I don't believe in past lives.'

Excellent. That was something he had in common with Mary-Kate. They could chat about their lack of belief in past lives. Perhaps they were sceptical lovers in ancient Rome.

'Or at least if I'd repressed some really shocking, traumatic memory from my childhood,' mused Alfred.

It was interesting how many clients with perfectly happy childhoods longed to find something dreadful in their past.

'The most trivial incident can be traumatic for a child,' said Ellen. 'And your subconscious retains those memories. That's what we're going to do at our next session. We're going to reprogram your subconscious. Alfred, you're going to be *amazed* at the new confidence you're going to experience.'

As she made this pronouncement she leaned forward and locked eyes with Alfred. She'd found that her clients remained extremely suggestible straight after they came out of a trance. It was a good opportunity for her to reinforce the session with some waking suggestions.

She looked at her watch. *Come on, Mary-Kate. Don't cancel. This could be your destiny waiting for you.*

She wrote out Alfred's receipt and as she slowly led him down the stairs the doorbell rang.

Yes!

'Ah! That will be my next appointment,' said Ellen joyously, as if it was a magnificent surprise to have another client show up.

'Oh, that's . . . good,' said Alfred, who was probably now wondering if she had cash-flow issues.

Ellen opened the door to reveal Mary-Kate's unsmiling, dour face. Alfred stood back courteously to let her in first.

'Hi, Mary-Kate!' carolled Ellen.

Mary-Kate looked at her suspiciously. 'Hi.'

'Oh!' Ellen slapped the side of her head (quite hard – she was a terrible actress). 'I meant to give you – something, Alfred. If you could just wait one moment, I'll be right back. My apologies, Mary-Kate. I won't be long. Just, ah, take a seat both of you.' She gestured at the two cane chairs she had sitting in the hallway next to a coffee table with magazines.

As she headed back up the stairs, she saw Mary-Kate plonk herself down and pick up a magazine from the coffee table.

Alfred coughed nervously and kept standing. He walked over to one of the prints Ellen had hanging on the wall and studied it intently as if he were considering buying it.

Ellen went back into her office and found some notes on self-hypnosis for public speaking. She also picked up a relaxation CD for good measure.

Then she stood at her window and watched the ocean. Was she putting her toe across that ethical line again? They probably weren't even talking to each other. She looked at her watch. How long before they'd start to worry that she'd collapsed or something?

She'd give them five minutes. Five minutes that could mean nothing at all in the stories of their lives, or five minutes that could potentially change everything, forever.

Which will it be, Alfred and Mary-Kate?

16

Do not dwell in the past, do not dream of the future,
concentrate the mind on the present moment.
— Buddhist quote on Ellen's bathroom mirror

'So, I guess I should, that is, I mean I assume you don't want . . . should I wait in the car?'

They had pulled up at the graveyard where Colleen was buried. Jack was in the back seat of the car, his head down, lips moving silently as he played with his Nintendo DS. He'd played for the whole hour and a half it had taken them to drive to Katoomba. Colleen's parents had moved to the Blue Mountains a few years before she'd died, and they'd wanted her to be buried close to them. On the seat next to Jack was a giant bunch of Colleen's favourite flowers (yellow gerberas) that Patrick had specially ordered and picked up from the florist that morning.

(It was not like Patrick was buying flowers for another woman. A rival for her affections. A mistress. Certainly not. And it was not as though Patrick had never bought flowers for Ellen before. He had. Many times. Beautiful bunches. So, then, why was she even thinking about the damned flowers, when there was nothing to think about them, nothing at all?)

'No, I want you to come.' Patrick turned off the ignition and unbuckled his seatbelt. He turned to look at her and smiled, awkwardly. All morning, he'd been in a jumpy, skittish mood, laughing too loudly at her jokes, overly stern with Jack, and then suddenly hugging him to make up. It was as though he had intense stage fright about an upcoming performance.

'I'd sort of like to introduce you to her,' he said quietly.

'Ah,' said Ellen.

'Is that too weird?' He put his hand over hers.

'Of course not,' she said, while silently shrieking, *OF COURSE IT'S WEIRD! ARE YOU OUT OF YOUR MIND?!!*

Patrick turned to the back seat. 'Ready to come and see Mum, mate?'

'Just let me . . .' said Jack without looking up, his thumbs moving rapidly.

'Jack,' said Patrick sharply.

Jack sighed and tossed aside the Nintendo. 'Fine.'

They all got out of the car. It was even colder than Ellen had expected outside the car and she pulled her coat more tightly round herself. She looked about, as she always did now, to see if Saskia had followed them today, but there wasn't anyone around except for an older couple, hand in hand, murmuring to each other as they walked back from the graveyard. The woman smiled at Ellen.

Since the book and the flower incident, Ellen had only seen Saskia once, when she and Patrick and Jack were at their local supermarket. Jack and Patrick were arguing over breakfast cereals, and Ellen had looked up to see Saskia walking down the aisle towards them, pushing an empty trolley. Their eyes had met, and Ellen had automatically smiled because it was Deborah Vandenberg she first saw: a client suffering chronic pain who was doing well with her treatment, who had chatted and joked with Ellen, a woman of a similar age to Ellen, who reminded her a little of Julia, who could so easily have been a friend.

A second later, she remembered the true, peculiar nature of their relationship, and for some reason her nervous system had reacted as if she was embarrassed, and her cheeks had flooded with colour. Her throat had dried up and her eyes flew to Patrick and Jack, who were still obliviously discussing crunchy nut cornflakes. Saskia shook her head, almost imperceptibly, as if to say, 'Don't tell them,' and glided silently past.

'Are you all right?' Patrick had looked round, just as Saskia turned her trolley at the end of the aisle.

'Feeling a bit dizzy,' she'd said. (Pregnancy was so handy in that way.)

She'd felt obscurely guilty about that ever since, as if she and Saskia were somehow in cahoots to deceive Patrick. But there had been no point mentioning it to Patrick. Ever since Noosa, his hatred of Saskia seemed to have reached a new, more intense level. Ellen was frightened sometimes by the look in his eyes when he spoke about her. The night she'd thrown her grandmother's plate against the wall, he'd come home with another lot of boxes to stack in the hallway (and flowers, to apologize for slamming out of the house earlier) and he'd said, 'She was at the house tonight. Psycho bitch.'

Why had Saskia shook her head at Ellen? There had definitely been something conspiratorial about it. But didn't she normally like Patrick to know she was there? Wasn't that the point? And if not, what *was* the point? Did she really think that Patrick would eventually take her back? When and how would this all end? Saskia was a puzzle Ellen couldn't stop trying to solve.

Now Patrick leaned in the back of the car and pulled out the bunch of flowers. He held them in front of him with both hands clasped round the stems, like a nervous beau about to walk up to his girlfriend's door. He gave Ellen a strange half-smile.

'So,' he said awkwardly.

Jack scuffed his foot against the grass and made a 'pow-pow' sound through his lips like a machine gun.

'Jack,' said Patrick.

'What?'

'Stop it.'

'Stop what?'

'Come on. Let's go.'

Jack ran ahead. Ellen walked alongside Patrick, looking at the names on gravestones, and wondered if it would be inappropriate to mention that she felt sick. She longed for the little pile of dry Vita-wheat biscuits she'd carefully wrapped in plastic for this morning's journey and then left on the kitchen counter.

She was exactly eleven weeks pregnant today and it seemed that the nausea, which up until now had just been like a mildly unpleasant background noise, had suddenly intensified. She'd vomited this morning. She never vomited. She didn't even like the word. It was horrendously uncomfortable and undignified, kneeling on the bathroom floor, bent over the toilet bowl. She'd wanted to cry for her mother, which was absurd, because her mother hadn't been at all sympathetic when Ellen was unwell as a child. She'd always tell Ellen about the much sicker children she'd treated that day.

Apparently Colleen hadn't been sick for a single moment when she was pregnant with Jack. She'd played tennis every week right up until she was eight months pregnant!

She wasn't imagining it. Patrick was definitely talking more about Colleen since their engagement. In fact, she'd started keeping a tally in her head and there had been at least one reference to Colleen every single day for the last week. She'd learned that Colleen had put headphones over her pregnant stomach and played classical music to the baby every night (Ellen had wanted to do the same thing for her baby, but she'd gone off the idea now); Colleen had craved salt and vinegar crisps throughout her pregnancy; Colleen had actually *lost* weight in the first few months of her pregnancy, which had worried Patrick; Colleen hadn't suffered any mood swings; Colleen had a completely natural childbirth; and so on and so forth.

If Colleen had been an ordinary living ex-wife or ex-girlfriend, Ellen could have banned all further mentions of her, but as she was dead, and as it was perfectly understandable that having another child would be bringing back memories for Patrick of Jack's birth, and as Colleen was Jack's mother and he loved hearing stories about when his mother was pregnant with him, Ellen felt she had to not only listen politely, but she even had to encourage further revelations about the seemingly perfect

Colleen by asking Patrick interested questions with a bright, loving, empathetic expression on her face.

Frankly, it was driving her bananas.

She loved Jack, and she loved the thought of him being a big brother to her baby, but she couldn't help imagining what it would have been like if Patrick had been a first-time father-to-be, if it could have been just the two of them, excited and apprehensive together.

Also, the nausea didn't help. She'd known that the nausea could be bad; she just didn't think it would actually *matter*, not as much as it did, or at all really. Even though her rational mind knew that it wouldn't last forever, this awful, seedy, off-colour feeling seemed to taint everything. When she thought of holding her baby, all she could think was, 'How could I possibly look after a baby feeling like this?'

'She's up in the far corner over here,' said Patrick.

Jack ran ahead. Patrick stopped and touched Ellen's shoulder.

'You OK, darling?' he said, and his eyes met hers. He did this sometimes, just when she least expected it. He would stop what he was doing, and really look at her, properly, his green eyes studying her with such intensity it was as if he was waiting for her to impart a crucial message.

It melted her heart every time.

'I'm fine,' she said. She didn't want him worrying about her nausea right now, hurrying her back to the car or whatever.

'You sure? Are you too cold?'

'I'm fine.'

'Well, it's just up here.'

They kept walking, past grave after grave; life after life. Ellen had occasionally walked through graveyards before, but she'd actually never been to visit a grave of someone she knew. Both her grandparents had been cremated and had their ashes scattered in the ocean from their favourite cliff-top walk. Of course she'd grieved for them, but it had been gentle, accepting grief; simple sadness for herself and the loss of their company. Not the sort of raw grief you'd feel for someone who died before their time. She'd managed to reach thirty-five years old without ever experiencing a shocking death.

She saw fresh flowers in front of one headstone and wondered if it had been the one visited by the couple she'd seen leaving.

She paused to read the inscription. It was the grave of a boy called Liam who was born in 1970 and died in 1980. She glanced back to the car park and saw the couple's car pulling away, the woman's profile only just visible through the car window.

She kept walking behind Jack and Patrick. Her stomach began to churn. Her mouth filled with saliva. At that moment, nothing mattered, not Patrick's loveliness, not even that poor woman's grief. All that mattered was this sickness; this awful, awful sickness.

Finally, they stopped in front of a shiny grey headstone with an oval-shaped picture frame built into the top. The frame contained a black and white photo of Colleen caught looking away from the photographer, smiling at someone (Patrick?), her hair blown by some long-ago breeze, love in her eyes.

For the first time Ellen came slam up against the reality of Colleen's death. This beautiful young girl shouldn't be dead! She should be in the car with her husband and son, driving up the mountains to see her parents, pregnant with her second child.

Or, better still, she should be Patrick's living ex-wife, not quite as pretty any more, making unreasonable demands about child support and access visits. That way Ellen could stay in the picture (and, after all, she would have excelled at dealing with an ordinary shrewish ex-wife – she'd be so tranquil and accepting – and Patrick would have found her all the more attractive!).

The carved inscription read:

COLLEEN SCOTT
1970 – 2002
BELOVED WIFE OF PATRICK, MOTHER TO JACK
AND DAUGHTER TO MILLIE AND FRANK.
LIFE IS NOT FOREVER. LOVE IS.

Right.

'That's my mum at my first birthday party,' said Jack to Ellen, putting his finger on the photo. 'She's looking at me opening a present from Grandma. The present was a dinosaur jigsaw. I've still got that jigsaw.'

'It's a lovely photo,' said Ellen.

'And by the way, in case you're wondering, the dinosaur is a tyrannosaurus,' said Jack. He paused, stuck his hands in the pockets of his jeans and considered. 'It's a pretty easy jigsaw. It's got like maybe five pieces or something. I can do it in maybe three seconds. Or even one second.'

'We, ah, we sort of talk to her,' said Patrick, without looking at Ellen. 'A bit silly –'

'Of course it's not,' said Ellen. She felt terribly, terribly sick. It would not do to throw up over Colleen's grave. She looked around. If the worst came to the worst she would quickly scoot over to Bill Taylor's grave. He was 'of tender heart, and generous spirit', so perhaps he wouldn't mind.

Patrick knelt down in front of Colleen's headstone. He leaned forward and kissed the photo.

Oh my goodness me.

Jack knelt down beside his father and casually, without any self-consciousness at all, did the same thing. 'Hi, Mum.'

What was the etiquette here? Should Ellen kneel down too and also kiss the photo? No, surely not. She'd never even met Colleen. That would be entirely inappropriate. A handshake would be better. Perhaps the alternative would be to give the headstone a polite little pat? 'Lovely to meet you.' Ellen imagined herself telling this story to Julia, who would be shrieking, her hand covering her eyes, the horror, the horror!

Patrick placed the flowers down in front of the headstone with a rustle of cellophane. He cleared his throat. Ellen breathed in and out through her nostrils.

'Well, it's us again, Colleen. We're just on our way up to have lunch with your mum and dad. Your mum is making that chicken risotto again.'

As Patrick spoke, his voice became more natural.

'Remember how offended she was when you told her it was too bland? Now it's got so much garlic you can smell it as soon as you walk in the front door. It's such a beautiful day. We wish you were – oh, and guess what? Jack's team won at soccer at the weekend. Their first game!'

Ellen squirmed. He'd been going to say: we wish you were here with us. But then he'd remembered his pregnant fiancée.

'We smashed those guys,' said Jack comfortably.

'They did,' said Patrick. 'And Jack played so well. You would have been so proud.'

'You were watching, right?' said Jack. 'From in heaven. You probably have this, like, giant grandstand where everyone goes to watch all their different relatives back on earth playing sports, and you get whatever food and drink you want, and if you've got more than one relative to watch at the same time, you've got this screen that sort of splits in two, and you can, like, switch back and forth –'

'OK, mate,' interrupted Patrick. 'Anyway, Colleen, we've got other big news too, haven't we, Jack?'

Jack looked blank. Patrick tilted his head at Ellen and said, 'The baby!'

'Oh, yeah,' said Jack. 'Maybe Mum knows already if it's a boy or a girl! She probably knows, right? Like maybe she saw it coming off the assembly line in heaven, like in a factory, and it's like a baby factory, and Mum was there, and she's like, hey, that's Ellen's new baby, you're going to be Jack's little brother! Or, you're going to be Jack's –'

'Right,' said Patrick. 'So, this is Ellen.'

He looked up at Ellen, reached up and took her hand in his.

Should I kneel down? I should kneel. But what if I'm sick? No, I should definitely kneel.

She knelt down. There would be grass stains on her

cream trousers. But it seemed the right thing to have done because Patrick's face suddenly filled with some complex emotion, and Jack slung an affectionate arm round Ellen's shoulders, something he'd never done before.

'Ellen and I are getting married and I know you'd be happy, Colleen, because I always remember that day, when you told me I had to find someone lovely.' Patrick's voice broke, and he squeezed Ellen's hand painfully hard. 'And I said I wouldn't. But I have. And she is lovely. She's so lovely. And she's made us very happy.'

'Yeah.' Jack banged his chin gently against Ellen's shoulder.

'Oh, you guys,' said Ellen, because she didn't know what else to say. She could smell cold damp earth and Patrick's aftershave and Jack's peanut-buttery breath. Patrick's hand was warm round hers and for a moment the waves of nausea receded and Ellen was filled with glorious relief.

No, this was not an excruciating story to laugh over with Julia. Its very awkwardness and awfulness made it somehow essentially human. It was one of those rare, poignant, pure moments that encapsulated everything that was wonderful and tragic about life.

Today was the fourth Sunday of the month. That means Patrick has lunch with Colleen's parents.

It never changed. We arranged our holidays round it.

I only went once, after we'd been together for a few months. It wasn't a success. It was too soon. I shouldn't have agreed to go, but Patrick seemed anxious to take me. He insisted, in fact. It was almost as if he was in a hurry, as if this was something that needed to be done, to be ticked off some checklist. I got the impression he thought it would somehow be good for his in-laws. I remember my mother telling me that it was a mistake. 'Oh, Saskia, you must not go – that would be too cruel,' she said. But like an idiot I thought that Patrick knew best.

And, of course, Mum was right. It was terrible for Frank and Millie to see me with Patrick, to see their grandson running to me. They were still raw with grief. You could sense it as soon as you walked in the house, as if tears had a scent that pervaded the air. They both had identical shocked expressions, as if they'd just a moment before been punched in the face. There were photos of her *everywhere*. It was like a museum with one subject: Colleen. Colleen as a baby. Colleen on her first day of school. Colleen and Patrick. Colleen and Jack. I couldn't let my eyes rest anywhere. Although, strangely, I remember not feeling any envy when I saw the photos of Colleen and Patrick together. I was utterly, idiotically confident of his love. It was the photos of Colleen and Jack that made me feel unsettled; the evidence that I wasn't really Jack's mother.

After that, I always let Patrick and Jack go up to the mountains without me, and I always spent that Sunday catching up on housework or seeing a friend or, in the time before I got my leg problem, doing some exercise. I quite enjoyed the break, having the house nice and quiet to myself. It seems completely foreign to me now, the idea of enjoying time on my own, when these days I have my whole life to myself, and time outside of work is a gigantic expanse of empty space, an endless desert I fill by watching Patrick.

Was I really that busy, happy girl? That girl who raced down the aisles of the shopping centre after work, who prepared nutritious meals for a toddler and gourmet meals for his father, who went to parties and barbecues and movies, who had sex on Sunday mornings, who was just another regular member of the human race?

That Saskia really does seem like someone else, someone I knew well, someone I quite liked – but not actually me.

I've never bothered following Patrick up the mountains on the fourth Sunday. I know where he's going. I know the flowers he'll take and the florist where he picks them up. I know how he'll stop at the graveyard where Colleen is buried. The day I went with him, he wanted me to come with him to see Colleen's grave. I refused. I thought it was a completely bizarre idea. I said, 'If I died I wouldn't want you bringing your new girlfriend to dance on my grave.' He said, 'I'm not suggesting you *dance* on it.' But, anyway, Jack had fallen asleep in his car seat so I said we shouldn't wake him, and I'd stay in the car with him.

I thought it was about time he took Ellen up the mountains with him. Now they've moved in together, and they're getting married and all that. Now he's in a *proper* relationship, now Jack has a *proper* stepmother.

I watched them from my car as they all came out of Ellen's house, looking like a proper little family. Jack wasn't dressed warmly enough for the mountains in the middle of winter. He was only wearing a long-sleeved T-shirt. I thought about calling out to Ellen, 'Get Jack a jacket!' but I didn't. I've always tried not to confuse or upset Jack.

Ellen didn't see me, but Patrick did. He actually held

my eyes for a few seconds and then he sniffed and shrugged and put his sunglasses on as if he was a gangster at a funeral catching sight of the police presence.

It was strange when I saw them at the supermarket the other day. I wasn't actually following them. I just happened to be there. It was a coincidence. Sort of. I was in their area, because I'd driven by the house on my way home from work, but then I'd decided to pick up a few groceries. I wasn't even thinking about Patrick and Ellen, which is a rare treat. I was looking for oats. I'd had a sudden craving for Anzac biscuits. I haven't baked biscuits in years. Not since I was with Patrick. He and Jack loved it when I made biscuits. Of course when I got home from the supermarket with the ingredients I couldn't be bothered to make them. What would be the point? Ellen was the one who should have been making biscuits, not me.

Ellen saw me and then quickly looked away, almost as if she was embarrassed or guilty, as if she was the stalker, not me.

That's what Patrick calls me. A stalker. I got such a shock the first time he said it. How could I be a stalker? I wasn't some deranged stranger. We'd lived together. We'd tried to have a baby together. The only reason I follow him is because I want to see him, to talk to him, to try and understand.

But perhaps, technically, that's what I've become. A stalker.

Never thought I'd be forty-three years old and alone. Never thought I'd be childless. Never thought I'd be a stalker.

I shook my head at Ellen because I didn't want to upset

Jack if Patrick started acting as if I was a potential murderer. I try to be invisible when they're together. It's my own personal code of stalker ethics.

I didn't see any point in following them all the way up to the mountains today. I don't like those winding roads, and also I didn't want Patrick speeding with Jack in the car. So, I got as far as the freeway, just to confirm that's where they were going, and then I took the next exit.

'Have fun!' I called to the back of their car as it disappeared into the distance. And then the whole of Sunday lay in front of me, like a malicious joke. As I drove home I imagined them talking in the car. So much to chat about and plan. The wedding. The baby. What they'll all have for dinner tonight. I wonder if Ellen prepares Jack's school lunch for him. Has she slipped into the Mummy role as easily and enthusiastically as I did? I can still remember the lunch I made for Jack's first day of school. Ham and cheese sandwich on wholemeal bread. A peach. He loved peaches. Little box of sultanas. Carton of apple juice. A buttered slice of his favourite banana loaf. I planned it so meticulously. Talked about it with Mum. 'Did he eat everything?' she rang up to ask that night. 'Everything except the sultanas,' I told her. Patrick had no idea what Jack had in his lunchbox. Food doesn't really interest him.

When you're responsible for a child, when your days are filled with the tiny details that make up a child's life – his lunchbox, his school bag, his shoes, his favourite T-shirt, his friends, his friends' mothers, his TV shows, his temper tantrums – and then you're told that you are no longer responsible, that you are no longer wanted, that your services are no longer required, that you have been made redundant, like an employee walked to the door by security, it is difficult.

It is quite profoundly difficult.

Jack must have asked for me. He must have been so confused.

I let him down. I blame myself for my mini breakdown or whatever it was that happened to me when Patrick broke it off. I couldn't stay in the same bed so I went to stay at my friend Tammy's place. Tammy. Whatever happened to Tammy? She tried so hard to stay friends with me, but then she sort of slid out of my life along with everyone else.

I remember waking up in Tammy's room five days later, and realizing it was Friday morning and that Jack had swimming lessons straight after school, and I always had to remember to pack his things the night before, and who would take him? I worked 9.30 to 2.30 p.m. I had rearranged my working hours so I could pick him up from school. I was happy to do this. I had more flexibility than Patrick and I loved picking him up. I was Jack's mother. I didn't mind when I missed out on a promotion because I wasn't working full hours. That's what all mothers do; they put their careers on hold for their children.

So I called Patrick, to remind him about swimming lessons, and that's when all this started: my habit. My 'stalking' of my old life.

Because Patrick treated me like a stranger. As if Jack's swimming lessons were nothing to do with me, *when just the week before* I'd been at swimming, helping Jack adjust his goggles, talking to his teacher about maybe moving him up a class, making arrangements with one of the other mothers for a play date with her son. 'It's fine,' Patrick said. All irritable and put out. As if I was interfering. As if I'd never had anything to do with Jack. 'We've got it all under control.' The rage that swept through me was like nothing I'd ever felt before. I hated him. I still loved him. But I hated him. And ever since then it's been hard to tell the difference between the two. If I didn't hate him so intensely maybe I would have been able to stop loving him. I know that doesn't make sense.

If he'd just let me *ease* my way out of being his wife – I thought of myself as his wife – and Jack's mother, if he'd just listened to me with the respect I deserved when I called up to remind him things about Jack, if he'd just sat down with me and let me talk and let me say how much he'd hurt me, if he'd ever just said, 'I'm sorry,' and meant it, then I think I could have let it go. Perhaps then I would have eventually healed, like people do. Instead, it got infected. It spread. Like gangrene. It took hold. It's his fault. I know what I do is unacceptable. Deep down I do know this. But he started it. Mum used to say that when she met my dad it was like a perfect love story. I thought Patrick was my perfect love story. Except he's not. He's the hypnotist's love story. I'm the ex-girlfriend in the hypnotist's love story. Not the heroine. I'm only a minor character.

Or perhaps I'm the villain.

No one spoke after they left the graveyard and drove towards Frank and Millie's place.

Jack sat quietly in the back seat, absorbed in his game again. Patrick concentrated on driving along the winding mountain road.

Ellen tipped her head back against the car seat. The nausea was still there, but it was manageable, as long as she didn't have to wait too long to eat once she got to Frank and Millie's place. One dry piece of bread would do the trick.

She watched the world whip by outside the window like a movie on fast forward. Quaint little mountain villages with cafés and second-hand bookshops and antique stores. She remembered a romantic weekend in the mountains with Jon in the very early days of their relationship. She let the memory slip away. He was getting married. So was she. Life was moving forward. She needed to keep her eyes on the road ahead. So did Saskia. So did Patrick, actually.

She wondered if he was thinking about Colleen right now, comparing her with Ellen, wondering what his life would have been like if she hadn't died.

If only she could read his mind. She glanced at his inscrutable profile.

Of course there was a way.

Most nights Patrick still asked for a relaxation exercise before they went to sleep. It was part of their routine. He trusted her completely. She could easily take him into a deep trance and ask him to tell her how he felt about Colleen, and then use a post-hypnotic suggestion so that he would never remember what she'd asked.

But that would be wrong. Totally unethical. She couldn't go poking about his mind without his permission. It would be like reading his diary.

And it would be unfair because he couldn't do the same thing to her. She wouldn't want him finding out that she still had complicated feelings about Jon.

So of course she would never do such a thing. It was the sort of thing Danny would do to a girlfriend if he were ever in a relationship.

She couldn't believe she'd even allowed such a thought to cross her mind. It wasn't like her. She was becoming increasingly disappointed with herself lately. She wasn't nearly as compassionate or moral or as patient a person as she'd always thought herself to be.

But, goodness me, it was tempting.

'Dad?' said Jack suddenly from the back seat.

Ellen started guiltily.

'After we've finished lunch, can we go for another bushwalk to that same place we went last time?'

'Sure,' said Patrick. 'Oh, actually, no, mate, we might have to leave straight away because I need to go back into the office this afternoon for a few hours.'

Jack sighed.

'Next time,' said Patrick.

'You're going into the office this afternoon?' said Ellen.

Patrick glanced over at her. 'Oh, yeah, sorry, didn't I tell you? I've got to catch up on some paperwork. I've just been swamped.'

So presumably that meant she would be the one taking care of Jack. She'd been planning to catch up with Julia this afternoon. It had been ages since she'd seen her, and Julia was looking forward to hearing all about the visit to Colleen's parents. She could hardly speak freely if she had Jack with her.

'So I'm looking after Jack this afternoon?' she double-checked.

'Well, he's big enough, he doesn't need a babysitter any

more, do you, mate?' said Patrick. 'He'll just do his own thing. Actually, you've got some homework to finish off, haven't you, Jack?'

Ellen suppressed a sigh. Since Patrick and Jack had moved into her house, she'd experienced the pleasure of homework supervision for the first time. It was awful. It was so hard to get Jack to just sit upright at the table with his pencil in hand and his books open in front of him. He would half slide off his chair, resting his cheek on the table, as if he were ill, or else he'd keep running off, disappearing on unexplained errands as they occurred to him.

She was still finding her way with Jack. It wasn't like he was rebelling against her, or treating her like a wicked stepmother. He was perfectly friendly and relaxed with Ellen; she was the one who felt on edge. She noticed that her voice got terribly *bouncy* whenever she talked to him. It reminded her of being fourteen and in love with the one-legged boy at the neighbouring school. Giles was kind to her, as he was to all the girls who adored him, and the patient, distracted expression he got on his face while Ellen babbled on at the railway station, trying desperately to make some sort of impression before the 3.45 train arrived, was identical to the one on Jack's face. It said: *I couldn't care less really, but I'm a nice person, and I don't want to hurt your feelings so I'm just going to keep smiling until you stop talking*.

And it was even worse when she tried to play it cool, to act as if she didn't care what Jack thought of her, because he was so self-contained, so busy with his own life, that he really did just completely forget about her existence, which was exactly what used to happened with Giles too.

Well, this was what she had signed up for. She'd loved the idea of a stepchild; of an instant family. She should be happy that Patrick was treating her like a wife and taking it for granted that she would be in charge of homework this afternoon. She should be focusing all her attention on poor little Jack, who had lost not one but *two* mothers by the age of five and was probably suffering from terrible abandonment issues.

'*YES!*' shouted Jack, holding his computer game aloft.

'Jesus,' said Patrick. 'Don't kick the back of my seat.'

But shouldn't Patrick have checked with her first? Wasn't he taking advantage of her? To assume she'd be available?

Of course, then again, she herself hadn't bothered to check with Patrick before she'd made the arrangement to have coffee with Julia. So she'd been acting like a single person, too, as if Jack wasn't her responsibility at all.

It was so difficult to work out what was fair and what wasn't. Presumably parents had some sort of procedure, an approval process when you were making arrangements. She'd have to ask her friend Madeline about this.

'I thought you said you'd clear out all the boxes from the hallway this afternoon,' said Ellen.

Saturday had been taken up with Jack's sports activities and Patrick had promised he'd have the boxes gone by the end of the weekend.

'Oh, sure, don't worry,' said Patrick. 'When I get back from the office I'll do it.'

He wouldn't. She knew he wouldn't. He'd be too tired after today's trip, and then the office. It would be too late. Jack would want his attention when he got home, and then Patrick would want to collapse on the couch in front of *60 Minutes*. It would be mean to remind him then. It would be considered 'nagging'. She would have to put up with another week of those boxes sitting in the hallway.

All that clutter was having a catastrophic effect on the *feng shui* of her house. She seemed to remember that the front entrance was called 'the mouth of chi' where all the energy was meant to flow through. No *wonder* she was feeling so irritable – all the energy was being stopped at the front door!

Of course, now was certainly not the time to push the issue of the boxes; not when Patrick was so uptight about the lunch with Frank and Millie.

But the words were as irresistible as the last chocolate in the box.

'You won't move them,' she murmured to the window, as if saying it quietly didn't really count.

'What did you say?' Patrick spoke sharply.

'Nothing.'

'Ellen! I just said I *would* move them.'

'So you did hear me.'

'Are you two fighting?' asked Jack with interest.

So much for beautiful poignant moments, thought Ellen.

I decided I would spend the rest of Sunday watching television. A few months ago Lance, who works in the office next to mine, lent me the series of *The Wire*. He and his wife are always developing obsessions with TV series and then he talks on and on about the fabulous character development and the amazing plotlines and the whatever – it's just television. I always want to say,

'Look, Lance, I'm not that interested in television. I have a life.'

Ha. Good one.

Such a pity that 'stalking' isn't a socially acceptable hobby.

For some reason he insisted on lending me the series, even though I'm sure I'd showed minimal interest. He wants me to watch it so we can talk at length about each episode. I know this because he lent the *West Wing* to another girl in the office, and then every time he saw her he wanted to know what episode she was up to, so he could do an in-depth analysis. Eventually she started hiding, leaping into nearby offices whenever she saw him coming down the corridor.

So I was never going to bother watching it and Lance has given up asking me if I've seen the 'pilot' yet, but suddenly it seemed like the perfect way to swallow up a whole Sunday. I would eat toast and chocolate and try to let the rest of the day go by without even thinking of Patrick, Ellen or Jack. I was even looking forward to it.

But, of course, like so many other things, it wasn't meant to be.

When I drove into my driveway, the new family from next door were pulling in too, with impeccably horrible timing.

They moved in on Friday, and they're just as bad as I knew they would be. A swinging-ponytail Mummy and a bald-in-a-cool-way Daddy. A little girl with freckles and curls. A little boy with dimples. They're adorable and athletic, friendly and frisky. It's going to be like living next door to four Labradors. They introduced themselves and said they hoped they wouldn't be too noisy, and I must tell them if they were, and they must have me over for drinks some time. I tried to be polite but stand-offish, so they would know that none of this was necessary, that all that was required was a friendly wave. Jeff or the real estate agent should have explained this to them. The garage door sticks, garbage night is Monday, the neighbour doesn't require conversation.

As soon as I got out of the car they all came bounding over to me, their tongues hanging out, tails wagging. I nearly held up a palm to ward them off.

'Do you want to come over to our place this afternoon?' asked the little girl.

'Give Saskia a minute,' said the mother, all loving laughter. She's at least fifteen years younger than me. Maybe more. I had no memory of her name. I hadn't even bothered to register it.

They wanted to know if I would like to come over for a 'house-warming barbecue' that afternoon.

'Just a few friends,' said the mother. 'Just very casual.'

'The next-door neighbour at our last house was called Mrs Short,' the little boy told me. 'But she actually wasn't short. She was actually pretty tall.'

'Huh,' I said.

The boy reminded me a little of Jack, something about the eyes maybe. Or perhaps it's just the age. He looks about five, the same age as Jack was when Patrick and I broke up. I didn't want to make friends with him. Just looking at him made my chest hurt.

'Or even if you just wanted to stop by for a quick drink,' suggested the father.

'We've got special sausages,' said the little girl. 'They've got chilli in them.'

'No pressure, don't feel obligated!' said the mother. 'We just thought – you know, if you didn't have anything else on, seeing as we're sort of sharing a house, we've never lived in a duplex before, so we thought – but of course you probably have other plans, or you might prefer to just relax on a Sunday.'

She stopped, a little flustered. I saw her husband give her a look. They could sense my resistance and they were giving me a way out. They're nice. Nice, polite, ordinary people. That's all I need. To be living next door to nice people. They make me feel so inferior.

So much for my day at home sedating myself with television. I told them I would have loved to have joined them but I had another commitment that would take up most of the day.

I overdid it with my regrets. I shouldn't have acted at all regretful.

'Another time!' said the father.

'Another time!' said the mother.

'Another time!' said I.

'Another time!' said the little boy, and we all laughed oh so heartily, and the poor kid frowned because, after all, why was it funny when he said it?

So, fabulous. Now there will be another time.

I went inside and spent quite a lot of time preparing for my fake social obligation. I decided I was going to an old friend's fortieth birthday party. It was just a casual but elegant event in their backyard. There would be lots of kids running about, and they were having it catered – I decided they were well-off friends; in fact, their house actually backed on to the harbour – so the food would be good. I would be doing a speech! It would be funny and sentimental. The sort of speech that Ellen would do at a friend's fortieth birthday party.

I dressed in jeans, boots, a really beautiful blue top that Tammy had bought me for my birthday just before Mum died, that I'd never found the right occasion to wear – a fortieth birthday by the harbour, perfect! – and a long scarf that Mum had made for me. I knew that everyone at the party would compliment me on the scarf. My mother was very talented, I would tell them. I even blow-dried my hair and put on make-up and a pair of big earrings that Patrick always said made me look sexy.

By the time I walked out the door I was feeling the most attractive I'd felt in a long time.

On impulse I grabbed together the ingredients I'd bought for the Anzac biscuits and put them in a plastic bag. I decided I would drop them off at Ellen's front door on my way to the party. She could make biscuits; I was too busy with my active social life.

As I walked to my car, a man and woman were walking up the driveway towards the neighbours' house for the house-warming barbecue. The man was holding a bottle of wine and the woman was carrying a large plate wrapped in aluminium foil.

I smiled at them, and said 'Hi!' as if I was a person too; a person off to a fortieth birthday party on a Sunday.

They smiled back. In fact the man's smile seemed especially friendly, not at all perfunctory, almost as if he knew me, and was trying to place me, or almost as if – could it be? – he found me attractive.

'Coming over to the party?' he said.

'No, I've got another one to go to,' I said. 'A fortieth.'

'Oh, well, have fun!' he said, at the same time as the neighbours' front door was opening and the next-door neighbours came out crying, 'Look who's here!' and 'So you found us OK?'

I went to my car quickly, before they felt they had to introduce me. There was none of this awkwardness when Jeff lived next door; neither of us ever had anyone over. As I turned on the ignition and waved goodbye, I saw the man was still watching me. He lifted his hand to wave goodbye and I felt a warm feeling, like the way I remembered happiness felt.

I reversed out on to the street and glanced back, smiling, ready to wave again if someone caught my eye, and saw that none of them were looking at me. The woman was handing over the aluminium-wrapped plate, and as she did so, I saw the man pulling her towards him, his hand on her hip, in the same mock-masterful way that Patrick used to do, and she was laughing up at him and the little boy from next door was pulling at his free hand, wanting to point something out to him.

The warm feeling vanished like a slap in the face.

He hadn't found me attractive at all. He was just one of those nice, friendly people who liked everyone. It made sense. The nice people next door would know other nice people. They tend to congregate.

Or possibly he had found me attractive, but in a slimy, sleazy, I'm-happy-to-cheat-on-my-girlfriend-if-you're-up-for-it way. He was probably the sort of man who smiled at every woman like that, just in case he was in with a chance.

And then I thought: *Where the fuck am I going to go now?*

The fortieth birthday party in the house by the harbour had begun to seem so real, I'd almost been looking forward to it.

I had nowhere to go. Once upon a time there were people I could have called. It's amazing how friends can slip through your fingers; how your social network can vanish as if it never existed. If you don't have a family, if you live in a city that is designed so that you don't need to connect with anyone, so you drive everywhere, so there is nowhere to walk and nod hello, so you can do all your shopping in soulless supermarkets with blank-faced teenagers scanning your groceries while they look right through you as if you don't exist, because you don't, not really.

If I lived in a town like the ones I once wanted to design, there would be somewhere I could go, where I wouldn't feel alone, somewhere open and light where I could drink a cup of coffee and read a book in a place that encouraged conversation.

Which is all such self-delusional crap because I could not bear to live somewhere lovely, where I would be forced to talk to people every day, a whole town of horrendously nice people, smiling their sunny smiles at me when I just wanted to buy a small carton of milk without anybody asking about my weekend.

I'm not lonely. I'm just alone. I choose to be alone.

I know exactly what I need to do if I want to step back into society. I could watch *The Wire* and talk to Lance about it, and then I could offer to lend him a DVD series, and then one day I could say, 'Do you and your wife want to come over for dinner some time?' Didn't I meet his wife once? I could say, 'Do you want to have a drink one night after work?' to any number of people in the office. I could have said 'yes' to that work party a few months back. I could have said 'yes' to the people next door. I could even get on the Internet and meet men who wanted a relationship, or at least sex.

I am not socially disabled. I am reserved, sometimes shy – but not in a debilitating way. I could do it. I did it when I moved to Sydney and didn't know a soul. I participated. I said 'yes' to invitations. I smiled and asked questions and made the first move.

But now I can't be bothered to do it again. I'm too old, and this is the crux of it – *it's not fair*. I shouldn't have to be in this position again.

I can't bear the pretence, the fraudulent cheeriness, like when I spoke to the people next door. I would be pretending all the time, because you have to fake it in the beginning – that's the way it works.

But once I had a real relationship with real friends. Once I was a mother and a wife and a friend and a daughter, and now I am nothing.

And if I moved on, if I lived a regular life, it would be like Patrick had got away with it, as if he was right: we weren't meant to be together.

I drove to Ellen's house, and my regular feeling, that permanent feeling of pain and loss and fury, felt even worse than usual because it had disappeared for a few seconds.

I was just going to leave the plastic bag with the ingredients at the front door – no need for a note, they would know they were from me – but as I was about to go back down the footpath, I saw she had a little miniature stone owl, with glasses, sitting up on the cornice above her door, and I thought, *I bet she keeps her spare key under the owl.*

And I was right.

17

DON'T THINK OF A DOG! You thought of a dog, didn't you? That's why it's so important to be careful with your language when you're structuring your suggestions. It's what's known as the law of reversed effect. The imagination ignores the word 'Don't' and just hears 'Dog'
— Excerpt from Ellen O'Farrell's *Introduction to Hypnotherapy* two-day course

Colleen's parents came out on to their front porch as soon as Patrick drove the car into the driveway.

'That's them. Frank and Millie.' Patrick spoke in an odd, strained voice and waved, smiling with his teeth clenched.

Jack threw open the car door and ran to his grandparents. Ellen and Patrick watched as he hugged them. It seemed like he was going to be the only one acting naturally today.

'Right,' said Patrick, and they got out of the car.

'Quick!' called out Millie from the doorway, beckoning to him, as Jack disappeared inside with his grandfather. 'Come inside, you two, where it's nice and warm!'

'Hi, Millie! Yes! Good idea!' called back Patrick in a jolly tone Ellen had never heard him use before.

Good Lord, she thought.

'Hel-*looo*!' she cried out, in a desperate rush to demonstrate to Colleen's parents she was a friendly, nice person and so very sorry for their loss.

(Oh God, why had she called out 'hello' in that echoey voice? As if she was shouting to them across a mountain top? She sounded deranged.)

Millie was right. The house seemed especially cosy and warm after the chilly visit to the graveyard. There was soft music playing, and Millie led Ellen to a seat right next to it.

'What can I get you to drink?' she asked. She was a tiny bird-like woman, wearing a younger person's outfit of jeans and a white jumper that hung on her thin frame. You could see that once she'd been beautiful, and there was something about her, a look of resigned acceptance, that said, *I know I'm no longer beautiful and I couldn't care less.*

Her husband, Frank, was thin too, and very tall, like an elderly, stooped basketball player. Ellen saw how grief had dragged at their faces, like faded claw marks.

They seemed like shy people but they were all smiles, gracious and welcoming, chatting about the traffic and the weather. It broke Ellen's heart. If only they weren't so damned nice.

'What Ellen really needs is a dry cracker,' said Patrick. 'She's feeling nauseous. The, ah, pregnancy, you know.' Did she imagine that he'd lowered his voice on the word 'pregnancy' as if it was a shameful disorder?

'I'll get you one straight away,' said Millie.

'I had some ready at home but then I forgot to bring them. I'm so sorry to be a nuisance,' Ellen babbled, as if asking for a cracker was a huge inconvenience, when what she really meant was that she was so sorry to be there at all, inconveniently alive and pregnant, taking their daughter's place.

'When I was pregnant with Colleen I ate dry biscuits all day long,' said Millie, as she handed over the plate. 'But then when she was pregnant with Jack the lucky girl didn't get any nausea at all.'

She smiled at her grandson. 'You were such a well-behaved baby, Jack, even before you were born.' She turned back to Ellen. 'Not that I mean your own little baby isn't well behaved.'

As Millie spoke, Ellen caught sight of a framed photo of Colleen on the wall, holding Jack when he must have been about six months old. She was smiling adoringly down at him, while Jack gnawed on the leg of a toy rabbit.

That's when it happened.

She burst into tears, choking on her cracker, spraying crumbs, causing everyone to stare at her with alarm and astonishment.

What are you doing? It was as if her body had done something unmentionable in polite company, like an explosive fart. *Stop it*, she ordered herself but the tears kept sliding down her face.

It was a combination of the adoration on Colleen's face in the picture, the exquisite relief of eating the cracker, the warmth of the house after the cold mountain air, Millie saying 'your own little baby', the strangeness and stress of the graveyard visit, the fact that she was meeting her father for the first time the following day – oh, who knew what it was, except that her emotions had never embarrassed her like that before.

'*Hey* now,' said Frank, and he came over to where she was sitting, squatted down on his long spidery legs and rubbed her back in gentle circular motions.

Lucky Colleen to have grown up with a lovely father like Frank.

'What's wrong, Ellen?' asked Jack.

He'd looked to his father, but Patrick was no help. He had the stunned expression of someone whose girl-friend has just knocked over a priceless vase. He'd kept up a steady stream of conversation ever since he'd walked in the house, his voice light and chatty, but with a panicky undertone, as if he was trying to distract some-one from jumping off a cliff by talking about ordinary things while he waited for the police. Ellen had never seen him talk so much, and she saw that these visits were a huge effort for him, and that he was determined to ensure there were no conversational gaps or uncomfort-able silences that might allow for horrible displays of grief. Now she'd upset the delicate balance he was work-ing so hard to maintain.

'So sorry,' she finally sniffed. 'It must be my hormones.'

Hormones, hormones, hormones. It was all she talked about lately and yet she'd never believed in blaming her body for her behaviour! She'd always believed that the mind–body connection was more likely to operate in the other direction: the mind affecting the body, not the body affecting the mind. If a client had described this irrational behaviour and then tried to blame it on hormones, she would have said (in such a soothing, know-it-all tone!), 'I suspect this is your body's way of trying to pass on a mes-sage from your subconscious.'

Patrick finally recovered enough to move over and hug her.

'You're probably just exhausted from the drive,' he said, speaking in his normal voice, and the relief of feeling his arms round her and breathing in his familiar Patrick scent nearly made her cry again.

'So sorry,' she said shakily.

'Don't think anything of it,' Frank and Millie soothed.

She worked hard to redeem herself over lunch, following Patrick's bright, chatty lead. They bounced the conversation rapidly back and forth across the table, without letting it drop once, as if they were playing hot potato. When they were ready to leave, she noticed that Frank and Millie looked drained. They probably wished the two of them had just shut up for a second.

'We hope to see you next month, my dear,' said Millie when they were leaving, and she'd put her hand on Ellen's arm. A voice in Ellen's head boomed: CRY AGAIN AND YOU'RE DEAD.

Nobody said anything as they drove out of Katoomba. Jack seemed to be slumbering in the back seat. Finally, Ellen couldn't bear it any longer.

'I'm sorry about my unexpected weeping back there,' she said, as if the word 'weeping' would turn it into a charming, rather fascinating little incident.

'It's fine,' said Patrick. 'Seriously. Don't worry about it.'

That's where she should have left it.

'They must have found it so difficult,' she said. 'Meeting me, and the new baby.'

'Yes,' he said. 'Although of course *you* were the one doing the crying!'

The sting was so sharp she caught her breath.

'I'm sorry,' he said almost immediately, taking one hand off the steering wheel to reach for her. 'That was meant to be a joke. A really stupid joke. Whenever I see Frank and Millie I feel guilty for being alive when Colleen is dead. I find those visits really hard. Awkward.'

No kidding.

'Yes. I found it very awkward myself,' she said. *I sat on your dead wife's grave! These grass stains will never come out!*

'I'm sorry,' he said again, putting his hand back on the steering wheel. 'Really. You were wonderful today. I'm so grateful to you for coming. I just wish . . .'

His voice drifted away, and then he stopped talking, and frowned at the road ahead, as if driving now required all his concentration.

What did he mean? I just wish you hadn't cried? I just wish Colleen wasn't dead? Ellen silently boiled and bubbled with different emotions she couldn't even properly define: shame, resentment and something like fear. *This is not me*, she kept thinking. *I am not like this.*

She broke the silence when they stopped at a red light. 'So, I guess you won't have time to move those boxes tonight.'

Even while she was saying it, another part of her looked on, coolly observing and shaking her head. *Oh, Ellen. You feel guilty about embarrassing him with your tears, so this is your childish way of pointing out that he's not perfect either. You're picking a fight because you want to make something happen.*

'I told you I've got to work this afternoon,' he said.

'So maybe we can make next weekend the new deadline?' she said, and her tone was light and humorous, but just like his joke, it had that fine thread of steel running though the centre of it.

'Don't nag me, Ellen,' he said, and as she turned to look at his profile she saw that he was clenching his jaw so tightly his cheek was hollow.

'*Nagging?* How am I nagging?'

'Not now. Not here,' he hissed, turning his head slightly to indicate Jack in the back seat, as if she'd deliberately picked a fight in front of his young, impressionable son.

They didn't say another word for the rest of the drive home. Ellen spent the entire time reliving that weekend in the mountains with Jon, deliberately lingering over the memories of their lovemaking. It was the most passive-aggressive thing she'd ever done.

By the time they got home, the air in the car was stuffy with silence.

'I'll see you later,' said Patrick shortly, before driving off and leaving Ellen to take Jack inside. She would have to remember to cancel her coffee with Julia before she got started on homework.

'What's this?' said Ellen as she opened the screen door.

There was a foil-wrapped package sitting next to the front door. She bent down and picked it up. It felt warm.

Her breath quickened. *Saskia.*

It was an impulse decision. I walked into her kitchen with the plastic bag full of ingredients and it was like I was returning home from the supermarket. I thought, *Why not cook some biscuits for them?*

I enjoyed being in her kitchen, using her mixing bowl,

her spoons, her baking trays. I have a feeling most of the things in her kitchen probably belonged to her grandmother. I remember her saying that she hadn't changed anything much when she inherited the house. 'I have sort of retro taste,' she told me once. I'd made some remark about liking the carpet. I guess that's something we have in common; apart from Patrick of course.

I felt strangely peaceful, as if I had every right to be in this house, as if I were Ellen, and Patrick and Jack were out somewhere and I was planning on surprising them with freshly baked biscuits, like I used to do when Jack was little and they went out to the park. I imagined them coming home, the sound of the key in the lock, the pounding of Jack's footsteps down the hallway.

Ellen's kitchen reminded me a lot of my mother's — perhaps that's why I felt so inappropriately comfortable, because I felt like I was in my childhood home. I remembered being a little girl, standing on a kitchen chair, one of Mum's aprons tied round my waist, helping her cook. I'd always imagined doing the same thing with my little girl one day.

In fact, I did do the same thing with Jack, except I never bothered with the apron, and I didn't stand him on a chair, I just let him sit up on the worktop next to me. He loved it. Flour in his hair, sticky fingers, eggshell in the mix. I let him use the beaters once and he lifted them up and splattered the entire kitchen with cake mix.

How could I have explained myself if they'd come home early?

I know this seems strange but I cannot bear my non-existence in your lives. If I could just move in with you, maybe? If I could just sit quietly in the corner over there and watch you live? So anyway, how was your day in the mountains? Biscuit, anyone?

They didn't come home but somebody did stop by.

I was just taking the biscuits out of the oven when the doorbell rang.

I jumped. Guiltily. I haven't completely lost my mind. I know that you're not meant to walk into someone else's house and start making biscuits.

After the bell rang, someone started banging on the front door.

My first thought was that it was Patrick, something about the angry tone of the knocking; even though that didn't make sense, because why wouldn't he just walk straight in?

And then I thought maybe it was the police. Someone had seen me take the key and called them. A friendly neighbour perhaps. Ellen is the sort to have a friendly neighbour.

I put down the biscuits and crept down the hallway, past all Patrick's boxes, piled up all higgledy-piggledy. Poor Ellen; her house doesn't have quite the same spiritual feel to it now, with all these dusty boxes. I wonder if she hates it, or if she is above such earthly matters. If I know Patrick they'll be sitting there for a long time.

I looked out the side window near Ellen's front door and I could see a man. He'd shoved his hands in his pockets and stuck his jaw out, as if he was ready for a confrontation. He was in his forties. There was something premium-looking about him, something that said money: maybe it was the suit, or the longish, carefully tousled haircut, or just the way he was standing with his feet firmly planted, as if he was in charge.

I was intrigued.

A customer in need of a hypnotic fix?

An ex-boyfriend of Ellen's? He didn't seem her type. I'm sure Patrick isn't her type either – he's too ordinary and blokey. She should be with a pale and interesting poet, and give me back my hale and hearty surveyor.

A lover? *Perhaps Patrick wasn't the baby's father.* That would be perfect. Could this visitor, this really quite angry-looking man, be a spanner in their works?

I opened the door.

18

It's funny that people call hypnotherapy 'new age'. Hieroglyphics found on tombs indicate that the Egyptians were using hypnosis as early as 3000 BC.

– Excerpt from www.EllenOFarrellHypnotherapy.com

'Listen to this, Madeline.'

Julia put her hand on Madeline's arm and Ellen watched Madeline flinch slightly. It was Wednesday night and the three of them were out having dinner at a crowded Thai restaurant before they saw a movie. They were squashed together in a booth table. The movie started at 9.00 p.m. and it was 7.30 p.m. now, and they'd only just managed to get their menus delivered. They were going to be late for the movie, which would irritate Madeline, while Julia would make a show of not letting it worry her, being the free and easy type that she wasn't.

Julia and Madeline didn't get on, and they only pretended to like each other for Ellen's sake. As the 'mutual friend', Ellen normally made a point of seeing them separately but she'd known that they both had wanted to see the new George Clooney movie, so it had seemed silly not to ask the two of them.

Now she reminded herself not to do it again. Julia always seemed to want to make it clear to Madeline that she was the longer-standing friend, bringing up stories from their school days, mentioning old friends and behaving in a slightly adolescent fashion. Madeline refused to take part in the *I'm the better friend of Ellen* competition and instead took refuge in her role as the only mother among the three of them. She maintained a permanent distracted, harried expression, as if she was listening out for a child's cry. At the moment she was eight months pregnant, so she was even worse than usual, with one hand permanently pressed to her belly. Now that Ellen was pregnant too, Madeline had the edge over Julia and she was using it to full advantage, constantly steering the conversation back to babies. As the only one drinking, Julia was working her way through a bottle of wine, and fighting back by using every opportunity to imply that she adored her child-free existence and high-flying career.

Ellen wanted to grab both their hands and say: *Relax!*

'What?' said Madeline. She moved her hand slightly away from Julia's. She wasn't a touchy-feely sort of person. Julia, picking up on this, was always touching Madeline's arm, and kissed her ostentatiously whenever they all met.

'Her stalker leaves her freshly baked biscuits at her front door – and does she toss them straight in the trash and call the police, like any normal, sane person would do?' said Julia. 'No, she makes herself a cup of tea and she *eats* them!'

'I hope they didn't have nuts in them,' said Madeline. 'You should be avoiding peanuts when you're pregnant, did you know that?'

'*Nuts* are the very *least* of her worries!' cried Julia. 'The stalker would have spat in them for sure. Or worse. Oh

God, I'm gagging at the thought of what she could have done, Ellen, at what she probably did do. Seriously.'

'Well, what sort of biscuits were they?' asked Madeline.

'Shit-flavoured,' said Julia. She giggled so hard she keeled over sideways.

Madeline shifted herself away from Julia and smiled stiffly. 'How did you know they were from her?' she asked Ellen.

From her prone position Julia said, 'Were they chocolate chip?'

'They were Anzac biscuits, and I know they were from her because there was a note,' said Ellen. 'It said: *I made these today and I thought you might like some, love Saskia.*'

'Oh, that's so creepy.' Madeline shuddered with distaste to show that this sort of thing wouldn't be allowed to happen in her own orderly life.

'It gets worse,' said Ellen.

'It does?' Julia sat up again. Ellen had only given her half the story before Madeline arrived.

'I think she cooked them in my house,' said Ellen.

'Oh. My. God,' said Julia.

'What made you think that?' asked Madeline, calmly, because Julia had taken on the dramatic role.

'There was a smell of cooking in my kitchen,' said Ellen.

She remembered standing in the kitchen, after that strange, awful day in the mountains, breathing in the distinctive fragrances of golden syrup and brown sugar, her heart hammering, reminded so strongly of visits when her grandmother was alive. Her grandmother used to make Anzac biscuits all the time. Saskia's had been nearly as good as hers, maybe better. Crunchier.

'You might have imagined it,' said Julia.

'Probably not,' said Madeline. 'Your sense of smell is so acute when you're pregnant. When I was having Isabella, I once smelled –'

'No crumbs?' interrupted Julia. 'Or any other signs? Things moved in your cupboard?'

'The opposite of crumbs,' said Ellen. 'My oven was too clean. I think she cleaned it after she used it.'

'Why would she come to your kitchen and cook?' mused Julia. 'What point is this lunatic trying to make? What's the *message* she's trying to give you?'

'I hate cooking in someone else's kitchen,' commented Madeline. 'I can never find what I want.'

Julia blinked slowly at her and then turned back to Ellen. 'What did Patrick say?'

'I didn't tell him,' said Ellen. 'When we got back from the mountains he had to go straight to the office. He just dropped Jack and me off. There's no point telling him. It just upsets him.'

She didn't tell them that she and Patrick hadn't been talking by the time they got back from the mountains.

'Did you tell Jack?' said Julia.

'I just said a friend of mine left them,' said Ellen. 'He wasn't that interested.'

'You didn't let Jack eat them, did you?' asked Madeline.

'No,' said Ellen. 'I thought I'd better not. I distracted him with chocolate biscuits instead. We ate them while we did his homework.'

'Biscuits before dinner,' murmured Madeline.

'But you ate them yourself! You shouldn't have even

touched them,' said Julia. 'They could have been poisoned.'

'Not to mention the danger to your unborn child,' said Madeline.

Now the two of them were nodding in complete agreement, both with serious, responsible expressions on their faces.

'I know,' said Ellen. 'I didn't even think.'

And they'd smelled so good. It was ironic but she'd been upset and disconcerted by the sight of the biscuits, and then, when she pulled one out and held it by her fingertips, it felt like *exactly* the thing she needed to make herself feel better. And then it was so good, she had another one. So eating the biscuits made her feel better for the shock of receiving them. It wasn't until after she'd eaten three in a row that it even occurred to her that they could have been poisoned, and then she'd spent the rest of the evening secretly hyperventilating and Googling things like 'How long till poison takes effect?'

'You've been so weirdly flippant about this whole thing from the beginning.' Julia spoke at the same time as she tried to catch a waiter's attention on the other side of the room. 'This woman came into your home. She violated your privacy. Why aren't you terrified? And why is this waiter pretending he can't see me? You can see me, oh yes, you can!'

'I don't know,' said Ellen. 'I am a little bit terrified.'

Ever since the incident with the biscuits, she'd felt a permanent sense of slight breathlessness, as if she was running late for something important. The previous night she'd woken up just before dawn with the thought clear in her head, *Something bad is going to happen*. Saskia wasn't going to stop until something happened. But what? What needed to happen?

It seemed to her that it wasn't about Saskia and Patrick any more. It was about Saskia and Ellen. It was between the two women. And if she could just work out the right thing to do, or the right words to say, maybe she could end it. But what to say? What to do? *What?* It felt like that endless moment just after you've knocked something breakable off a table, and instead of grabbing it from the air you freeze with one arm outstretched, and after it smashes you think, 'I could have stopped that from happening.'

'You should be *completely* terrified,' said Madeline sternly. 'All the time.'

'Thank you so much,' said Ellen. 'That's extremely comforting.'

'What I don't understand is why you haven't got the police involved,' said Julia. 'There should be a restraining order out against her, and then each time she breaks it, you call the cops, *wham*, she's in handcuffs. Problem solved.'

'Patrick did go to the police once,' said Ellen. 'And he keeps talking about going again, but then he doesn't ever seem to get round to it. Also, I don't think it's quite as easy as you describe.'

'I've heard restraining orders are pretty useless,' agreed Madeline.

'*You* go to the police then,' ordered Julia, pointing at Ellen and ignoring Madeline.

There had been a moment, when she was holding her oven mitt, her *grandmother's* oven mitt, thinking about the fact that Saskia had probably used it, slid her hands inside its soft cloth to protect her hands, when Ellen had been filled with outrage at the sheer audacity of this woman. She'd marched towards the phone to call the police, but then she'd stopped before she even picked up the receiver. How could she prove it? *Sniff the air, officer, can't you smell the scent of baking? And just look how clean my oven is! I never left it that clean!* She would have looked like a fool.

And besides, it was up to Patrick, and for whatever reason, he still wasn't ready to get the police involved.

'She's never shown any signs of being violent,' she said feebly.

'Not yet,' said Madeline.

'You do realize she's going to turn up at your wedding,' said Julia. 'When the priest says that "if anyone here present knows of any reason why these two should not be joined in holy matrimony", she'll pipe up, "Oh, me, me!"'

'I don't think they actually say that any more,' said Ellen.

Julia talked over the top of her. 'She'll come charging down the aisle saying "I'm the reason!"'

'She might bring a gun,' said Madeline enthusiastically.

'You'll have to wear a bullet-proof vest under your gown,' said Julia.

'I don't think I'll bring my children,' mused Madeline.

'Mmmm,' said Ellen. This was why she and Patrick hadn't got very far with their wedding plans. Every time they started talking about it, the conversation came back to Saskia. 'Even if we go overseas she'll probably track us down,' Patrick had said.

He'd seemed relieved when Ellen suggested perhaps they should just wait until after the baby was born, even though his mother would probably 'have kittens' about the child being 'born out of wedlock'.

Ellen's nausea wasn't making her feel very bridal anyway.

'You must hate her,' said Madeline. '*I* hate her on your behalf. You can't even plan your own wedding!'

'I don't hate her,' said Ellen. 'Not really. I'd actually quite like to talk to her.'

'Yes, good idea, ask your stalker out for coffee,' guffawed Julia.

'Ring her up now and ask her to join us at the movies,' said Madeline, with a quick, shy grin at Julia.

Julia laughed harder than was necessary. They were bonding over Ellen's foolishness.

'I might ring her one day,' said Ellen thoughtfully. She stirred her glass of mineral water with her straw and watched the bubbles. 'I just might.'

Ever since Sunday I've been thinking about the man who came to Ellen's house.

'Ellen O'Farrell?' he said when I opened the door and he sort of lunged at me. I stepped back and kept the screen door shut.

'No,' I said. 'She's not here.'

'OK, who are you?' He had the tone of voice of someone who demands and receives the very best service. He reminded me of the developers I deal with at work. Men who are so very, very sure of their place in the world.

'Well, who are you?' I said, quite snootily, which is funny, seeing as I was actually the intruder.

'I'm someone who needs to talk to her,' he said. His nostrils flared. 'Urgently.'

'I could give her a message,' I offered, imagining a jaunty little note left on a Post-it on her fridge. *Angry man dropped by who needs to see you urgently, love Saskia.*

'Don't bother.' He looked like he was trying hard not to punch a wall. 'I'll come back another time.'

'You do that,' I said spiritedly.

And then he left.

It was strange but, as I closed the door, I actually felt defensive on Ellen's behalf. There's something so guileless about her, as if she believes everyone is as sweet and sincere as her. When clearly we're not.

Also, I had a strong feeling that I knew that man from somewhere. I just couldn't quite pin it down.

'So what was it like meeting the dead wife's family?' asked Julia. Her cheeks were flushed from all the wine she was drinking, and she'd rubbed her eyes so her mascara was faintly smudged under her eyes, giving her a sexily dishevelled look. In the restaurant's shadowy mood lighting she looked the way she had when Ellen and she used to take their fake IDs so they could go out drinking together in high school, during their not especially impressive, short-lived rebellious phase. (Her mother and godmothers had got up to much worse when they were teenagers.)

'Oh, but wait, I want to hear about meeting your dad!' Madeline sat back and laced her hands together under her breasts and across the top of her big belly. As she moved, Ellen's elbow bumped against the firm flesh of her belly, and she was shocked by the reality of Madeline's baby. There was an actual baby just centimetres away from Ellen's elbow. Not just the idea of a baby. A real live baby curled up under the striped fabric of Madeline's maternity top and the stretched skin of her stomach. Ellen secretly laced her own hands together in imitation of Madeline, and placed them across her own stomach, which was still soft and only faintly, implausibly rounded, as if she'd just been enjoying a few too many pizzas. Her clothes were starting to feel tighter but it was impossible to imagine that in a few months she'd have an enormous stomach like Madeline's, one that would give her that characteristic pregnant sway-backed gait, one that would cause people to smile and offer a chair and ask, 'How much longer now?'

'Her life is like a soap opera, these days, isn't it?' said Julia.

'Like sand through the hour glass, so are the days of Ellen's lives,' intoned Madeline in a quite good American accent. Ellen had never heard her put on a voice before to make a joke.

'Remember when she was so calm and Zen? Nothing messy ever happened to her?' said Julia.

'That's not true!' protested Ellen. 'I had messy relationship break-ups.'

'No, even your break-ups seemed to happen on a higher level of existence to the rest of us,' said Madeline.

'That makes me sound annoying,' said Ellen. She was hurt, as if she had overheard a conversation that revealed what her friends really thought of her.

Julia and Madeline were too busy liking each for the first time to notice.

'Oh, not that annoying. Anyway, me first,' said Julia. 'The wife's family?'

'Maybe we should just concentrate on eating quickly

and efficiently,' said Ellen, as a waiter appeared at their table with three giant plates balanced on his forearm.

'Let's skip the movie,' said Madeline. 'Let's just relax.'

'Excellent idea.' Julia settled back in her booth and smiled at Madeline.

Watching them talking to the waiter, confirming what each dish was, leaning back politely to let him spoon out their rice, Ellen saw for the first time that the two of them were actually quite similar. Their carefully relaxed demeanours hid a fragile defensiveness, as if they expected to be criticized at any moment and they weren't going to stand for it. They both seemed to cling so hard to their chosen personalities. *I am this sort of person and therefore I believe this, I think this, I do this and I'm right, I'm right, I'm sure I'm right!*

Although then again maybe everybody did that to some extent. Perhaps all grown-ups were just children carefully putting on their grown-up disguises each day and then acting accordingly. Perhaps it was a necessary part of being a grown-up. Or perhaps it was just that Ellen felt herself to have a more nebulous, less defined sort of personality than both Madeline and Julia.

Or perhaps this was all a load of rubbish, and Madeline and Julia were just being themselves. Lately, Ellen was becoming increasingly impatient with the way she never just accepted anything at face value. She couldn't quite understand her impatience. It was as if she'd suddenly turned against a dear old friend for no good reason.

'It must have been so awkward,' said Madeline. 'Meeting Patrick's old in-laws.'

'Do you think they hated you?' asked Julia. 'Replacing their beloved daughter?'

'They were lovely,' said Ellen. 'They seemed perfectly relaxed about it, but I made a fool of myself.'

'Oh, *no*,' said Julia, as if Ellen was in the habit of making a fool of herself. 'What did you do?'

'I saw a photo on the wall of Colleen holding Jack when he was a baby and I . . .'

'You *criticized* her?' said Julia. 'You spoke ill of the dead!'

Julia was terrified of death. Whenever she was confronted with it, she became skittish and weird, as if she could somehow ward it off.

'Does that sound like something I'd do?' said Ellen, as she lifted her spoon to her mouth.

'Shellfish!' screeched Madeline, and knocked the spoon from Ellen's mouth.

'It's not!' Ellen indicated the plate in front of her. 'It's the chicken.'

'Oh, sorry, you're right,' said Madeline. 'Carry on.'

'Anyway, I think this whole thing with what you can and can't eat when you're pregnant has gone too far,' said Ellen. 'The French still eat soft cheeses and drink wine, the Japanese still eat sushi – and their babies are all fine.'

Madeline pursed her lips, as if she wasn't quite convinced about the quality of French and Japanese babies. 'I wouldn't be taking any risks in the first trimester.'

Julia's face closed down slightly at the pregnancy talk. 'So what did you do when you saw the photo?'

'I cried,' said Ellen.

'You *cried*? You didn't even know the girl!' Madeline put down her fork, as if she'd just tasted something disgusting; she was clearly mortified on Ellen's behalf.

'Why would you cry?' asked Julia with interest.

'Pregnancy hormones,' said Madeline wisely. 'Although you can't spend the next nine months behaving like that! Couldn't you, I don't know, hypnotize yourself or something?'

It was clear just how seriously Madeline was taking this that she'd suggested self-hypnosis. Ellen knew that Madeline thought hypnotherapy was a load of new age nonsense, a waste of people's time, a waste of money, quackery, plain silly, misguided but well meaning, or something like that anyway; she didn't know which actual phrases Madeline would use, but she knew, from the carefully polite blank expression that crossed Madeline's face whenever Ellen's career came up, that it would be something along those lines. Ellen had never pushed because she knew Madeline would lie to be polite, and she'd lie badly, and Ellen didn't see the need to make her uncomfortable. She knew that Madeline was fond of her, and that she would never want to hurt Ellen's feelings.

Up until now, Ellen hadn't minded about the lack of balance in their conversation. In fact, she'd enjoyed a slightly superior feeling about her maturity in the face of Madeline's prejudice. Her sense of self-worth didn't rely on other people's approval. But now she felt a powerful surge of resentment. Her work was important to her. It was a huge part of her life. Why hadn't Madeline at least tried to learn more about hypnotherapy? She'd never even asked a single question about her work! What was that about? It was disrespectful. In fact, it was infuriating.

'Have I got something in my teeth?' asked Madeline, flustered. She turned to the mirrored wall. 'Why are you staring at me like that?'

Ellen cleared her throat. It would not be appropriate to suddenly shriek, 'Why have we never talked about my *job*, Madeline?'

What was wrong with her lately? Pregnancy seemed to be stripping away all her emotional maturity. She had all these new, raw, out-of-control feelings. Moments of pure fury followed by hopeless despair. Good Lord. She was behaving like a *client*.

'Sorry,' said Ellen. 'I drifted off.'

'Well, I think there must have been more to it than just hormones,' said Julia. 'Did it make you feel guilty? Knowing that you were having a baby with her husband? Of course, you're the expert on repressed feelings.'

Ellen gave Julia a grateful look. Unlike Madeline, Julia had always been entirely respectful and proud of Ellen's work. Over the years she'd referred dozens of friends and acquaintances to her. Yes, she was a dear, dear friend.

'Goodness, are you crying *now*?' asked Julia. 'Just remembering it?'

'No, sorry, I just –' Ellen began to giggle hopelessly.

She saw Julia and Madeline exchange looks.

'I know pregnant women go a bit crazy,' said Julia, 'but isn't this excessive?'

'Yes,' said Madeline.

'I hate to think what you did when you met your father for the first time,' said Julia. 'You must have needed a sedative.' She put the back of her hand to her forehead. 'Daddy, Daddy! My long lost daddy!'

Madeline chortled, and then looked guilty. 'Although, I guess, maybe meeting your father probably was quite emotional, wasn't it?'

'Actually,' said Ellen, 'I had the opposite problem. I felt nothing. Absolutely nothing.'

'Really?' Madeline looked relieved. That was more like it.

'He was just a man,' said Ellen. 'A dull, ordinary man. Like your dentist. Or your accountant. Receding hairline. Glasses. I just didn't find him that interesting.'

'Poor Daddy,' said Julia into her wine glass.

'You know what I really want to talk about?' Ellen put down her knife and fork. 'Boxes. Boxes clogging up my hallway.'

'That doesn't sound especially interesting,' said Julia.

'They're Patrick's, right?' Madeline immediately grasped the situation.

'Yes,' said Ellen. 'I've asked and asked and he won't move them. It's driving me crazy. How do you make a man do something without nagging?'

'That,' said Madeline, 'is the billion-dollar question.'

I was watching the late news tonight when it suddenly came to me.

I knew exactly who that man was.

So what did *he* want with Ellen? And why was he so angry with her?

Ellen sat in the car in the dark without turning the keys in the ignition and luxuriated in the sudden silence after the noisy babble of the restaurant. Her ears were buzzing and she felt over-stimulated, as if she'd just been having a crazy drunken night out in a nightclub, not a sedate, alcohol-free dinner with two old friends. For some reason she had found Julia and Madeline a little overwhelming tonight. Their faces in that crowded booth had been so close to hers: Julia's fine-boned face with the surprising lines around the eyes (surprising because she'd always think of her as a fourteen-year-old schoolgirl) and Madeline's plumper, softer features with the upturned nose and the rosebud lips. Ellen could still smell Julia's perfume, and hear the rhythms of Madeline's slightly hoarse voice (she had the beginnings of a cold).

'I'm seeing Sam tomorrow night,' Julia had said to her, as they stood on the pavement outside the restaurant, after Madeline had hurried off.

'Stinky? He really did have the flu that time? I knew it! You've been seeing him? Why didn't you tell me earlier?'

'We don't call him that,' said Julia. 'Anyway, don't get all excited and start planning cosy little double dates. We're just friends.'

Ellen could see hope shining bright in Julia's eyes.

'Stop it,' said Julia when she saw the expression on Ellen's face. 'Not a word.' But her arms tightened round Ellen when she hugged her goodbye.

Now Ellen glanced at her watch. It was only nine o'clock. Jack would still be up when she got home. He seemed to stay up very late for an eight-year-old, but what did she know?

She knew that Patrick would be entirely respectful if she was to suggest that Jack's bedtime was changed, but she felt so self-conscious when it came to parenting this self-sufficient little boy, as if she was just play-acting. She should have asked Madeline what time Isabella went to bed. She would have set her straight.

It was so nice to not be going home to an empty house. The lights would be blazing as she pulled up in the driveway. When she opened the door there would be the smell of tacos or popcorn or some other late-night snack. Patrick and Jack would be watching television together or playing some game on the Wii or chasing each other through the house, brandishing the branch that had once hung on her ceiling to remind her to practise mindfulness and had now somehow become a sword or a laser gun or something (they seemed so violent sometimes!). Patrick would ask about the movie. Jack would want to tell her something about his day. They would have hot chocolate and some of the fundraiser chocolates Jack was meant to be selling for school. Patrick would tell Jack to go to bed about twenty times and he finally would.

Yes, it was so very nice to be going home to the hubbub of the family life she'd always wanted.

But she still didn't turn the keys in the ignition.

Fine. Think it out loud, Ellen.

It would also be quite nice to be going home to an empty house, to calming silence and a hallway free of boxes, to a cup of tea with a book, to a long hot bath without anyone asking if she was coming to bed soon.

It would be lovely, in fact, the way she was feeling right now, to have her own house to herself, to have her own bed to herself, to have her old life back for just tonight.

She thought of all those nights over the last year when she'd come home alone and she'd fumbled in the dark with her key to unlock the door and, as she'd fumbled, she'd *longed* for someone to be waiting inside for her, someone exactly like Patrick.

She thought about Saskia, so single-minded in her desire to have Patrick back. She'd held on for all those years. She was an attractive, intelligent woman. She could have met plenty of other men, but she only wanted Patrick. It might be crazy, but it was committed.

Ellen knew that she didn't love Patrick with that same ferocity. Actually, she'd never loved anyone that much. She would never break into anyone's house. She'd never be so overcome by a feeling that she'd break a law, or do anything that was socially unacceptable. She could hear Julia and Madeline saying, *That's a good thing, you fool! That's sanity! That's maturity!*

She sighed and reached out to turn the key in the ignition, and then she dropped her hand back in her lap. A young couple walked by on the pavement outside the car. They were arguing over something. Suddenly the girl turned on her heel and walked away, making a flicking motion with her hand. The boy watched her go. *Follow her*, thought Ellen. *That's what she wants you to do.* But he clenched his jaw, shrugged, shoved his hand in his pockets and walked away from her.

She thought about everything she'd said to her friends at dinner that night and everything she'd left out.

All those years she'd sanctimoniously told clients that 'relationships are hard work', she'd never truly understood the truth of what she was saying.

(In fact, she'd probably subconsciously thought that the relationships were hard work for other people, not for her, not with her knowledge and skills and emotional intelligence. Oh, the conceit!)

She and Patrick had made up after their trip to the

mountains, of course, later that night. The relief had been exquisite, almost worth the argument.

'It was my fault,' Ellen had said nobly.

'It was absolutely my fault,' said Patrick, and he'd explained about a problem he was having at work: a client who was refusing to pay a big bill. Also, he'd seen Saskia waiting outside in her car when they left for the mountains. Patrick said, 'I think I was subconsciously taking out my stress on you.' He was trying his best to speak her language, which was sort of adorable.

Then he'd been horrified to learn that she'd had to cancel her coffee with Julia to stay home with Jack.

'Why didn't you tell me?' he said. 'That's ridiculous!'

'I don't know,' said Ellen. 'I guess I just wanted to be like a proper mother.'

'You *are* a proper mother,' said Patrick. 'I love the way you are with him. You couldn't be any better. I should never have assumed you were free.'

'Well, I guess I should have told you earlier.'

'Shut up, woman. I'm taking the fall for this one,' said Patrick, and he'd spent the next twenty minutes rubbing her feet.

There was no way she was going to mention Saskia's biscuits then. The foot rubbing would have ended instantly, while he paced and fretted and swore.

And late that night he'd actually moved two of the boxes.

He'd dragged them into the dining room, leaving what looked like the tyre marks of a monster truck right across her grandmother's carpet. Ellen had a vision of her grandmother's horror-struck face, remembering all the time she'd spent on her hands and knees scrubbing away at some tiny spot visible only to her eyes.

Sorry, Grandma.

The rest of the boxes were still there. They had a settled, slumped look about them now. It was becoming impossible to imagine them moving.

Now she turned on the ignition and switched on the headlights, illuminating the street in front of her.

The boy she'd seen earlier was running back along the street, his chin down, his arms pumping as if he was on the football field. Yes! Ellen felt a tingle. He was running back after his girlfriend to swoop her up into his arms and bury his face in her hair. How lovely.

Or perhaps he was going back to knock her teeth out. Life wasn't always as romantic as it seemed. She pulled out into the traffic.

Like, for example, you would think that meeting your father for the first time ever would be an occasion filled with tender, tremulous emotion.

Monday lunchtime had been such a mistake. Why in the world had she thought that daytime would be better than night? It was so obvious that dinner would have been more appropriate. They had ended up meeting at a café in North Sydney because all three of them had various appointments around that area that day and it seemed to make sense. The problem was that it gave the lunch the feeling of it being another appointment in their day, an errand to be crossed off the list. Ellen kept feeling like they were doing the small talk business acquaintances do before someone takes out their notepad, and says, 'Right, let's get started.'

Also, the lighting was all wrong. It was too sunny and real. She didn't want to notice the minuscule black dots of hair on her father's upper lip. She didn't want to see the pores on his nose or the glimpses of pink mottled scalp beneath his hair. She didn't want to see the sauce from his Moroccan chicken wrap on his lip. She certainly didn't want to see her mother gaily wiping it away with her serviette! (Her mother! So soft and accommodating and feminine. At one point in the conversation, she'd actually fiddled with her hair.)

Ellen's nausea hadn't helped either. It really coloured the way she saw the world. A horrible beige colour. It seemed to get better at night. Why hadn't she remembered that?

When she'd walked into the café it had reminded her of Internet dating: that intensely peculiar feeling of searching the room for the face of a stranger, a stranger who you were imagining as a potential life partner. *Could I imagine kissing you, waking up with you, arguing with you?* Except that there was no escape clause with this meeting, because it didn't actually matter what she thought of him. She wouldn't be able to go back online and choose another potential father.

Her eyes had skimmed right past him at first. He was just another one of the ubiquitous grey-haired businessmen in good suits that filled the café. And then she saw her mother sitting opposite him. She almost hadn't recognized her. She was used to seeing her mother with Mel and Pip, the three of them making a minor spectacle of themselves: talking and laughing louder than anyone else. Her mother seemed somehow diminished sitting opposite this grey-haired man. Instead of sitting back in her chair, with perfect posture, like a queen, she was leaning forward, both her forearms resting on the table, her head tilted at a subservient angle.

When she saw Ellen, she sat up abruptly, as if she'd been caught doing something wrong, and then she smiled and waved, and Ellen saw pride, followed almost instantaneously by fear, cross her face.

David, her father, stood up as Ellen walked towards them, and kissed her graciously on both cheeks, in the way that men of a certain age and income level did these days. ('The kissing thing has got out of control in this city lately,' Madeline had said tonight at dinner. 'Next thing you know you'll have to kiss the checkout chick goodbye as you're picking up your groceries.')

'It's a pleasure to meet you, Ellen,' he'd said, and then as they sat down he said, formally, 'You're a very welcome surprise in my life.' But at the moment he said it, a waitress appeared, talking over the top of him, tossing down laminated menus on their table, and then he obviously wasn't sure if Ellen had heard him, and he didn't know if he should say it again, and Ellen was too busy asking if the waitress could bring some plain bread as quickly as possible please, so the moment passed for her to reassure him, and to say that he was a welcome surprise in her life too. That tiny little moment of social awkwardness had caused his urbane façade to slip a little, and that had given her the squirmy feeling of seeing something she shouldn't have seen, as though she'd suddenly noticed that he was wearing a toupee.

After that they'd stuck to small talk. They'd chatted about the weekend away in the Whitsundays (*Glorious!*

Amazing! Her mother's voice was so shrill. She sounded like someone else's mother) and the play they'd seen, about what it was like for David to be living back in Sydney after all these years. He was an orthopaedic surgeon and planned to practise for only a few more years before he retired.

'Then I might buy a boat and sail round the world for a year,' he said. He looked at Anne. 'Fancy being my first mate?'

Anne glowed. 'As long as there's an espresso machine on board.'

Every now and then Ellen would think, *These are my parents. I'm out having lunch with my parents.* She imagined meeting a friend or a client, someone who didn't know her history. 'This is my mum and dad.'

How extraordinarily ordinary.

Her father had asked her lots of searching questions about hypnotherapy, with elaborately casual references to articles he'd recently read. It was obvious that he'd spent some time researching hypnotherapy specifically for this meeting, which was touching, almost painfully so. Ellen got a prickling sensation behind her eyes as he listened so courteously and attentively to her answers.

It was also obvious that he was relatively open-minded on the subject of 'alternative therapies', especially for a surgeon of his age and background. Her mother didn't make any of her normal sharp comments. She even made some vaguely complimentary remarks. 'Ellen often has a waiting list, you know,' she told David, and a few minutes later, in a doctor-to-another-doctor tone: 'Apparently, she's had some quite good results with idiopathic pain management.'

Although you've never once referred a patient to me, Mum, thought Ellen. Did her mother feel she needed to sell Ellen to him? As if Anne was a single mother and her kid was part of the package, like Jack was part of Patrick's package?

David spoke about his two sons with a father's casual tenderness; just using their names caused him to smile involuntarily.

'Do they have children yet?' asked Ellen. She was refusing to think too hard about the fact that these two strange men – one was in real estate and the other was in marketing – a few years younger than her, living on the other side of the world, presumably with English accents and English complexions, were her half-brothers. It was like hearing that the imaginary friends of your childhood had actually existed all along. When she was a child she was always asking her mother if her father had other children and her mother would answer, depending on her mood, airily or tersely, 'Probably.'

She had created sisters and brothers in her imagination: a sexy older brother, who wore a leather jacket and rode a motorbike and had lots of handsome friends, a younger sister who adored her, an older sister who lent her make-up. She'd grown out of it, of course. There was really no necessity for two younger brothers now. She was busy. She had enough trouble keeping up with her own friends. What was she meant to do: look them up on Facebook?

'No grandchildren yet,' said David. 'Callum is married, but his wife doesn't seem too interested in having children, and Lachlan seems to be settling into bachelorhood.' He stopped and frowned. 'So this –' he made an awkward sweeping motion with his teaspoon towards Ellen's stomach. 'So this is my first grandchild!'

Then he flushed slightly as if he'd overstepped the line. 'Yes,' said Ellen, trying to be generous.

'Who would have thought we'd be grandparents,' murmured Ellen's mother, and Ellen watched as her parents (her *parents*!) exchanged secretive, loaded looks.

Throughout the lunch Ellen had stared at her father's features, searching for evidence of their shared DNA. She noted the small ears and good teeth that her mother had put on his list of attributes. (She couldn't see any evidence of his 'strange sense of humour' but that was probably because he was nervous. They all were. None of the three of them were really being themselves.) David must have been covertly studying her too, because at one point he suddenly said, 'I think you have my mother's eyes.'

That was the one time when she hovered on the edge of feeling something momentous. A sense of loss for everything that could have been? The family she never knew? Grandparents were her soft spot.

'Your mother who read tarot cards?' said Ellen.

He looked startled. 'That's right. She did. It was a funny hobby of hers. How in the world did you –'

'Your mother read my cards once,' said Anne quickly. (Presumably David didn't know about the scoring system.) 'Don't you remember? She told me she saw a journey to far-off lands in my future. I think she was hoping I would take a long journey far away from you. She didn't like me much.'

'I think she saw you as a threat,' smiled David. 'She was fond of Jane.'

'Was Jane your wife?' said Ellen, and then she'd flushed, because his wife had been the woman he'd cheated on when Ellen was conceived, and Ellen felt weirdly culpable.

David cleared his throat. 'Yes.' He lifted his cappuccino to his mouth. Ellen's mother tapped her teaspoon against the rim of her saucer. At the table next to them, two women were looking at a laptop together and speaking passionately about 'poor response rates'.

'My mother died in 1998,' said David. 'She would have been fond of you. She would have been very interested in your choice of career.'

'She might not have approved of my existence,' said Ellen, and smiled, to show that he didn't need to worry, none of this really mattered to her, she was not a mixed-up teenager, that it was all such a long time ago.

'Still,' said her father. He chewed on his lip. 'Still . . .'

He glanced at his watch. 'I must run. This was a pleasure, Ellen. I hope we can do it again. And, of course, I'd like to meet, perhaps, your husband-to-be, ah, Patrick, isn't it? That is, if you would like that.'

Oh, the awful strangeness of it all! It was just like the end of an Internet date, one where the man was trying to ascertain her interest in a second date, when he was pretty sure he had no chance, but thought it might be worth a shot anyway.

'Of course!' said Ellen, all false smiles, in Internet date mode.

He'd kissed them both, and left, stopping at the counter to swiftly, efficiently, pay their bill. He was clearly a man who always automatically paid the bill.

'So, what did you think?' asked Anne, her eyes on

David's back as he left the café. He didn't look back. He was looking at the screen of his iPhone as he walked. There was something about the look in her mother's beautiful violet eyes that reminded Ellen of the expression on Patrick's face at Colleen's grave. Was it a yearning look? It made her feel grumpy.

'Did you go to their wedding?' she said abruptly.

'Whose wedding?' said Anne.

'His. David's wedding to Jane.'

'Oh.' Her mother had regained her normal posture and her voice had gone back down a few decibels. 'Well, I did actually. Mel, Pip and I were all there. We were all in the same group of friends. A dreadful day. I felt so sick.'

'With guilt?'

'Well, no. I meant because I was three months pregnant with you.'

'Oh, *Mum*.' Imagine if that poor girl had known that one of her guests was pregnant to her brand-new husband.

'I'm not sure why you're acting as if this is a surprise to you,' said her mother. 'You always knew that he was engaged to someone else.'

'I know I did,' said Ellen. 'I'm sorry. I just hadn't thought about the fact that you were at their wedding.'

She knew what she was doing. She was over-identifying with the bride. It was because she was subconsciously – no, actually, quite consciously – worried that she might be marrying a man who was still in love with someone else, albeit a dead someone else.

'Did you ever think about telling him that you were pregnant?' said Ellen.

'Not really,' said Anne. 'I barely admitted to myself how

much I cared about him. I repressed it – to use your language. I pretended I was the tough feminist who just wanted a baby.'

But I liked it when you were the tough feminist, thought Ellen. *I liked it when you were so different from me. It made me more me.*

'I thought you'd find this all so romantic!' continued Anne. 'I thought it was right up your alley! I said to Pip and Mel, Ellen is going to love this! And yet, you've been so strangely negative about it all. My daughter, Miss Positivity! Miss I-empathize-with-the-whole-world! Even your fiancé's crazy stalking ex-girlfriend! Well, how about a little empathy for your own mother?'

'My hormones,' began Ellen tentatively.

'Oh, please. Don't give me hormones!'

'OK,' said Ellen. And then she knew what she needed to say. Her mother had just introduced her to a new man.

'He's lovely,' she said. 'David, that is. Charming. Handsome. I really liked him.' It was actually not untrue.

It was like switching on a light bulb. Her mother had glowed. 'I *know*!'

And then they'd spent the next half-hour talking about David's positive attributes in comparison to all the men her mother had ever dated.

'Of course, none of those poor unfortunate men ever had a chance,' said her mother. 'I see that now. How could they, when I was still in love with your father? I was subconsciously holding back, wasn't I? I should have let you hypnotize me! We could have worked on my *issues*.'

'As if that would have ever happened in a million years,' said Ellen.

It had been strangely comforting seeing the snarky glint

in her mother's eyes when she used the word 'issues'. It would have been just too much if her mother had started coming over all respectful about hypnotherapy.

Now Ellen pulled up in front of her house and saw all the lights blazing.

There would be no fumbling in the dark for the key. The front-door porch had been broken for years, but like so many other things around the house, it had been quietly, magically fixed by Patrick, within a week of him moving in.

She laughed when she saw the silhouettes of Patrick and Jack suddenly dash by the window, their arms waving in the air. *We're home*, she said to the baby. *Looks like your dad and your big brother are still up.*

She put her hands over her stomach and suddenly, like a message from her future, she felt an exquisitely painful, hot, tingling rush envelop her breasts. It was a revelation that her body could experience such new sensations.

'Hi, in there.' This time she spoke out loud. 'That sort of hurts. But that's OK, I don't mind. You just rest up. Keep growing.'

There was that blinding feeling of joy again. A baby. For heaven's sake, she was having a *baby* with a man who adored her. None of the rest of it mattered.

19

Every day, in every way, I am getting better and better.
  – The classic conscious auto-suggestion created by
    the famous French psychologist and pharmacist
    (the 'father of auto hypnosis'), Émile Coué
                                    (1857–1926)

'Did you sleep OK last night, Jack?' asked Ellen.

It was Tuesday morning and she and Patrick and Jack were eating breakfast. Patrick was reading the paper, and Jack was being uncharacteristically quiet. He was normally bouncing about at breakfast time, as if he'd banked up a whole lot of thoughts through the night and they all had to come spilling out as he ate his corn-flakes, but today he was dully banging his spoon against the side of his bowl, and Ellen noticed shadows under his eyes. They looked especially wrong on his smooth little-boy face.

'I had a really big long dream,' said Jack. 'It went on and on for, like, the whole night. It was like a movie that went on forever.'

'Huh,' said Patrick without looking up from his news-paper. 'Eat your breakfast.'

'What was the movie in your dream about?' asked Ellen.

'Armageddon,' said Jack.

Patrick put his paper down and raised an eyebrow at Ellen. 'Do you even know what that means?'

'Yeah, of course,' said Jack. *He looks pale*, thought Ellen. 'It means the end of the world. I've been looking it up on the Internet.'

'I'm sure you picked up lots of sensible stuff there,' sighed Patrick.

'Yeah,' said Jack obliviously. 'It's coming, you know. Armageddon.'

'Well, it's not,' said Patrick.

'How do you know?' said Jack. 'You said just the other day that you don't know everything.'

Patrick briskly folded up his newspaper. 'I know this.'

'In my dream everyone I know died,' said Jack. 'It was pretty scary.' He stood up and took his half-eaten bowl of cereal over to the sink. 'I'll have to tell Ethan about the dream. We've got an Armageddon Club.'

Patrick shook his head. 'I was in a spy club when I was at school. Can't you change your club to a spy club?'

Jack looked at his father like he was deranged. 'No, Dad, I really could not do that.' He sounded like he was about thirty; a stressed-out business executive who could not possibly take on another project as much as he'd like to help out.

He left the room; the weight of the world on his narrow little shoulders.

'So, Armageddon, eh? That's a cheerful topic of conversation for breakfast, isn't it?' said Patrick, as they listened to Jack clumping up the stairs to his room.

He took his own plate to the sink and smiled at her. 'Are you excited?'

They were going for Ellen's first ultrasound.

'Yes,' said Ellen. 'I can't wait to see it. At the moment this baby just feels like some sort of horrendous stomach bug. I want proof that there's an actual baby making me feel so sick.'

She thought, *Please don't say anything about Colleen's lack of nausea, or Colleen's first ultrasound.*

Patrick went to speak and Ellen interrupted him hurriedly, afraid she might scream if the word 'Colleen' came out of his mouth.

'So you remember it's at eleven o'clock? You'll meet me there? At the ultrasound place?'

'That's what I was about to say,' said Patrick. 'We can go together. After I drop Jack off at school, I'm going to come back here and finally move those boxes. When I woke up this morning I thought, what's the point of working for myself if I can't take a few hours off when I need it? And you've put up with those boxes for long enough.'

Before Ellen had a chance to answer, Jack called from upstairs. 'Da-aaad!'

'Better go see what Mr Armageddon wants,' said Patrick. He paused and frowned. 'I wonder if the club was his idea. What would make a kid develop an interest in *Armageddon*? What do you think? Isn't it a bit –'

'Da-adddd!' The first time Jack had shrieked like this Ellen had gone skidding down the hallway, her heart pounding, assuming he was lying in a pool of his own blood. Now she knew better. He'd probably lost a sock.

'I'm *coming*!' roared back Patrick and he went clumping up the stairs in exactly the same way as his son, except possibly even louder.

Ellen put down her spoon and contemplated her porridge and her conscience.

He was taking the morning off work to move the boxes.

She felt herself smile: a satisfied, creamy, cat-like smile. Oh, she was good. She was damned good. Every day, in every way, she was making him better and better.

The smile vanished almost immediately. Oh my goodness, it was a wonder she wasn't waggling her fingertips together while tossing her head back and cackling fiendishly! She was a witch! A manipulative, unethical –

But actually, that was all bluster. She didn't really feel any of that. Deep down she felt nothing but cool, crisp satisfaction at a job well done.

The only guilt she felt was over her lack of guilt.

It hadn't been planned; at least as far as she knew. She'd had no conscious intention of hypnotizing Patrick into moving the boxes. Patrick had been upset again about the client who wasn't paying his bill. 'He doesn't return my calls or answer my emails,' Patrick had ranted as they lay together in bed that night. 'He ignores me, as if I'm the one in the wrong. He treats me like *I'm* stalking *him*, like I'm *Saskia*!'

'Do you want me to do a relaxation?' Ellen had asked. After the night before the proposal she'd stopped offering, and they'd been so distracted by so many things: the pregnancy, meeting her father, Patrick and Jack moving into the house.

Patrick had been so grateful, and he was such a good subject; that was the thing. He was like Julia. He had the ability to focus and visualize. He was more imaginative than he knew.

She got him to imagine himself climbing to the top of a mountain. He was carrying a backpack filled with the worry and the fury and the stress that the horrible client was causing him, and as he climbed the mountain he gradually discarded each one of those negative emotions, until he finally took off the backpack completely and then he reached the summit where he took in deep breaths of pure relaxing mountain air, and with each breath he went deeper and deeper into himself.

And as she'd watched his forehead smoothing, and seen his chest rise and fall as he breathed in so deeply, it had felt as if they were together at the top of that mountain, breathing the same air. She'd talked about how that clean, crisp mountain air was going to help him take clean, crisp decisive action. 'You'll do exactly what you need to do to get your life under control,' she'd said. 'Whether it's calling your solicitor or delegating paperwork or moving those boxes that you've been wanting to move. You will systematically de-clutter your life, so that by the end of the week you'll feel completely in control, able to breathe, energetic and exhilarated, as if you're standing on that summit with your arms held high!'

You cannot be hypnotized into doing something that goes against your intrinsic values or, in fact, doing anything that you don't want to do.

She'd explained that so many times to her clients.

Patrick *wanted* to move the boxes. He *wanted* to get through his paperwork. He *wanted* to call the solicitor. He freely admitted that he was a procrastinator when it came to unpleasant tasks.

Her own self-interest didn't change the fact that he would feel great once he'd moved the boxes.

'Bribe him with sexual favours,' Julia had said at dinner the other night.

'Refuse sex until he moves them,' said Madeline.

Surely a gentle suggestion during an enjoyable hypnosis session was better than nagging or yelling or manipulating him with sex? That was so 1950s.

Also, she had not instructed his conscious mind to forget her suggestion about moving the boxes. So he should be fully aware of what she'd said. She would ask him about it. 'Did you mind me mentioning the boxes last night?' she'd say, lightly, casually.

Once he'd moved them, of course. No point mentioning it until it actually happened.

'Bye, Ellen!' Jack came running into the kitchen carrying his school bag.

'Did you get your lunch?' asked Ellen.

She'd taken over the making of school lunches when she'd seen what Patrick had been giving him every day: a slapped-together Vegemite sandwich on limp white bread (who ate white bread any more, wasn't it sort of against the law?) and a green apple. 'He should have protein with every meal,' she'd told Patrick. He'd protested, saying that he wasn't so sexist as to expect her to take on making Jack's lunch just because she was a woman, and he'd been in charge of Jack's lunches for years, and anyway Jack wouldn't eat anything else, and wasn't Vegemite sort of protein-ish? But she'd insisted, surprised at her forcefulness. As soon as Jack had moved into her home she'd felt like his diet had become her responsibility. It was something to do with the sight of his heartbreakingly skinny little-boy body. Every time she managed to get him to eat something healthy she found herself deeply satisfied, her lips virtually chewing along with his, as if some innate biological need was being met. At the end of each day she would mentally list everything that Jack had eaten during the day, as though she were presenting a report on his diet to somebody. It certainly wasn't for Patrick; it must be for his mother. *This is what I fed your son today, Colleen; a good mix of complex carbohydrates and protein.*

Today she'd made him a tuna-rice wrap and a little container of fruit salad to have with yoghurt. Jack took the lunch she gave him from the fridge without noticeable enthusiasm.

'You could pour the yoghurt over the fruit,' she told him.

Jack looked at her blankly.

She sighed. Perhaps he was still worried about Armageddon, or else the poor child was missing his Vegemite sandwich. Her attempts to give him a healthy diet didn't appear to be paying off; he looked exhausted.

'Are you feeling OK?' she said to him. 'Maybe you should stay home today.'

'Nah,' said Jack. 'I'm going to Ethan's place after school.'

She met Patrick's eyes over Jack's head. If she insisted Jack stayed home, he would make a point of agreeing with her. He backed her up any time she made the slightest show of authority.

'Well, an early night tonight then.'

'Definitely.' Patrick ruffled Jack's hair in that rough, loving Dad way. 'And no more looking at the computer without adult supervision. We'll research spy clubs.'

Jack rolled his eyes.

After they left for school, Ellen checked her diary to remind herself who she was seeing that morning before the ultrasound.

Luisa Bell.

How sadly inappropriate that on the day she was going for her first ultrasound she was treating someone for 'unexplained infertility'.

Or maybe it was happily appropriate. She would put her heart and soul into doing what she could for Luisa.

A wave of nausea swept over her, and Ellen looked around for her 'wellness stone'. It was the pleasingly shaped white stone she'd found on the beach soon after meeting Patrick. She'd decided to use it as part of the self-hypnosis she was doing to try to handle the morning sickness, or the every-minute-of-the-whole-bloody-day sickness. The idea was that every time she rolled the stone across her stomach her subconscious would help the wave of nausea to recede. The only problem was that she couldn't find the stone. The last time she'd seen it Patrick had been tossing it up in the air while he walked around the house swearing to someone on the phone. The conversation had sounded too serious for her to say, 'Hey, give me back my wellness stone!'

She sighed, and made herself a cup of ginger tea instead, while she imagined her mother snorting, 'Wellness stone indeed; drink your tea!'

An hour later, Luisa walked up the path and nearly

collided with Patrick, who was barrelling out of the front door down the footpath with his arms stretched round a box of random items he'd announced he was donating to charity. He stepped aside for Luisa, nodded grimly at her and kept walking towards the car. His brow was sweaty and his eyes were crazed. Ever since he'd got back from dropping Jack at school he'd been working at a frenzied pace, as though he'd been set an impossible deadline he was determined to meet.

If you ever wanted proof that hypnosis worked . . .

'Sorry about that,' said Ellen. 'My, ah, fiancé is having a clean-out.'

'Oh, yes, I heard that you were getting married.' Luisa dabbed at her nose with a soggy-looking tissue. She was the very essence of a woman with a cold, as if she'd been cast for the role in a TV commercial for cold and flu tablets. Her nose was red and her eyes were bloodshot and puffy. Ellen felt her own sinuses block up in sympathy.

'You heard I was getting married?' said Ellen, as she led Luisa up the stairs. For some reason she thought of Saskia. Was she passing on the news to all of her clients?

'Patricia Bradbury,' said Luisa shortly.

Julia's mother. Ellen had forgotten that Luisa was the daughter of one of Julia's mother's friends.

If Luisa knew about the engagement, did she know about the pregnancy too? Surely people knew better than to pass on random pregnancy news to a woman who was desperately trying to have a baby.

'Would you like me to make you a cup of herbal tea?' she asked Luisa, as she gestured towards the client chair.

'I could make you one with lemon and honey for your cold?'

'So *I'm* not pregnant,' said Luisa. 'But apparently *you* are.'

It appeared people did not know better.

'Well, yes, actually. It's only early days –' began Ellen.

'I heard it was an accident,' said Luisa. She sniffed and grabbed a handful of Ellen's tissues. She wiped her nose aggressively.

'It's true that it wasn't planned,' said Ellen carefully. She sat down and picked up Luisa's file that she had taken out beforehand and placed on the coffee table ready for her session.

'Maybe you accidentally hypnotized yourself when you were meant to be hypnotizing me.' Luisa gave a bitter little laugh that turned into a spluttering cough.

'This must seem very unfair to you,' said Ellen.

'You said you could get me pregnant,' said Luisa.

'I did not!' said Ellen involuntarily. She would never have said that. Although it was true that she did have high hopes for her success with Luisa. Over the years she had helped a number of women with similar case histories. They had sent her effusive letters, and photos of their babies; one had even named her baby Ellen in her honour.

'I want my money back,' said Luisa. 'That's the only reason I came today. You're a fraud. You take advantage of people when they're suffering, when they're at their most vulnerable. I can't believe you were recommended to me.'

Ellen felt a rush of prickly heat flood her whole body

like an instant allergic reaction. 'Luisa,' she began. 'I'm so sorry –'

'Just give me my money back.'

Never ever give a client a refund. Flynn had drummed that into her. *This is a professional service you're offering. Professionals do not give a refund for no reason. Respect yourself. Respect what you do.*

'You're a quack,' said Luisa. Her voice quivered on the edge of tears. 'Why should I help fund stuff for your baby; your baby's *clothes*, your baby's *nappies*. Do you think with all the money we're spending on IVF that we need this extra expense? My husband told me, he said, all this alternative stuff is a load of crap, and he was *right*.'

She was sobbing now, rocking back and forth, as if she was wracked with pain. Ellen's eyes filled with sympathetic tears. What to say, what to say?

'Luisa, I really believe that we could still –'

'Just give me my money back.'

'All right,' said Ellen. 'I will. Just give me a minute. I'll write you a cheque.'

She took her chequebook from the drawer of her desk and watched her hand shake slightly as she wrote Luisa's name. All her pregnancy symptoms suddenly intensified: her breasts hardened and burned, her mouth filled with metal – as if her body wanted to make her feel even guiltier for being pregnant when Luisa wasn't.

'It better not bounce.' Luisa stuffed the cheque in her handbag.

'It won't,' said Ellen. One part of her wanted to slap the woman and the other part wanted to hug her.

'Right, well, I'll be . . .' Luisa sneezed three times in row.

She pressed her sodden tissue to her nose and looked at Ellen with streaming eyes.

'Bless you,' said Ellen. Her hand went out involuntarily to touch Luisa's arm in a gesture of sympathy. The poor woman looked so pitiful.

'Don't touch me,' said Luisa. She turned and walked down the stairs, blowing her nose the whole way. Patrick looked up from the hallway where he was in the process of straightening up while he hefted two giant garbage bags over his shoulders like a weightlifter. He smiled politely up at Luisa, and then his smile vanished as he saw her clearly unhappy demeanour. His eyes moved questioningly to Ellen's and she silently shrugged.

Ellen opened the door for Luisa and she left without saying a word, walking briskly down the path, her chin jutting forward, arms swinging, as if she was on her way to put a stop to something.

'What's her problem?' asked Patrick, coming to stand beside her at the door.

'She's mad at me for being pregnant when she's not,' said Ellen. 'She – who's that?'

Luisa had stopped near the top of the path to talk to a tall man in dark sunglasses and a stylish suit.

'Do you know him?' asked Patrick.

'I don't think so,' said Ellen.

She had a strong sense of foreboding as she watched Luisa fling back her arm towards the house, while the man bent towards her, listening with his whole body. He was far too interested in what Luisa was saying; whoever he was, Ellen didn't want him talking to Luisa right now.

'It's not a new client, is it?' said Patrick. 'Because it looks like she's giving him an earful.'

'I'm not expecting anyone,' said Ellen. She squinted. The man turned so she could see his face in profile. He had a big, beaky nose. There was something familiar about him.

'I feel like I know him from somewhere.' Patrick shifted the garbage bags more comfortably on his shoulders.

'Me too,' said Ellen. 'Is he a newsreader or something? An actor?'

They watched as Luisa reached into her handbag and held something up to the man.

'I think she's showing him the cheque I gave her,' said Ellen.

'Why did you give her a cheque?'

'It's a refund,' said Ellen.

'A refund? You gave her a refund because you're pregnant?'

'I'll explain later. What's he doing now?'

The man reached into the pocket of his jacket and took out something that appeared to be a business card. Luisa glanced at it and then smiled.

'Oh God,' said Ellen. 'Who *is* this man?'

'I'll go and find out,' said Patrick. 'They can't just stand there chatting on your property.'

'No, wait.' Ellen chewed a fingernail and watched as Luisa carefully put the man's card in her bag, as if she was filing away an important document, before walking off. The man lifted a hand to wave goodbye and then came striding down the footpath, smoothly removing his sunglasses with one hand. He looked angry and determined, as if he were walking straight to the lost-luggage counter at the airport.

'Right,' said Patrick. He set down the garbage bags and opened the screen door. 'Can I help you, mate?'

There was an aggressive edge to his voice. Ellen tugged at the back of his T-shirt. 'Patrick, don't –'

'I'm here to see Ellen O'Farrell,' said the man. He didn't smile. Most people couldn't help but give at least a perfunctory smile when they walked to the door of a strange house.

'Have you got an appointment?' Patrick squared his shoulders.

'Nope.' The man lifted his chin as if to say, *What if I don't?*

Patrick puffed out his chest and Ellen thought, *Look at him being all chivalrous.* He said, 'Why don't you come back when you've got one?'

This was getting ridiculous. Ellen stepped forward. 'I'm Ellen. Can I –' The man turned to her with such hatred in his eyes, Ellen faltered. 'Can I help you?' she said.

'I'm Ian Roman. My wife is a "patient" of yours. Rosie. Remember her? You were helping her stop smoking, although, funnily enough, she's still going through a pack a day.'

That's why she recognized him. Rosie's wealthy husband. A 'bigwig'. That's how Rosie had described him. He was in real estate, wasn't he? Or some sort of media tycoon? Ellen couldn't remember which. She just knew she'd seen his face in the papers.

'I don't care who you are,' said Patrick, although Ellen could tell by the subtle change of tone in his voice that he knew exactly who Ian Roman was and where he sat on the social hierarchy. 'You can't come barging in here without an appointment.'

'It's fine,' said Ellen. 'I have a few minutes.' She stepped in between the two men and gave Patrick a look that was meant to say, *Thank you, my darling, but you can back off now.* 'My office is this way, Ian.' She put deliberate emphasis on his name. 'I can see you for ten minutes or so.'

'I'll be just down here,' said Patrick warningly.

'So this is where you supposedly hypnotize people,' said Ian Roman. He glanced around her lovely office and his nostrils flared as if he was seeing something unhygienic and unsavoury.

'Have a seat.' Ellen indicated the green recliner, and for some reason, perhaps fear, she said flippantly, 'Have a chocolate too.'

Ian took a seat and didn't even bother to glance at the chocolates. He pulled on his trouser legs. Ellen sat down in front of him. She was mentally replaying her last session with Rosie.

Ian suddenly leaned forward. 'So, Rosie has her sister over the other night. I come home early and I stop in the hallway to look at some mail and I can hear them talking. I'm not really listening, but then it starts to register, and you know what I hear?'

He didn't wait for an answer.

'I hear my wife say that she discovered under hypnosis that she doesn't really love me. Great! But you know what, that's OK, that's no problem, because now she's being hypnotized *into loving me*. One hundred and fifty dollars a pop! Let's forget about helping you to stop smoking, that's too hard, let's help you love your husband. The one you married five fucking minutes ago!'

Ellen took a deep, shaky breath. *What was in the air today?* She tried to keep her voice detached and professional, yet caring and empathetic. 'Obviously, it would be unethical of me to discuss your wife's treatment with you. However, I do understand –'

'Oh, obviously, because you're so very ethical.'

There was thump and a crash from downstairs. It sounded like Patrick had dropped one of the boxes. Ellen's cheeks felt hot.

I am not a quack. I have nothing to feel guilty about.

Except maybe she did.

'Have you spoken to Rosie about this?' she said.

'I have nothing to say to her,' said Ian. 'Clearly, our marriage is over. I don't need a woman who needs to be hypnotized into loving me. For Christ's sake. What a joke. What an *absolute* joke.'

His mask of controlled fury slipped for a fleeting second and that was all it took for Ellen to understand everything. He loved Rosie and he was desperately hurt, but overriding everything else was his shattered pride. That was what was driving him. His ego had taken a violent blow, and he was going to fight back until it stopped hurting.

'Never hurt their pride,' Ellen's grandmother had once told her. 'A man with hurt pride is like a wounded bear thrashing about in the forest.'

Ellen massaged her stomach. Before she saw Luisa, she'd drunk two glasses of water in preparation for this morning's ultrasound. She desperately needed to empty her bladder.

'I had the pleasure of meeting another one of your satisfied clients on the way in,' said Ian. 'Great little operation you've got going here. Regularly hand out refunds, do you?'

'You really need to talk to your wife about this,' said Ellen. She floundered; her professional identity suddenly seemed slippery and tenuous. She saw her mother's face all those years ago: 'Ellen, you can't seriously be considering a career in this.' She thought of all the jokes and the sneers and the doubts she'd ever endured. It suddenly felt like she *was* a quack, a charlatan. 'This is not the way it seems.'

'I bet you're involved with these ridiculous hypnoparties, aren't you?' said Ian. 'I guess it makes it easier to rip people off en masse.'

Oh God, if he knew her connection to Danny. How would he handle this sort of attack? Or Flynn? Both of them would do a better job than she was doing now.

'I expect you cure cancer, do you?' said Ian. 'Forget chemo. Just use the power of your mind.'

'I have never, ever made unsubstantiated claims,' said Ellen. 'Look, for heaven's sake, I'm not a faith healer. I'm a fully qualified clinical hypnotherapist and counsellor. I belong to the Australian Society of Clinical Hypnotherapists and the Australian Hypnotherapists' Association. Hypnotherapy has been recognized by the Australian Medical Association. *Doctors* refer their patients to me.'

(*Although not my own mother.*)

'I expect you give them a nice little kick-back for that.'

'I don't, actually.' (Although she had sent Lena Peterson a nice box of chocolates for Christmas last year. Was that wrong?)

Ian stood up and went to the window. He tapped the glass as if he was testing its strength. 'Ocean view. This is a great house. Business is obviously good.'

'This was actually my grandmother's house –' began Ellen. She could hear Flynn: you do not need to explain your financial situation to him.

Ian turned round to look at her. He spoke gently, almost kindly, as if he was paying her a nice compliment. 'I'm bringing you down.'

'I beg your pardon?' She nearly laughed out loud. It just sounded so dramatic. What was he talking about?

He smiled sweetly. 'I'm putting you out of business.'

20

*All that we are is a result of what we have thought. If a
man speaks or acts with an evil thought, pain follows him.
If a man speaks or acts with a pure thought, happiness
follows him, like a shadow that never leaves him.*
  – Buddhist quote on Ellen O'Farrell's refrigerator

I was driving back to the office from an on-site meeting
when it occurred to me that I was only a few minutes away
from the hypnotist's house.

Don't do it, I thought. You've got that meeting with
Toby later. A million emails waiting for you. You're in
a good mood. Why do you always do this when you're
in a good mood?

But I was already turning left instead of right, as if I
had no choice in the matter, as if her house had some sort
of irresistible magnetic force.

I've been feeling a bit strange about what I did on Sunday. I keep thinking about it and feeling amazed at myself;
that I could go into someone else's house and make biscuits. I imagine how that sort of behaviour would sound
to someone else. Like the people I just met at that development site. One of the women told me that she'd spent
last weekend in Mudgee, and I thought: imagine if you
knew what I did on Sunday; how your face would change,

how you'd take a careful step away — how I'd be instantly transformed from fellow professional to strange, crazy woman.

It never really felt like I was doing anything wrong when I went into Patrick's house, because it never stopped feeling like home. That's where I spent the happiest years of my life. I scrubbed that bathroom every Saturday morning. I painted Jack's room. I chose the rug for the dining room. It never felt illegal or wrong; I felt like I had a right to be there, even if nobody else would agree.

But going into Ellen's house and cooking biscuits, and opening the door to angry visitors as if I lived there — I feel like I've possibly crossed a line.

I woke up at 3.00 a.m. on Sunday night with this thought clear in my head: I have to get help. Therapy. Proper therapy. I have to stop. I even went and looked up counselling services on the Internet. I wrote down names and numbers. It was the responsible thing to do.

And then I woke up Monday morning to go to work, and everything seemed so ordinary in the daylight and I thought, oh, look, I don't really need *therapy*. I hold down a job. I'm not suicidal or bulimic or hearing voices. I'll just stop. The biscuits will be my last hurrah. My *au revoir* gift.

And that feeling lasted all through yesterday, and I felt great last night. I even went next door and reminded the happy Labrador family that it was garbage night. Which was a caring, neighbourly thing to do; not the act of someone who needs therapy. They bounced about, all grateful because they'd forgotten that it was garbage night, and they had so much rubbish from the move, and oh, by the way, how was Sunday? For a moment I completely forgot the mythical fortieth birthday party, but then I did a completely believable act of remembering it, and saying how it was a great party, and the weekend already seemed like such a long time ago, even though it was only Monday, that's what work did to you, and oh, ha ha ha, and tra la la la, isn't life a hoot.

And then today I went to work without thinking about Patrick or Jack or Ellen or the new baby at all. I enjoyed the meeting.

It was for a new shopping complex. It's in a great spot, high up with views of the ocean, and I thought of Ellen's office with those big glass windows, and the way the sun reflects off the water, and I told the developers that we need an area like a village square, with big glass windows, somewhere where you could sit and have a cup of coffee and see the sky, with enough space for your toddler to run around in circles and pretend to be an aeroplane. It would be the sort of place I needed when Jack was a toddler and I took him shopping. It's strange how I still feel like I'm the mother of a toddler, even though he's a schoolboy now, and he doesn't belong to me any more. It's like I'm frozen in time. The developers said, OK, chuckle, chuckle, we'll call it Saskia's Serenity Spot, with just a touch of that condescending but flirtatious 'yes dear' tone they get, as if the little lady was asking for a bigger kitchen, but I'm going to fight tooth and nail to make sure it stays there. I'm doing it for the mothers.

So I was filled with vigorous professional satisfaction, and remembering what I loved about town planning, and when I got in the car I had a phone call, and it was Tammy.

My old friend Tammy Cook. The one who let me stay in her spare room after Patrick said, 'It's over.'

She was a good friend to me at that time; taking care of me as if I was an invalid. She made me chicken soup and cups of tea, and held my hand while I lay on the bed and stared at the ceiling and tried to breathe, even though I felt like a lorry had parked on my chest. I remember asking her if life would ever feel the same again, and she said, 'Of course it will, honey.' She was wrong of course, but still, she was a nice girl, the sort of girl who calls you 'honey' and says 'I love you'. I can't actually believe I once had a friend like that. It's like remembering that I once spoke fluent French, when now I can't understand a single word.

After I moved out of her place and into the duplex she kept trying to be my friend. She wanted me to go dancing and drinking in nightclubs and bars. She wanted me to snap out of it, to pull myself together, to show him, to get back out there.

I remember thinking that it wasn't fair. If Patrick had been killed in a car accident I would have been allowed to grieve for him for years. People would have sent me flowers and sympathy cards; they would have dropped off casseroles. I would have been allowed to keep his photos up, to talk about him, to remember the good times. But because he dumped me, because he was still alive, my sadness was considered undignified and pathetic. I wasn't being a proper feminist when I talked about how much I loved him. He stopped loving me so therefore I had to stop loving him. *Immediately.* Chop, chop. Turn those silly feelings off right now. Your love is no longer reciprocated, so it is now foolish.

He and Jack were both gone from my life as if they

were dead, but that was hardly a tragedy. Break-ups happen to everyone. It was the same with Mum's death. Old people die all the time. And she was sick! So, a blessing really. So what that you'll never hear her voice again. So what that you'll never read Jack another bedtime story. So what that you'll never make love to Patrick again.

Get over it, get on with it, get a grip, girl. Everyone wanted me to hurry up and make myself happy again – cut my hair, sign up for evening classes – and it was just plain irritating when I wouldn't; when I couldn't. It was no wonder that Tammy slipped out of my life.

And now here she was again, after all these years, her voice on my mobile phone sounding exactly the same; Tammy always sounded slightly puffed out, as if she'd just run round the block.

'Saskia, honey, I'm back in Sydney!' she said. I didn't know she'd left Sydney. 'You're not on Facebook!' she said. 'How are your old friends meant to find you if you're not on Facebook, you philistine!'

She acted as if we'd just lost touch the way ordinary people do. She didn't even mention Patrick. She asked if I'd have a drink with her on Wednesday night. And I said sure, while I sat in the car and felt the sun on my face, and I thought, no way do I need therapy! I'm meeting an old friend for a drink tomorrow night! I'm perfectly normal.

Then five minutes later I found myself driving to the hypnotist's house.

I'll just drive by, I told myself. I won't stop the car. Jack will be at school, and Patrick will be at work, and Ellen will be sitting in her striped chair, in her cosy little glass haven, offering chocolates, letting her liquid voice rise and fall while the sunlight dances around the walls.

As I drove there I wished I was still Deborah going for another appointment about my leg pain. It's strange how much I enjoyed those sessions. The pain has been worse again lately. I haven't even bothered with any of Ellen's techniques. Now I'm not Deborah to her, I don't feel entitled to use them.

But Patrick was there.

As I turned the corner into her street, I saw them coming out of the house together, hurrying as if they were running late for an appointment. Patrick was wearing jeans. He had the day off; why? He never took a day off during the week. Ellen was wearing jeans too, and a beautiful long grey fitted coat with cute pompoms bouncing about on little strings. The sort of coat only someone quirky and delightful could wear. You couldn't tell she was pregnant yet.

They looked like a couple; nobody looking at them would think that they didn't belong together. And there it was, that strange feeling of exquisite, tender pain: delicate but fierce, like a long, thin, gleaming needle slowly piercing my flesh.

Where could they be going? I didn't even bother fighting it; I had to know. If I could just know, it wouldn't hurt so much. I always think that, even though the knowledge always hurts more.

So I followed them. I was driving one of the work cars, because mine was playing up again, so Patrick didn't see me or do any of his clever manoeuvres to get rid of me.

They drove to Jack's school.

A school concert perhaps? Or a soccer game? One that I'd missed? I thought about texting him to ask, not that he would answer of course, but then Ellen stayed in the car while Patrick went into the school. He was half running. Was Jack sick?

But then only a few minutes later, he reappeared, walking quickly, carrying Jack's school bag while Jack ran to keep up with him. They jumped in the car and off they went again.

I couldn't think where they'd be going at this time of day and my desire to know was now a raging thirst. I was leaning forward, my hands clenched hard round the steering wheel, my vision focused entirely on the number plate of Patrick's car.

I dream about that number plate.

Toby from work rang on my mobile and I let it go to voicemail. Following them was all that mattered. I lost them at a set of lights on Military Road, when some idiot driver slammed on her brake at an orange light, as if her sole purpose was to thwart me. I screamed with frustration and slammed my hands so hard on the steering wheel they will probably bruise. It was pure luck that I found them again. When I got to the end of Military Road I turned left on to the Pacific Highway, for no particular reason, just because I was in the left-hand lane, and I saw the three of them walking along a footpath. Ellen pointed at a building and they disappeared inside.

I found a spot nearby and didn't bother putting money in the meter. I walked back to the same building while pain grabbed and twisted at my leg.

When I got to the empty lobby I stopped at the directory

board that listed various business names. Dental surgery. Chartered accountants. Immigration specialists. It could have been anything.

And then I saw: *Sydney Ultrasound.*

That's where they were going. To see the baby.

The baby.

It felt personal, as if they were all three of them doing this to hurt me, as if this entire building had been placed here for the sole purpose of hurting me.

He would hold her hand, and they would listen to the heartbeat and exchange teary, radiant smiles. I've seen the movies. I know how it works. Jack would see his little brother or sister for the first time.

You'll be the best big brother in the world, I used to tell him, when Patrick and I were trying to get pregnant. Jack said he'd prefer a little sister. His best friends were all girls at pre-school. 'I want a little sister called Jemima,' he said. 'With black hair.' And then he added, 'Please.' I was teaching him manners at the time. I said that would be fine. I quite liked the name Jemima.

I thought, thank God I followed them. Otherwise I might never even have known what day it was that they went for the ultrasound. It would have suddenly occurred to me, probably at 3.00 a.m. one night, that they must have been due for an ultrasound by now, and then I would have laid awake, obsessing over the details, wondering when it was, and where, and what they wore. At least this way I had some control. I was still part of it; I still existed. Even if they didn't know I was there, *I* would know. I could say, 'Fancy seeing you here!' as they came out of the office, or I could send a text tonight saying,

'How was the ultrasound?', or I could do nothing at all, but I would be a part of it from the beginning: from that very first pregnancy test, of course.

Perhaps they'll make me godmother.

Oh, I'm a riot.

It was a big, busy waiting room, filled with plump pregnant bellies and couples holding hands while they chatted softly, and slim women reading magazines while secretive smiles played across their faces. These were all people who fitted as snugly into society as the pieces of a jigsaw puzzle: clean, wholesome people who loved and were loved back.

I sat down on the first seat I saw, close to the door, and picked up a magazine. As I did, I heard a nurse say, 'Ellen O'Farrell.' There was a pause and then again, louder this time, 'Ellen O'Farrell.'

I looked up and saw that Ellen had been in the middle of helping herself to two plastic cups of water from one of those water cylinders, and now she was flustered, in that charming, girlish way of hers, uncertain what to do with the cups, her bag slipping off her shoulder as she straightened up too quickly. I saw Patrick and Jack walk towards her, and Jack lifted the strap of the bag back up over her shoulder – so grown-up, so well-mannered; I taught him manners – and Patrick took the cups. Then the nurse said something I didn't hear, and they all smiled, and off they went down a corridor, the three of them; they hadn't noticed me at all.

A woman sitting next to me said, 'Are you all right?'

I hadn't even realized I was crying.

*

'If you died,' said Jack to Ellen, 'would the baby die too?'

'Jack!' said Patrick. 'What sort of question is that?'

They'd gone out for an early dinner at a local pizza restaurant and Jack was studying the ultrasound photos while they waited for their pizza to arrive.

'The baby needs me to be alive to keep growing,' said Ellen. Should she reassure him that she wasn't going to die, like his mother? Or was he just interested? Or was he hoping she *would* die? Maybe he was sick to death of the healthy lunches.

'Did you eat your lunch today, Jack?' she asked.

'So, like, when Armageddon comes, and all the pregnant women die –' began Jack.

'Jesus! Enough with the Armageddon,' said Patrick. 'This is why you're having nightmares and this is why you're falling asleep in class.'

'I didn't actually fall asleep,' said Jack. He put the ultrasound photos down and Ellen slid her finger across the table and pulled them back towards her. 'I just closed my eyes for a minute to concentrate.'

'They couldn't wake you up, mate,' said Patrick.

Just before Ellen and Patrick had been due to leave for the ultrasound, the school had called to say that Jack had put his head on the desk and fallen so soundly asleep that the teacher had carried him all the way to sick bay without being able to wake him up. They'd assumed he was coming down with something, but he seemed in perfectly high spirits now, thrilled to have been given the day off school and taken along for the ultrasound.

'You were probably snoring,' said Patrick. 'Nobody else could concentrate.'

He put his head on one side and gave a convincing rumbly snore.

Jack grinned. '*You* snore. I never snore.'

'Me? I don't snore,' said Patrick. 'Do I, Ellen?'

'No,' said Ellen. He did snore, in fact; she was considering earplugs. She picked up the ultrasound photo and studied it. *Mine*, she thought. *My baby*. She glanced at Patrick and amended it: *Our baby*. The photo had a ghostly look to it, as if it was a photo of some supernatural phenomenon. 'Everything looks just as it should,' the woman doing the ultrasound had said. 'Congratulations.' And then she'd said, 'Oh, look! He or she is waving at you!' and she'd pointed out a tiny, ghostly hand, and Patrick, Ellen and Jack had all waved back.

'You snore like an earthquake!' Jack jabbed his finger at Patrick. He leaned forward with his elbows on the table and the tablecloth began to slip. 'You snore like a volcano!'

'Careful, mate.' Patrick adjusted the cloth. 'Actually, your mum taped me snoring once. I did sound a bit like a volcano.'

Ding! Fourth Colleen reference in the last hour, thought Ellen. She couldn't seem to stop noticing it, no matter how hard she tried.

'There's a volcano in America called the Yellowstone Super Volcano,' said Jack. 'And when it erupts – POW!' He banged his fist on the table and a glass full of sugar packets tipped over. 'That's the end of the world. It could happen any minute.'

'Really?' said Ellen.

'I don't think so,' said Patrick. 'Where's our pizza? Don't

they know we're starving over here? Let's see that photo again.' He took the photo from Ellen.

'Have you got a photo of me like that somewhere?' said Jack.

'Yeah, your mum put it in your baby book, remember? You've seen it before.'

Ding!

Oh, Ellen, give it a rest. What was the poor man meant to do? Ignore his son's questions? Pretend Colleen never existed?

'I'm going to the toilet,' announced Jack.

He always went to the toilet whenever they went out. It was his excuse for wandering around the restaurant, checking out whatever interested him.

'I bet he stops right there, where you can see into the kitchen,' said Ellen.

Jack stopped on cue, looking nonchalantly casual, as he pressed himself up against a pot plant and stood on tippy-toes so he could see over a ledge into where they were tossing pizza dough up into the air.

Ellen and Patrick laughed, and for a moment it felt like they were both his parents. Patrick smiled. 'Funny kid.' He lifted up the photo and looked at it. 'I wonder if you'll be worried about Armageddon one day, kid? Or will you be a serene, spiritual soul like your mother?'

'I'm not feeling that serene at the moment,' said Ellen. 'What a day. First Luisa wanting her money back and then Ian Roman threatening to "bring me down". I think this qualifies as the worst day in my professional life.'

'Ian Roman is just throwing his weight around,' said Patrick. 'Don't worry about him. He'll get distracted buying his next television station or whatever.' He paused. 'So are you really hypnotizing his wife to fall in love with him?'

'Of course not,' said Ellen. 'I can't make anyone feel something that isn't genuine. Rosie *asked* me to do that and I suggested that we do some work on her self-esteem issues instead. You can't love someone unless you feel good about yourself. I can't say too much but I just said I would try and help give her enough self-confidence to either leave him or to try and make it work.'

'Mmmm,' said Patrick. He looked doubtful.

'What?' said Ellen.

'I don't know. I guess it sounds a bit . . . airy-fairy?'

Ellen felt quite profoundly irritated. 'Oh, so now you think I'm some sort of charlatan as well, do you?'

'Of course not. Look. I'm a simple surveyor. A man of the land. Obviously I have no idea what I'm talking about.'

'Mmmm,' said Ellen.

'Quick! Change of subject! How about our beautiful baby? Hey?' He handed her the photo, and Ellen smiled in spite of herself.

After a second, Patrick said, his tone changed, 'Did you see her?'

Ellen kept looking at the photo. She knew exactly who he was talking about.

'Yes,' she said.

'I have to do something about it,' said Patrick. 'With the baby coming . . .' He pressed a fingertip to the photo. 'I've never thought of her as dangerous, but she looked a bit . . . I don't know, unhinged. Crazier than usual.'

Ellen thought of Luisa today; crazy with grief and envy

over Ellen's pregnancy. She thought of Saskia's face when she walked into the waiting room. Ellen had seen her immediately. She had a feverish, desperate look about her, as if she was hurrying to catch an important flight.

'Did Saskia want to have a baby with you?' she asked.

'Who cares if she did?' said Patrick roughly. 'There is no justification for this!'

'I just wondered,' said Ellen. *I just want to understand.*

'Family-sized supreme?' interrupted a waitress.

When they got home, there was a message on Ellen's voicemail from a journalist, called Lisa Hamilton. She said she was working on a story for the *Daily News* about hypnotherapy and 'its claims' and had been speaking to some of Ellen's clients. 'I wondered if you would care to comment about some of the allegations that are being made,' she said.

Her voice was cold and clipped; full of certainty and authority with a faint edge of disgust.

Ellen put down the phone.

'Everything OK?' said Patrick.

'I think I know how Ian Roman is planning to put me out of business.'

21

Dreams are the royal road to the unconscious.

— Freud, 1900

'What's that old cliché? All publicity is good publicity?' said Patrick.

Ellen was already in bed and Patrick had just come in from checking on Jack.

'This isn't going to be good publicity,' said Ellen. She'd called back the journalist and had agreed to meet her for an interview the following morning at eleven. Ellen had talked to plenty of journalists over the years, and normally she quite enjoyed it. Ever since she'd attended a seminar a few years back called 'Marketing Your Hypnotherapy Practice', she'd actively looked for opportunities and made herself available for comment. Every December she was called up by journalists writing articles to appear in the new year with headlines like, 'How to stick to those resolutions: We ask our panel of experts!' She'd been interviewed for health magazines about weight loss, and business magazines about overcoming public-speaking nerves. She contributed to a weekly 'mental health' column for her local paper and she was a regular guest on various mid-morning radio shows. She'd even been on television a few times.

In every case the journalists she'd dealt with had been, if

not respectful, at least perfectly friendly and interested. She was soft news. The human interest angle. Something a bit different for the women readers. A bit of fun. Nobody was really too fussed about what she had to say. They didn't *really* believe in hypnosis, but they didn't care too much either way.

But as soon as she spoke to Lisa Hamilton, she knew that this was going to be a different sort of interview to anything she'd done before. Her voice didn't even soften when Ellen, in a blatant plea for sympathy, had mentioned that she was pregnant and suffering terrible morning sickness and would therefore prefer not to meet too early in the morning. Lisa was clearly not the sort of person who could fake the charm in order to get Ellen to reveal more. If she was going to write an article trashing Ellen, she had to hate her.

Ellen had no experience being hated.

It wasn't helping her nausea.

'I remember Colleen saying that they didn't mind if they got a bad product review because the only part that stuck in people's minds was the name of the product.' Patrick pulled back the quilt and climbed in next to her.

Colleen had been a marketing assistant. Ellen wondered if she just imagined that Patrick's face automatically softened whenever he mentioned Colleen's name, in the same way that her father's face had softened when he mentioned his real children.

And so what if it did?

(And just what did she mean by '*real* children'? How sulky and silly and obvious of her. She was behaving as if her father had deserted her. Was that what she subconsciously thought? She thought her subconscious was more mature than that.)

'I'm not a product,' said Ellen, although the marketing course she'd done had encouraged her to think of herself as a 'brand'.

'You know what I mean,' said Patrick. 'I just don't want you getting yourself worked up about this when it probably means nothing. It might not even be related to Ian I've-got-a-big-dick Roman.'

'He owns that paper,' said Ellen. 'I looked it up on the Internet. It's too much of a coincidence.'

'Have you called his wife?' said Patrick. 'She's the one who needs to put a stop to all this.'

'I've left two messages,' said Ellen. 'I don't think she could help now anyway. He's got me in his sights.' She paused. 'Did I just say, "He's got me in his sights"? I can't believe I said that.'

Patrick didn't answer. He was lying back on his pillow looking at his BlackBerry. He was addicted to it. It made Ellen laugh when he complained about Jack spending too much time on his DS.

'Jesus,' said Patrick. He sat up.

'What?' said Ellen, thinking *Saskia*.

'The bastard wants to take *me* to court.'

'What bastard?'

Patrick was still looking incredulously at the tiny screen. 'That client who is refusing to pay his bill.' He tapped furiously with his thumbs. 'I got my solicitor to send over a Letter of Demand today. And now this guy is not only refusing to pay, but he reckons he's going to sue us because we took too long to complete the work. What a joke.'

'It's probably just a, what do you call it, a countermove,' said Ellen.

'God almighty! The *injustice* of it.' Patrick's whole body had become almost rigid with rage. 'He wanted this job fast-tracked. We worked overtime for him. I missed Jack's soccer game because of this prick, and then he has the *audacity* to say we took too long?'

'Your solicitor will know what to do,' said Ellen.

His rage made her feel nervous. She'd always found male anger intimidating. It was so physical.

She said, 'You can call him first thing in the morning.'

'Yes,' said Patrick. He turned off his BlackBerry, took a deep breath and glanced at her. 'We're not having a great day, are we?'

Ellen pointed at her stomach. 'Shhhh. It was a great day, remember?'

Patrick put his hand briefly on Ellen's stomach. 'Of course it was.'

He put the BlackBerry down on his bedside table and folded the quilt back so that it was covering Ellen, but not him.

'Flat pillow,' he said.

'Oops,' said Ellen. They swapped pillows.

They snapped off their bedside lamps at the same time, lay down and turned away from each other, their backs pressed together. Patrick tapped her leg with his heel to say goodnight, she tapped back with her heel.

They'd been in a relationship for less than a year, and already they had so many routines, customs and procedures. It was like each new couple created a new kingdom together.

Saskia couldn't let her kingdom go.

She closed her eyes and Ian Roman's face immediately loomed in front of her, as if he'd been waiting behind a curtain, ready to jump out the moment she tried to fall asleep.

I'm putting you out of business.

He couldn't really put her out of business, could he? Even if the article did imply terrible things about her, she wouldn't lose all her clients, would she? All the goodwill she'd built up over the years couldn't vanish overnight, could it?

From just one article?

And for heaven's sake, how bad could that one article be? She wasn't some sort of evil con artist. She hadn't done anything wrong.

They couldn't just make things up, could they?

Well, of course they could. She thought about all those celebrity articles announcing that Jennifer Aniston and Brad Pitt were getting back together, when they clearly weren't. But she wasn't a celebrity. Nobody actually cared about her life, whereas everybody wanted Brad and Jennifer to get back together; that's why they wrote those articles, because that's what people wanted to hear.

(She herself was quite keen for Brad and Jennifer to get back together.)

Surely this Lisa Hamilton would have enough journalistic integrity to talk to clients other than Luisa. Or did she have no choice? Had Ian Roman called her up and said, 'I want this woman's reputation trashed or it's your job'?

And the poor journalist had an abusive husband and three small children, one of them requiring some sort of expensive transplant, and she had to keep her job at all costs, so Ellen would have to be sacrificed.

'Can you sleep?' said Patrick, his voice suddenly loud in the quiet room.

'No.'

'Me neither.'

He switched his light back on. 'Should I get us some milk or something? Tea?'

'No thanks,' yawned Ellen. She sat up.

He said, without any real enthusiasm, 'Should we have sex do you think?'

Ellen laughed. 'I'm not feeling especially amorous.'

'No,' agreed Patrick. 'I think I'll go write an abusive email to that client. Or punch something. Or run round the block.'

'Let me do you a relaxation,' said Ellen. She would be glad of the distraction.

'You've got enough on your mind,' said Patrick.

'I don't mind,' said Ellen. 'I go into a trance too.'

'Oh God, thank you, I didn't want to ask.' Patrick lay down next to her. 'I can't believe how hooked I've got on this.'

Ten minutes later, he was in a medium trance, and Ellen herself was in that lovely liquid state she seemed to reach whenever she hypnotized Patrick.

'I want you to go back to a time when you felt completely relaxed. A time long before the stresses of running your own business. Think of a time when you felt completely relaxed and happy. Are you there yet?'

He nodded.

'Where are you?'

'Honeymoon,' said Patrick. His voice had that stupid drugged quality.

Ellen went very still.

Stop right there, said Flynn's voice in her head. She paused, considering, listening to Patrick's deep, even breaths.

Ask him, said Danny. *Ask him what you want to know.*

'What are you doing?' she said to Patrick. There was nothing wrong with that.

In the soft lamplight Patrick looked ten years younger. The lines between his eyes had smoothed out and his cheeks looked plumper.

'We're snorkelling,' he said.

'You and Colleen,' checked Ellen.

Who else? Julia snorted in her head. *Oh, what a load of rubbish*, said her mother. *He's just describing a memory to you. This isn't time travel.*

'Yes. It's stunning.' Patrick smiled. 'Col is wearing a blue bikini.'

'Is she?' said Ellen faintly.

'She looks gorgeous.'

'Great,' said Ellen. Julia was rolling about laughing in her head. *You asked for it, you idiot.*

Highly unprofessional, said Flynn.

'Describe what you're feeling,' said Ellen, trying to get him back on track.

'I've never been snorkelling before. Everything feels slowed down and still and all I can hear is my breathing. The coral is – oh, but I have to tell her!'

His face changed. The lines reappeared, dragging down his cheeks.

'Tell her what?' said Ellen. Sometimes a simple relaxation

exercise could bring up repressed negative feelings; it had never happened before with Patrick, it wasn't meant to happen with Patrick. This wasn't a proper session; this was just helping him forget about the horrible client so he could go to sleep.

And this is exactly why we don't recommend hypnotizing your partner, said Flynn.

'To see the doctor! Now. Right now. We have to go and see a doctor and catch it, the cancer, before it's too late.' Patrick's hand opened and closed reflexively round the bed sheet. 'She's so *stupid*, so stubborn. She felt that lump and she never said a word, for months, just hoping it was nothing, hoping it would go away. Just like she hoped the oil light would stop flashing in her car. Jesus Christ. You idiot, I said to her. You *idiot*. I made her cry. I shouldn't have made her cry. But she had a responsibility. To Jack. To *me*.'

Grief ravaged his face.

'It's time to let this memory slip away,' said Ellen. Her voice did not have the appropriate level of authority. She sounded like a beginner: shaky and forced.

'I will never love another woman like her.'

'On the count of five,' said Ellen.

'I look at Ellen,' said Patrick.

Ellen froze.

'And I think: It's not the same. It's just not the same.'

After they walked in to have their ultrasound, I couldn't stop crying. I had to leave. I was making a spectacle of myself. A woman came out from behind the reception desk and started walking towards me with a kind, purposeful expression on her face that meant: *I sympathize but please shut the hell up.*

I guess people aren't always crying tears of joy here. Ultrasounds don't always mean good news. The woman probably thought I'd lost a baby.

What could I have said to her? No, I've never actually been pregnant, but I did lose my stepson. Does that count? He's that beautiful kid over there helping his new stepmother with her handbag. He looks tired. I don't think she's feeding him right. Too much tofu and lentils. Not enough protein. And although I didn't lose an actual baby, I did lose a dream baby, because that man over there stopped loving me, and now I'm too old, and he's found someone younger and nicer.

They would say: No, that certainly does not count. Stop embarrassing yourself. Show some dignity. Some self-respect.

Fair enough too.

As I went down in the lift, I was still crying, but wasn't really aware of feeling any particular emotion. The tears were like a symptom of some peculiar disease. I was just waiting for them to stop.

I was walking back to my car when the pain in my leg suddenly became unbearable. If I used Ellen's dial metaphor, it was like someone had twisted it up to high.

It was impossible to walk. I had to sit down. I looked around for a bus stop or a wall, but there wasn't anywhere, so I just sat down in the gutter, like a drunk. I couldn't believe that just half an hour earlier I was dealing so efficiently with those developers and now here I was, crying in a gutter.

A man who had parked his car just in front of where I sat down came over to ask if I was OK. He looked like he was in his late sixties. One of those weathered friendly faces, like a man from the outback. He reminded me of Patrick's dad. He seemed convinced that he'd seen me twist my ankle, and was talking about getting ice for it, and how I needed to keep it elevated, and it took quite a while for him to be convinced that my ankle was fine. I finally had to explain to him that I had a pain in my leg that could not be explained or cured, and that I wasn't crying because of the pain but because of 'something personal'. He pulled his wallet out of his pocket and took out a card. For a moment I thought he was giving me the name of a therapist, but he said, 'This guy is a brilliant physio. I had terrible back pain a few months ago. Excruciating. Nearly brought *me* to tears. He fixed me right up. Good as new!'

I thanked him, and didn't bother telling him that I'd already been to seven different physiotherapists and I wasn't going to waste any more of my money.

'In the meantime, take a really strong painkiller,' he said. 'And forget that schmuck! His loss, right? Plenty more fish in the sea for a gorgeous girl like you!' He gave me a little pat on the shoulder and then he suddenly seemed embarrassed, as if he was worried he might be acting inappropriately, and he stood up quickly and his knees made a loud cracking sound, which his brilliant physio might need to take a look at.

Nice people! How do they get so nice? And how do they *sustain* it? All that smiling and caring and sharing? It must be exhausting and so time consuming – keeping an eye out for strangers in need.

As I watched him go I thought, for the first time in years: It must be nice to have a dad.

I bet Ellen has a lovely father, a daddy who bounced her on his knee and called her his Princess. She has the look of someone who has been adored by her father.

I called up the office from the gutter and told them that I was going to work from home for the day.

I managed to hobble back to the car, and when I got home I took the nice dad-like man's advice and found some Panadeine Forte in my medicine cupboard. I took two and then I feel asleep. When I woke up, the brother and sister from the nice family next door were home from school and they were in the backyard. I tried to do some work but my head felt so fuzzy and peculiar, and I kept getting distracted by the sounds of their playing. For nice children they didn't seem to be playing so nicely. It sounded like a toxic relationship: one minute laughter and singing and the next tears and screams of 'Stop it!' I was under the impression that children stayed indoors these days and played computer games.

Eventually I gave up trying to work and I opened a bottle of red wine. I thought I would toast Patrick's new baby.

That was my mistake. I've never been much of a drinker.

Ellen dreamed.

Her dreams were vivid and endless and exhausting. She knew she was dreaming and she kept trying to wake up properly so the dreams would stop, and every now and then she would find herself back in the reality of the dark room, turning over to readjust her pillow, nudging Patrick to stop him snoring, but then before she could stop herself, she'd find herself falling asleep again, toppling head first into a canyon of swirling thoughts and faces and sounds.

Her mother and her godmothers were running along a

beach, naked, laughing in that schoolgirl way that always made her feel left out.

'They're showing off,' she said to her father, who was sitting on the beach next to her, fully dressed, thankfully, in his suit and tie. He had sauce from his Moroccan chicken wrap on his lip.

Ellen said, 'The daughter's relationship with her father is the model for all her future relationships.' She felt proud, as if she were making some sort of incredibly subtle, ironic, witty point.

Her father was reading the newspaper now. He glanced up at her with an expression of pure disgust on his face. 'This article is about you,' he said.

'It's not true,' said Ellen, filled with shame and hurt beyond belief.

'It is true,' said a girl who was sitting in front of Ellen patting a sandcastle into shape with a yellow spade.

'Colleen!' said Ellen. She was going to be extremely nice to her because that was the sort of person she was. 'How *are* you?'

She tried to think of a topic of conversation that would interest Colleen. 'I hear that you sewed your own wedding dress,' she said. 'You must be so *talented*!'

'You're being condescending,' said Julia. She was sunbathing on her stomach and lifted her head from her towel to speak.

'She should never have got pregnant,' said Colleen to Julia. 'That was unethical of her.'

'Probably,' yawned Julia. 'But she means well.'

'It was unethical because he's still in love with me,' said Colleen complacently.

'But you're dead!' cried Ellen, suddenly remembering and filled with the injustice of her accusation.

'You're a very pretty girl,' said Ellen's father to Colleen.

Colleen tilted her head. 'Thank you, David.'

'Well, I'm so sorry for getting pregnant,' said Ellen. She knew she was acting petulantly because she was jealous of her father complimenting Colleen but she couldn't seem to stop herself. She began to fling handfuls of sand at her own face. 'How can I redeem myself? What can I do to make it up to you?'

'Ellen. Stop it. You are making an absolute fool of yourself,' said Madeline, who was sitting on the old couch they had when they shared a flat.

'Did you hear something?' said Patrick. Ellen woke to see Patrick sitting up next to her in bed, rubbing his eyes.

'It's just the wind, I think,' said Ellen.

Outside, the wind was howling, making the windows rattle. She sat up and reached for the glass of water on the bedside table.

'Sorry,' said Patrick. He lay back down.

Ellen tipped back her water glass. It was empty. She didn't remember drinking it. She looked at the clock: only 4.00 a.m. This night would never end.

'I'm having all these peculiar dreams,' said Ellen.

There was a bang as a branch or something landed on the roof.

'Me too,' said Patrick. 'It's the wind.'

'You said something when I was doing your relaxation,' said Ellen.

'Mmmm?' said Patrick.

'About Colleen.'

She waited. Patrick snored.

Ellen lay back down and instantly dreamed again.

This time she was walking down the aisle on her wedding day, wearing her grandmother's dress. She was carrying the baby in the palm of her outstretched hand. The baby was the size of a bead and it was rolling back and forth across her palm.

'Keep your hand flat! You'll drop it!' said one of the wedding guests. Ellen turned her head to see that it was her client Luisa, wearing a big hat. 'You don't even know how to look after a baby! I should be the pregnant one! Give it to me!'

'I gave you your money back,' said Ellen briskly. 'There is nothing more I can do. I am a good person.'

She kept walking. She could see Patrick at the end of the aisle, facing away from her. He turned round to look at her and Ellen smiled at him, but his face changed.

'Stop following me!' he yelled. His voice echoed throughout the whole church. 'It's *over*! Can't you understand? I never loved you!'

Ellen was mortified. 'Patrick, it's not Saskia, it's me!' she called out. She tried to keep her voice light and cheery, because it was a wedding after all, but loud enough for Patrick to hear right down the other end of the aisle, which had become as long as an airport runway.

'Leave me alone!' shouted Patrick.

'Darling, I don't think he loves you any more,' said her mother. She and the godmothers were dressed up like bridesmaids from the eighties, in pink taffeta dresses with big shoulders and bows.

'Men!' said Pip. 'Who needs them? Let's get drunk.'

'You'll meet someone else,' said Mel.

'I never really liked him much anyway,' sniffed Ellen's mother.

'He thinks I'm Saskia,' said Ellen. 'I'm sure it's just a mix-up.'

But actually she wasn't sure. Had *she* been the one stalking Patrick all along?

'You hypnotized me into moving those boxes!' shouted Patrick. 'You manipulated me!'

'I'm sorry!' cried Ellen. He was breaking up with her. This relationship was going to end just like all her other relationships. She was going to have to bring up this baby on her own and it was so teeny-tiny! She closed her hand carefully round the baby-bead and began to run, but as soon as she did her legs lurched sickeningly, as if she'd run off a cliff.

She opened her eyes.

She couldn't tell if it was morning or night; the bedroom seemed to be filled with a strange, eerie orange-yellow light.

It was like there'd been a fire, except there was no smell of smoke. She could hear Patrick's rattly breathing that was not quite snoring, and the hollow, rhythmic sound of waves crashing on the beach.

And she could hear or sense something else. Something not right.

There was a long dark shape at the end of the bed. Ellen stared, her heart hammering, waiting for her eyes to adjust and for the shape to become a familiar object, like a chair or a dressing gown hanging on a door.

It moved.

Ellen's lungs filled with air.

A woman was standing in their bedroom, at the foot of their bed, watching them sleep. Ellen scrabbled back so fast that her head banged painfully against the headboard.

Colleen. Colleen back from the dead to claim her husband.

'What is it?' said Patrick sleepily.

He sat up and rubbed his eyes with the heels of his hands. Then suddenly he flung back the covers and crawled straight across the bed.

'Get out!' he roared. 'Get *out*!'

It wasn't Colleen. It was Saskia. She was wearing pyjama bottoms with a football jersey over the top. Her hair was wet and plastered to her head; her feet were bare.

'Patrick,' she said. She stepped back to avoid his grasp. 'I just wanted –'

Patrick fell out of the bed and on to the floor in an ungainly sprawl.

Ellen saw that Saskia was holding something in her hand. It was the ultrasound pictures that they'd left on the kitchen table.

'Hey!' She'd never heard her voice sound like that before: as if it had been scraped raw. 'Give those back!'

She got out of bed and moved towards Saskia. 'They're *mine*!'

There was a terrified shriek from down the hallway. 'Daddy!'

'Jack,' said Saskia. She half turned towards the door.

Patrick got to his feet and grabbed Saskia by both arms. He lifted her up into the air as if he was going to slam her against the wall. The ultrasound photos fell from her hand on to the floor. Ellen saw that Patrick was trembling all over, his eyes wild and crazed.

He's going to kill her, she thought. *It's my job to stop him killing her.*

She grabbed for the back of Patrick's T-shirt, as Saskia tried to drape her arms round Patrick's neck.

'I just want to explain!' she said.

Patrick pulled her hands away from his neck.

'Dad!' screamed Jack. 'Ellen! What's happening?'

'Get out!' Patrick dragged Saskia back to her feet. 'Get out now.'

'I'm sorry,' sobbed Saskia. She fell against Patrick's chest again, and with Ellen still clutching the back of his T-shirt, they shuffled out into the hallway in a strangely intimate dance.

Dawn was breaking and through the open door of her office opposite their bedroom, where Ellen would normally see the beach and the ocean, all she could see was a haze of apocalyptic orange. Yellow light poured into the house. She let go of Patrick's T-shirt and stared.

What was going on? Was it war?

'Daddy! It's *Armageddon*!'

Ellen turned her eyes back in time to see Patrick shove Saskia away from him at the same time as Jack came pounding down the hallway in his pyjamas, his eyes gigantic with fear.

Saskia slipped on the landing runner and she flung an arm out to save herself.

Her flailing hand clutched at Jack's pyjama top and the two of them fell together; toppling, crashing, rolling.

22

Careful!
— Mothers throughout the world, throughout time

For one long, endless, silent moment Ellen and Patrick stood at the top of the staircase, their hands gripped on the landing banister, their eyes fixed on Jack and Saskia below.

Saskia was on her back. One leg was bent at a sickeningly strange angle. Her head lolled; her face was obscured by her hair.

Jack was flat on his stomach, his legs straight, his palms down on the floor as if he were asleep in bed.

They're both dead, thought Ellen with certainty, and she was seized by the terrifying revelation that this actually happened, exactly like this, all the time, every day. People died, *children* died, in clumsy, stupid accidents that took only a few seconds, and afterwards you kept breathing, and your heart kept pumping, and everything was still exactly the same. The unacceptable happened and you were expected to accept it.

Patrick made a sound like a dog's whimper.

Then Jack moved, and Patrick reacted instantly. He went clattering down the stairs so fast that as Ellen ran behind him she called out, 'Careful!'

Jack sat up on his haunches, cradling his arm. His face was dead white.

'I think I broke it,' he said in a matter-of-fact tone, and then he turned his head and was sick all over the floor.

Ellen and Patrick fell to their knees on either side of him.

'Oh, darling,' said Ellen. She lifted the sleeve of his pyjamas and saw the bone poking out through the skin.

'You're OK, mate,' said Patrick unconvincingly. He looked like he might faint.

Jack lifted his head and wiped his hand across his mouth. He looked at them with streaming, baffled eyes.

'What's happened? I don't understand. Why is Saskia here?'

'Don't worry about that,' said Patrick. He went to reach for Jack as if to pick him up. 'I'm going to take you to emergency.'

'No, you mustn't move him,' said Ellen. 'He might have a back or head injury. Just lie him down and keep that arm still. I'll call an ambulance. Let me just check on Saskia.'

'Forget Saskia,' hissed Patrick.

'Why is she here?' said Jack again. His eyes widened as he saw her over Ellen's shoulder. 'Is she all right?'

'Just forget about her,' said Patrick.

'No!' yelled Jack. His voice was unexpectedly loud in the silent house.

Patrick blanched. 'It's all right, mate.'

Jack pulled away from him. 'You can't just *forget* about her! Stop saying that! Just because *you* don't like her. It's not fair!'

'Everything is OK,' said Patrick soothingly.

'Check on her!' Jack's face went from white to bright red, his small chest heaved beneath his pyjama top and his eyes glittered with fury. Ellen stared; she'd never seen a small child experiencing such grown-up emotions.

She said, 'I'll make sure she's OK, Jack.'

There are some parts that I know I'll never forget, and some parts that I expect I'll never remember.

Like, I don't remember calling a taxi, but I do remember pulling up in front of Ellen's house and paying the driver. I gave him a ten-dollar tip and we talked about the wind. It was howling. I remember the trees swaying back and forth, like women lamenting their dead children.

I felt exhilarated and wild; a woman in the forest embracing my inner something-or-other. I remember touching my hair and realizing it was dripping wet and being confused because it wasn't raining. I must have stepped straight out of the shower and called a cab.

At least I didn't drive when I was drunk. Some rational part of my mind knew enough to call a cab.

I don't remember why I decided to go to Ellen's house, but I can guess my train of thought. I was probably standing in the shower and imagining Ellen and Patrick getting ready to go to bed at the same time, and how they would have been talking about their day, how exciting it was to see the baby for the first time, and I would have thought: *I wish I could see them.*

And at that point I must have thought: *Why not go there right now?*

Or maybe I felt an overwhelming desire to tell Patrick something: that I loved him or I hated him, that I understood or that I would never understand, that I was letting him go, finally, this was it, I would never go near him again, or that I would never let him go, I would love him for the rest of my life.

Who knows?

The next thing I remember is standing at the foot of their bed.

Patrick was flat on his back, his mouth open, snoring in that way of his, where each snore goes further up the scale in volume, until there is an enormous shuddery one that half wakes him up and he stops, and then a few seconds later it starts again. Ellen was lying on her side, with her hands folded in prayer under her cheek, just like you'd expect her to sleep, although she was snoring too, in a gentler, more regular rhythm than Patrick. Their snoring sounded comical; as if they were trying to play a tune together and kept getting it wrong and having to start again.

I didn't feel envy or anger or pain. I felt calm and quite friendly towards them. I think it was because of the snoring. So I got a shock when they woke up and I saw their reactions. The fear on their faces! I wanted to say, 'No, no, relax, it's only *me*!'

It was like Patrick had seen some sort of dangerous animal. As if I was a grizzly bear looming over him. Me! Just me. Saskia! I don't even kill cockroaches. He knows that.

And then Ellen was yelling at me about something in my hand and I looked down and saw that I was holding their baby's ultrasound pictures, although I didn't remember picking them up, or looking at them.

She reacted as if I was stealing her baby.

Technically, she stole my baby. I could have got pregnant with Patrick's baby, if we'd kept trying. I might have.

They woke Jack up with all their noise. I heard him call out. So then I just wanted everyone to calm down. I wanted them to know that there was no need for anyone to be upset.

It was like a nightmare, where you suddenly realize you're naked in a shopping centre. A tiny voice in my head said: *Saskia, you've gone too far. What would Mum think?*

Mum would not approve of me upsetting Jack.

Nobody would calm down. Patrick refused to listen. He was pushing me, shoving me. I noticed that everything had turned sepia, as if we were in an old photograph. It added to that nightmarish, surreal feeling.

I remember Jack running down the hallway in his pyjamas, his eyes and mouth huge with terror. That voice in my head saying: *This is your fault, Saskia.*

And then somehow, we were falling together, and I was trying to hold on to him, to stop him hurting himself. It was terrible.

That was the last thing I remember before I woke up in the hospital and felt the most unbearable pain shatter the lower half of my body, as if someone was dropping bricks on me from a great height, and I saw Ellen, standing with her back to me at the hospital window. I must have made some sort of a noise, because she turned round and smiled at me. She didn't look frightened. She smiled at me, as if I were a normal person, not a grizzly bear.

She said, 'There's been a big dust storm.'

It was the first thing that came into her head.

'Sydney is covered in dust,' she said. 'It really looks quite apocalyptic out there. No wonder Jack thought it was the end of the world. I actually thought there had been a nuclear bomb myself.'

Saskia stared up at her blankly, as if she was speaking a foreign language.

'They can see it from space, apparently,' said Ellen. She took a deep breath and sat down on the chair next to Saskia's bed. 'That's why it took a while for the ambulance to come this morning. The city is in chaos.'

Saskia's eyes moved slowly down the bed and the white hospital blanket covering her body.

'You've fractured your pelvis,' said Ellen. 'And your right ankle. You might need surgery for the ankle, but they think the pelvis should heal itself. You can press the little button here for more pain relief.'

There was silence. Ellen's eyes locked with Saskia's. It felt shocking, as if the strange connection between the two of them was more intimate than that of two sexual partners. Saskia had light brown eyes. They were almost gold.

'I don't know if you remember what happened,' began Ellen.

'Jack,' said Saskia clearly.

'He's broken his arm,' said Ellen. 'But other than that he's fine.'

Saskia's face crumpled. 'My fault.'

'Well,' said Ellen. 'Yes.'

Jack went through a stage when he was a toddler when he seemed to be constantly hurting himself. He'd bang his head on the coffee table, his elbow against the door frame. As soon as one bruise or graze healed he'd get another one. I'd be down the other end of the house and hear the crash, the pause and then the anguished scream that shredded my heart. I'd think: *Not again.*

Once Patrick was playing with him when it was past his bedtime and I was saying, 'OK that's enough now,' because I knew Jack was getting overtired and he'd hurt himself soon, and, sure enough, next thing Jack's yelling and spitting out blood because he'd banged his chin and bitten his tongue, and I was *furious* with Patrick.

I must have said it a thousand times: 'Careful.'

And now, because of *me*, Jack had a broken arm. There was no denying my responsibility. There was no way I could twist the events of the previous evening round to make it someone else's fault.

Ellen sat there, just looking at me steadily. She looked exhausted: grey shadows under her eyes, pale lips. No make-up. Messy hair. Her face plain. Ordinary even. Except that there was something so pristine about her. Looking at her was like looking at something natural and true.

I caused Jack to break his arm.

It was like someone was holding a screen right up close to my face, and it was playing a movie of everything I'd done for the last three years: every text message, every phone call, every letter I knew he'd never read, leading up to the final sepia-coloured moment when Jack and I crashed down the stairs.

I closed my eyes to try to escape from it, but I could still see it. It was unflinching and unrelenting.

I was being suffocated by shame.

'Breathe,' said Ellen. 'Just concentrate on your breathing. Inhale and exhale. Inhale and exhale.' The sound of her voice was like an old familiar tune. It took me straight back to her little glass room overlooking the ocean. I listened greedily, as if her voice was oxygen.

'That's it. In. And out.'

I opened my eyes, and saw that she'd leaned in closer, so that her face was only inches from mine. She took my hand. Her hands were cold. My mother always had cold hands. *Cold hands, warm heart*, she used to say.

'Have you heard the phrase "hitting rock bottom"?' she said.

She didn't wait for an answer. I noticed her voice had changed subtly. She was speaking in her 'professional' voice.

'It's something that happens to addicts when they finally break down in every way possible: physically, spiritually, emotionally. I think that's sort of what's happening to you right now, Saskia. And I don't know, but I think it probably feels terrible. I think it probably feels like the end of the world.'

I felt a wild, flapping sensation in my chest, like a trapped bird.

Ellen kept talking. 'But it's good, it's a good thing, it's even a great thing, because it's the turning point. It's the beginning of getting better. It's the beginning of getting your life back. I think you've probably tried to stop before, haven't you?'

Once again, she didn't seem to expect an answer.

'But this time it's going to work. For one thing, you're going to be stuck.' Ellen's eyes sparkled, as if it was all a great joke. 'They tell me you won't be walking for six to eight weeks, and after that you'll be on crutches.

'And during that time you'll get counselling,' continued Ellen confidently, happily, as if we were discussing shared holiday plans that were already in place. 'It will be a good way to pass the time.

'And then, once you're back on your feet, I think you should move.' She smiled. 'That might seem a bit presumptuous of me, but, well, I've got the right to be presumptuous. I think you need to move somewhere far away from Sydney. So you won't be tempted.'

Her hand tightened round mine. 'I expect Patrick will finally take out a restraining order against you. So, legally, you won't be able to come near us. He's going to need to do that, but what I need is a promise from you, a promise right now, that this is it, that last night was the end and today is the beginning. The end of your old life and the beginning of your new life. Can you promise me that?'

I felt my head jerk up and down, as if I was a puppet and she was pulling the strings. I said, 'I promise.'

She patted my hand and said, 'Good.'

I became aware of the pain again. It gripped and viciously squeezed the lower half of my body, and it felt personal, as if someone was doing it on purpose. I tried not to resist it, to accept it as my punishment, but frankly, it hurt too much.

'Give yourself a hit,' said Ellen. She put something like a light switch in my hand. I pressed the button. A few seconds later I felt a sensation of fuzzy warmth, like pins and needles creeping up my legs, and the pain receded. I said, 'Why are you here? Why are you being nice to me?'

My mouth felt as if it was full of marbles, as if I hadn't spoken for a very long time.

Ellen went to speak and then she stopped, as if she were reconsidering.

She said, 'I don't really know. You frightened me, but at the same time you intrigued me. I even found it strangely validating. You watching us made my life seem more interesting.' She shook her head. 'I was sort of addicted to you.'

'You should hate me,' I said. My voice sounded unfamiliar: slurred, like a stroke victim. 'Patrick hates me.'

'That's because I didn't have the emotional connection that Patrick has to you. Patrick hates you because he once loved you.'

'That's nice of you to say that,' I said. My nose was running. I went to wipe it with the back of my hand and saw I had the drip attached. I sniffed noisily. I didn't even care. I had no dignity left to lose.

'I'm not that nice,' said Ellen. 'When I saw you holding the ultrasound photos I wanted to kill you. It turns out that I do have limits. I don't want you near my baby.'

Her eyes had turned steely.

The words *I'm sorry* came into my mind but they seemed insultingly inadequate.

I said instead, 'Patrick is lucky to have you.' And it occurred to me that I might actually mean it, that in a far-off, more generous part of my mind, I could even be happy for him.

Her face shifted in some tiny, subtle way. She said, 'He's still in love with his first wife.'

'Yes, of course,' I said. I could feel my senses starting to drift. 'He still loves Colleen. First love and all that, but, so what, she's dead, isn't she? I always knew that I loved him more than he loved me, but I didn't care, I just loved him so much.'

A great wave of tiredness was dragging me somewhere far away.

'I know you did.' Ellen stood up, adjusting my blankets, like a mother. 'You loved him. And you loved Jack.'

For a moment I seemed to swim back up to lucidity again and I said, 'Have you hypnotized me?'

She smiled. 'I've been trying to *un*hypnotize you, Saskia.'

And then I was drifting away again, and I heard her say, 'It's time to move on now, Saskia, and let go of all those memories of Patrick and Jack. It doesn't mean it didn't happen, or that Patrick didn't love you, or that you weren't a wonderful mother to Jack. I know that you were. It doesn't mean that he didn't hurt you terribly. But now it's time to close that door. Imagine an actual door. A big heavy wooden door with an old-fashioned gold lock. Now close it. *Bang*. Lock it. Throw away the key. It's closed, Saskia. Closed forever.'

When I woke up again, the room was empty and the hypnotist's visit seemed like a dream.

23

Love! Give me chocolate any day!

— Ellen's godmother, Pip

*The suffragettes didn't starve themselves for the vote,
so that you girls could starve yourselves for a man.*

— Ellen's godmother, Mel

Oh Lord, what superficial nonsense she'd been dishing out. *Close the door. Close it forever.*

For heaven's sake, the woman had broken into their house in the middle of the night and watched them sleep. She was probably schizophrenic or bipolar or who knew what. She probably needed antipsychotic medication combined with intensive ongoing therapy. Ellen's sappy little comments were like giving her vitamins when she needed surgery.

Also, closing the door wasn't quite the right metaphor. You didn't close the door on your memories. That was encouraging repression! Something to do with water might have been better. Cleanse yourself . . . oh, whatever.

Ellen yawned hugely without bothering to put her hand over her mouth. She was driving back from the hospital.

There wasn't as much traffic as usual on the roads; people were staying home because of the dust storm. It was still windy, although not as bad as the previous night. The sky was heavy with gloomy cloud, and the entire city was covered in a fine layer of orange dust. Everything looked grimy. She drove by an empty outdoor café and saw a woman wearing a hospital mask and mopping the floor. A mother hurried from her car carrying a toddler with a sheet draped over its head, like one of Michael Jackson's children. Then a young man wearing shorts and a T-shirt jogged by, as if he'd jogged straight through from another day, a sunny, blue-skied, clean and ordinary day.

Why were you even talking to her? That's what everyone would say. *You must be crazier than her! Did you take her chocolates and flowers? A 'get well' card?*

She looked at her watch. It was noon. She thought back to early that morning: it seemed like days had passed since then, not hours.

When it became obvious that Jack was well enough to move around, Patrick had decided to drive him to the hospital. It was clear to Ellen that he couldn't bear to sit and wait for an ambulance, he needed to be moving, taking action, and most important of all, he needed to be far away from Saskia. Ellen could sense the heat of his simmering fury emanating from his body like a low-grade fever. She'd offered to stay at home and wait for Saskia's ambulance. 'You can't stay with her,' Patrick had said, but Ellen had pointed out that as she was barely conscious (breathing shallowly and obviously in a great deal of pain), she wasn't a danger to anyone, and besides, they could hardly just leave her there alone, with a note pinned to the door for the paramedics. Patrick hadn't been in the mood for light-hearted remarks of that nature. Let's call the police, he'd said, and hand her over. But Ellen had convinced him to concentrate on Jack.

When the ambulance arrived the paramedics had told Ellen they were taking Saskia to Mona Vale hospital, and told her not to try to follow them but to take her time driving there, and that Saskia was in good hands. They seemed to take it for granted that Ellen would also be coming. So she had got dressed and driven to the hospital, and then sat for hours in a crowded waiting room, reading trashy magazines without absorbing a single word, surrounded by wheezing asthmatics who had been affected by the dust storm. Finally, a nurse had told her that she could see Saskia for a few minutes.

In the meantime she'd spoken to Patrick once on his mobile. He'd taken Jack to a private hospital in Manly and they were waiting for someone to put a cast on his arm. He hadn't even asked about Saskia, and he'd obviously assumed that Ellen was still at home, because he'd told her to try to get some sleep.

How would he react when he heard she'd actually been at the hospital, and that she'd talked to Saskia? Would he see it as a betrayal? Was it a betrayal?

The thing was, talking to Saskia hadn't just felt like the right thing to do, it had felt somehow imperative, for both of them.

Ellen thought about the despair on Saskia's face as she lay in that narrow hospital bed. She seemed to Ellen like someone who had lost everything in a natural disaster, someone who was trying to grapple with the fact that the entire framework of their life no longer existed.

Had she really hit 'rock bottom'? Perhaps that despair Ellen thought she saw was just the pain (which the nurse had said would be considerable) and that once she was back on her feet, she'd be back to her old ways.

Her phone rang on the passenger seat beside her and she saw that it was Patrick calling. He must be home with Jack by now and was wondering where she was. She was only a few minutes away, so she didn't bother pulling over to answer.

There was no question that this would mark a turning point for him. Now that Jack had been hurt he would definitely want to get the police involved. If Ellen tried telling him that she thought Saskia may have reached her own turning point, he probably wouldn't believe her. She remembered him crawling across the bed in that eerie dawn light, his face ugly with fear and fury.

If she was wrong, if Saskia continued to stalk them, then Patrick's hatred for her was gradually going to destroy him. It was like acid, corroding him from the inside. She felt that it had already given his personality sharp edges. Most of the time those edges were hidden by the identity he liked to show the world: the easy-going, straightforward Aussie bloke. But over the last few months, as she'd got to know him, to truly know him, as they both moved beyond the infatuation stage, she'd seen the edges reveal themselves. The bitterness. The mistrustfulness. The anxiety. And he'd already suffered so much grief in his life before he even met Saskia.

She wondered what sort of person Patrick would have

been if Colleen had lived. They probably would have had more children after Jack. Patrick would have been a typical dad, involved with the school, leaving the domestic decisions to the wife – a simpler, sweeter person. A happier person.

And the tiny baby who had waved at them yesterday would never have existed.

Well, whatever. A foolish and pointless line of thought.

She yawned again. She was not only exhausted but starving: that urgent, ravenous hunger she'd never experienced before pregnancy. When she got home, she wanted to climb into bed with a *huge* plate of toast and a cup of tea, and then she wanted to pull the covers up and fall straight into a deep, dreamless sleep. She would tell Patrick she was too tired to talk; too tired to talk about anything – the past, the future, the present.

He doesn't . . .

Don't think about it, she ordered herself sharply.

But it was useless because she knew that on some level she hadn't thought about anything else ever since last night, even in spite of everything that had happened. It had added to the nightmarish quality.

He doesn't love me as much as he loved Colleen. He has doubts. He looks at me and thinks of her and sees that it's 'not the same'. He will never love another woman the way he loved Colleen.

She examined her feelings: slowly and tentatively, as if she was lifting a piece of clothing to examine a gunshot wound.

Did it hurt?

Yes, quite a lot.

She thought about Saskia's matter-of-fact acceptance

that Patrick would always love Colleen best, and she understood something with simple, startling clarity: *I don't love Patrick as much as Saskia does.*

Saskia hadn't cared if she loved him more than he loved her, whereas Ellen did care. If she was handing over a slice of her heart, she wanted the exact same size given back in return. Actually, she really preferred a bigger piece, thank you very much.

What she really wanted was to be *adored*. She was having a baby. She deserved to be adored.

Well, that was just infantile, wasn't it?

Women had babies all the time without the support of an adoring partner. She had a *loving* partner. That should be enough! Her own mother had given birth without a man.

Ellen was lucky. She'd had more than her fair share of love. In fact, perhaps that was the problem. She'd been spoiled with far too much adoration.

She would forget about what Patrick had said about Colleen. She would never think about it, or tell a friend, and she would certainly never mention it to him.

Yes, it might be difficult, but it was the right thing to do.

There was a polite toot of a horn from the car behind her, and she realized that the traffic light she'd been waiting at had turned green while she'd been sitting there feeling virtuous. She lifted her hand in apology and put her foot on the accelerator.

Lucky, she reminded herself.

'So you're going to need a lot of support over the next couple of months,' finished up my doctor. He seemed very young, with flushed, baby-smooth cheeks. I must be getting old.

I remember when Mum was in hospital she couldn't get over the youth of her doctors. 'I get the giggles,' she told me. 'They sound so serious but they just look like kids playing dressing-up!' she whispered to me.

The kids knew what they were talking about though. *She'll probably make it through Christmas*, one of them told me. *But not much longer.*

I wasn't there when she died. I had to go home because Jack was starting school. Funny that I thought it was 'home'.

My doctor confirmed what Ellen had already told me. Fractured pelvis. Broken ankle. They were scheduling me for surgery the next day. I was going to be on bed rest for the next six weeks.

I wondered how long Jack's arm would take to heal.

'I don't have any family,' I told him. I don't know why I said that. Perhaps I thought he could prescribe me one.

'Well, you're going to need to rely on your friends,' he said. 'I noticed you had a visitor earlier. She seemed like a close friend, very concerned about you.'

He was talking about Ellen.

'Mmmm,' I said. 'I don't think she'll actually be visiting again.'

'Oh,' he said. 'Well, as I say, you're going to need support, so you might want to call in some favours. Don't worry. People love to help in a crisis. It makes them feel good. You know, useful. You'll be surprised at how your friends will step up.'

'I'm sure I will be,' I said.

I couldn't tell him that there was no one to step up, that I didn't have that ordinary social framework, that there was just me, that there was no one I could possibly ask for help. This man had no idea that people like me existed: people who look and sound well educated and normal on the outside, but are actually as lonely and crazy as a homeless bum.

Then I remembered that the difference between me and a homeless person is that I have money. I'll pay someone to be supportive, I thought. There must be some sort of a service, for people like me.

'You'll get through this,' said the doctor.

I tried to smile politely, but my facial muscles rebelled, as if it was an unfamiliar move, as if I'd never smiled before.

The doctor pressed the morphine clicker into my hand, and patted my shoulder. 'Give yourself some pain relief. Enjoy it while it lasts. We'll be weaning you off soon enough.'

I pressed the red button.

Jack was sound asleep when Ellen got home. He was lying in his bed curled up on his side, looking tiny and pale, the arm in the cast over the blanket.

'The doctor prescribed him some strong painkillers,' said Patrick quietly as they stood together in his bedroom looking down at him. He pulled the quilt up and let his hand rest briefly on Jack's forehead. 'He'll probably sleep for hours.'

As they walked down the stairs together, Ellen felt Patrick's fury rise steadily like a boiling jug. They went into the living room and he began pacing back and forth, talking nonstop. He hadn't yet asked where Ellen had been. He wanted to tell her about how he'd already phoned the police and they'd told him to come in to make a full report and begin the process of taking out a restraining order against Saskia, how Jack's injuries could have been so much worse, how he'd thought Jack was dead when he saw him lying at the bottom of the stairs, and did she think that too, and he should have taken the order out so much sooner, and he'd never forgive himself for that, never.

'I've been trying to work out how she got in,' he said finally.

'I don't know,' said Ellen tiredly. While Patrick had been talking she had laid down on her grandfather's leather couch and put her forearm over her eyes. Patrick had offered her a cup of tea when she first got home but so far it hadn't materialized. 'I moved the key after the last time.'

'What?' said Patrick.

Ellen realized her mistake too late. She opened her eyes. Patrick had stopped pacing and was standing frozen in the middle of the room. 'What "last time"?'

She opened her mouth to speak and closed it again. She was desperately trying to find the right balance between honesty and enraging him further. She gave up.

'She left biscuits on the doorstep when we went up to the mountains,' she said. 'I think she might have cooked them in my kitchen.'

'*What?* She broke in before and you neglected to tell me?'

'Well, I might have been wrong.' Ellen sat up and folded

her arms protectively across her stomach. 'I just had a feeling.' Patrick was looking at her almost as if he wanted to hit her. An image came into her mind of the way he'd grabbed Saskia by the shoulders as if he was about to throw her up against the wall.

'I'm not Saskia,' she said involuntarily.

'I know you're not,' he said with an impatient, disgusted move of his hand. 'But why did you not mention this to me?'

'I didn't want to upset you,' said Ellen. 'I know how much it upsets you.'

'You threw them out straight away, of course.'

'Of course,' said Ellen. Honesty was often overrated.

'Because they probably had rat poison in them. Or, Christ, I don't know, anthrax!'

'She doesn't want to kill you, Patrick. She loves you.'

'How do you know what she wants?' said Patrick. 'You have no idea what she wants. God Almighty, the woman watched us sleep last night!'

'I just talked to her at the hospital,' said Ellen. 'I think it's finished. I really do. She promised me. Anyway, she's going to be stuck in bed for a long time.'

Patrick sat down on the chair in front of Ellen. It was the chair where her grandmother always used to sit to watch TV. Patrick looked too big and rough for it. Ellen had to stop herself from saying: *Don't sit there*.

'You talked to her,' said Patrick slowly. 'Why would you do that?'

'I just felt if I talked to her, I might be able to make a difference.'

'Right,' said Patrick. He ran the palm of his hand

roughly across his face, pulling at the stubbled skin. 'So, you two girls have a nice chat?'

'I really think she's hit rock bottom,' began Ellen.

'Oh dear, the *poor* thing,' said Patrick.

Ellen went silent. He'd earned the right to be sarcastic.

They locked eyes for a few seconds and then Patrick looked away and shook his head.

He took a deep breath. 'You're meant to be on my side.'

'I am!' said Ellen immediately.

'It feels like you're on her side.'

'That's – silly.'

'If you had some ex-boyfriend stalking you the way Saskia stalks me, I wouldn't hesitate. I'd knock his head off.'

'You're saying I should have *punched* Saskia?' said Ellen, unfairly and ridiculously, but needing all the points she could get.

'Of course not,' said Patrick tiredly. He sat back and closed his eyes.

There was a pounding sensation at the very centre of Ellen's forehead. Her wrist itched unbearably.

Guilt. That's what she was feeling, because he was partly right. She'd tried harder to understand what it must be like to be Saskia than she'd tried to understand what it would be like to be Patrick.

The mature thing would be to say nothing, to not try to defend herself, and to certainly stop aligning herself with Saskia.

Instead she said, 'Are you thinking it now?'

'Thinking what?' Patrick opened his eyes.

'Are you thinking about Colleen?'

'What are you talking about? Why would I be thinking about Colleen? What has she got to do with anything?'

He looked completely, innocently baffled.

So much for her virtuous decision in the car. Part of her longed to rewind and take it back, but the other part, her basic, instinctual self, wanted everything, every single thing, out in the open.

'You said last night that sometimes you look at me and you think about Colleen, and you think that it's not the same and that you'll never love anyone as much as you loved Colleen.'

'I said that?' said Patrick. He paused. 'I never said that!'

'You were in a hypnotic state,' admitted Ellen.

He didn't say: I would never have said that.

'So it was like I was sleep talking,' said Patrick slowly.

'Sort of,' said Ellen. 'You were somewhere between asleep and awake.'

'So when we do these hypnosis sessions, do you ask me stuff?' said Patrick. 'You ask me stuff about Colleen? Is that why you do it? So you can go ferreting about in my head?'

'Of course not,' said Ellen. The phone began to ring. She wondered if she should use it as an opportunity to escape from this conversation, which did not seem to be going well. She looked down and saw that she'd been scratching at her wrist so hard there were little flecks of blood.

'Let them leave a message,' said Patrick.

They sat there looking at each other while the phone rang and rang.

*

The morphine made everything melt. The ceiling softened and swirled; the white blanket covering my body rippled like water.

When I closed my eyes to get away from the melting room I saw images from my life, slapped in front of me like playing cards, one after the other, in rapid succession.

Patrick, waiting for me outside the movie theatre, deep in thought, looking so sad, and then his face changing, lighting up, when he saw me arrive; my mother, when her hair was still blonde, driving me home from school, looking at the road ahead and laughing over something I'd said; the kids who moved in next door, looking up at me with their trusting, nonchalant eyes; Lance from work, standing in my office, eagerly handing over *The Wire* DVD series.

I opened my eyes and remembered I had a job and that I should probably let them know that I wouldn't be coming in for a while.

I called on the phone next to my bed. Nina answered, and when I heard her familiar, cheery voice I had a sensation of horror, as if I was in a dream and I'd walked into the office naked. The game was up. They were going to find out the truth.

I heard myself say, 'Nina, it's me, Saskia.'

'Oh, hey, Saskia, I didn't know you were out this morning. Look, I've been wanting to ask you about –'

'Nina,' I said. It felt like I was talking underwater. I gripped the phone hard. I must have waited too long to speak because she said, 'Are you still there?'

'I hit rock bottom,' I said.

'I beg your pardon?'

*

'I don't know what to say to you,' said Patrick. His eyes looked glassy. 'My head is too full of last night. I have no memory of saying that, that thing about Colleen.'

'I shouldn't have mentioned it,' said Ellen. She was desperately disappointed with herself. Her mobile phone began to ring somewhere in the house.

'Can we talk about it later?' asked Patrick. 'I want to go to the police station while Jack is asleep and make that report.'

'Of course,' said Ellen. 'Actually, let's just forget I ever –'

'We're not going to forget it,' said Patrick. 'We're going to talk about it later.' He smiled at her and the unexpectedness of it made her want to cry. 'I promise, we're going to talk about everything at *length* later and we're going to fix it.'

'Right.'

Now her office phone was ringing again.

'Sounds like someone needs to talk to you,' said Patrick.

'Yes,' said Ellen, and then the air rushed from her lungs. 'Oh God, I forgot. I completely forgot.'

'What?'

Ellen looked at the clock above Patrick's head and tried to will the hands to move backwards. It was 2.30 p.m. 'That journalist. I was meeting her at a café at eleven this morning.'

She imagined the journalist sitting in the café, tapping her fingers and irritably checking and re-checking her watch. She was already ill-disposed towards Ellen. Now she would think that she'd deliberately not turned up. She would think that she had something to hide.

'Reschedule,' said Patrick. 'Tell her there was an accident. It's not your fault.'

'Yes,' said Ellen, because of course that was logical, but she already knew that it was going to be a disaster, and when she listened to the messages on both her office phone and mobile, she knew she was right.

'I'm waiting in the café you suggested,' said Lisa, with a faint emphasis on the word 'you' and the sounds of the café in the background adding to Ellen's guilt. 'I'll be filing this story this afternoon, so if I don't hear from you soon, I'll assume you have no comment, and you're not interested in responding to the issues raised by your former clients.'

As Ellen hung up, the phone immediately rang again, and she snatched it up, desperate for the chance at redemption. It was her mother.

'I've been trying to call you all morning,' she said accusingly. 'I really need to talk to you.'

'I can't talk,' said Ellen. 'I'll call you back.'

The phone rang again. It was Julia, her voice low and throaty. 'Guess who just left my bed.'

'I can't talk right now,' said Ellen again. This was becoming like some sort of awful comedy. 'I'm sorry.'

She hung up.

'Breathe,' said Patrick.

'Shut up.'

She called the journalist's mobile number. The phone went straight to voicemail. Ellen tried to keep the panic out of her voice as she left a message.

'My stepson had an accident,' she said. 'I've been at the hospital.' Her voice didn't sound authentic. It sounded forced and fraudulent. She felt like she was lying because she'd never called Jack her 'stepson' before and because she hadn't been at the hospital with him, she'd been at the hospital seeing Saskia.

Patrick mimed deep breaths at her. Ellen waved him away.

The guilt she was feeling was all out of proportion: she hadn't murdered anyone. In fact, she hadn't actually done anything except forgotten an appointment.

As she completed her message – *I'd still love the opportunity to talk to you!* ('love the opportunity': she sounded like a telemarketer) – she heard the doorbell ring.

Patrick went to open the door and Ellen's heart sank as she recognized the client's voice. It was Mary-Kate for her 2.30 p.m. appointment. Mary-Kate certainly deserved a paragraph in the article exposing Ellen. The journalist could calculate how much Mary-Kate had spent over the last few months without any progress. Then they could mention how much Ellen had spent on those boots that she'd only worn once.

I'm a bad person, thought Ellen. *A bad, bad person.*

(He'll never love me the way he loved Colleen.)

(He'll eventually leave me and I'll be a single mother like Mum.)

(Without a job.)

(And to top it all off, in five very short years I'll be forty. Forty!)

'Mary-Kate,' she called out, filled with decisiveness. She walked briskly out into the hallway as Patrick ushered Mary-Kate inside. 'I'm very sorry but I can't see you today. In fact, I can't see you again.'

Mary-Kate looked startled. Ellen registered that there was something different about Mary-Kate today. Her face didn't look as doughy as usual. Also, she was carrying a bunch of flowers and she was wearing a long buttercup-yellow scarf.

'I'll just check on Jack before I go out.' Patrick raised his eyebrows questioningly at Ellen over the top of Mary-Kate's head, his tired eyes clearly trying something along the lines of *Are you sacking all your clients now?* He gave a minute shrug and disappeared up the stairs.

'Is everything OK?' asked Mary-Kate.

'Not really,' said Ellen. 'I think there's going to be an article in the paper tomorrow that's going to destroy my reputation.'

'Which paper?' said Mary-Kate immediately, as if she was going to rush out and buy a copy.

'The *Daily News*,' said Ellen. 'I'd really rather you didn't read it, to be honest, but look, my point is –'

'Well, let's see what we can do about it,' said Mary-Kate. 'Oh, and by the way, these are for you.' She handed over the flowers.

'Thank you.' Ellen stared at the flowers. They were yellow, like Mary-Kate's scarf. 'I really don't think there's anything you can do, although I appreciate –'

'Tell me everything.'

'Pardon?'

'To the extent that you can do so without breaching confidentiality, tell me everything that has happened.'

'I'm sorry, I'm not sure I understand.'

'I'm a barrister,' said Mary-Kate. 'I specialize in defamation law.'

24

But I have a little boy.
  — Colleen Scott's first words upon being told that
                                    she only had a few months to live

I dreamed that Lance from the office was sitting next to my hospital bed, together with a pale, red-haired woman I didn't know.

'No, Lance, I still haven't watched *The Wire*,' I said, for my own entertainment.

'That's OK,' he said. It wasn't a dream. Lance really was sitting next to my bed.

'Are you in a lot of pain?' said the red-headed woman. 'My cousin broke her pelvis years ago. She said the pain was worse than childbirth.'

'I haven't experienced childbirth,' I said. Who was this woman?

'Me neither,' said the woman. 'It's the universal pain benchmark, isn't it? It's like you can't talk about pain unless you've experienced childbirth. Although, apparently, passing a kidney stone is worse.'

'We should be taking her mind off the subject of pain,' said Lance.

'I was trying to show empathy,' said the woman. 'I always say the wrong thing at hospital visits.' She glanced at me and said, 'I'm Kate, by the way, Lance's wife, if you can't place me. We met at last year's Christmas party.'

'Of course,' I said, although I wasn't sure I could remember meeting her before. Didn't I usually find an excuse for the Christmas party?

'We just thought we'd stop by,' said Lance.

'We're on our way to the movies,' said Kate.

There was silence. I couldn't think of anything to say. I didn't understand why they were visiting me.

Then I said, 'What movie are you seeing?' at the same time as Lance said, 'I've got a card from everyone at the office.'

He handed me a white envelope with my name on it.

'And chocolates.' Kate held up a box and waved a hand in front of it, like a game show hostess. 'And trashy magazines. Oh, and grapes. Very unoriginal.'

I tried to open the card, but I couldn't seem to manage it, my hands were shaking too much.

'Let me do that,' said Lance gently.

'Would you like a chocolate?' said Kate.

'Maybe later,' I said.

'Do you mind if I have one?'

'Kate,' said Lance.

'Sorry,' she said.

'You can have one,' I said.

I looked at the card Lance had given me and read some of the scribbled messages.

Saskia! No need to throw yourself down the stairs just to get out of the Eastgate project! Get well SOON! Malcolm

'Is there anything you need us to pick up for you?' said Kate, who was helping herself to a second chocolate. 'I remember you saying that your family is in Tasmania, so . . .' She glanced briefly at Lance as if she was worried she was saying the wrong thing. Lance cleared his throat awkwardly and looked up at the blank television screen next to my bed. Kate kept talking.

'My family is in Brisbane, so I understand what it's like, you know, other people have sisters and mothers and cousins and what not. Really. It's no trouble.'

I stared at them. At Lance. He had kind, sleepy eyes and big shoulders, as if he worked out. I don't think I'd ever properly looked at him before. I looked at his wife. She was extremely thin and flat-chested – 'gamine' my mother would have called her – with very short hair and big eyes like a woodland creature. She was sitting at a strange angle on the chair, still eating my chocolates. Maybe I did remember talking to her at the Christmas party, about a holiday she'd taken to Cradle Mountain. I'd left the party early to sit outside Patrick's house in my car. I saw him come home and carry Jack inside, asleep on his shoulder, his head lolling.

I thought of Jack again, and his broken arm, and Ellen telling me that I should move away from Sydney, and what would these two nice people visiting me think if they knew what I'd done last night, what I'd been doing for the last three years, and I felt a plummeting sensation.

'It's a shock, isn't it, when something like this happens,' said Kate. 'Your life is going along one way, and then, wham, you get thrown a curve ball.' She jerked her head to demonstrate herself avoiding a curve ball and half the chocolates went flying from the open box on her lap.

'Kate,' said Lance. He crouched down to pick up the chocolates.

'Oops,' said Kate.

'I'm not . . .' I was trying to say: *You don't understand. You think I'm a normal person like you, but I'm not.*

The words dried up. It was as if my entire personality had disintegrated. I was still breathing, my heart was still beating, but I was no longer there. There had been the brisk professional Saskia that Lance had known, and the crazy Saskia that Patrick had known, but now it was as though neither of them had existed. I had no idea what sort of person I was: funny or serious, quiet or loud. If I stopped wanting Patrick, what did I want? What was I interested in? Did I exist at all? These two odd, sweet people were looking at me as if I did exist, but my very existence seemed questionable.

'Boogie boarding,' I said suddenly.

'Oh, yes,' said Kate amiably, as if that was a perfectly normal thing to say out of the blue.

'I thought Nina said you fell down a flight of stairs,' frowned Lance. 'She said you were walking in your sleep.'

I had no memory of telling Nina that, but it was logical.

'Boogie boarding is an interest of mine,' I said, and then I thought: *Did I just say that out loud?*

'Me too!' said Kate. 'Well, not that I've ever actually *been* boogie boarding, but I'd like to try it, or, well, to be accurate, I'd really like to try proper surfing, on a proper surfboard. I've been meaning to have lessons.'

Lance snorted and Kate slapped him on the arm and looked at me brightly.

'Looks like they've got you on some pretty good painkillers, have they then, Saskia?' said Lance.

'Don't be rude,' said Kate. 'She's making perfect sense.'

'I didn't say she wasn't,' said Lance.

'Whose phone is that?' said Kate.

I recognized the sound of my mobile phone. Kate lifted up my leather bag. 'Should I answer it?'

I looked at the bag. How was it possible that I still had my bag? After all that had happened? For some reason it struck me as amusing that I still had my bag. I laughed out loud.

'I really want some of what you're having,' said Lance.

'I'll answer it.' Kate burrowed in my bag and pulled out the phone.

'She didn't say she wanted it answered,' said Lance.

'Saskia's phone!' Kate stood up and walked away from the hospital bed with my phone pressed to her ear. I heard her say, 'Well, yes she is here but, now don't worry, she's *fine*, it's just that she's actually in hospital at the moment.'

'Sorry,' said Lance. 'Kate can be a bit . . .' He shrugged, unable to find the right word to describe his wife. 'Sure you don't want a chocolate?'

'All right,' I said. I took a chocolate and listened to Kate. A few minutes later she came back and put the phone next to my bedside table.

'That was your friend Tammy,' she said. 'You were meant to be meeting her for a drink tonight? Anyway, she's on her way here. I gave her directions.'

'We should get going.' Lance slapped his hands to his knees and half rose from his chair. 'We don't want to tire you out, Saskia.'

'I guess we should.' Kate looked at her watch. 'Although, we've got plenty of time. We could wait until Tammy gets here if you want the company, Saskia?'

I had every intention of saying something like: *Oh, you'd better not miss your movie*, but the words that came out of my mouth were, 'Please stay.'

'Of course,' said Lance and Kate at the same time.

It was early evening and Ellen's house was unexpectedly full of people.

Patrick's parents and brother had come over to sign Jack's cast and give him get-well gifts, and so, to Ellen's mild irritation, although she couldn't explain why, had her own mother. Anne had given Jack the *Guinness World Records* book, which had proved to be a huge hit.

They were all crammed round Ellen's dining-room table eating sausages that Patrick had cooked on the BBQ. Patrick had come back from the police station in a better frame of mind. The police had praised him for his 'Stalking Incident Log': a ring folder full of meticulously kept records of Saskia's actions over the last three years including print-outs of emails, letters and descriptions of 'incidents'. (Ellen had flipped through it, marvelling at Patrick's terse comments: '12.30 a.m., 27 July: *S banged on front door, demanding entry, ignoring repeated requests to leave.*')

Patrick had been told that an interim restraining order would be issued and that Saskia would be given the option to appear in court to contest it. She would also most likely be charged with trespass. It seemed that this time, whoever had been on the desk at Patrick's local police station had given Patrick exactly the right level of respectful, authoritative sympathy. He was no longer seething. He had the look of a man who was finally about to be vindicated after a long fight for justice.

Ellen had her mobile phone on the sideboard within hearing distance. She was waiting for a phone call from Mary-Kate, who had said she was going to try to get the newspaper article stopped. Ellen wasn't holding out much hope. It seemed highly unlikely that Mary-Kate – stodgy, morose Mary-Kate – would be able to take on someone as powerful and shiny-teethed as Ian Roman.

'I'm not making any promises,' Mary-Kate had said after she'd listened to Ellen's story, using a small leather notebook to take down cursory, decisive notes. 'But as soon as I leave here, I'll file for an interlocutory injunction. There's not a chance in hell we'll get one – the courts have this thing about freedom of speech so you basically can't ever get one – but I'm aiming to convince the *Daily News*'s lawyers that we will. It's clear the story's motivated by malice, and sounds like it'd *really* flush your reputation down the toilet. But, anyway, I'll go in tough.'

'I thought you were a legal secretary,' said Ellen faintly.

'Nope,' said Mary-Kate, most unbarrister-ish.

A memory resurfaced now of Mary-Kate saying she worked in the 'legal profession'. Ellen had just assumed she was a legal secretary. Would she have been more patient and respectful with Mary-Kate if she'd known she was dealing with a barrister? Shamefully, the answer was yes.

'Do you know the world record for the most broken bones?' said Jack now. He had the *Guinness World Records* book open on the table next to him and was turning the pages while he ate. He didn't wait for anyone to answer.

'Thirty-five! Some dude called Evel Knievel.'

'Really! I didn't think we had that many bones!' said Maureen. She was acting particularly interested in the book to show that she didn't mind that Jack had put aside her gift for Anne's.

'We've actually got two hundred and six bones,' said Anne.

'Well, fancy that!' Maureen smiled fiercely.

'Babies have around three hundred bones. They fuse together as they grow,' said Anne.

'It must have been wonderful bringing up a child with your medical expertise,' said Maureen. 'I was always bundling them into the car to take them off to the doctor and then feeling like a fool when there was nothing wrong.'

Please don't be condescending, Mum, thought Ellen.

'Actually, I think it made it worse.' To Ellen's relief, the smile Anne gave Maureen had only minimal queenliness. 'I knew everything that could go wrong. Every temperature meant certain death.'

'Speaking of temperatures,' said Patrick's father, 'well, not temperatures so much, but *aches*, I've had this really strange ache in my –'

'Dad,' said Patrick.

'George refuses to make an appointment to see a doctor,' said Maureen, 'but whenever he meets one he starts telling them about his medical problems.'

'I just thought she'd find it interesting,' said George.

'Would you find it interesting if people started talking to you about their electrical problems?' said Maureen.

'I certainly would,' said George. 'Blown any fuses lately, Anne?'

'So, *anyway*, it must have been nice for you, Ellen, growing up with a mother who was a doctor,' said Maureen.

'Mum,' said Patrick.

'What?'

Patrick shrugged and took a bite of his sausage sandwich.

'She was always sort of cranky with me when I got sick,' said Ellen.

'Our mum was exactly the same!' spoke up Patrick's brother. 'The angriest I have ever seen Mum was the time I got knocked out by a cricket ball. I come to, and the first thing I see is Mum, and she's yelling, "*Simon! WAKE UP THIS MINUTE!*"'

'I thought he was dead,' said Maureen.

'So you thought yelling at me would bring me back to life.'

'I understand completely,' said Anne. 'The fear makes you furious.'

'You'll understand when you have your baby, Ellen,' said Maureen.

Ellen, who was actually looking forward to being the very opposite of her own mother, and fondly imagined herself soothing her child's feverish brow with a gentle, cool hand, said, 'I'm sure I will.'

'Dad wasn't mad at me when I broke my arm,' said Jack. 'He was mad with Saskia.'

There was an instant strained silence around the table.

'That's because it was Saskia's fault,' said Patrick.

'It was an accident,' said Jack. 'Actually, *you* were sort of pushing *her*.'

'Yes, darling, it was an accident, but what your dad means is that Saskia should not have been here in the middle of the night,' said Maureen.

'How'd you go with the police?' said George to Patrick.

'You told the police about Saskia!' Jack's head whipped round to look accusingly at his father. 'She's not going to jail, is she?'

'She won't go to jail,' said Patrick. 'But you understand, mate, she can't break into our house again. The police will just tell her that she can't come anywhere near us any more.'

'Right, but I guess she'll still come and watch me play soccer though,' said Jack.

Ellen drew in her breath.

'Good Lord,' said George.

'What are you talking about, Jack?' Patrick carefully placed his sausage sandwich back on the plate in front of him.

'She watches all my games,' said Jack.

'I've never seen her there,' said Patrick.

'You've got bad eyes,' said Jack dismissively. 'She stands way off. Near a tree or whatever. She always wears this blue knitted hat, like a pancake.'

'Beret?' murmured Anne.

'Goodness, I think I knitted it for her,' said Maureen.

'If I see her anywhere near you again I'll have her arrested,' said Patrick.

'You will not!' said Jack.

'I will.'

'If you do, I will never speak to you again.'

'Fine,' said Patrick. 'Don't!'

'Boys!' Maureen held out her hands to each of them helplessly.

Ellen's phone began to ring.

'I'll just – excuse me.'

She rushed into the kitchen with the phone. 'Mary-Kate?'

'Yes, hi, Ellen. Right, they're holding off on publication. The journalist has agreed to hear your side of the story first. And I get the impression she's ready to drop the whole thing. Most journalists do have integrity – and this one is hating the idea that she could be being used by Ian Roman for some personal vendetta. Even if Ian Roman does rule her world.'

Ellen felt her whole body sag with relief.

'Thank you,' she said. 'I can't thank you enough, Mary-Kate.'

'No problem,' said Mary-Kate.

Ellen heard the deep rumble of a man's voice in the background. 'By the way, Alfred says to say hi.'

'Alfred?' said Ellen. 'Alfred Boyle?'

Mary-Kate chuckled. Ellen didn't think she'd ever heard her laugh before. 'Don't pretend to be so surprised, Ellen.'

Ellen laughed. A little nervously.

'Alfred said to tell you that he gave a speech to two

hundred accountants today, and he had them in stitches. That's really saying something. He made accountants laugh.'

'That's great,' said Ellen.

'I'll be in touch about where we go next with this,' said Mary-Kate. 'But I expect once the journalist and editor know the full story, it will be shelved.'

'You'll have to bill me for your work,' said Ellen. (Didn't barristers charge by the minute?)

'Don't be ridiculous,' said Mary-Kate joyfully, and then she abruptly hung up.

Ellen dropped her head, closed her eyes and tapped the phone against her forehead. So her matchmaking with Mary-Kate and Alfred had paid off. She must remember to tell the journalist about it, if she ever got to speak to her again. Clinical hypnotherapist hypnotizes her patients to fall in love with each other. That would really add to her credibility.

'Everything OK?'

Ellen opened her eyes. Her mother was standing in front of her holding a salad bowl. 'Thought I'd start clearing up. It's getting a bit tense in there. I'm not surprised. This Saskia is clearly deranged.'

'Saskia is finished with us,' said Ellen. 'I talked to her today.'

'Hypnotized her, did you?' said Anne smartly but automatically, as if she was just doing it out of habit, and then before Ellen could answer, she put the bowl down on the table and said, 'Listen. I need to talk to you about something. About your father.'

'You're getting married,' guessed Ellen.

She could just imagine the discreetly elegant wedding.

Her mother would wear violet to match her eyes. There would be designer labels galore, flutes of champagne held between manicured fingers. It would be the sort of wedding that made it into the society pages. Ellen's face would ache from faking her smile.

'Will you have Pip and Mel as bridesmaids?' she said. 'I could be flower girl! Your daughter as your flower girl. Your cute little pregnant flower girl.'

'Ellen.'

'My stepbrothers could be page boys. Giant page boys.'

'We broke up.'

'Oh, no!' The one time Ellen was enjoying being a bitch and it was entirely inappropriate and hurtful. (And, in fact, she would have been perfectly happy for her parents to be married! Their wedding would have been moving and lovely. What was wrong with her?)

'What happened?' she asked. He went back to his wife, of course. Or he moved on to a younger model. Or was it somehow Ellen's fault? Did he not like Ellen? (Ah, listen to the Inner Child piping up for attention.)

'I broke it off,' said Anne. She sat down at the kitchen table and extracted a cherry tomato from the salad bowl.

'But why?' Ellen pulled out a chair and sat down opposite her mother. 'You seemed – well, you seemed completely besotted.'

'I know,' said her mother. She looked at Ellen and gave a little half-smile and shrug. 'I was. Look, I'm utterly mortified.'

Ellen was momentarily distracted by the sound of Patrick's voice rising in the dining room. 'Can we please talk about something else other than Saskia? Like, I don't know, Armageddon? Who wants to talk about Armageddon?'

'You don't need to feel embarrassed,' she said to her mother.

'I've been such a twit,' said Anne. 'With everything you've got going on in your life at the moment.' She inclined her head towards the dining room. 'Getting married, new stepson, baby on the way, deranged stalkers and what have you – and I decide to throw your father into the mix!'

'Mum, I'm a grown-up,' said Ellen gravely, and extremely fraudulently, seeing as she'd thought exactly the same thing. 'Tell me why you broke it off.'

'I've spent the last thirty-five years being in love with a memory,' said Anne. 'It's crazy, and I would have denied it, but every time I went out with anyone, I was comparing him to your father. Your father who I had never actually dated, who I really didn't even know that well. So, of course, every man came up short.' She giggled. 'In more ways than one.'

'Mother.' Ellen recoiled. 'Please.'

'Sorry. So, when David and I finally got together, I was deliriously happy. He was every bit as lovely as I recalled. Actually, let me make this clear. He *is* lovely. He still qualifies as the loveliest man I've ever met.'

'So? What's the problem?' said Ellen.

'Well, I started noticing this feeling creeping over me after we'd spent more than an hour together. At first I couldn't put a name to it, and then, last week, it hit me. I was bored.'

'Bored,' said Ellen. She was suddenly feeling very sorry for her father.

'Bored out of my mind,' confirmed Anne.

'Well, but that can happen –'

'No,' said Anne decidedly. 'He's not right for me. He never was right for me. He doesn't have enough to *say*! And he has these periods of time when he literally does nothing. The other morning, he sat in an armchair for twenty minutes, literally twenty minutes, without doing *anything*. Not reading. Not talking. Just staring at a tree. What's that about?'

'Perhaps he was silently contemplating the beauty of nature,' offered Ellen. 'Or just taking a few moments to meditate, and be thankful for his life. Or he was practising mindfulness –'

'It was a rhetorical question, Ellen. Honestly, I thought he'd lost brain function. Anyway, as the young people say so eloquently: whatever. I don't care what he's doing, I just know it drives me nuts. We will be friends, of course. It's all perfectly amicable. And he says that he would love to see you again, if you'd like that.'

'That would be nice,' said Ellen. Actually, the thought of meeting up with her father now seemed perfectly acceptable, even quite soothing. She thought of rainy Sunday afternoons as a child, when she would lie on a rug on the floor mesmerized by the raindrops sliding down the windowpane, and her mother would keep walking in and out of the room, saying, 'Ellen, what are you doing? Let's go out! Let's talk! Let's *do* something.'

Perhaps she and her father could linger together, without the need to say a word. No need for awkward 'getting to know you' conversations. They could just be. Father and daughter. And if they didn't feel a thing for each other except a mild friendliness, then that would be perfectly fine.

'So, at the tender age of sixty-six,' said Anne, 'I might be finally ready for a real relationship, now that I can let go of my ridiculous obsession with a romance that never really was. I might even do a little online shopping for a new man. Apparently it's the latest thing for the over-sixties. And look how successful it's been for you!'

'Yes!' said Ellen. He would never love another woman as much as he loved Colleen. Maybe not that successful.

'Speaking of which,' Anne lowered her voice, 'I've been meaning to say for a while that I've become very fond of Patrick. Really. Very fond. I took a while to warm to him –'

'He's right there!' hissed Ellen.

'Well, that's OK, I'm saying nice things about him. I like the way he looks at you. You're right. Jon was entertaining but he didn't look at you the way Patrick looks at you.'

'How does Patrick look at me?' asked Ellen.

'And he's a good father.'

'Am I interrupting?'

Ellen and her mother turned to see Maureen at the door, with her arms full of plates.

'I was just saying what a good father your son is.' Anne stood up and took some of the plates from her.

Maureen beamed. There was a sound of running footsteps and they heard Jack scream, 'I hate you!'

'Fine!' shouted back Patrick. 'Break your other arm for all I care!'

Maureen's beam wavered. She got it back under control

and began scraping left-over food from the plates with the edge of a knife.

'This windy weather really puts people on edge, doesn't it? I wonder, is there a medical reason for that, Anne?'

I must have fallen asleep because it seemed like I just blinked my eyes and Tammy had materialized. She and Lance and Kate were sitting in a little semicircle of chairs next to my bed, eating chocolates.

Tammy had changed her hair from long and dark to short and strawberry blonde. A mistake, I thought.

Lance and Tammy were talking excitedly to each other in peculiar accents, shrugging their shoulders and jutting out their chins.

'They're trying to talk like Baltimore drug dealers,' explained Kate when she saw I'd woken up. 'They've discovered they're both obsessed with *The Wire*.' She lowered her voice. 'Some weekends Lance talks like that for an entire *day*. Can you imagine? I mean, fine, if he actually did sound like a drug dealer, that might be quite sexy.'

'Tammy?' I said.

'Saskia, honey!' She stood up and leaned over to kiss me on the cheek. She must have still been using the same fragrance as she had five years ago, because I was immediately taken back to a different time and place.

'It's so good to see you!' she said. 'But you're meant to be sitting next to me in a bar, not lying in a hospital bed. Lance and Kate said you were sleepwalking and fell down some stairs? That's terrible! How long have you been sleepwalking for?'

'Since I last saw you,' I said, profoundly – the sort of comment that Ellen would appreciate – but Tammy took it at face value.

'Really? Is there a cure? You know, I was thinking on the way here about the last time I saw you. You'd just had your heart broken by some guy. That surveyor? What was his name? Pete? Patrick? It's been so long you probably don't even remember the guy.'

Oh, how I laughed.

'El-*len*!'

It was Patrick, shouting from the second floor.

'Goodness, is he all right?' said Ellen's mother, startled.

'I expect he needs your help working things out with Jack,' said Maureen to Ellen. 'A woman's touch, you know.' She gave Anne a 'you-know-what-I-mean' smile, which was totally lost on Anne.

Ellen dried her hands briskly on a tea towel, bustling a little for Anne's benefit, because she knew it would bug her to see her behaving so housewifely, and hurried upstairs to Jack's room. Patrick and Jack were sitting on the floor, their backs up against Jack's single bed with its Ben Ten bedspread, their hands dangling between their propped-up knees, not looking at each other.

'Can you explain to this stubborn kid why Saskia can't break into our house in the middle of the night?' said Patrick to Ellen, when he saw her standing at the doorway. He mouthed silently, '*Help!*'

'I'm not *stupid*, Dad,' said Jack hotly. 'I know she shouldn't have done that.'

'Right, good then, so what's the problem?' said Patrick. 'Why are you so mad with *me*?'

Ellen went and sat on the floor next to them. She looked at Jack's skinny, vulnerable little legs in tracksuit pants stuck out in front of him.

She said, 'How did you feel when your dad and Saskia broke up, Jack?'

Jack and Patrick both went very still, as if she'd brought up something deeply shameful. *For heaven's sake*, thought Ellen. She felt filled with feistiness. Everything might as well be out in the open now! There would be no more pussyfooting around the subject of Saskia.

'Well, that's not –' began Patrick.

'I'd like to know,' said Ellen. *You asked for my help, buddy*.

'I don't really remember,' said Jack. 'I was really little, like, *five*.' He gazed ahead, looking back over the vast expanse of time that separated five from eight.

'That's right, you were very little.' Patrick gave Ellen a triumphant look. 'So, the point is –'

'Oh, yeah, I remember one thing,' interrupted Jack. 'I thought it was to do with her lucky marble.'

Patrick's face changed. 'What?'

Jack banged his knuckles against the cast on his arm.

'Her lucky marble?' asked Ellen.

Patrick answered her, his eyes on Jack as he spoke. 'She had this big, colourful marble that belonged to her father, and she held it in the palm of her hand whenever she was nervous about something. She gave it to Jack when he started school.' He paused and cleared his throat. 'She said to carry it in his pocket, and the marble would give him magic powers.'

'It wasn't a weapon,' clarified Jack. He looked up at Ellen. 'It didn't transform into a laser gun or anything like that. It didn't really do anything at all, actually.'

'I took Saskia's lucky marble with me when I saw my first ever Scott Surveys client,' said Patrick. 'I held it while I waited in reception.'

He'd never before referred to a nice memory involving Saskia. It was Ellen's first glimpse of the other side of their story.

'I lost the marble at school,' said Jack. 'I looked and looked, and a teacher tried to help me but we couldn't find it. I didn't want to tell Saskia because I knew she'd be sad, and then the next day she was gone. So I thought, uh-oh, she found out I lost it.'

Patrick's eyes met Ellen's over the top of Jack's head.

'You thought it was your fault,' said Ellen to Jack.

'I thought she must have been so mad at me,' said Jack. 'And I thought Dad was mad at me for making her go, and that's why we couldn't talk about her.'

'Oh, mate.' Patrick pressed two fingers to his forehead. 'You didn't.'

'Yeah, I did,' said Jack cheerfully.

'But it was absolutely nothing to do with you!' Patrick's eyes were glistening. He went to put his arm round Jack's shoulders. 'Mate, Saskia *adored* you! She would have done anything for you! She —'

Jack shrugged his father's arm away. 'Take a chill pill, Dad. I know it wasn't my fault. You and Saskia broke up, like Ethan's parents did. I was telling you what I thought when I was a dumb little kid.' He yawned. 'Anyway, I might go look at my *Guinness World Records* again.'

'We haven't finished talking!' protested Patrick.

Jack shrugged. 'Whatever.'

'I just want to make sure you understand –'

'You don't have to be so mean about her.' Jack went to fold his arms and then realized he couldn't because of his cast. 'That's all I want to say. You act like she's an actual murderer of actual people! She didn't break my arm on purpose. It was an accident.'

'Yeah,' said Patrick tiredly. 'I know, mate, you're right, but it's complicated –'

'Hey, guys.' Patrick's brother appeared at Jack's doorway. 'I've got to get going. Meeting some friends.'

Jack took Simon's arrival as his opportunity to escape back downstairs. 'See ya!' he said, giving his uncle a high five on the way out.

'You two look totally trashed.' Simon looked down at them on the floor and shook his head in wonder, before heading back downstairs.

'Thanks so much,' Ellen called after him.

Patrick stood up, and gave his hand to Ellen to haul her up.

She grunted. 'Oof. I feel trashed.'

Patrick pulled her to him and she rested her head briefly against his chest for a moment. Her head swirled. *Poor little Jack thinking it was his fault; poor Saskia losing her lucky marble; poor David being dumped by Mum for being boring; poor me, because Patrick doesn't really love me and I'm having a teeny-tiny baby and oh my God in heaven my breasts hurt.*

'Everything is going to be fine,' said Patrick quietly in her ear.

'Is it?' she said.

When they got downstairs they found Anne had given up on her half-hearted attempt to help Patrick's mother and was sitting at the kitchen table drinking a glass of wine while Maureen kept packing the dishwasher.

'Well, I have to dash,' she said when she saw Ellen. 'Pip and Mel and I are meeting up for a drink. There's a new wine bar in the city we've been meaning to try.'

'You're going into the city *now*?' Maureen looked at the clock on Ellen's kitchen wall. It was 8.00 p.m. 'Goodness.'

'Oh, we three are night owls!' said Anne.

It was like her romance with Ellen's father had never happened. His appearance hadn't been a giant upheaval in Ellen's life at all, just an odd little ripple.

Anne ended up leaving together with Simon, who coincidentally was meeting friends at a club in the same street as Anne's wine bar, and was thrilled to save on cab money into the city. 'Well, that's just *so* nice of you, Anne,' said Maureen unhappily.

After Ellen and Maureen had finished clearing up the kitchen (Ellen's kitchen cabinets hadn't been so sparkling clean since before her grandmother had died), Patrick's father suggested a game of Monopoly. He'd spotted the box sitting on Ellen's grandmother's shelf, and was rubbing his hands and promising to send them all bankrupt within the hour.

While George was setting up the board, carefully stacking banknotes into neat piles, Patrick asked if he and Ellen could be excused from the game.

'We might take a quick walk on the beach,' he said, raising his eyebrows questioningly at Ellen. She nodded. Maybe that would clear her head.

'It's a cold, windy night in the middle of winter and the middle of the night!' protested Maureen. 'And your wife is pregnant!'

'It's spring and it's half past eight,' said Patrick. 'It's quite balmy and I don't think the baby will mind.'

'And I'm not his wife,' said Ellen.

There was an uncomfortable silence.

'Yet!' she amended hastily. 'I mean, obviously, I will be.'

'Off you go then.' Maureen gave Patrick and Ellen a swift, searching look, a specialist appraising their relationship for hairline cracks that might cause trouble. Then she rearranged her face and said, 'After you come back, George and I might duck out for a game of tennis in the moonlight.'

'Ooh, my wife is so sarcastic!' said George. 'Here, darling, I've got the iron for you.' He held up the miniature iron from the Monopoly set.

'You know perfectly well I always have the battleship.' Maureen sat down at the head of the table and rattled the dice in her cupped hands. 'Come on, Jack! Don't think I'm going easy on you because of one broken bone!'

Patrick was right. The wind had dropped and it felt good to walk out on to the deserted beach in their jackets and scarves. The sand was still orange from the dust, but the salty cold air seemed dust free, and they both took big, bracing breaths, before tramping straight down towards the hard sand close to the water.

They walked side by side without touching. Ellen concentrated on the rhythmic hollow sound of the waves crashing on the beach and her own breathing.

'So,' said Patrick finally.

'So.'

'So that threw me for a six.'

'Jack.'

'Yes. I mean, I thought the fact that he never asked for Saskia was a good thing! It *never* occurred to me that he blamed himself for her leaving.' His voice cracked. 'Poor little tacker.'

Ellen had noticed that in times of stress Patrick spoke more like his father: the language of Australia in the 1950s.

'Children think they're the centre of the universe,' said Ellen. 'That's why they blame themselves.'

'I think,' said Patrick, 'that he's been angry with me about Saskia for years.'

'It's possible.' Ellen stopped herself from saying anything more. He needed to work this out for himself.

They walked in silence for a few minutes and then Patrick said quietly, 'She *was* a good mother to him. She . . .'

His words drifted away, and he looked up to the stars as if for inspiration. Then he took a deep breath and began to speak quickly, without looking at her, as if they were secret agents who had met on a beach and he only had limited time to brief her on this urgent information.

'When Colleen died I didn't cope very well. I'd never felt that sort of pain before, it scared the crap out of me. I thought, what's this? This hurts! So my brilliant strategy was to resist it. I remember thinking, *I'm* not going through that seven stages of grieving bullshit. If it hurts to think about her, then don't. Get busy. That's why I started the business. It was like I thought if I tried hard enough, if I was mentally strong enough, I could avoid the pain. So that worked out really well, as you can imagine. I was a walking, talking, breathing robot. But people thought I was coping great. They complimented me. And it was sort of true, I was coping. And then I met Saskia at that conference, and you know, I liked her; I probably even loved her, in my weird, robotic way. But she didn't seem to notice I was a robot! We'd be doing stuff, and she'd be smiling at me, and every now and then I'd think, in a sort of surprised way, she's really happy, she's not putting it on, she's genuinely happy. And I thought, well, it doesn't matter, because this is who I am now, and Jack's happy – watch your feet there.'

A wave had broken further in than the others and white, foamy water rushed towards them. Patrick used one arm to lift Ellen briefly in the air, saving her shoes, before depositing her back on to the dry sand. The sudden unexpected warmth of his body filled Ellen with a strange yearning for him, as if they weren't in a relationship, as if she was taking a walk with a non-available man who was just a friend.

'Saskia took on so much of the parenting,' said Patrick. 'I blame Colleen for that.'

'Pardon?' said Ellen, confused, but somewhat happy to hear poor Colleen blamed for anything.

'Colleen was a great mother, but she was very much: This is *my* territory. She was so condescending whenever I tried to help with Jack, as if I was an adorable buffoon, as if he wasn't really completely safe with me. So when she died, I was terrified, thinking, I can't bring up this kid on my own! I'll dress him the wrong way, he'll be cold or too hot, and I won't feed him right, or buy the right nappy cream or whatever. I had no idea, and my mother and Colleen's mother were over all the time, taking care of him, and of course they were even worse than Colleen, as if no man was capable of changing a nappy. And then I met Saskia, and she seemed so happy to step right into Colleen's place, to take on the Mummy role, and I let her do that. I just sat back and let it happen. Jack loved her, and she loved him. I shouldn't have done that.' He glanced over at Ellen. 'Although, I don't know, maybe I'm doing it again with you, letting you make Jack's lunches.'

'I like making his lunches,' said Ellen carefully. She could feel the presence of all those other women in Jack's life – the grandmothers, Colleen, Saskia – gathered round her, shaking their heads at Patrick and tutting in their condescending, womanly way, all thinking the same thing: *You'd feed him white bread sandwiches!*

'Well,' said Patrick. 'I guess I'm trying to find a better balance this time. Not just handing over my son and saying, Here, you look after him. And when our new little baby is born, I want to be involved, right? From the beginning.'

'You've got more experience with babies than me,' said Ellen.

Patrick shot her a grateful smile. 'That's right. I'll be the expert. I'll train you up, darlin', tell you what's what.'

'So, you stopped being a robot?' said Ellen. 'Is that why you broke up with Saskia?' *And are you still a robot? Am I just another Saskia?*

'One day, I started crying,' said Patrick. 'In the car. It was the strangest thing. I cried all way from Gordon to Mascot. And it kept happening. Each time I was alone in the car, I started crying. Sometimes I caught people staring at me at traffic lights. This grown man sobbing away at the steering wheel. It went on for weeks. And then, one morning, I woke up and I felt different. Like when you've been really sick and you wake up and you realize you're better. It wasn't that I felt happy so much, I just felt as if maybe happiness was possible. And I looked at Saskia lying next to me, and I just knew that I had to break up with her, that it was absolutely the right thing to do, that it needed to be just Jack and me for a while. It was so blindingly clear to me. But she'd only just found out that her mother was sick, so I kept putting it off.'

'And then her mother died.'

'Yes,' said Patrick. 'And then I finally told her. I think I had this stupid idea that she wouldn't be that upset, that I was almost doing her a favour, because she could find someone who loved her properly. I was shocked by her reaction, and I guess I didn't take it seriously. It was like I thought: But you can't *really* have loved me because I haven't even *been* here. You know what I mean?'

'I think so,' said Ellen. She was a bit breathless. The more Patrick had talked, the faster he had walked, and she'd been struggling to keep up with him.

'Sorry,' said Patrick. 'Let's sit down for a few moments.'

They walked up to the softer sand and sat down together facing the sea, their shoulders touching.

'I think that's why I kept putting off taking out the restraining order,' said Patrick. 'Because, deep down, I knew I'd treated her badly, even though I didn't admit it, even to myself. I'd start driving towards the police station and I'd think, geez, the woman *toilet-trained* my kid. She put her career on hold so she could take care of him. I'm in debt to her. And then I'd think, oh, she has to stop *eventually*. I should have taken her more seriously. I should have done something straight after Noosa, as soon as I knew you were involved. When I think what could have happened last night, to you or Jack or the baby.' He shuddered.

'It might not have made any difference,' said Ellen. 'Even if you had been to the police.'

Patrick lifted one shoulder in a 'Who knows?' gesture.

'Anyway,' he said. 'Enough of Saskia.' He lifted his chin and looked at the starry sky. 'Please God, *enough* of Saskia.'

'Yes,' said Ellen, thinking of Saskia's white face and wondering what she was doing right at the moment, if she had friends or family visiting her at the hospital, and what was going on in her strange, mixed-up mind.

Patrick took a deep breath. 'Anyway, the reason I suggested a walk was so I could talk to you about last night and that, ah, thing that I said. About Colleen.' His tone had changed completely. He spoke stiffly and formally, as if he were taking part in unfamiliar legal proceedings.

'All right,' said Ellen. Her stomach knotted, and she found that she actually didn't want him to speak about it. Words would just tangle things up further and make them feel worse. How strange. She had always thought words were the answer to everything; after all, she treated people with nothing but words.

Keep those lines of communication open! That's what she

always told her clients experiencing relationship difficulties. And now she couldn't think of anything worse than talking. This must be what it was like to be a man, his heart sinking each time a woman said, 'We need to talk,' thinking, JUST SHUT UP, WOMAN, as she revealed her soul in all its naked glory, when he really wanted her to keep it covered up.

'The thing is,' began Patrick.

Ellen said, 'Is that your mother?'

She could just make out the figure of Maureen picking her way carefully across the sand as if watching out for landmines.

'Phone call for Ellen!' Her voice, surprisingly clear, floated down the beach. 'She says it's urgent!'

25

Friendship is the only cure for hatred, the only guarantee of peace.
— Buddhist quote on Ellen O'Farrell's noticeboard

In the end, Tammy left at the same time as Lance and Kate. She'd invited herself along to the movies with them. It was clear that they were all three going to become friends. I'd forgotten how Tammy had that childlike ability to make instant friends. She'd done the same to me years ago.

A nurse came in to see me, just as they were all standing up to go. When she opened the door, everyone was laughing at something Kate had just said, and the nurse apologized and said, 'I'll come back when your friends are gone.'

She thought I was a normal person with normal friends, who were fond of me, who had rushed straight to my bedside when they heard I'd had an accident. She didn't know that Lance was someone I worked with, but had never seen socially, who, to be honest, I'd never really even noticed as a person, and that his wife was a complete stranger to me, and their visiting me was really sort of odd, and that Tammy was someone I'd lost touch with for three years, and that none of the people there knew the truth about how I'd broken my pelvis.

The really strange thing was that Lance, Kate and Tammy seemed determined to continue this performance. They all had plans to visit me again. Helping me through my six weeks of forced bed rest had become a project for them. I wondered, had they all signed up for some sort of self-improvement project doing the rounds of the Internet – random philanthropic acts?

Lance was going to bring me a portable DVD player so I could finally watch *The Wire* series. 'You've got no excuse now,' he'd said, with a gentle, teasing note in his voice that made me think he possibly, bizarrely, *liked* me.

Also, Kate was coming back to teach me how to knit, of all things. This had come about because Tammy had said that I should use this time to do something I'd always wanted to do but never had the time for – like learning Spanish or whatever. I said that I'd always wanted to know how to knit, which was sort of half true. It was something that I'd always *said* I'd wanted to do anyway, without really ever having the intention of doing anything about it. But as soon as I said it, Kate's eyes had lit up with the same evangelical glint that Lance got when he talked about *The Wire*, and she was now all set to give me knitting lessons.

And it had somehow transpired that Tammy was going to live in my townhouse while I was in hospital. Since she'd come back to Sydney, she'd been staying with her sister, who was driving her crazy, and so offering her my place had seemed the obvious thing to do. She was going to pick up clothes for me and bring them back after I had the operation on my ankle the next day.

I wondered what she'd think of my home. No books or pictures or photos on the fridge. If I'd known she was coming, I would have styled it in preparation. The bottle of wine I'd been drinking and the packet of painkillers would still be sitting on the kitchen table. Apart from that, every surface was bare and extremely, weirdly clean. The fridge and pantry were filled with functional food: milk, bread, butter. No biscuits or cakes, no treats at all. She would notice how I'd changed, remark on it. She used to visit me when I was living with Patrick and tease me about my domesticity: the cut flowers arranged in vases, freshly baked biscuits always ready in the tin. Now my home looked like it belonged to an obsessive-compulsive loner, a serial killer.

After I'd eaten my dinner – it was described on the docket placed on the tray as a 'light' meal, but it was actually the most substantial meal I'd had in months: I normally ate a bowl of cereal for dinner – I put my head back against the pillow and listened to the industrious sounds of the hospital: quick footsteps down hallways, the clunk of trolleys against doorways, voices rising and falling.

Most people would have felt lonely, suddenly alone in a hospital room, but I didn't. I found the noise strangely comforting. This was my village. The village for sick, sad, broken people like me.

The pain began to roll in again and, like a well-trained rat, I automatically clicked for more morphine.

I wondered, as I habitually did, what Patrick and Ellen and Jack were doing right at that moment, whether Jack's arm was giving him a lot of pain, whether Patrick had been to the police about me. But the morphine made me lazy. My wondering was idle. I had no desire to actually be there, watching them.

And anyway, then my mind drifted away from them, to Kate, Lance and Tammy, and whether they'd enjoyed the movie, and if they'd gone out to that Korean restaurant they'd talked about, and I imagined Lance and Tammy doing their Baltimore drug-dealer impressions while Kate rolled her eyes.

I think I actually laughed out loud before I fell asleep.

'I didn't catch her name, I'm sorry,' said Maureen, as she handed Ellen the phone. 'Sorry to interrupt your walk, but she sounds like she's crying.'

'Of course, of course.' Ellen took the phone nervously. What now?

She cleared her throat. 'Hello?'

A woman's snuffly voice bubbled from the phone.

'Ellen, listen, I'm so sorry to call you at this time of night, but I only just found out and I had to call you straight away, to tell you, and to apologize for my shocking behaviour yesterday. It was just inexcusable.'

The voice was familiar but Ellen couldn't place it. Someone with a bad cold. She'd seen someone with a bad cold just recently. Who was it?

'I'm not sure —'

'I'm *pregnant*, Ellen.'

'Luisa!' Ellen thought back to Luisa's furious, pale face as she'd demanded her money back. In hindsight, it was obvious. Of course she was pregnant. She'd had that particular washed-out look about her that Ellen had seen on her own face in the bathroom mirror. It was just that Luisa had been so angry about *not* being pregnant that Ellen hadn't noticed it.

'My doctor had been trying to call me. We were meant to be starting our next round of IVF, and my doctor called and said, "You can't start this cycle," and I said, "What's the problem?" and she said, "The problem is you're pregnant." A natural pregnancy! After all these years! And it's all due to you! You got me pregnant!'

'I think your husband might have something to do with it,' said Ellen.

'I can't believe I asked you for my money back. I'm horrified by my behaviour. I was crazy with jealousy and I don't know – just crazy!' She lowered her voice slightly. 'Also, I don't know if you know, but the *Daily News* is writing a story about you.'

'Yes,' said Ellen. 'I know.'

'I'm so, so sorry, but I ran into Ian Roman when I was leaving your place, and maybe he intimidated me a bit, or I was sort of star-struck, well, I'm just looking for excuses for my inexcusable behaviour really. He gave my details to a journalist and she interviewed me, and now I'm just sick about the things that I said. I've left her about thirty messages trying to withdraw my comments. If it's too late and this story appears, you'll have to sue me. I'm serious. It's the only answer. Sue me for *every penny* I've got. I haven't got that many pennies, but you sue me for them. I deserve it.'

She paused and her voice became muffled as she spoke to someone else. 'But it's true! I deserve it!' It seemed like Luisa's husband wasn't quite so keen on being sued.

'I think I've managed to get the story stopped for a few days,' said Ellen.

'Oh, thank God! Well, when the journalist calls me

back, I'm going to set her straight. I'm going to tell her that you're a miracle worker.'

'Please don't tell her that,' said Ellen. 'Seriously.'

'Well, I'm just going to tell her the truth. This is a miracle baby. Oh, sorry, Ellen, I've got to go, my parents have just arrived, but thank you, seriously, and once again my deepest, *deepest* apologies.' Her voice skidded up with delight. '*Dad*, I can't drink *champagne!*'

Ellen heard a man's voice say, 'Well, Grandpa sure can!'

'Congratulations,' she said, 'congratulations to all of you,' but Luisa had already put the phone down.

She inhaled. Exhaled. She got a bit teary thinking about the Grandpa-to-be with the bottle of champagne. Oh God, it was still early days. If she was getting the credit for Luisa's pregnancy would she get the blame if something went wrong? But still, her professional reputation appeared to be safe for a few more days.

She went back into the dining room. Patrick was leaning over his mother's chair following the progress of the Monopoly game, while his father marched his token round the board, shaking his head dolefully.

'Pay up! Pay up!' shouted Jack. 'Triple the rent!'

'I think you've bankrupted him, darling,' said Maureen hopefully. 'Does that mean we're done?'

'Everything OK?' Patrick looked at Ellen.

'It's good,' said Ellen. 'Tell you later.'

'Hand over the cash, dude.' Jack held his palm out to his grandfather.

'It's late, we probably should wrap this game up soon,' said Patrick.

'But you said I was having the day off school tomorrow,' protested Jack.

'Yes, but the point was so you could rest.'

'I slept all day,' said Jack. He did appear to be bursting with good health now, his eyes bright and clear.

'He's full of beans,' said Maureen. 'But you two look exhausted. Why don't you let him stay with us tonight?'

'I don't know,' said Patrick. 'After last night, I'd rather –'

'We'll take him to McDonald's for breakfast as a special treat,' said Maureen casually. She concentrated on rattling the dice in her cupped hands.

'Yes!' said Jack. 'Hash browns!'

'Mum,' said Patrick, but Ellen could see he didn't have the energy to argue. Her own mother would be up against a formidable adversary in the battle for ruling grandma.

An hour later, Ellen and Patrick had the place to themselves, but instead of sleeping they were eating their way through a bag of marshmallows and playing the *Dragon Blade Chronicles* on Jack's PlayStation. Since having a stepson, she'd done a lot of Ninja fighting.

'You're getting pretty good,' said Patrick, after he'd defeated her for the fifth time. 'For a lentil-eating hippie girl.'

'It's strangely addictive,' said Ellen. 'And, actually, lentils are not my favourite legume.'

'Leg– what?'

'Just shut up and eat your marshmallows.'

They sat silently for a few seconds, chewing.

Finally Patrick cleared his throat and said carefully, 'OK, enough is enough. We still haven't got to the main item on the agenda.'

'Just forget about it,' said Ellen. 'Honestly. Let's play another game.' She picked up the console. Patrick took it off her and put it back on the coffee table.

'Is that the first time I've said anything like that under hypnosis?'

'Yes.'

'It's just that you once said to me that hypnotherapy was completely consensual,' said Patrick, 'that no hypnotist could make you do or say anything that you didn't want, and I certainly did not want to say that in front of you.'

Maybe your subconscious wanted to tell me, thought Ellen.

'Well, this is where it gets messy because I'm not just your therapist, I'm your partner,' she said in her professional voice. 'I don't normally lie in bed with my clients!' She gave a horrible fake little laugh, but Patrick wasn't smiling. 'I think you were probably half asleep, half in a trance. Anyway, it really doesn't matter –'

'Doesn't matter? Of course it matters!' said Patrick. 'What a thing for you to hear! And the thing is, it gives you a completely skewed idea of how I do feel, and ever since you told me I've been struggling to think of the right way to put this.'

'It's OK,' murmured Ellen. If she hadn't compromised her professional integrity so badly, this horribly awkward conversation would never have had to take place.

'Have you ever had any doubts about this relationship? Ever compared me to one of your previous exes? Ever had a thought cross your mind that you wouldn't want me to know?'

'I don't know, I guess.' She squirmed. Throughout the course of their relationship there had been a whole plethora of thoughts and feelings that she wouldn't want him to know about.

'What about that day after we visited Colleen's parents and I was being a bastard, did you think to yourself, geez, what have I got myself into here?'

'I – don't really remember.' She remembered how she'd relived the weekend in the mountains with Jon the whole way home.

'Of *course* you've had moments of doubt. You probably felt like strangling me when I left those boxes in the hallway, but the thing is, you don't say every single thought that crosses your mind out loud.'

'Yes,' said Ellen. His eyes held hers. She looked away. 'I mean no.'

A feeling of misery swept over her. All day she'd been waiting for him to deny what he'd said, to somehow explain it away, and even though she wouldn't have believed him, she'd been perfectly prepared to begin the process of deluding herself. Now she just had to grin and bear it: her husband would always be looking at her and wishing she was his first wife.

'I understand,' she began bravely.

'You do not,' said Patrick.

'Oh, OK.'

'You think love is black and white. All women think that. And they're wrong. Women are really intelligent except for when they're being really stupid.'

She punched him, quite hard, on the arm.

'Ow. Look, I'm still not saying this right.' He chewed on the inside of his mouth with an expression that was so frustrated it was almost anguished.

'It's all right.' She rubbed his arm where she'd punched him. 'I do understand.'

'Have I been talking too much about Colleen lately?' said Patrick abruptly.

Ellen shrugged and smiled.

'I'm sorry.' He picked up her hand. 'She's been on my mind, ever since we got engaged and you told me about the baby. It's because I've felt so happy. Even with Saskia still hanging about. I haven't felt this happy since Colleen was pregnant with Jack. And that's made me think about her, remembering things.'

He ran his thumb over her knuckles.

'Colleen told me I'd fall in love again, and have more babies, and I said I wouldn't. I said I'd never be happy again. But I am. Sometimes I think, actually, this is *better* than it ever was with Colleen. It's deeper, it's more grown-up. It's just . . . better. And then I thank God and the Internet that I met you! And then I feel bad for Colleen, because it's like I'm thinking, thank God she died.'

'Right.' She wasn't sure if she believed him, or if he just wanted to make her feel better.

'I'm not sure if you believe me, but it's the truth. Don't you ever have thoughts that totally contradict each other? Isn't it possible to feel one thing one day and the opposite the next?'

'I guess. Well, yes.' She really wasn't enjoying this role. It was mildly humiliating. *She* was the one who was meant to ask the wise questions, to gently lead the less emotionally intelligent to new insights.

'And the stupid thing is, when I have those thoughts, I feel like I should make up for it to Colleen, by remembering all the good times I had with her. As penance. So the better it is with you, the more I think about her. Does that make sense? I don't know. Maybe it's a Catholic thing.'

'No, that makes sense.'

'Anyway, obviously I do not spend my days comparing you and Colleen, like you're in some sort of permanent Ninja-fighting contest. To be honest, most of the time my thoughts are pretty superficial, like: mmm, I feel like lamb chops, or how can I beat Jack to level four on *Tomb Raiders*. That sort of thing.'

Ellen picked up two marshmallows and squished them together between her fingertips.

'When Colleen died everyone started talking about her as if she was a saint. People put on these mournful faces as if our marriage had been amazing, as if we never had a fight. And I think I bought into that. I was younger. Everything was simpler. So I guess that's why I said what I said, last night. Of course I'll never love another woman the way I loved Colleen, because I'll never be eighteen and falling in love for the first time again, but that doesn't mean I'm not in love with you. And exactly the same thing applies in reverse. I never loved Colleen the way I love you.'

Ellen suddenly, unexpectedly yawned and Patrick laughed. 'Aren't I meant to be the one yawning, while you talk on about your feelings? Anyway, the bottom line is that I love you with all my heart. Not in a half-hearted, second-best way. I love *you*. And all I can do is spend the rest of my life proving that to you. Do you get that, my crazy hypnotist?'

He put his hand to the back of her head and kissed her,

hard, as if they were saying goodbye at a railway station and he were going off to war.

A deeply peaceful feeling surged through her veins. It wasn't so much what he'd said, but the two lines of fierce concentration between his eyes the whole time he was speaking, as if it really, really mattered that she understood. Or maybe it was just because she was so very, very sleepy, and Luisa was pregnant, and the newspaper article wasn't running.

'I think I get it,' she said when they came up for air.

'Thank God, because I don't think I've ever talked about "feelings" so much in my entire life as I have over the last two hours.' He handed her a marshmallow. 'See. The last marshmallow. That's love. Now let's go to bed.'

26

Enrique Penalose, the former mayor of Bogotá, Colombia, believed that we should strive to create 'Cities of Joy'. His objective was to create urban infrastructure with one objective: happiness. As town planners, can we plan for happiness? Are we planning for happiness?

— Quote from a speaker at a seminar attended by Saskia Brown following the death of her mother.

'Plan for happiness' she wrote in her notebook

It was a warm Saturday afternoon, two weeks after the accident, or the event, or whatever you want to call it. I'd been moved to a new room adjoining a courtyard where they sometimes wheeled me out for some fresh air. I could smell jasmine and the possibility of summer.

The surgery on my ankle had gone well, according to the doctors, and my pelvis fracture was healing as expected. No more morphine clicker. Just ordinary pain relief doled out in little plastic cups.

Lance's wife, Kate, sat on the visitor's chair next to me. We were both knitting. She'd been twice before to give me lessons, refusing to accept any money for the new needles she'd bought especially for me, or the wool. My first project was to be a scarlet beanie with a big white pom-pom on top. It was for me. The thought had crossed my mind to knit something for Jack, or even for Patrick's mother, Maureen, because she'd once knitted me a beret. An apology gift, I thought. Something to say goodbye. It would be a nice gesture. But as soon as I thought of it I saw an image in my head of a huge oak door, like something you'd see on a mediaeval castle. The door slammed shut in my face.

Kate said I was a 'natural knitter'. I didn't understand why she was being so kind to me. She didn't seem like a 'do-gooder', as my mother used to call certain ladies from our church; the ones with saintly smiles, who dropped off casseroles and bags of second-hand clothes, but were always too busy being charitable to other needy folk to accept Mum's offer of a cup of tea. I've always blamed those women for my godlessness.

I liked Kate. She was a tiny bit odd. Not eccentric, just a bit off-kilter. She always spoke a beat too late or too soon, and she dropped things a lot. She was friendly, but not in that look-at-me-demonstrating-my-excellent-social-skills way. I felt strangely comfortable with her.

She told me that after we'd met at the Christmas party last year, she'd been telling Lance to invite me over for dinner one night, but that Lance was too shy. She and Lance were from Melbourne and they'd only been in Sydney for a year.

'We're on the hunt for new friends,' said Kate. 'See, now you're trapped in your bed you can't get away from me. I'm stalking you.'

I laughed a bit too loudly at that.

Kate cleared her throat, and we fell silent. I listened to the gentle clack-clack of our knitting needles and the muted busy sounds of the hospital that had become the backdrop of my life.

'Speaking of making new friends, Tammy and I did a yoga class on the weekend,' said Kate suddenly. 'I picked her up from your place.'

'I know,' I said. 'She told me.'

Tammy had been coming in every few days, bringing books and DVDs, takeaway food, and gossip about our old circle of friends she was re-joining. I enjoyed seeing her but I was always tired after she left. Kate's visits were somehow more restful. Maybe it was the knitting.

'Is that weird?' said Kate. 'That I've been to your house without you there?'

It was a bit weird, but I didn't really care.

'Of course not,' I said.

'I was a bit worried you might feel like I'm stealing your friend,' said Kate, in her odd, almost childlike way. I realized what made her odd was her honesty. She didn't seem to filter her comments. She was a bit like the hypnotist.

'Tammy and I have been out of touch for years,' I said to Kate. 'She's up for grabs.'

Kate smiled. 'When you're back on your feet, we could all three go to yoga. We had coffee afterwards at this café which makes the best chocolate mud cake I have ever had in my entire life. It brought tears to my eyes it was that good.'

I didn't say anything. I didn't want to imagine facing my life again after leaving the hospital. 'You must be counting the days,' one of the nurses had said to me, and I said yes, I was, but not in the way she meant. The thought of returning home, to my real life, made me feel sick.

'You should have had herbal tea after a yoga class,' I said.

'I know. We probably ruined the energy flow with caffeine,' said Kate.

We knitted again in silence. I liked the rhythmic feel of the needles sliding in, up and over, the sense of achievement as the rows multiplied.

'You're getting hooked.' Kate nodded her head at my knitting.

'It's sort of hypnotic,' I said, and I saw the hypnotist's face, the day I first visited her as 'Deborah' and we stood together looking out of her window at the ocean. It felt like a very long time ago.

The police had been to see me the day after my ankle operation. A man and a woman. They both seemed very young to me, which didn't stop me from feeling terrified, and humiliated, and full of burning shame. What would Mum think? She was so respectful of the police. They read me a caution. It was a bit different from the one you hear on the American cop shows, drier, not as glamorous, and therefore scarier.

'So how did you end up here?' said the policeman, indicating the hospital bed, and he took out a notepad. I told him, and they both listened, their faces expressionless.

I guess they'd heard worse.

They asked me if I was aware that stalking was now a criminal offence. They said that they were serving me with an interim Apprehended Violence Order, on Patrick's behalf, effective immediately, and that I wouldn't be able to go within one hundred metres of him, his home or his workplace, and that I was legally bound not to 'assault, molest, harass, threaten, intimidate or stalk' him. I would have the option to contest the order at a court hearing. They said this in a tone of voice that made it obvious I would not succeed. The penalty for breaking the terms of the order was a five-thousand-dollar fine or two years' jail.

Assault. Molest. Harass. Threaten. Intimidate. Stalk.

Those words are burned permanently in my head. They were using those words in relation to me: A good girl. A school prefect. A pacifist. I cried when I got my first and only speeding ticket.

There was more.

In addition to the restraining order, I was also charged with breaking and entering. The policewoman handed me a court attendance notice, which I took with such badly trembling fingers it slipped from my hand and nearly fell to the floor. She grabbed it just in time, and placed it carefully on my bedside cabinet, and for a moment her eyes lost their official sheen and I saw just a hint of pity.

Then they left, their blue hats under their arms, their guns in their holsters. My heart was still hammering three hours later.

'Knitting is how I met Lance,' said Kate. 'He sat next to me on a tram and he said, "What are you knitting?"'

'Great pick-up line.'

'I know. So creative,' said Kate. 'What about you? You're single, right?'

I said, 'I haven't been in a relationship for three years, but I guess I haven't really felt single for that time.'

'What do you mean?' Kate glanced up. Her needles kept moving.

I wasn't going to say anything, I barely knew the girl, I

had the right to remain silent, but all of a sudden the words came pouring, tumbling out.

He's early, thought Ellen, as she went to the door.

Her father was coming to take her out. They were going, bizarrely, to some event in Parramatta called 'The Festival of the Olive'.

It was David's idea. 'Might be interesting,' he'd said when he rang to suggest it. 'It's at Elizabeth Farm. Don't know if you've been there. It's Australia's oldest surviving European dwelling.' He was obviously reading aloud from something. He cleared his throat. 'Sounds like a bit of fun. Something different.'

She wished she could stop comparing her meetings with her father to Internet dating (it was so inappropriate) but she couldn't help being reminded of a certain type of needy man, one who was overly eager to impress, and tried too hard to think of 'different, interesting' dates.

It broke her heart a little to think of her father looking up 'events' on the Internet, searching for something that would appeal to his 35-year-old daughter, in the same way that he probably would have taken her off to an amusement park and bought her a stuffed toy if they'd met thirty years earlier. 'We don't need to do anything, we can just talk,' she wanted to say to him, but actually, she wasn't sure what they would talk about anyway. Damn her mother to hell.

She opened the door with a fond, daughterly smile on her face, to be greeted by a woman wearing dark sunglasses and a baseball cap pulled low over her eyes.

'Quick,' said the woman. 'Let me in.'

'Sorry?'

The woman tipped her glasses down to reveal familiar round blue eyes. 'Sorry to be so dramatic. It's me, Rosie. I've had photographers chasing me all day.'

Ellen opened the door. She hadn't heard anything from Ian Roman since his visit two weeks earlier, or the journalist, and she'd given up leaving messages for Rosie.

'Why are there photographers chasing you?' asked Ellen.

'You haven't seen today's paper?' Rosie pulled off her cap and sunglasses. She looked tanned and pretty; happier than Ellen had ever seen her.

'No,' said Ellen. Her heart rate picked up. Mary-Kate had said the newspaper story had been dropped, but Ellen still felt sick each time she turned the pages of a newspaper, imagining how it would feel to be confronted by her own face and name, under some horrible headline. She had a new-found empathy for anyone who had ever been the brunt of bad press. It was funny how she'd always thought she had ample supplies of empathy; it turned out that to be truly empathetic she had to experience it.

Rosie pulled out a tabloid paper from her bag, folded in half. She held it up and tapped a finger on the front page.

It was a black-and-white photo of Ian Roman with a tall, leggy woman as they left what looked like a hotel lobby. The implication was obvious even without the headline, which read: ROMAN IS ROAMING!

Ellen read the first paragraph:

High-profile media magnate Ian Roman was married only three months ago, but the honeymoon appears to be well and truly over.

'Ian is having an affair with some supermodel,' said Rosie. 'They need a photo of me looking heartbroken and dowdy.'

'I'm so sorry,' said Ellen.

'It's fine,' said Rosie dismissively. 'He's just saving face. He thought I was about to break up with him so he wanted to get in first. He would have tipped off the photographers. But listen. Ian told me he visited you.'

'I did have the pleasure of his company,' said Ellen, in her mother's dry, cool voice. It came in useful sometimes. She led Rosie into the living room. 'Tea? Coffee? Cold drink?'

'No, no, I'm not staying. I'm sorry for turning up out of the blue.' Rosie sat down in front of Ellen on her grandfather's leather chair. Her legs were so short the tips of her ballet shoes only just reached the floor. She leaned forward, her hands clasped together as if begging for forgiveness. 'I just wanted to talk to you face to face and apologize for what I've put you through. I've been away, you see, and I didn't take my mobile with me. I only just got your messages this morning and I drove straight here.'

Ellen winced as she remembered that awful day. 'I probably sounded hysterical –'

'Oh God, you had reason! I can just imagine the things he said. He acts like, I don't know, Rambo or Tony Soprano.'

'He was quite . . . intimidating. He said he was going to "bring me down".'

'What a tosser.' Rosie took some gum out of her bag, unwrapped it and began chewing rapidly. She pointed at her mouth. 'Nicotine gum. I'm finally off the cigarettes.'

'Well, as your husband pointed out, I wasn't much help there.'

'Are you kidding? I would recommend you to anyone!' Rosie chewed vigorously and looked off into the distance, presumably trying to think of a good reason as to why she'd recommend Ellen.

'So Ian overheard you talking to your sister about me,' prompted Ellen.

'I had no idea.' Rosie leaned back; now her feet didn't reach the floor. 'I would have thought eavesdropping on my trivial conversations was beneath him. And he got it wrong, of course. I was just telling my sister how I'd *asked* you to hypnotize me into falling in love with him, and she was telling me I was an idiot.'

'Anyway, then she convinced me to go and join her on a family holiday in Queensland. It was wonderful. Just your average beach holiday, building sandcastles with my nieces. Prawn sandwiches. Ian would have hated it. It sort of confirmed everything that is different between us. I'm just so . . . average.'

'Nobody is average,' said Ellen automatically.

'I am,' said Rosie. 'I'm extremely average. I don't know why he even showed an interest in a hobbit like me. I'm not his type. That supermodel in the paper. That's his type. She'll look good on his yacht.'

'I don't know, Rosie,' said Ellen. 'I think he really loved you. That's why he was so angry.'

'No,' said Rosie. 'It was just his pride. Anyway, it's over. It was a big mistake on both our parts. I never really loved him. You know that. You helped me work that out.'

'I think,' said Ellen, 'that you never even let yourself

love him, or like him, or even know him at all, because you were so busy wondering why he chose you. I think you were blinded by the Ian Roman image. The money. The power. His big tycoon act. He might love an average beach holiday.'

Rosie blinked. Chewed some more.

'He chose you,' said Ellen. 'A man in his position could have any sort of trophy wife. He didn't choose a supermodel, he chose you.'

She was trying to say: *The fact that he chose someone ordinary-looking like you means that he saw something extraordinary in you, and THAT means maybe there is more to him than we think.*

She thought of Patrick's words: *You women think love is black and white.*

Rosie frowned. Something flickered in her eyes. She looked down at her hands and kicked her legs. Then Ellen saw her face close down, as she made her decision. No. She lacked the self-esteem or the courage or the some-thing; her marriage to Ian Roman died in that instant.

'Whatever,' said Rosie. 'He's cheated on me now any-way. We're done. Don't worry about it. I'm not. As I said, I came here to apologize and to let you know that he won't be coming after you. I told him that if I ever saw anything negative about you in the papers, I'd do a tell-all interview about my marriage to Ian Roman and that I could proba-bly come up with some really interesting sexual fetishes that he'd never live down. You're safe.'

'Thank you,' said Ellen.

'He doesn't have any strange sexual fetishes by the way,' said Rosie, as she stood up and picked up her bag. 'Actu-ally, the sex was quite good.'

It was ridiculous that Ellen felt sad about the end of this marriage. Rosie didn't love Ian Roman, and the horrible Ian Roman was probably out on his yacht right now, drinking champagne with his supermodel. Except that maybe Rosie and Ian could have been happy together if it wasn't for their pride.

Rosie held out her hand. She smiled. She really did have a very pretty smile. 'Back to my average life.'

As Rosie was leaving, Ellen's father was coming down the footpath. He stopped to hold the gate open for her.

'Patient?' he said, as Ellen ushered him in.

'Client,' Ellen corrected him. 'We don't call them patients.' She watched Rosie walking off, and said, 'With hindsight I would have treated her completely differently.'

'Hindsight,' said her father. 'It's always just a fraction too late.'

'Well,' said Kate. She paused, looked around the room for inspiration. Her eyes didn't meet mine. 'Holy shit.'

She hadn't said a word the whole time I'd been talking. She'd just kept knitting, nodding her head occasionally, and sometimes lifting her eyebrows. I had no idea what she was thinking. I'd told her everything that had happened and everything I'd done. I didn't try to mitigate myself in any way. If only I'd had a terrible childhood, I could have put it down to that, but I couldn't actually blame anyone or anything. My guilt, I told her, was absolute.

'You didn't know you were visiting a crazy person,' I said at last.

It had felt so good telling her. I couldn't stop. It was like I was tearing away at a horrible scab with my fingernails, but now I'd done it, and I was sitting in front of her, red-raw and exposed, I was filled with regret and a terrible sense of loss. I'd really liked her. We could have been friends. Now I'd ruined everything.

'Oh, well,' said Kate. 'I've done some pretty crazy things.'

'Really?'

Kate put her head on one side, considered. 'Well, no, not really. Not compared to that. I was just trying to make you feel better.'

'Thank you.'

She kept knitting.

'I bet you're a Scorpio, hey?' she said without looking up.

'Well, yes, actually, but I don't –'

'You don't believe in astrology. Scorpios never do. But anyway, you're very passionate, you Scorpios. All brooding and mysterious. I always wished I was a Scorpio. Or a Leo. I'm a Libra. We're indecisive.' She kept knitting. 'I don't really believe in any of it either.'

She unwound some wool from round her wrist. 'You must have really loved him,' she said. 'And the little boy.'

'Yes,' I said. 'But I guess if I really loved them I should have "set them free", or whatever that stupid line is. Loving them is no excuse.'

Ever since that night I'd kept seeing a recurring image of Patrick's face when he saw me standing at the end of his bed. It wasn't just that there was someone standing there, it was that it was *me*. *I was his nightmare*. I'd made myself his nightmare.

'You know what I think you should do?' said Kate.

'You think I should get counselling,' I said tiredly. She and the hypnotist were right, of course. 'Professional help' was required.

'I guess, if you want,' said Kate. 'But I was just going to say, I think you should stop it.'

'Stop it.'

'Yes, that's my extremely wise advice. Stop it.'

'Just . . . stop it.'

Kate began to giggle. 'That's what I'd say if I was your therapist. Saskia, just *stop it*. Take up knitting instead.'

I picked up my needles again. Kate smiled. 'That's it. See, you're cured. That'll be two hundred dollars please.'

It seemed that the universe had seen fit to send me a brand-new friend. I wondered if my mother had arranged it. I imagined her in the Afterlife, dancing with my father in a starry ballroom. Maybe they'd been talking about me, shaking their heads at my shocking behaviour. Maybe after Jack and I went crashing down the stairs, my mum said, 'I *told* you she wasn't going to grow out of it! What she needs is a brand-new friend.' Then she'd had an inspiration: 'I know! A knitter! I always wanted her to learn to knit.' And she'd rushed off to fill in the appropriate paperwork.

'Knit don't stalk,' murmured Kate. 'Repeat after me: Knit don't stalk.'

The 'Festival of the Olive' was unexpectedly delightful.

Of course it was; Ellen couldn't think why it was unexpected. She'd always enjoyed this sort of thing: school fêtes, craft shows, outdoor markets. She loved little stalls, and the gentle, earnest people who presented their organic, home-grown wares on white tablecloths: honey, jam, chutney, wine, or in this case olives and olive oil. She loved the sound of wind chimes and the smells of essential oils. These were her people; this was her thing. ('Hippies with money,' Julia would say.)

She and her father walked through rows of white tents, the white canvas flapping gently in the breeze, breathing in the Mediterranean fragrances of garlic, fresh bread and wisteria, while the spring sunshine gently caressed their shoulders. Ellen was filled with a deep, sleepy feeling of contentment.

Partly it was because it had gradually dawned on her that this wasn't in fact a date, and there was no danger at all (presumably) of her father suddenly trying to kiss her. Partly it was because her nausea had seemingly gone for good, and the relief was as glorious as waving goodbye to an annoying house guest.

And perhaps it was really because her father had got tears in his eyes when he looked at the pictures of Ellen's baby and then he'd been embarrassed, and at that moment he'd become a real person; not the punchline of a joke about Ellen's life. All the way here in the car, as she'd sat in the passenger seat and watched her father drive (capably, casually – like Patrick), she'd felt something softening in the very core of her body. *Why not be sentimental about this*, she thought. *He's your father. It's allowed. You can like him if you want. You can let yourself feel fond of him.*

They stopped in front of a stall and a small, intense woman immediately launched into a passionate explanation of the Australian Olive Association's criteria for Extra Virgin Olive Oil status. She spoke in such meticulous detail it was as if she believed they were about to apply for Extra Virgin Olive Oil status, and probably wouldn't get it.

'Right!' said David, when she finally finished. 'Well, that's . . . Ellen, why don't we try some?'

Ellen dipped a piece of bread into a small square of golden olive oil.

'Fantastic.' She rolled her eyes heavenward with exaggerated pleasure. And it was fantastic, although she knew from past experience that everything always seemed to taste particularly delicious at these sorts of things, and then once she got back home it would probably taste much the same as the mass-produced stuff she got from the supermarket. It was the fresh air and the power of suggestion at work. She was being gently hypnotized.

'Let me buy you a bottle.' David pulled a fifty-dollar note out of his wallet.

'What a nice dad,' said the woman.

David coughed into his fist, and Ellen smiled sympathetically at him.

The woman frowned. 'Oh, I'm sorry, you're not father and daughter?'

'No, you're right, we are,' said Ellen.

'Well, I knew it,' said the woman, in a tone of mild rebuke, as if they'd tried to put one over her. She handed over David's change and the olive oil in a white paper bag. 'You've got identical chins.'

Ellen and her father simultaneously touched their chins with the tips of their fingers and then dropped their hands.

They ate spaghetti sitting at a white plastic table under a big marquee. The conversation was pleasant but a bit of an effort, as if they were two strangers who had struck up a conversation at a bus stop, and now the bus was taking too long to arrive but they felt obliged to keep talking.

'I'm sorry about you and Mum breaking up,' said Ellen, after a long discussion about spring in Australia as compared to spring in the UK.

'So am I,' said David. 'It was probably my fault. I shouldn't have rushed into a relationship when I was still a bit battered and bruised.'

'Battered and bruised,' repeated Ellen, confused.

'Well, my wife left me after thirty-five years of marriage,' said David. 'It threw me for a loop. There wasn't even another man. She said she'd "forgotten how to be herself". I said, "*Be* yourself. I'm not stopping you!" But apparently I was.' He looped his spaghetti expertly round his fork and contemplated it sadly.

'I'm sorry,' said Ellen. She was struggling to readjust her perceptions. 'I think I was under the impression that you'd left your wife, or that it was mutual.'

'It certainly wasn't mutual.'

'Mum didn't say,' began Ellen.

'I sort of played down the "I'm so heartbroken about my wife" side of things,' said David.

'She said you'd been thinking about *her* throughout your marriage.' She hoped he didn't notice the sound of accusation in her voice.

Her father gave her a rueful look. 'She told you that.' He pushed his plate away from him and settled his arms on the sides of his chair. 'I wasn't lying. Over the years, I did think about your mother occasionally, or even dreamed about her, but that doesn't mean I didn't love Jane.'

Ellen pushed her own plate away.

'Although, of course, you did cheat on her when you were engaged,' she said briskly, but jokily, to show she wasn't judging. She gestured at herself to indicate the results of his infidelity. 'More than once, I hear.'

'Yes,' said David. 'I was young and stupid and your mother was gorgeous. Those *eyes* of hers!' He gave a boyish, 'awww shucks' shrug. 'Lucky I did, hey?'

Ellen couldn't decide whether to be charmed or not.

These were the muddled, imprecise facts of her conception: not quite a great love story, not quite a seedy indiscretion, not quite a brave feminist act.

'Anyway,' said David. 'Your mother and I are still friends, and between you and me, I'm not giving up hope just yet.'

'Really?' said Ellen. She wondered if she should tell him that she didn't think he had a chance at all, but then what did she know? Over the last few months she'd learned that anything she thought she knew to be true could shift and change in an instant. Nothing was permanent: the Buddhists knew what they were talking about.

They sat in silence for a while, watching the preparations for some sort of performance that was obviously about to take place in the centre of the marquee.

'Patrick seems like a good man,' said David. 'He's got a son too, hasn't he? From a previous marriage?'

'Jack,' said Ellen. 'He's at a party today. His mother died when Jack was little.'

'Testing,' said someone over a microphone. 'Testing, two, three, four.'

'So obviously my relationship with Patrick is a bit complicated,' Ellen heard herself say. This was what happened when you talked for too long to a stranger at a bus stop. The conversation suddenly took an inappropriately intimate turn.

'Why?' said David. Ellen was a bit thrown by the question. Wasn't it obvious? (Most women she knew would have said something like, 'Oh, well, *yes*, of *course*, I can just *imagine*, my sister's friend dated a widower and it was a disaster...')

'I just mean, I guess, that his first wife passed away, and that —'

She was interrupted by a high-pitched shrieking from the sound system. Everyone winced and stuck their fingers in their ears.

It finally stopped and someone said, 'Apologies!' over the microphone.

David said, 'I don't think you've got anything to worry about.'

'Why?'

He turned to look at her. 'Ellen,' he said. (She thought it might have been the first time he'd used her name, whereas she'd been 'David' this and 'David' that, because she always overused people's names when she didn't know them that well.)

'Ellen, the man was *hanging curtains* for you this morning.'

'Yes, I know —'

'That's a mongrel of a job. As my dad would have said.'

'Is it?'

'And he was pretty keen to show me the ultrasound pictures. Doesn't seem like a complicated relationship to me.'

The marquee filled with the sound of a thrumming

guitar. Three flamenco dancers stalked on to the stage flicking their gorgeous dresses and tossing their heads, their beautiful young faces fierce and regal.

'*Olé*!' said Ellen's father. He lifted his hands above his head and pretended to click imaginary castanets. It was a profoundly dorky dad-like move that would have caused any self-respecting teenage son or daughter to die with shame.

'*Olé*,' said Ellen agreeably.

She settled back in her chair to watch the dancing and as she did she felt a last lingering doubt over Patrick's love – a doubt she didn't know she'd had – quietly drift away.

So this was what it was like to have a father.

'Knock, knock?'

It was Tammy's voice outside my hospital room.

'Don't mention –' I said to Kate. It wasn't so much that I thought Tammy would judge me, although of course she would, but that I knew she'd be far too interested, too intrigued and fascinated. She'd gasp and shriek and ask question after question. She'd want to explore my motivations and Patrick's reactions for hours at a time. She'd never let the topic die.

'Of course not.' Kate put down her knitting. 'I won't even tell Lance.'

She would tell Lance. She would tell him as soon as they got home tonight. There was no way you could keep that sort of secret from your partner.

But I had a feeling that although Lance would think I was one crazy bitch for a while, and he'd be glad he'd never dated me, and he'd feel sorry for Patrick, in a few years' time, if Kate happened to bring it up, he'd say vaguely, 'Oh, that's right, what was that story again?' He wasn't the type to hoard personal information, and I also felt that some sort of innate integrity or morality or dislike of gossip would prevent him from telling people at the office. Anyway, I had a feeling that I wouldn't be going back to work there. Things were going to change.

'What up, bitches,' said Tammy.

Kate and I rolled our eyes at each other: Tammy and Lance still insisted on trying to talk like Baltimore drug dealers.

Tammy reverted to her normal voice. 'Look at you two grandmas with your knitting.'

She tossed a pile of mail on the bed in front of me. 'By the way, Janet and Peter said hi.'

'Janet and Peter?' I said blankly.

'Your *neighbours*,' said Tammy. Ah, the Labrador family from next door. I tried to visualize their faces and couldn't. Perhaps I'd never really looked at them.

'I went over there for dinner last night,' said Tammy.

It was interesting, watching someone else living in my home and living my life, showing me how easy and natural it could be. She wouldn't have hesitated when they asked her over. 'Sure! What will I bring?' she would have said.

'They're fun,' she continued. 'We played Monopoly with the kids.'

'I hate Monopoly,' commented Kate, picking up her needles again.

'Anyway, we're planning a welcome home party for you,' said Tammy.

'A party?' I said. 'I don't really do parties.'

'What are you talking about?' said Tammy. 'I was telling Janet and Peter about that Hallowe'en party you had years ago. Remember? It was one of the best parties I've ever been to.'

I did remember. It was when Patrick and I had just started dating but before we'd moved in together. I'd gone all out and decorated my flat with pumpkin lights and cobwebs. I even put dry ice in tubs for a creepy, smoky effect. Everyone dressed up. Patrick came as Dracula and kept bending me over so he could sink his fangs into my neck. I was Morticia, with a long black wig and a spider choker round my neck. I remember the photos: you'd never seen a happier Morticia.

But the girl who hosted that party doesn't exist any more, I thought.

'You made pumpkin pie,' said Tammy. 'It was divine.'

'I've never eaten pumpkin pie,' said Kate.

'I'll make it for you,' I said, and suddenly I was listing the ingredients in my head: cream cheese, cinnamon, ginger. And then I was struck by how very much I wanted to make pumpkin pie for Kate and Lance and Tammy and maybe even the family next door, to see people enjoying my food and asking for second helpings. How long had it been since I'd been the hostess, since I'd cooked for someone?

I remembered the Anzac biscuits I'd baked in Ellen's kitchen and I shuddered at the memory. I picked up the mail to distract myself.

'Apparently Janet's brother has taken a shine to you,' said Tammy. 'So we're going to match you up at this party.'

'Janet's brother?' She was talking nonsense. 'I've never

even met her brother.' As she talked I sorted my mail: bills; junk mail; more bills.

'He met you once on your way out,' said Tammy. 'He thinks he's seen you before, at Avalon Beach, boogie boarding? Could that be right?'

I picked up an envelope with my address in neat handwriting that was vaguely familiar.

'I tried boogie boarding a few times,' I said. I flicked the envelope back and forth between my fingertips as I remembered that woolly-haired man at the beach, the way his shadow fell over me that morning when I lay in the sand in my red dress, the night after I'd turned up at Patrick's parents' house when Ellen was there.

Then I thought back to the man with the baseball cap coming up the path of the next-door neighbours as I'd left for the pretend fortieth birthday party. I remembered how he'd looked at me as if he knew me.

I morphed together the two images from my memory and saw that they could easily be the same person. It gave me a peculiar feeling, as if I needed to go back and examine my whole life and look for all the things I'd missed.

'But he's got a girlfriend,' I said, remembering the way he'd put his arm round the woman he was with, and how bereft I'd felt when I'd seen it.

'He just broke up with someone,' said Tammy. 'He's back on the market. You'll have to move fast before he's snapped up by someone else.'

'What's he do for a living?' said Kate. 'Or is that a superficial question? What are his dreams, his hopes?'

'Wait for it,' said Tammy dramatically. 'He's a . . . *carpenter*.'

'He is *not*.' Kate dropped her knitting.

'He *is*!'

'Be still my beating heart!'

I laughed at them. I'd forgotten that sort of laughter. Silly, girly, helpless giggling. I'd thought I'd grown too old for giggling, but actually you never really grow out of it. I should have known that. When Mum was in her seventies she used to meet up with her old tennis club once a month for lunch. I was staying with her once when it was her turn to host and I remember walking in the front door and hearing *peals* of laughter coming from the living room. They sounded like teenagers.

I'd forgotten that the best part of dating wasn't the actual dating at all, but the talking about it; the analysis of potential new boyfriends with your girlfriends.

'Can I come to this party?' said Kate. 'So I can meet the carpenter?'

'Of course,' said Tammy. 'I wonder if we could think up an excuse so he'll need to do some actual *carpentry* at the party?'

'Like putting up a bookshelf?'

'Ideally something that makes Saskia seem helpless and vulnerable.'

'So much for feminism,' I said.

Kate snapped her fingers. 'A disabled ramp! For her wheelchair!'

'They say I'll be walking by the time I go home,' I said. They were going to try to get me on crutches next week.

'Oh,' said Kate, disappointed. 'Are you sure?'

I forgot about the envelope with the familiar handwriting until later that night after they'd left. I turned it over and saw the sender's details on the back: *Mrs Maureen Scott.*

Patrick's mother. Of course. She was like my own mother. A card sender. She'd often sent cards when I'd been with Patrick. '*Dear Patrick, Saskia and Jack, thank you for the lovely evening on Saturday night. We thoroughly enjoyed Saskia's "Thai Beef Salad". It was delicious.*'

Why was she writing to me now? To tell me *enough was enough*? *You broke my grandson's arm, you evil bitch*?

I opened it. The pale purple stationery with a border of lavender sprigs looked familiar. She'd probably been using the same notepaper for years.

I read:

Dear Saskia,

Jack wanted to send you this 'get well' card (he bought it himself with his own money) and I promised I would find your address and post it to you. Patrick doesn't know he has written to you, so I would be very grateful (given the current circumstances) if you didn't write back. I should have said this before, Saskia, but you were a wonderful mother to Jack and, as his grandmother, I should have done more to make sure you stayed in touch. I'm very sorry. I will always regret this. Jack has grown into a lovely young boy. He is a credit to you.

I hope and I pray that you can find a way to move on with your life now, and be happy. I know that's what your own mum would have wanted.

With love,
Maureen

The card showed a picture of a giraffe sitting up in bed with a thermometer in its mouth. Jack had written:

Dear Saskia,

    Get well soon. I'm OK. My cast comes off next week.

    Dad won't let me visit you. Sorry about that.

Love from Jack

PS I remember the playdough cities. They were awesome.

PPS Here is another lucky marble for you to make up for the one I lost.

At the bottom of the envelope was a marble.

I held it up between my fingertips to the light and studied the intricate, intertwined paint splashes of colour, and my eyes blurred.

I cried for such a long time. There were no wrenching, painful sobs, just quiet, cleansing tears, like a long, soft rainfall on a Sunday afternoon.

When the tears finally stopped, I blew my nose and turned off the light, and I slept more deeply than I think I'd slept in years. I don't think I dreamed at all. It was as if I were an animal that had gone into hibernation for the winter. Waking up was like emerging from a deep, dark cave into the fresh spring air.

I rubbed my eyes with the heels of my hands and smelled undercooked bacon and bad coffee. Sally, the wonderfully grumpy aide who brought in my breakfast most mornings, was standing at the end of my bed. She dumped the tray on my table with her usual ungracious clatter and raised her eyebrows at me.

'Sleep well?' she said.

'Wonderfully,' I said.

27

'Yes, that is my nose and, yes, it's very funny. Now could you focus?'

The baby let go of Ellen's nose and placed her palm over Ellen's mouth.

Ellen pretended to eat it. 'Umm, umm.'

The baby grinned. She turned her head and fastened her mouth back round Ellen's nipple, drinking with greedy concentration, one finger lifted in the air, as if to say: *Hold that thought. I'll be right back with you.*

Ellen closed her eyes briefly as she felt the tingling warm rush of a thousand tiny magnets pulling down the milk. Six months ago she'd never felt this; now it was as familiar a sensation as a sneeze.

Except that every time, it still felt marginally extraordinary.

For a few minutes Grace fed, her tiny hand circling as if she were conducting a symphony. She tipped her head back and her eyelids fluttered, as though the music was touching her soul.

'Where's my little girl?'

At the sound of her father's voice, the baby swung her head so fast in his direction she wrenched on Ellen's nipple and droplets of milk flew.

'*Hello*, my little Gracie girl, hello, hello, *hello*!' Patrick crouched down on the floor next to where Ellen was sitting. The baby crowed and gurgled and wriggled in an ecstasy of love. Patrick held out his hands and looked up at Ellen for approval.

'It's OK. She was just snacking really.'

Patrick took the baby into his arms and buried his face in her neck. 'Fee fi fo fum, I smell the blood of a yummy, yummy baby.'

Ellen re-fastened her bra and the buttons of her shirt, watching Patrick.

'Goodness, I've never seen such a besotted father,' Anne had said the previous night after watching him play with Grace. She sounded mildly disapproving, even cranky. Ellen wondered if it was regret that Ellen had missed out on a besotted daddy, or envy because Anne had been a single mother, or if she thought there was something unmanly or unseemly about Patrick's behaviour.

'Sorry.' Patrick stood up with the baby on his hip and kissed the top of Ellen's head. 'Hello, you.'

'Oh, yes, don't mind me,' shrugged Ellen.

She didn't think it was unmanly. She couldn't get enough of seeing Patrick interact with Grace. The very first moment she'd been wheeled back into her hospital room and seen him cradling the new baby to his bare chest (the nurses had told him to give Grace skin-to-skin contact while Ellen was in recovery, and so he'd unbuttoned his shirt and tucked her up against his bare chest like a sleepy koala) she'd felt such a powerful rush of feeling – something like lust, except not. It was just like the breastfeeding, an entirely new sensation. She wondered if it was biology: the satisfaction of seeing your mate bond with your offspring, so you knew that he would be likely to stick around and keep clubbing lions and tigers for you or whatever. Or was it because she was identifying with Grace, and Patrick was filling Ellen's repressed need for paternal love?

Whatever it was, she was grateful for it. Now all that fuss over whether or not Patrick still had feelings for Colleen seemed so silly. Ellen looked back tenderly and condescendingly on herself a year ago: all that unnecessary drama! There was enough love to go around for everyone.

There was even enough love to cope with last Monday morning's phone call from Harriet to say that Jon's new wife was pregnant with twins.

(Nearly enough love anyway. It helped to imagine how badly Jon would cope with sleep deprivation. He'd always liked his sleep. She hoped his twin babies would be healthy and lively; particularly at 3.00 a.m.)

After Harriet's phone call it had occurred to her how rarely she thought about her ex-boyfriends now. Gracie's arrival had kicked them clean out of her head. It used to be that a big part of her satisfaction with her love for Patrick was because it compared so favourably to her feelings for her previous partners. It was like she'd entered their relationship in a permanent contest with all her past relationships. *Yes, yet again, we're the winners! Look at our superior sex life! Look at how happy we are!*

Except no one was watching (not any more) and no one cared.

Now her love for Patrick was just a fact, an intrinsic part of her life, as if it had always been so.

She did sometimes wonder if all this blissful contentment might be due to the fact that breastfeeding released the 'love hormone' – oxytocin – which increased trust and empathy, and reduced fear. Oh well. She was going to breastfeed for as long as Grace wanted. ('Promise me you won't be one of those freaky hippie mothers, still feeding her when she starts school,' said Anne. 'What's wrong with that?' asked Ellen innocently.)

Grace Lily Scott, named in honour of her maternal great-grandmothers, was born on Valentine's Day by a planned C-section. A natural birth wasn't an option because of the baby's 'low-lying placenta'. For a while there, that had seemed like the end of the world. Ellen had always imagined herself having a drug-free, natural labour, using the hypnosis skills she'd successfully taught so many other mothers-to-be. It had never occurred to her that she might not even get to *try* a natural birth.

'Yes, I can see you'd be upset,' said Julia at the time. (She had just recently moved in with Stinky and was incandescent with happiness, due also to the news that her ex-husband's new wife had left him for another man: karma of the most satisfying sort.) 'It's because a caesarean doesn't fit with your brand identity. You should be having a home birth with chanting and candles and incense.'

'It's not exactly that,' sniffed Ellen, although Julia was exactly right.

'I always knew you'd be too posh to push,' said Madeline, before admitting that she was just jealous, because her sixteen-hour labour to bring little Harry into the world wasn't exactly one of her favourite memories. (Madeline had also recently admitted that the reason she'd never asked Ellen about her hypnotherapy work was because she thought Ellen didn't consider her 'spiritual or deep enough' to understand. Ellen had been astonished.)

'Labour doesn't make you a mother, darling,' said Patrick's mother.

'If *only* you were born a hundred years ago, when you could have gone through days of natural labour before bleeding naturally to death,' said Ellen's mother.

Of course, in the end, it hadn't mattered. She'd used self-hypnosis to help keep her blood pressure stable through the surgery and there had been no complications. 'Your wife is the most calm, serene patient I've ever had,' said the anaesthetist to Patrick.

'You should see her when she's Ninja fighting,' replied Patrick.

Ellen had stayed in her own peaceful little zone until the obstetrician held up her baby, at which point she'd gasped for air like she'd just been pulled from the bottom of a swimming pool, and everyone got concerned, and she couldn't speak properly to tell them she was perfectly fine, it was just that: Oh my God, did you see, that's an actual *baby*.

Apparently, while her conscious mind had been reading books and setting up a nursery, her subconscious mind had been thinking she was giving birth to a fish or a teddy bear or something other than a baby.

'What are we going to do while Mummy is busy hypnotizing?' said Patrick now to Grace. 'Do you want to go down to the beach with me and your big brother? Or just hang out and shoot the breeze?'

Grace launched into a long conversation in baby talk, her big eyes fixed on Patrick. She had inherited Ellen's mother's violet eyes. Ellen was very vain about Gracie's eyes; deliberately dressing her in colours that would make them even more startling. She had literally never been out in public without someone stopping to compliment her on them, although each time she would act surprised and flattered as if it was the first time someone had noticed. 'They come from her grandma,' she'd say modestly.

'Right.' Patrick nodded along respectfully as Grace continued to babble. 'Yep. I see. Gotcha. So you're not sure. You can't make up your mind? Well, that's because you're a woman, you see.'

'Hey,' said Ellen.

'Actually, it's probably because you take after your mother and you're over-analysing the situation. You're thinking, but what does it *mean* if Daddy takes me to the beach? Is he subconsciously trying to say something else? Is he repressing his real desires?'

'I'm not even listening to you.' Ellen stood up and stretched her arms high above her head.

She had just recently started treating clients again on a part-time basis. Her mother and the godmothers took Grace every Wednesday morning. They dressed her up like a princess and took her out to restaurants where they fed her tiny morsels of smoked salmon and shaved chocolate and who knew what else. Patrick's mother minded both Jack and the baby after school every Thursday afternoon. Maureen gave Grace long warm baths and fed her mashed pumpkin and never sent her home without a pink bow pinned to her wispy, sweet-smelling hair. Jack had found Grace of only mild interest when she was a tiny baby, but now she was starting to respond to him he'd made it his life mission to make her laugh with increasingly crazy versions of 'peek-a-boo'. Gracie had a very specific wicked chuckle she reserved especially for Jack.

Patrick was in charge on Saturdays, when Ellen did her longest stint and saw four clients.

There was a three-month waiting list to see her at the moment, but for now she didn't want to do any more hours than this. Having a baby had been like starting a demanding new job and beginning a passionate love affair and moving to a new country with a different language and culture all at the same time. The baby filled her mind, her heart and her senses. She wanted to inhale her, to gobble her up.

The love she felt for Grace seemed to permanently hover on a knife's edge between joy and terror. 'Babies are pretty resilient,' Patrick's mother would say when Ellen expressed her concern about anything, and Ellen wanted to say, 'Are you kidding? They can *die in their sleep*!'

Once, when her mother was visiting without the godmothers, Ellen came out of the nursery from checking on Grace and said, 'I love her so much it's just . . .'

'Excruciating,' supplied her mother. 'I know. It doesn't really get any better. You just learn to live with it.'

Ellen met her mother's eyes, which now reminded her of her daughter's eyes. She'd always known that the fierce, furious way Anne looked at her was because she was trying to hide how much she loved her, as if love was a weakness. She had always considered it one of her mother's more adorable flaws. *If only she could be more like me! Open to love!* Now for the first time she understood that her mother wasn't resisting love so much as bearing it. Now she knew that you could love so much it literally hurt: an actual pain in the centre of her chest.

Fortunately, whenever her feelings threatened to become impossibly transcendent, the banalities of mother-hood were there to bring her back down to earth. You couldn't be carried away by sentiment when you were dealing with an exploding nappy or trying to work out why avocado and cottage cheese were no longer acceptable, and the constant wondering: is she tired or hungry or teething, and what *is* that monotonous 'uh, uh, uh' sound she's making and how can we make it stop?

'I think I'll take her and Jack down to the beach,' said Patrick. 'Get Jack away from that computer.'

'OK. Gracie's hat is on the chest of drawers,' said Ellen. 'And the sun cream is –'

'We're all under control,' said Patrick.

'Good,' said Ellen. 'There is a bit of a breeze so –'

'Ellen. Respect the Dad.'

'OK. Just – okey-dokey.'

'Oooh, it's killing her,' said Patrick to the baby. 'There's so much more she wants to say. So many further instructions.'

Ellen rolled her eyes. 'I'm going to get changed for

work.' She was wearing jeans and a T-shirt covered in baby-food stains. 'You two have fun.'

Patrick lifted Grace's hand and waved it at her. 'Bye, Mummy.'

Ellen lingered and looked at the two pairs of eyes staring back at her. 'Her eyes are the same shape as yours. Mum's colour, but your shape.'

'And look at our identical bald spots.' Patrick lifted Grace up under the armpits and bent his own head.

Ellen left the room but when she got halfway down the hallway she ran back and poked her head round the doorway. She spoke very quickly. 'If-you-want-her-blue-cardigan-it's-in-the-bag-at-the-front-door-and-that's-all-I'm-going-to-say!'

As she walked up the stairs she could hear him muttering, 'She can't help herself, Gracie. She really can't.'

Twenty minutes later, she was dressed and standing at the window of her office, her hand on the curtain that Patrick had put up. She could see him walking on the beach with the baby on his hip, a sun umbrella under his arm, the beach bag over his shoulder. Jack was walking backwards in front of them, probably trying to make Grace laugh. Ellen squinted: Patrick had dressed the baby in the blue cardigan.

She watched them stop at a spot near the water. Patrick handed over the baby to Jack, and got down on his knees and began to dig a hole for the umbrella. He always took such care setting up the beach umbrella it would probably stay put during a cyclone.

'Hurry up,' she said to the window. 'She's out in the sun.'

Patrick stopped digging and looked up at the house as if he'd heard her. He lifted both arms and waved them high above his head as if he was waving from a mountain-top. Ellen laughed and waved back pointlessly.

Even the way Patrick inhabited his body was different now than when she'd first met him: his movements were bigger, freer, looser. It had been over a year since they'd had any contact with Saskia, and every month that had gone by Patrick had changed more: relaxing, becoming sillier, happier, more trusting, less irritable and angry. He sang country music songs with an American accent as he did stuff around the house – songs about 'cheatin' women' and 'cold stone hearts'. It was as though Ellen hadn't known the real Patrick at all, as if she'd fallen in love with a sick person, and now he was healthy. It felt like a sur-prise bonus; an unexpected free gift with her order.

It also made her belatedly angry with Saskia, and with herself for being so oblivious to the true extent of how much it had affected him, and how much it might always affect him.

Once, when Gracie was only a few weeks old, she and Patrick were watching a documentary together about a woman who had been stalked for years by her ex-husband.

'That's what I felt like,' said Patrick at one point.

Ellen had been startled. She hadn't been thinking about Patrick at all. She was horrified with herself. *She hadn't even registered that he would be thinking about his own experiences with Saskia.* Her sympathies had been entirely with the woman in the documentary. How terrible for her! There was no excuse for the ex-husband's behaviour; she had no inter-est in wondering about his motivations. He was just plain bad: a villain who should be punished to the full extent of the law. As Ellen sat there with Gracie asleep on her shoulder, while the woman on the television cried, it struck her that she'd given Patrick none of the empathy or concern she was currently giving to a woman she'd never met. Her prejudice, her blindness, had been quite breath-taking.

'I'm sorry you had to go through that,' she'd said to Patrick.

'Oh, well, worse for a woman,' Patrick had shrugged.

When they were driving Patrick still automatically checked the rear-vision mirror more than the average driver, and whenever they walked into a restaurant his eyes still swept the room, as if he'd been a spy in a past life, but he did it without that furrowed brow and that wary, defensive look. His insomnia had gone and he was more energetic. He looked younger. 'I feel like I'm in remission from some terrible illness,' he told Ellen. 'Every time I check my phone or my email and I don't see Saskia's name, it's like I've won a prize.'

Ellen and Patrick hadn't got round to getting married but they had begun idly, pleasantly talking about it again, and what sort of day they'd like. Patrick was keen on an overseas wedding, which meant, Ellen guessed, that he wasn't completely cured – he still thought there was a chance that Saskia could turn up.

Ellen wondered if Saskia had moved out of Sydney, as she'd suggested. She wondered if she was still suffering from her leg pain, and if she'd finally met someone new. These were facts she would have really liked to know, but she was too superstitious to even Google Saskia's name, in case doing so somehow made her materialize back into their lives.

She watched as Patrick finished putting up the umbrella and took the baby from Jack. He swung her up into the air. Ellen knew how she'd be giggling, clutching at his hair. Her giggles were fat and delicious; the most edible sound Ellen had ever heard.

Jack went running across the sand near the water and did a handstand, walking on his hands for a few seconds, his legs straight and tall.

'Careful,' she murmured to the glass.

This morning at breakfast he'd been talking with her about the upcoming Athletics carnival. 'I told everyone that you'll win the mothers' race because you'll hypnotize all the other mums! Pow, pow, pow! They'll fall to the ground!'

She'd been thrilled by the casual, unconscious way he'd referred to her as one of the mums, and she'd sent a mental note of apology to Colleen.

She thought of how it would feel if she knew she was going to die, and someone else was going to be there to bring up Grace. Before she had a baby she'd taken a secret, melancholy pleasure in imagining her own funeral. Now the thought of someone else making decisions about Gracie's life was unbearable.

I'm so sorry it worked out this way, Colleen, but I promise I'm doing my best. And I love Jack. I really do love him.

Although not so much that it hurt, not the way that she loved Gracie.

But that was OK, she thought, that wasn't something to lie awake at night worrying about. There were all sorts of ways to love. She thought of the new relationship she was forming with her own father; the growing fondness and respect. Just because it wasn't the same as the relationship he had with his sons didn't mean that it wasn't something special.

Of course, Jack was a child, not an adult, and perhaps if he unconsciously sensed that Ellen didn't love him in the same painful way as she loved Gracie it would do untold damage to his psyche. So she probably should devote a few late nights to worrying about whether or not she was an evil stepmother.

She sighed. If only she could win the mothers' race! Unfortunately, she was a terrible runner. She was seriously considering faking an injury.

Now Jack was sprinting round the umbrella in circles, probably kicking sand on to Patrick and into the baby's eyes. Hmmm. He didn't look too damaged.

The doorbell rang.

She was seeing a new client who had found her on the Internet. On the phone he'd sounded abrupt and doubtful – and desperate. He said he wanted help quitting smoking, but Ellen suspected that something else was really the problem. She knew she was his last resort.

Ellen gave her family a final glance and turned round to go downstairs, to see how she could help.

28

Will you please tell my daughter how much I love her?
– Saskia's mother's last words, whispered to a nurse
who was crouched down by the side of the bed,
trying to untangle a cord on the drip. 'Pardon?' the
nurse said irritably, but it was too late.

I didn't do everything the hypnotist told me, but I did see a psychiatrist, once a week for over a year.

I didn't have a choice.

After I got out of hospital last year, in the early summer, I went to my court hearing in the city, wearing my most responsible, non-crazy clothes, and while I waited for my name to be called, I thought of the first time I'd ever seen Patrick in Noosa. I was sitting in a workshop on 'Ecologically Friendly Building Design' and he came in late, looking for a seat. I saw his eyes scan the room, and I thought, *Sit next to me*, and his eyes caught mine, and he smiled.

That was the beginning and this was the end.

It was over and done with in a remarkably short time. I didn't contest the restraining order and I pleaded guilty to the criminal charge of breaking and entering. I was given a one-year good behaviour bond on the condition that I undertook psychological counselling.

My psychiatrist never said much, just let me drone on

and on, but when she did talk, I felt like I was a butterfly being pinned to a page. In the beginning it was always about Patrick.

'How do you think Patrick felt when you kept ringing him?'

'What do you think was going through Patrick's mind when you turned up that day?'

'Do you think Patrick was frightened that night?'

It was ironic that I'd spent the last three years doing nothing but thinking about Patrick and yet I hadn't really thought about him at all.

'I was never violent,' I'd say.

'Violence isn't just physical,' she'd say. 'You took away all his power.'

'It was never about *power*. I loved him. I just wanted to get back together.'

'Think about it, Saskia.'

She wouldn't let me get away with anything. It was like she was making me stand in front of a mirror, and I'd keep trying to turn round and look the other away, and each time I did she would take me by the shoulders and turn me back round to face the mirror again. And when I put my hands over my eyes she'd gently remove them and put them back by my side.

And, finally, I stood still and looked.

It wasn't very enjoyable.

She listed, in a dry, clinical voice, the possible impact of my behaviour on Patrick: anxiety, depression, post-traumatic stress.

'I really don't think –' I said, and then I stopped.

'It's very well documented,' she said.

'Fancy that,' I said.

'You knew this,' she said. 'I think a part of you knew exactly what you were doing to him.'

'I could send him a card to apologize,' I said at last, in a stupid, silly voice.

It was such a bad joke she didn't even bother to react. She just looked at me, driving that pin straight through my heart again, so I fluttered and squirmed and finally grew still.

I was only joking about the card. After I came home from the hospital, I never tried to see or contact Patrick again. I stopped going to Jack's games. I wasn't even tempted. Not really. It was like a particular food I'd once loved had made me violently ill. So although I could remember how good it tasted, whenever I thought of it, or automatically reached for it, I remembered how sick it had made me, so the desire was outweighed by the revulsion.

We talked a lot about grief: for the loss of my mother and Patrick and Jack and the children I wouldn't ever have. We talked about how I'd taken my grief and used it like a weapon against Patrick, how I'd directed the pain and the rage outwards, away from me, as if I'd been handed a flaming sword and I'd turned it on Patrick in a desperate, frenzied and ultimately useless attempt to avoid being burned myself.

I used up a lot of her tissues.

We talked about how Patrick's decision to break up really wasn't anything to do with me at all; it was about him and his own grief for Colleen. 'If Ellen had met him at that conference he probably would have broken up with her in exactly the same way,' said my psychiatrist.

'No, they're *soul mates*,' I said. 'It was true love for them.'

'It was timing,' she said.

We talked about friendship and how I'd let myself slip out of a social network. We talked about hobbies – other than stalking your ex-boyfriend. We talked about ways to deal with future relationships and future rejection.

I stopped using quite so many tissues.

Then one day I turned up and we chatted about a movie I'd seen at the weekend, and a new fish recipe I'd tried, and how we both wanted to eat more fish, and at the end of the session my psychiatrist said that she thought I probably didn't need to make an appointment for the following week, and so I didn't. I had a pedicure instead.

Ellen told me that I should leave Sydney, but I haven't. I'd miss my friends too much.

Tammy is living in the townhouse with me now, and we see a lot of our neighbours, Janet and Pete. Their kids are in and out of our place all the time. Tammy and I looked after them last weekend so Janet and Pete could go away for a couple of days.

I did end up going out with Janet's brother for a few months. The boogie-boarding guy. Toby. He was fun and it was a good distraction for a while, but he'd just come out of a relationship, and in strange way I had too, so we were both weird and fragile, and the relationship amiably petered out.

We're still good friends, which is an odd experience for me. I've never been friends with an ex-boyfriend before. I don't really understand how it works, or what the rules are, but so far it's been fine, if sometimes a bit awkward. We chat but we avoid eye contact.

Kate says she thinks Toby and I are destined to end up together, because of some complicated thing to do with the way he looks at me (I didn't think he did look at me but apparently he does when I'm distracted), but I don't know. She's pregnant at the moment and overly sentimental. She rang me last night to tell me that she and Lance had been for the ultrasound, and the baby was a boy, and that they'd like me to be the baby's godmother. *Me*. She said, 'I know I haven't known you that long so tell me if it's an imposition.' Then she said, 'Saskia? Are you still there?'

My godson will be born next year.

Speaking of babies, I saw the hypnotist with her baby today.

It wasn't deliberate. I've never breached the terms of my order, and I make a point of avoiding areas where I'm likely to run into them again.

It was early evening and I was at Circular Quay. I was meeting Tammy and Kate for a drink at the Opera Bar before we saw a play. Kate had got cheap tickets from some website. It was a beautiful evening and the Quay was crowded with people walking back and forth between the ferries and the Opera House.

Ellen was walking straight towards me pushing a stroller, one of those big, colourful contraptions. I only caught a glimpse of the baby. Patrick's baby. It was a girl. She was wearing a purple dress. Little legs stuck straight out in front of her with white socks.

I stopped dead and someone behind me said, 'Hey, watch out.'

I saw Ellen's face light up. It was as if she were looking straight at me. I smiled back, because I'd always thought we could have been friends in a different world, and I really wanted to tell her that it was the strangest thing, but since I'd broken my pelvis and ankle my mysterious leg pain had vanished.

And then I realized that she was smiling at someone behind me; lifting a hand to wave. I didn't even turn my head to see if it was Patrick or Jack or someone else. I kept walking and let myself melt into the crowd.

Acknowledgements

Thank you so much to all the talented people at Penguin who transformed this manuscript into a book, especially Celine Kelly and Karen Whitlock. Thank you also to my wonderfully supportive agent, Jonathan Lloyd, and everyone at Curtis Brown.

Writing this book gave me the excuse to learn about the amazing world of hypnotherapy. I'm so grateful to Lyn Macintosh for all the time she spent introducing me to her fascinating profession. Errors and flights of fancy are most definitely my responsibility.

Thank you to my friends: Mark Davidson for explaining police procedures, Janelle Atkins for answering questions about town planning and Jackie Mikhael for getting herself hypnotized just so she could report back to me.

Thank you to my father, Bernie Moriarty, for telling me about surveying, and my mother, Diane Moriarty, for telling every single person she meets about my books.

Thank you as always to my sisters, Jaclyn Moriarty and Nicola Moriarty, who read my first drafts, and Katrina Harrington who helps proofread my last draft.

The following books were very helpful to me in the writing of this novel: *Hypnosis and Hypnotherapy* (2001) by C. Banyan and G. Kein; *Hypnosis: A Comprehensive Guide* (2008) by Tad James with Lorraine Flores & Jack Schober;

Finding True Magic (2006) by Jack Elias; *The Art of Hypnosis* (2010) by C. Roy Hunter; *The Psychology of Stalking* (1998) by J. Reid Meloy.

One house. Nine strangers. Ten days that will change everything . . .

Read on for the first chapter of this twisty tale of deception from the bestselling author of *Big Little Lies*

Out now

I

Yao

'I'm fine,' said the woman. 'There's nothing wrong with me.'

She didn't look fine to Yao.

It was his first day as a trainee paramedic. His third call-out. Yao wasn't nervous, but he was in a hyper-vigilant state because he couldn't bear to make even an inconsequential mistake. When he was a child, mistakes had made him wail inconsolably, and they still made his stomach cramp.

A single bead of perspiration rolled down the woman's face, leaving a snail's trail through her make-up. Yao wondered why women painted their faces orange, but that was not relevant.

'I'm fine. Maybe just twenty-four-hour virus,' she said, with the hint of an Eastern European accent.

'Observe everything about your patient and their environment,' Yao's supervisor, Finn, had told him. 'Think of yourself as a secret agent looking for diagnostic clues.'

Yao observed a middle-aged, overweight woman with pronounced pink shadows under distinctive sea-green eyes and wispy brown hair pulled into a sad little knot at the back of her neck. She was pale and clammy, her breathing ragged. A heavy smoker, judging by her ashtray scent. She sat in a high-backed leather chair behind a gigantic desk. It seemed like she was something of a bigwig, if the size of this plush corner office and its floor-to-ceiling harbour views were any indication of corporate status. They were on the seventeenth floor and the sails of the Opera House were so close you could see the diamond-shaped cream-and-white tiles.

The woman had one hand on her mouse. She scrolled

through emails on her oversized computer screen, as if the two paramedics checking her over were a minor inconvenience, repairmen there to fix a power point. She wore a tailored navy business suit like a punishment, the jacket pulled uncomfortably tight across her shoulders.

Yao took the woman's free hand and clipped a pulse oximeter onto her finger. He noted a shiny, scaly patch of reddish skin on her forearm. Pre-diabetic?

Finn asked, 'Are you on any medication, Masha?' He had a chatty, loose manner with patients, as if he were making small talk at a barbecue, beer in hand.

Yao noticed that Finn always used the names of patients, whereas Yao felt shy talking to them as though they were old friends, but if it enhanced patient outcomes, he would learn to overcome his shyness.

'I am on no medication at all,' said Masha, her gaze fixed on the computer. She clicked on something decisively then looked away from her monitor and back up at Finn. Her eyes looked like they'd been borrowed from someone beautiful. Yao assumed they were coloured contact lenses. 'I am in good health. I apologise for taking up your time. I certainly didn't ask for an ambulance.'

'I called the ambulance,' said a very pretty, dark-haired young woman in high heels and a tight checked skirt with interlocking diamond shapes similar to the Opera House tiles. The skirt looked excellent on her but that was obviously of no relevance right now, even though she was, technically, part of the surrounding environment Yao was meant to be observing. The girl chewed on the fingernail of her little finger. 'I'm her PA. She . . . ah . . .' She lowered her voice as if she were about to reveal something shameful. 'Her face went dead white and then she fell off her chair.'

'I did not fall off my chair!' snapped Masha.

'She kind of slid off it,' amended the girl.

'I momentarily felt dizzy, that is all,' said Masha to Finn.

'And then I got straight back to work. Could we cut this short? I'm happy to pay your full, you know, cost or *rate*, or however it is you charge for your services. I have private health cover, of course. I just really don't have time for this right now.' She turned her attention back to her assistant. 'Don't I have an eleven o'clock with Ryan?'

'I'll cancel him.'

'Did I hear my name?' said a man from the doorway. 'What's going on?' A guy in a too-tight purple shirt swaggered in carrying a bundle of manila folders. He spoke with a plummy British accent, like he was a member of the royal family.

'Nothing,' said Masha. 'Take a seat.'

'Masha is clearly not available right now!' said the poor PA.

Yao sympathised. He didn't appreciate flippancy about matters of health, and he thought his profession deserved more respect. He also had a strong aversion to spiky-haired guys with posh accents who wore purple shirts a size too small to show off their overly developed pecs.

'No, no, just sit down, Ryan! This won't take long. I'm fine.' Masha beckoned impatiently.

'Can I check your blood pressure, please, ah, Masha?' said Yao, bravely mumbling her name as he went to strap the cuff around her upper arm.

'Let's take that jacket off first.' Finn sounded amused. 'You're a busy lady, Masha.'

'I actually really do need her sign-off on these,' said the young guy to the PA in a low voice.

Yao thought, *I actually really do need to check your boss's vital signs right now, motherfucker.*

Finn helped Masha out of her jacket and put it over the back of her chair in a courtly way.

'Let's see those documents, Ryan.' Masha adjusted the buttons on her cream silk shirt.

'I just need signatures on the top two pages.' The guy held out the folder.

'Are you kidding me?' The PA lifted both hands incredulously.

'Mate, you need to come back another time,' said Finn, with a definite edge to his barbecue voice.

The guy stepped back but Masha clicked her fingers at him for the folder, and he instantly jumped forward and handed it over. He obviously considered Masha scarier than Finn, which was saying something, because Finn was a big, strong guy.

'This will take fourteen seconds at the most,' she said to Finn. Her voice thickened on the word 'most' so that it sounded like 'mosht'.

Yao, the blood-pressure cuff still in his hand, made eye contact with Finn.

Masha's head lolled to one side, as though she'd just nodded off. The manila folder slipped from her fingers.

'Masha?' Finn spoke in a loud, commanding voice.

She slumped forward, arms akimbo, like a puppet.

'Just like that!' screeched the PA with satisfaction. 'That's exactly what she did before!'

'Jesus!' The purple-shirt guy retreated. *Jesus*. Sorry! I'll just . . .'

'Okay, Masha, let's get you onto the floor,' said Finn.

Finn lifted her under the armpits and Yao took her legs, grunting with the effort. She was a very tall woman, Yao realised; much taller than him. At least six feet and a dead weight. Together, he and Finn laid her on her side on the grey carpet. Finn folded her jacket into a pillow and put it behind her head.

Masha's left arm rose stiff and zombie-like above her head. Her hands curled into spastic fists. She continued to breathe in jerky gasps as her body postured.

She was having a seizure.

Seizures were disquieting to watch but Yao knew you just had to wait them out. There was nothing around Masha's neck that Yao could loosen. He scanned the space around her, and saw nowhere she could bang her head.

'Is this what happened earlier?' Finn looked up at the assistant.

'*No*. No, before she just sort of fainted.' The wide-eyed PA watched with appalled fascination.

'Does she have a history of seizures?' asked Finn.

'I don't think so. I don't know.' As she spoke, the PA was shuffling back towards the door of the office, where a crowd of other corporate-types had now gathered. Someone held up a mobile phone, filming, as if their boss's seizure were a rock concert.

'Start compressions.' Finn's eyes were flat and smooth like stones.

There was a moment – no more than a second, but still a moment – in which Yao did nothing as his brain scrambled to process what had just happened. He would remember that moment of frozen incomprehension forever. He *knew* that a cardiac arrest could present with seizure-like symptoms and yet he'd still missed it because his brain had been so utterly, erroneously convinced of one reality: *This patient is having a seizure*. If Finn hadn't been there, Yao may have sat back on his haunches and observed a woman in cardiac arrest *without acting*, like an airline pilot flying a jet into the ground because he is overly reliant on his faulty instruments. Yao's finest instrument was his brain, and on this day it was faulty.

They shocked her twice but were unable to establish a consistent heart rhythm. Masha Dmitrichenko was in full cardiac arrest as they carried her out of the corner office to which she would never return.

2

Ten years later

Frances

On a hot, cloudless January day, Frances Welty, the formerly bestselling romantic novelist, drove alone through scrubby bushland six hours north-west of her Sydney home.

The black ribbon of highway unrolled hypnotically ahead of her as the air-conditioning vents roared arctic air full-blast at her face. The sky was a giant deep blue dome surrounding her tiny solitary car. There was far too *much* sky for her liking.

She smiled because she reminded herself of one of those peevish TripAdvisor reviewers: *So I called reception and asked for a lower, cloudier, more comfortable sky. A woman with a strong foreign accent said there were no other skies available! She was very rude about it too! NEVER AGAIN. DON'T WASTE YOUR MONEY.*

It occurred to Frances that she was possibly quite close to losing her mind.

No, she wasn't. She was fine. Perfectly sane. Really and truly.

She flexed her hands around the steering wheel, blinked dry eyes behind her sunglasses and yawned so hugely her jaw clicked.

'Ow,' she said, although it didn't hurt.

She sighed, looked out the window for something to break the monotony of the landscape. It would be so harsh and unforgiving out there. She could just imagine it: the drone of blowflies, the mournful cry of crows, and all that glaring white-hot light. Wide brown land indeed.

Come on. Give me a cow, a crop, a shed. I spy with my little eye something beginning with . . .

N. Nothing.

She shifted in her seat, and her lower back rewarded her with a jolt of pain so violent and personal it brought tears to her eyes.

'For God's *sake*,' she said pitifully.

The back pain had begun two weeks ago, on the day she finally accepted that Paul Drabble had disappeared. She was dialling the number for the police and trying to work out how to refer to Paul – her partner, boyfriend, lover, her 'special friend'? – when she felt the first twinge. It was the most obvious example of psychosomatic pain ever, except knowing it was psychosomatic didn't make it hurt any less.

It was strange to look in the mirror each night and see the reflection of her lower back looking as soft, white and gently plump as it always had. She expected to see something dreadful, like a gnarled mass of tree roots.

She checked the time on the dashboard: 2.57 pm. The turn-off should be coming up any minute. She'd told the reservations people at Tranquillum House that she'd be there around 3.30 to 4 pm and she hadn't made any unscheduled stops.

Tranquillum House was a 'boutique health and wellness resort'. Her friend Ellen had suggested it. 'You need to *heal*,' she'd told Frances after their third cocktail (an excellent white peach Bellini) at lunch last week. 'You look like *shit*.'

Ellen had done a 'cleanse' at Tranquillum House three years ago when she, too, had been 'burnt out' and 'run-down' and 'out of condition' and – 'Yes, yes, I get it,' Frances had said.

'It's quite . . . unusual, this place,' Ellen had told Frances. 'Their approach is kind of unconventional. Life-changing.'

'How exactly did your life change?' Frances had asked, reasonably, but she'd never got a clear answer to that question. In the end, it all seemed to come down to the whites of Ellen's eyes, which had become really white, like, freakily white! Also, she lost three kilos! Although Tranquillum House wasn't about weight loss – Ellen was at great pains to point that out. It was about *wellness*, but, you know, what woman complains about losing three kilos? Not Ellen, that's for sure. Not Frances either.

Frances had gone home and looked up the website. She'd never been a fan of self-denial, never been on a diet, rarely said no if she felt like saying yes or yes if she felt like saying no. According to her mother, Frances's first greedy word was 'more'. She always wanted more.

Yet the photos of Tranquillum House had filled her with a strange, unexpected yearning. They were golden-hued, all taken at sunset or sunrise, or else filtered to make it look that way. Pleasantly middle-aged people did warrior poses in a garden of white roses next to a beautiful country house. A couple sat in one of the 'natural hot springs' that surrounded the property. Their eyes were closed, heads tipped back, and they were smiling ecstatically as water bubbled around them. Another photo showed a woman enjoying a 'hot stone massage' on a deckchair next to an aquamarine swimming pool. Frances had imagined those hot stones placed with delightful symmetry down her own spine, their magical heat melting away her pain.

As she dreamed of hot springs and gentle yoga, a message flashed urgently on her screen: *Only one place remaining for the exclusive Ten-Day Mind and Body Total Transformation Retreat!* It had made her feel stupidly competitive and she clicked *Book now*, even though she didn't *really* believe there was only one place remaining. Still, she keyed in her credit card details pretty damned fast, just in case.

It seemed that in a mere ten days she would be 'transformed' in ways she 'never thought possible'. There would be fasting, meditation, yoga, creative 'emotional release exercises'. There would be no alcohol, sugar, caffeine, gluten or dairy – but as she'd just had the tasting menu at the Four Seasons, she was stuffed full of alcohol, sugar, caffeine, gluten and dairy, and the thought of giving them up didn't seem that big a deal. Meals would be 'personalised' to her 'unique needs'.

Before her booking was 'accepted', she had to answer a very long, rather invasive online questionnaire about her relationship status, diet, medical history, alcohol consumption in the previous week, and so on. She cheerfully lied her way through it. It was really none of their business. She even had to upload a photo taken in the last two weeks. She sent one of herself from her lunch with Ellen at the Four Seasons, holding up a Bellini.

There were boxes to tick for what she hoped to achieve during her ten days: everything from 'intensive couples counselling' to 'significant weight loss'. Frances ticked only the nice-sounding boxes, like 'spiritual nourishment'.

Like so many things in life, it had seemed like an excellent idea at the time.

The TripAdvisor reviews for Tranquillum House, which she'd looked at *after* she'd paid her non-refundable fee, had been noticeably mixed. It was either the best, most incredible experience people had ever had, they wished they could give it more than five stars, they were evangelical about the food, the hot springs, the staff, or it was the worst experience of their entire lives, there was talk of legal action, post-traumatic stress and dire warnings of 'enter at your own peril'.

Frances looked again at the dashboard, hoping to catch the clock tick over to three.

Stop it. Focus. Eyes on the road, Frances. You're the one in charge of this car.

Something flickered in her peripheral vision and she flinched, ready for the massive thud of a kangaroo smashing her windscreen.

It was nothing. These imaginary wildlife collisions were all in her head. If it happened, it happened. There probably wouldn't be time to react.

She remembered a long-ago road trip with a boyfriend. They'd come across a dying emu that had been hit by a car in the middle of a highway. Frances had stayed in the passenger seat, a passive princess, while her boyfriend got out and killed the poor emu with a rock. One sharp blow to the head. When he returned to the driver's seat he was sweaty and exhilarated, a city boy thrilled with his own humane pragmatism. Frances never quite forgave him for the sweaty exhilaration. He'd *liked* killing the emu.

Frances wasn't sure if she could kill a dying animal, even now when she was fifty-two years old, financially secure and too old to be a princess.

'You could kill the emu,' she said out loud. 'Certainly you could.'

Goodness. She'd just remembered that the boyfriend was dead. Wait, was he? Yes, definitely dead. She'd heard it on the grapevine a few years back. Complications from pneumonia, supposedly. Gary always did suffer terribly from colds. Frances had never been especially sympathetic.

At that very moment her nose dripped like a tap. Perfect timing. She held the steering wheel with one hand and wiped her nose with the back of her other hand. Disgusting. It was probably Gary vindictively making her nose drip from the afterlife. Fair enough too. They'd once been on road trips and professed their love and now she couldn't even be bothered to remember he was dead.

She apologised to Gary, although, really, if he was able to access her thoughts, then he should know that it wasn't her fault; if he'd made it to this age, he'd know how extraordinarily vague and forgetful one became. Not all the time. Just sometimes.

Sometimes I'm as sharp as a tack, Gary.

She sniffed again. It seemed like she'd had this truly horrendous head cold even longer than the back pain. Hadn't she been sniffling the day she delivered her manuscript? Three weeks ago. Her nineteenth novel. She was still waiting to hear what her publisher thought. Once upon a time, back in the late nineties, her 'heyday', her editor would have sent champagne and flowers within two days of delivery, together with a handwritten note. *Another masterpiece!*

She understood she was no longer in her heyday, but she was still a solid, mid-level performer. An effusive email would be nice.

Or just a friendly one.

Even a brisk one-liner: *Sorry, haven't got to it yet but can't wait!* That would have been polite.

A fear she refused to acknowledge tried to worm its way up from her subconscious. No. No. Absolutely not.

She clutched the steering wheel and tried to calm her breathing. She'd been throwing back cold and flu tablets to try to clear her nose and the pseudoephedrine was making her heart race, as if something wonderful or terrible was about to happen. It reminded her of the feeling of walking down the aisle on both her wedding days.

She was probably addicted to the cold and flu tablets. She was easily addicted. Men. Food. Wine. In fact, she felt like a glass of wine right now and the sun was still high in the sky. Lately, she'd been drinking, maybe not excessively, but certainly more enthusiastically than usual. She was on that slippery slope, hurtling towards drug and alcohol addiction! Exciting to know she could still change in significant ways. Back home there was a half-empty bottle of pinot noir sitting brazenly on her writing desk for anyone (only the cleaning lady) to see. She was Ernest frigging Hemingway. Didn't he have a bad back too? They had so much in common.

Except that Frances had a weakness for adjectives and adverbs. Apparently she scattered them about her novels like throw cushions. What was that Mark Twain quote Sol used to murmur to himself, just loud enough for her to hear, while reading her manuscripts? *When you catch an adjective, kill it.*

Sol was a real man who didn't like adjectives or throw cushions. She had an image of Sol, in bed, on top of her, swearing comically as he pulled out yet another cushion from behind her head, chucking it across the room while she giggled. She shook her head as if to shake off the memory. Fond sexual memories felt like a point for her first husband.

When everything was good in Frances's life she wished both her ex-husbands nothing but happiness and excellent erectile function. Right now, she wished plagues of locusts to rain down upon their silvery heads.

She sucked on the tiny, vicious paper cut on the tip of her right thumb. Every now and then it throbbed to remind her that it might be the smallest of her ailments but it could still ruin her day.

Her car veered to the bumpy side of the road and she removed her thumb from her mouth and clung to the steering wheel. 'Whoops-a-daisy.'

She had quite short legs, so she had to move the driver's seat close to the steering wheel. Henry used to say she looked like she was driving a dodgem car. He said it was cute. But after five years or so he stopped finding it cute and swore every time he got in the car and had to slide the seat back.

She found his sleep-talking charming for about five years or so too.

Focus!

The countryside flew by. At last a sign: *Welcome to the town of Jarribong. We're proud to be a TIDY TOWN.*

She slowed down to the speed limit of fifty, which felt almost absurdly slow.

Her head swivelled from side to side as she studied the town. A Chinese restaurant with a faded red-and-gold dragon on the door. A service station that looked closed. A red-brick post office. A drive-through bottle shop that looked open. A police station that seemed entirely unnecessary. Not a person in sight. It might have been tidy but it felt post-apocalyptic.

She thought of her latest manuscript. It was set in a small town. *This* was the gritty, bleak reality of small towns! Not the charming village she'd created, nestled in the mountains, with a warm, bustling café that smelled of cinnamon and, most fanciful of all, a *bookstore* supposedly making a profit. The reviewers would rightly call it 'twee', but it probably wouldn't get reviewed and she never read her reviews anyway.

So that was it for poor old Jarribong. Goodbye, sad little tidy town.

She put her foot on the accelerator and watched her speed slide back up to one hundred. The website had said that the turn-off was twenty minutes outside of Jarribong.

There was a sign ahead. She narrowed her eyes, hunched over the wheel to read it: *Tranquillum House next turn on the left*.

Her heart lifted. She'd done it. She'd driven six hours without quite losing her mind. Then her heart sank, because now she was going to have to go through with this thing.

'Turn left in one kilometre,' ordered her GPS.

'I don't want to turn left in one kilometre,' said Frances dolefully.

She wasn't even meant to be here, in this season or hemisphere. She was meant to be with her 'special friend' Paul Drabble in Santa Barbara, the Californian winter sun warm upon their faces as they visited wineries, restaurants and museums. She was meant to be spending long lingering afternoons getting to know Paul's twelve-year-old son, Ari, hearing his dry little chuckle as he taught her how to play some violent PlayStation game he loved. Frances's friends with kids had laughed and scoffed over that, but she'd been looking *forward* to learning the game; the storylines sounded really quite rich and complex.

An image came to her of that detective's earnest young face. He had freckles left over from childhood and he wrote down everything she said in laborious longhand using a scratchy blue ballpoint. His spelling was atrocious. He spelled 'tomorrow' with two m's. He couldn't meet her eye.

A sudden rush of intense heat enveloped her body at the memory.

Humiliation?

Probably.

Her head swam. She shivered and shook. Her hands were instantly slippery on the steering wheel.

Pull over, she told herself. *You need to pull over right now.*

She indicated, even though there was no-one behind her, and came to a stop on the side of the road. She had the sense to switch on her hazard lights. Sweat poured from her face. Within seconds her shirt was drenched. She pulled at the fabric and smeared back strands of wet hair from her forehead. A cold chill made her shake.

She sneezed, and the act of sneezing caused her back to spasm. The pain was of such truly biblical proportions that she began to laugh as tears streamed down her face. Oh yes, she *was* losing her mind. She certainly was.

A great wave of unfocused primal rage swept over her. She banged her fist against her car horn over and over, closed her eyes, threw back her head and screamed in unison with the horn, because she had this cold and this back pain and this broken bloody heart and –

'Hey!'

She opened her eyes and jumped back in her seat.

A man crouched next to her car window, rapping hard on the glass. She saw what must be his car pulled up on the opposite side of the road, with its hazard lights also on.

'You okay?' he shouted. 'Do you need help?'

For God's sake. This was meant to be a private moment of despair. How deeply embarrassing. She pressed the button to lower the window.

A very large, unpleasant, unkempt, unshaven man peered in at her. He wore a t-shirt with the faded emblem of some ancient band over a proud, solid beer belly and low-slung blue jeans. He was probably one of those outback serial killers. Even though this wasn't technically the outback. He was probably on holiday from the outback.

'Got car trouble?' he asked.

'No,' said Frances. She sat up straighter and tried to smile. She ran a hand through her damp hair. 'Thank you. I'm fine. The car is fine. Everything is fine.'

'Are you *sick*?' said the man. He looked faintly disgusted.

'No,' said Frances. 'Not really. Just a bad cold.'

'Maybe you've got the proper flu. You look *really* sick,' said the man. He frowned, and his eyes moved to the back of her car. 'And you were screaming and sounding your horn like you . . . were in trouble.'

'Yes,' said Frances. 'Well. I thought I was alone in the middle of nowhere. I was just . . . having a bad moment.' She tried to keep the resentment from her voice. He was a good citizen who had done the right thing. He'd done what anyone would do.

'Thank you for stopping but I'm fine,' she said nicely, with her sweetest, most placatory smile. One must placate large strange men in the middle of nowhere.

'Okay then.' The man straightened with a groan of effort, his hands on his thighs to give himself leverage, but then he rapped the top of her car with his knuckles and bent down again, suddenly decisive. *I'm a man, I know what's what.* 'Look, are you too sick to drive? Because if you're not safe to drive, if you're a danger to other drivers on the road, I really can't in good conscience let you –'

Frances sat up straight. For heaven's sake. 'I just had a hot flash,' she snapped.

The man blanched. 'Oh!' He studied her. Paused. 'I always thought it was a hot *flush*,' he said.

'I believe both terms are used,' said Frances. This was her third one. She'd done a lot of reading, spoken to every woman she knew over the age of forty-five and had a double appointment with her GP, where she had cried, 'But no-one ever said it was like this!' For now they were monitoring things. She was taking supplements, cutting back on alcohol and spicy foods. Ha ha.

'So you're okay,' said the man. He looked up and down the highway, as if for help.

'I really am perfectly fine,' said Frances. Her back gave a friendly little spasm and she tried not to flinch.

'I didn't realise that hot flashes – flushes – were so . . .'

'Dramatic? Well, they're not for everyone. Just a lucky few.'

'Isn't there . . . what's it called? Hormone replacement therapy?'

Oh my Lord.

'Can you prescribe me something?' asked Frances brightly.

The man took a little step back from the car, hands up in surrender. 'Sorry. It's just, I think that was what my wife . . . Anyway, none of my business. If everything is okay, I'll just be on my way.'

'Great,' said Frances. 'Thank you for stopping.'

'No worries.'

He lifted a hand, went to say something else, evidently changed his mind and walked back towards his car. There were sweat marks on the back of his t-shirt. A mountain of a man. Lucky he decided she wasn't worth killing and raping. He probably preferred his victims less sweaty.

She watched him start his car and pull out onto the highway. He tipped one finger to his forehead as he drove off.

She waited until his car was a tiny speck in her rear-view mirror and then she reached over for the change of clothes she had waiting on the passenger seat ready for this exact situation.

'Menopause?' her eighty-year-old mother had said vaguely, on the phone from the other side of the world, where she now lived blissfully in the south of France 'Oh, I don't think it gave me too much trouble, darling. I got it all over and done with in a weekend, as I recall. I'm sure you'll be the same. I never had those hot flushes. I think they're a myth, to be honest.'

Hmmph, thought Frances as she used a towel to wipe away her mythical sweat.

She thought of texting a photo of her tomato-red face to her group of schoolfriends, some of whom she'd known since kindergarten. Now when they went out to dinner they discussed menopause symptoms with the same avid horror they'd once discussed their first periods. Nobody else was getting these over-the-top hot flushes like Frances, so she was taking it for the team. Like everything in life, their reactions to menopause were driven by their personalities: Di said she was in a permanent state of rage and if her gynaecologist didn't agree to a hysterectomy soon she was going to grab the little fucker by the collar and slam him up against the wall, Mònica was embracing the 'beautiful intensity' of her emotions and Natalie was wondering anxiously if it was contributing to her anxiety. They all agreed it was totally typical of their friend Gillian to die so she could get out of menopause and then they cried into their Prosecco.

No, she wouldn't text her schoolfriends, because she suddenly remembered how at that last dinner she'd looked up from her menu to catch an exchange of glances that most definitely meant: 'Poor Frances.' She could not bear pity. That particular group of solidly married friends was meant to *envy* her, or they'd pretended to envy her anyway, for all these years, but it seemed that being childless and single in your thirties was very different from being childless and single in your fifties. No longer glamorous. Now kind of tragic.

I'm only temporarily tragic, she told herself as she pulled on a clean blouse that showed a lot of cleavage. She tossed the sweaty shirt onto the back seat, restarted the car, looked over her shoulder and pulled out onto the highway. *Temporarily Tragic*. It could the name of a band.

There was a sign. She squinted. *Tranquillum House*, it said.

'Left turn ahead,' said her GPS.

'Yes, I *know*, I see it.'

She met her own eyes in the rear-view mirror and tried to give herself a wry 'isn't life interesting!' look.

Frances had always enjoyed the idea of parallel universes in which multiple versions of herself tried out different lives – one where she was a CEO instead of an author; one where she was a mother of two or four or six kids instead of none; one where she hadn't divorced Sol and one where she hadn't divorced Henry – but for the most part she'd always felt satisfied or at least accepting of the universe in which she found herself . . . except for right now, because right now it felt like there had been some sort of cataclysmic quantum-physics administrative error. She'd slipped universes. She was meant to be high on lust and love in America, not pain-ridden and grief-stricken in Australia. It was just wrong. Unacceptable.

And yet here she was. There was nothing else to do, nowhere else to turn.

'Goddamn it,' she said, and turned left.